THE SOCIETY OF BLOOD

OBSIDIAN HEART
BOOK TWO

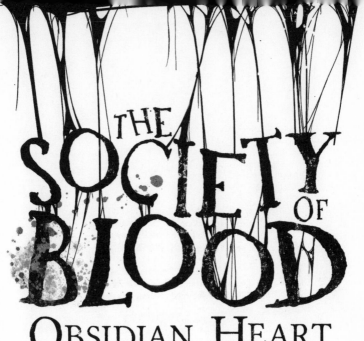

THE SOCIETY OF BLOOD

OBSIDIAN HEART
BOOK TWO

MARK MORRIS

TITAN BOOKS

Obsidian Heart Book Two: Society of Blood
Print edition ISBN: 9781781168707
E-book edition ISBN: 9781781168738

Published by Titan Books
A division of Titan Publishing Group Ltd
144 Southwark Street, London SE1 0UP

First edition: October 2015
1 3 5 7 9 10 8 6 4 2

This is a work of fiction. Names, characters, places, and incidents either are the product of the author's imagination or are used fictitiously, and any resemblance to actual persons, living or dead, business establishments, events, or locales is entirely coincidental. The publisher does not have any control over and does not assume any responsibility for author or third-party websites or their content.

Mark Morris asserts the moral right to be identified as the author of this work.

Visit our website:
www.titanbooks.com

A CIP catalogue record for this title is available from the British Library.

Printed and bound in the United States.

To Tim and Tracey Lebbon, with love.
"Get away from her, you *bitch!*"

ONE

DEEP AND CRISP AND EVEN

The little girl with the mechanical arm reached for the brightly wrapped package that was almost as big as she was. Then she paused and looked up at me.

'It's all right, Hope,' I said gently. 'It's for you. Merry Christmas.'

A radiant smile appeared on the girl's pinched and delicate features – she still looked under-nourished despite devouring every last scrap of food placed in front of her over the past three months – and then she dragged the package out from beneath the tree. She had eyed the tree warily at first, watching from the top of the stairs as Hawkins and I had manoeuvred it through the front door, its piney aroma causing her nose to wrinkle with suspicion. When Clover and I had dressed it on the night before Christmas Eve, bedecking its green-needled branches with trinkets and strips of coloured paper and small cloth bags containing fruit and nuts and sweets, she had sidled into the drawing room and stood silently beside the log fire for a while, eyeing us in bewilderment.

'What are you doing?' she had asked finally.

It was Clover who answered. In her long coral-coloured skirt and matching fitted jacket over a high-collared blouse and black, buttoned-up boots, she looked like a kindly schoolteacher or governess. Her formerly maroon hair was now a deep chestnut-brown, and held in place with various pins and grips and a tortoiseshell comb.

'We're decorating the tree,' she said. 'Haven't you seen a Christmas tree before?'

Hope thought about it for a moment, then shook her head.

'Would you like to help?' Clover asked.

Hope considered the question carefully. We waited. We had learned to give her time, and that to rush her was often to panic her.

'What is its purpose?' she asked eventually.

'Its purpose?' At a loss, Clover glanced at me.

'Well, it's... traditional to bring a tree into the house at this time of year. Especially an evergreen like this one.' My fingers brushed the tip of one spiny-needled branch.

'Why?'

I glanced towards the row of windows on the far side of the room, but the heavy damask drapes had already been drawn, shutting out the night. 'You know how cold and dark it is outside, how all the flowers are dead at this time of year, and how all the trees have shed their leaves?'

Hope nodded.

'Well, the evergreens keep their leaves all year round. And so we bring them into our homes as a reminder of renewal and rebirth.' To be honest, I had no idea if I was making this up or if I'd read it somewhere. 'Also it reminds us of the birth of baby Jesus in Bethlehem.'

Hope looked at me blankly. 'Who is baby Jesus?'

'Blimey, you really *do* have a lot to learn, don't you?'

Smirking, Clover said, 'Baby Jesus was born a long, long time ago. His mother and father followed a star to a place called Bethlehem, and baby Jesus was born in a stable on Christmas Day, and that's why we celebrate Christmas.' Under her breath she murmured, 'Or so the story goes.'

Hope frowned. As she involuntarily flexed the muscles in the stump of her skinny right arm the metal pistons and pulleys in the artificial limb began to creak and move, causing the pincer-like claw that served as her hand to open and close.

'Why do you decorate the tree?' she asked.

'To make it look pretty. Don't you think it's pretty?' said Clover.

Another moment's thought, then Hope nodded. 'Yes, but not as pretty as you.'

Clover laughed. 'What a little charmer you've become.' She shook a tiny bell, which she'd been about to hang on the tree, making it tinkle. 'So – *do* you want to help?'

This time Hope nodded eagerly.

As Clover lifted Hope up so she could hang decorations on the higher branches, I reflected, not for the first time, what an open book this little girl was, and how much her naivety and lack of knowledge shocked me.

It wasn't her fault, of course. For as long as Hope could remember – or was prepared to remember – she had lived in a tiny cage in a basement laboratory beneath a hospital, her existence as a living subject for the vile experiments of a surgeon called Dr Tallarian dominated by misery, pain and fear.

When I'd rescued her and brought her home (though in truth it had been Hawkins who'd done that; I'd been overcome by smoke inhalation, having attacked Tallarian's henchman with an oil lamp and inadvertently set the laboratory on fire), she'd been all but feral, tearing up sheets and clothing to build nests in cupboards and under the bed we'd provided for her, and using the corner of her room, instead of the chamber pot, as a toilet. She couldn't dress herself, had barely been able to speak, and had gone crazy at the feel of soap and water on her skin. She'd been terrified and mistrustful, spitting and snarling and lashing out at anyone who came near.

But in the three months since then her progress had been remarkable. Hope was like a sponge, absorbing knowledge, responding to the kindness and patience shown to her not only by Clover and me, but by the rest of the household staff (particularly Mrs Peake, the housekeeper, and Polly, one of the maidservants), and latching on quickly to whatever was required of her. She'd learned to speak, or at least had found her voice, since when she had barely stopped asking questions. She had begun to dress herself, to wash regularly, to sleep in her bed instead of under it, and to use a fork or a spoon to eat with – which, of course, she held in her left hand, as her right, the pincer-like claw, was little more than an encumbrance.

But it wasn't the claw's inefficiency that bothered me. The real concern was the artificial arm to which the claw was attached, and not only because it was heavy and impractical. Where the metal was grafted into Hope's flesh, halfway between her shoulder and elbow, the skin was red and inflamed, prone to infection. Mrs Peake and her staff fought a constant battle to keep the wound clean, though there was a danger in that too, because we were all aware that if the metal became too wet too often it would start to corrode, which could, if the rust seeped into Hope's bloodstream, cause septicaemia.

In my view, Hope's metal arm was therefore not all that different to having a bomb attached to her body – one that was currently dormant, but that might start ticking at any time. The obvious solution would be to have it amputated, but in this day and age such an operation was too risky. Anaesthesia, in the form of ether, chloroform, even cocaine, was hit and miss, and the body trauma to patients was often considerable. It was still common for patients to die of shock or blood loss or of later infections contracted during surgery. Of course, if we'd had twenty-first century techniques at our disposal it would have been a doddle. But we didn't.

I watched Hope opening the largest of the Christmas presents we'd bought for her – to be honest, we'd spoiled her, but if there was ever a child who deserved to be spoiled, it was her – and tried to put my anxieties out of my head, at least for today. Admittedly it wasn't easy. It wasn't just Hope I was worried about, but my youngest daughter, Kate. Kate had been abducted by an individual or group who were after an artefact in the form of a small obsidian heart, which until recently had been in my possession. If I didn't recover the heart, which I'd last seen in the hands of DI Jensen, the detective leading the enquiry into my daughter's disappearance – or, more likely, a shape-shifter in the form of Jensen – I would never be able to get back to my own time. And if I didn't get back, then the likelihood was that I would never see Kate again.

But even if I *did* recover the heart, I knew it would still be only the first step on the long road towards a reunion with my daughter. Of course, the fact that the heart was no longer in my hands could mean that, in the twenty-first century, Kate had been released by her captors. On the other hand it could be an entirely different group that had snatched the heart – but I had no way of even beginning the process of finding that out until the thing was back in my possession. But who was to say the heart was still even in this time period? Whoever possessed it now had the potential to use it to travel in time, in which case it could already be permanently beyond my reach. There'd been periods in the past few months when my problems had seemed so insurmountable that I'd sunk into despair. It was at these times when Clover's calm, reassuring presence had been invaluable.

'Forget about the bigger picture,' she'd said to me more than once. 'Take it one step at a time.'

The first time she'd said that I'd lost my rag with her, had accused her of being insensitive. 'It's not your daughter who's missing,' I'd snapped. 'Every day that passes feels like a day where she's getting further away from me.'

'Except she isn't, is she?' Clover said calmly. 'Think about it, Alex. Just because time's passing here doesn't mean it's passing at the same rate for Kate. If you get the heart back, even if it takes six months, you could theoretically use it to travel back to the moment after you left.'

It was true, and her words were a comfort. The knowledge that the heart could make the passage of time irrelevant, that somewhere, in the future, Kate's existence was not necessarily continuing without me, but was, to all intents and purposes, suspended, was, I think, the only thing that kept me from going mad.

Using both her real hand and her metal claw, Hope was now tearing the paper from the parcel. Beneath was a doll's house, a real beauty, lovingly hand-carved and painted, breathtaking in its attention to detail.

'Do you like it?' Clover asked. The doll's house had been her idea.

'Yes,' said Hope automatically. Her nose wrinkled. 'What is it?'

'What does it look like?' I said.

'A house. Like this one. But little. Too little to live in.'

Clover knelt on the carpet beside her and leaned forward, dragging another couple of smaller parcels out from beneath the tree. 'Open these.'

Obediently Hope tore the paper from one parcel, and then the other. The first contained miniature items of furniture – tables and chairs, beds and wardrobes, a bath on four tiny clawed feet, a dressing table, a foot stool, a writing desk, a pair of washstands – and a bunch of even smaller items, all carved out of wood: bottles, hairbrushes, a joint of meat, ornaments, paintings, chamber pots, houseplants. The second parcel contained the house's occupants: a mother, a father and three children (one boy, one girl, one indeterminately gendered baby), plus a number of servants, including a chauffeur and a gardener.

'It's your very own house,' Clover said. 'And all these things are for you to put in it. You've even got your own family, look.' She held up the little girl and jiggled her from side to side. 'Hello, Hope,' she said in a squeaky voice.

Hope was fascinated. She reached for the wooden figure Clover was holding, but then paused, her hand hovering in the air. Uncertainly she said, 'Aren't *you* my family?'

'Well... yes, of course,' said Clover. 'We're your *real* family. But this is a pretend family for you to play with.'

'But what do I do with them?'

'Whatever you like. You're in control, so you can give them names and decide who they are. You can use your voice to make them speak to each other, and your imagination to make up stories about them and send them off on wild adventures.'

'Remember what we said about imagination?' I prompted.

'It's when you make up things that aren't real. Not lies,' Hope added hastily. 'Lies are different. They're bad.'

'That's right,' said Clover. 'But imagination is good. Because making up stories is fun. And it forces you to think.'

'It exercises the little grey cells,' said Hope solemnly, repeating something I'd told her, making both of us laugh.

'Exactly,' said Clover. 'And the more you think the quicker your mind works and the cleverer you become. Because you need to think to make decisions, to decide what's right and wrong. You see?'

Hope nodded slowly, looking at the doll's house. 'So do *I* decide where all these things go in the house?'

Clover nodded. 'You can put things where you like. And if you decide afterwards you don't like them where they are, you can move them around.'

'Same with the people,' I said. 'You can decide what sort of people they are. You can decide whether they're happy or sad, or nice or nasty, or...' I floundered.

'Brave or cowardly,' Clover offered.

Thoughtfully Hope picked up the father and brought him up close to her face, staring at him as if trying to read his personality in his painted eyes.

'Can he be an explorer?' she asked.

I smiled. 'If that's what you want.'

'What are you going to call him?' asked Clover.

Hope looked at me. 'I shall call him... Alex.'

My smile widened. 'And what about the mother?'

'Clover,' Hope said without hesitation.

Clover glanced my way, raising her eyebrows in amusement. Since finding ourselves here, we had decided, for the sake of decorum, that it would be best if we posed as husband and wife. To live together under any other circumstances would have been regarded as dubious at best, scandalous at worst. It would have led to adverse attention, unneeded hostility, maybe even a downturn in my business interests and investments – all of which had been set up before I got here, and which thankfully managed to tick over quite nicely with the minimum of involvement from me.

But even having established a veneer of respectability, Clover and I still occasionally caused eyebrows to be raised. I'd known vaguely before finding myself here that the Victorian era was an age when gender equality was still in its infancy, when women didn't yet have the right to vote, and when Emmeline Pankhurst and her suffragettes, their movement still very much in its earliest days, spent most of their time battling against an overwhelmingly hostile tide of public opinion. But it wasn't until I was actually living *among* the Victorians that I realised just *how* chauvinistic a society it was, and how entrenched was the notion that women were second-class citizens in all departments. It was honestly believed among the majority of men – or at least the ones I'd encountered – that women who refused to conform to the expected role of being a demure housewife were thought to be suffering from an 'affliction of the brain'.

Clover had adapted to Victorian society quickly and was well aware of the need to rein in her usual garrulousness, but even so, she could not exactly be described as demure, at least not by the standards of the day. Several of my business colleagues who had visited the house had been shocked when she had answered questions directed at me. One of them, the managing director of a shipping company in which I had shares, had even taken me aside and suggested I encourage my wife to make house calls on other ladies in the neighbourhood, or perhaps become involved in charitable work, in order to curb what he described as her 'tendency towards vulgarity'.

Clover had laughed when I'd told her this, but it had annoyed her too. 'If he thinks it's vulgar just for a woman to express an opinion,' she said, 'maybe we ought to take him back with us when we find the heart. It would blow his tiny mind.'

Clover had been here when I'd arrived, installed apparently by an older version of me, who had been in possession of the heart I was currently searching for. He had explained just enough of the situation to prepare her for my arrival, and this had helped to cement my trust in her. Before her appearance, despite all we'd been through together, I'd harboured a lingering thread of doubt – in fact, if I was honest with myself, I still did, but it was now gossamer thin, and appeared only when I was overly stressed or tired, which in turn tended to bring out the paranoia in me. I reasoned that if a *future* version of me had brought her here to help, then she *must* be trustworthy – at least according to my older self. It followed, therefore, that if Clover *did* have a hidden agenda, she must be playing a long game – a *very* long game, in fact.

This, of course, was assuming that Clover's claim to have been transported here by an older me was true. However, as Hawkins had confirmed her story, I was inclined to believe it. Now and again it did occur to me to wonder whether *both* of them might be in league with my enemies, and were protecting me only to preserve me for an even bigger fall somewhere down the line. But that was a ridiculous and destructive way to think, wasn't it? I mean, what, for them, would be the point?

And believing Clover's story gave me a reason to be optimistic about my own personal future, and that was something I was loath to relinquish. The idea that an older me had brought her here, together with evidence that future versions of me had used the heart to perform other deeds – not least buy this house and set up an entire portfolio of business interests – enabled me to cling to the hope that, whatever happened, eventually everything would turn out okay.

Was it really that simple, though? Was my fate already mapped out? I'd seen dozens of movies where the hero or villain went back in time and changed history, thus altering the future they'd come from. But in truth I had no idea how time really worked, how flexible it was. Whenever I tried to think it through, it tied my head in knots. It always came back to variations on that age-old conundrum: what if you travelled back in time and killed your grandfather – would you cease to exist? The impossibility of that suggested that time travel was a nonsense, that it couldn't be feasible. Yet it *was* feasible; I was proof of it. But maybe time had its own rules that couldn't be broken? Maybe the person who *tried* to kill their grandfather would find themselves constantly thwarted for one reason or another?

The fact that I didn't know, *couldn't* know, meant that I couldn't afford to be blasé about my future. I couldn't assume that just because I had 'evidence' that my future self was in possession of the heart it automatically meant I was destined to find it.

Once Hope had opened her other presents – a doll; a stuffed horse; a drawing set comprising paper, pencils and an India rubber; a toy theatre with cardboard figures on sticks; a music box; a magic lantern with slides of animals and famous buildings – she sat in a kind of stupor, her eyes dazzled and dreamy. For a girl who'd had nothing her whole life, who had no concept of the notion of 'Christmas', and didn't even know how old she was, this was probably too much. Yet Clover and I had wanted to treat her, had wanted to try to roll all the Christmases she'd missed into one glorious celebration. Of course, material things didn't bring happiness, they didn't heal a scarred soul, but we were doing our best to deal with that too. We were providing Hope with love and kindness and security, and hoping it would be enough.

Clover, still kneeling beside Hope, said brightly, 'Right, what shall we play with first?' She reached for the magic lantern, her eyes shining, as though showing Hope how to play the role of Eager Child on Christmas Morning. 'How about this?'

With something to focus on, Hope blinked and nodded, a smile creeping across her face. Watching her I was hit with a sudden, unexpected wave of sadness. Although I wasn't missing out on Christmas morning with Kate – that was a different time, a different world, away – it felt as though I was. I couldn't shake the notion that Christmas was a time for family, and that Kate should be here with me, with us, opening presents and joining in the celebrations. For a moment I saw her, sitting on the carpet with Hope, squinting adorably behind her pink-framed spectacles. I remembered last Christmas morning – or at least, *my* last Christmas morning: Kate's excitement; her squeals of delight as she opened her presents. I'd made us both pancakes for breakfast, and then we'd sat on the settee in our pyjamas, my daughter burrowing into the gap between my arm and my hip like a warm puppy as we watched – for about the hundredth time – *Toy Story* on the telly.

My eyes blurred with tears; my head went stuffy and hot. I sniffed and Clover glanced at me. Her eyes flashed a question: *Are you all right?*

I stood up as unobtrusively as possible. Hope was still preoccupied with the magic lantern, gazing with awe as the first image – a springing tiger, mouth open in a snarl – appeared in faint, broken patches on furniture and the wall beyond.

'I... er... just have to deal with something,' I muttered. 'I'll be back soon.'

Clover nodded her understanding as I crossed the room and slipped out of the door.

In the corridor, I leaned against the wall, pressed my cool fingers to my closed eyelids and took a shuddering breath. I exhaled hard, opening my eyes in time to glimpse my breath as a faint curl of mist in the air. This house on the edge of Kensington Gardens, which I had suddenly found myself rich enough to own, was big and high-ceilinged, its walls adorned with paintings, mirrors and stuffed animal heads, its many rooms crammed with furniture, fabrics and artefacts from China and the Far East. Sumptuous as it was, though, like the majority of homes at this time it didn't have central heating. Hot running water, yes – that was heated from the kitchen range. But for now we lived, as Clover had put it, 'like cavemen', Mrs Peake and her staff having to stoke up the fires in every room each morning to stave off the biting winter cold.

Twitching my nose at the smell of slowly roasting turkey drifting up from the basement kitchen, I crossed the icy hall, bypassing the foot of the wide staircase, which faced the front door across an expanse of patterned floor tiles. The first door I came to on the opposite side of the hallway opened into the morning room, but I ignored that and continued along the corridor leading to the rear of the house. Wall-mounted gas lamps, whose paraffin-like fumes overwhelmed the delectable aroma of our Christmas dinner, dispelled the deepening gloom here. Gaslight might look pretty in films and TV dramas, but as well as being whiffy it gobbled up huge amounts of oxygen, which meant that unless the room you were in was well ventilated (and who wants a well ventilated room in the dead of winter?) you invariably ended up with a stinker of a headache. I'd told Hawkins and the household staff that as soon as electricity became domestically available I'd be signing up for it. Mrs Peake was dubious; she thought electricity was dangerous and unreliable, that it would never catch on. When I tried to assure her that it was the way forward she gave me pitying looks.

Pushing open the solid oak door into the library, I was met with a billow of warmth. It enfolded me like an arm around the shoulders, drawing me towards the log fire, which danced and crackled behind the dark mesh of the fireguard. Although real fires were cosy, they left a thin layer of sooty grime on every surface – not good for the hundreds of leather-bound books lining the floor-to-ceiling shelves. This had been one of the things that had most surprised me about Victorian London – how horribly *dirty* it was. I'd known about the Industrial Revolution, the dark, satanic mills, the growth of mechanisation, all that. I'd even known about the rookeries, the workhouses, the terrible poverty – and yet there had still been a part of my brain that associated the Victorian era with elegance and innocence and romanticism.

Not so. Victorian London was *filthy*. And it wasn't just the poor areas of London that were bad, it was *everywhere*. Coal was used not only in industry, but to heat virtually every household in the city. This meant that every day thousands of fires belched out soot and fumes, as a result of which the stonework of most of the buildings was black, the pavements muddy underfoot, the air itself not only gritty and hazy, but often so smoky it was sometimes hard to breathe. On days when the air was particularly damp, the smog was so brown and dense you couldn't see more than a couple of feet in any direction. Also there was shit everywhere – dog shit on the pavements, horse shit in the road. And the people smelled. Because there was no deodorant, few showers, or bathrooms even, and clothes were hand-washed and often hung out to dry in smoky environments, even those who were lucky enough (or scrupulous enough) to wash regularly had a slightly musty, sweaty, smoky odour about them. It wasn't nice, but it was something you had to accept and get used to.

And I *had* got used to it in many ways. It's amazing how quickly you can adapt to a new environment. Which didn't mean I wasn't still often struck by how amazing and terrifying and disorientating this situation was. I had *travelled in time*. I was *living in history*. Queen Victoria was on the throne (and next year would become the longest-reigning monarch in British history); the Jack the Ripper murders had happened only seven years ago, which meant that the killer, whoever he was, could still be alive. Arthur Conan Doyle was on hiatus from writing his Sherlock Holmes stories, but was yet to write his most famous, *The Hound of the Baskervilles*. Elsewhere in the world, the likes of Monet, Lenin, H.G. Wells, Oscar Wilde, Sigmund Freud and Joseph Lister were going about their business. The Eiffel Tower was a mere six years old; last year the Lumière brothers had invented the cinematograph; somewhere in Germany X-rays had just been discovered.

Sometimes I would literally get the shakes thinking about it all. I thought about it now as I walked slowly across to the windows that overlooked the stretch of lawn at the side of the house. I was a man who could see into the future. If I wanted I could use my foreknowledge in all sorts of ways to earn myself a fortune – or rather, a greater fortune than the one I had *already* earned.

The snow outside was a foot deep, even deeper where it had banked up against the trees and bushes at the perimeter of my property. Though I couldn't see anyone, I knew there were people watching the house; people patrolling the area *around* the house, on the lookout for anything suspicious. They constituted a small fraction of the vast army I employed, or at least paid, not only to guard my interests but to keep their eyes and ears open for any news of the heart. It was an army that had been recruited from all walks of life.

Those who guarded the house did so on a rotational basis, and had instructions to be as circumspect as possible. They'd been handpicked by Hawkins – tough men who would otherwise be working on the docks or the railways, or even keeping themselves afloat by nefarious means. In view of the weather, I'd instructed Mrs Peake to keep them supplied with bread and cheese and beef tea. I'd even told Hawkins to make sure they took turns to come inside now and again to warm themselves by the kitchen range.

How effective the guard would be if the Wolves of London decided to launch an attack I had no idea, but their presence gave me some peace of mind. I watched the snow drift lazily down from a sky so colourless it was as if God had forgotten to fill it in. The snow formed spirals, helixes; it was mesmerising. After a while I wondered if the patterns were trying to tell me something.

I felt calmer now, less friable. *White Christmas*, I thought, and smiled at the idea of becoming an internationally renowned songwriter. I wondered what would happen if I were to 'write' songs I knew from the future – songs by Burt Bacharach, Irving Berlin, say – and claim them as my own. Would time warp and crack and shatter? Would reality unravel?

Something popped in the fire – a rusty nail, a knot of wood. I turned away from the window and went back to spend Christmas with my 'family'.

Later, after turkey and plum pudding had been eaten, after charades had been played, after Hope had collapsed into bed, exhausted but happy, after Mrs Peake and the girls – Polly, Florence and Hattie – had retired to their rooms at the top of the house, and Clover and Hawkins were in the drawing room, sharing a bottle of port and chatting in front of the fire, I went outside.

I did this most nights. It had become a habit. I was like a crusty old colonel in some far-flung outpost, patrolling the perimeter of his domain to check on the morale of his men and ensure that all was well before sealing the lid on another day.

I went armed. Both Hawkins and Clover insisted on it. I carried a howdah pistol, a large-calibre handgun, which had been designed for use against the lions, tigers and other dangerous animals in colonial Africa and India. Hawkins had acquired it for me – I didn't ask from where. Again I had no idea how useful it would be against the Wolves of London – Tallarian and his mechanical army, the shape-shifter – but at least it *felt* reassuring, and it allowed Clover and Hawkins to convince themselves I was as well-protected as I could be.

As it was Christmas night I went out armed not only with my trusty pistol, but with a hamper of goodies – turkey sandwiches, a quarter wheel of cheese, mince pies, Christmas cake, a bottle of good brandy – with which to feed the troops. Although it had stopped snowing it was still bitterly cold and my breath hung on the air like a Yuletide apparition. My feet made soft crumping sounds as I plodded through the snow, the shadows in the depressions I left behind shimmering blue in the moonlight. From the front door I turned left, trudging parallel to the front of the house, before turning left again into deeper shadow when I reached the first corner. As I plodded along the side of the house, taking exaggerated, clown-like steps, I scanned the black, jagged screen of trees and bushes at the edge of the property, but all was still.

Then something shifted, black on black. I peered harder, my right hand slipping inside my fur-collared topcoat – all my coats and jackets had been fitted with a special pocket in which I could carry my pistol. Like a globule of oil breaking free from a slick, a shape detached itself from the larger clump of blackness behind it. As it moved towards me the snow creaked like polystyrene.

'Name yourself,' I challenged.

'Frith, sir.' The voice was gruff and phlegmy, with a pronounced Scottish accent. 'Donald Frith.'

I relaxed, though not entirely. The shape-shifter could adopt the guise of anyone so perfectly it was impossible to tell the fake from the real thing. Already I had seen it in the forms of Clover, Barnaby McCallum and DI Jensen. Who was to say it couldn't catch me off-guard by taking on the form of one of my protectors?

'Tell me today's word, Mr Frith.'

I heard the man clear his throat in the darkness, as if about to make an important proclamation. 'Crackerjack.'

I smiled. My hand slipped from beneath my coat. 'Do you have a lantern?'

'I do, sir.'

'Then light it, by all means.'

It hadn't taken me long to adopt the Victorian speech patterns I heard around me every day, though I sometimes wondered whether the idioms and rhythms I found myself slipping into had more to do with Sherlock Holmes movies and TV period dramas than actual reality. If the natives ever thought I spoke a bit oddly they didn't mention it. Perhaps they were too polite. Or perhaps they thought I was a foreigner and that English was my second language. I was purposely vague about my origins.

After a few seconds of fumbling, a Lucifer flared in the darkness and next moment a brass lantern in Frith's other hand was glowing brightly. Frith held it up, as if to emphasise that he'd complied with my suggestion, his black form acquiring a flickering orange definition, which gave the snow around him the appearance of softly glowing lava. When he grinned, his craggy, bewhiskered face crumpled up like an old leather shoe, full of pits and grooves.

'There you are, sir,' he said. 'A very Merry Christmas to you.'

'And to you, Mr Frith. Though I'm afraid that yours can't have been as merry as all that. I'm sorry that you drew the short straw today.'

'The short straw, sir?'

'What I mean is, I'm sorry that you're out here alone on Christmas night.'

Frith shook his grizzled, leonine head. Like the rest of the men that Hawkins had selected, he was tall and bulky, though some of his bulk could be attributed to the fact that in order to keep warm he wore numerous layers of clothing. Much of it, in common with the majority of London's population, was baggy, colourless, patched, threadbare, ragged at the edges. The cap on his head, from which his badly cut hair jabbed like dark straw, resembled a cowpat with a brim; the scarf around his neck was not much more than a length of grey rag. The pockets of his brownish jacket sagged and gaped, as though full of stones, and his boots were wrapped with cloth and twine to prevent them from falling apart.

'Not at all, sir, not at all,' he said amiably. 'I've little else to do. And gainful employment keeps me from indulging in certain devilish temptations, if you get my drift.' He tilted a hand towards his mouth in a drinking gesture.

I thought of the brandy in my hamper, and wondered whether it might be best to keep it there. 'I hope I'm not depriving your family of your company, though, Mr Frith?'

'All gone, sir,' he said bluntly. 'My wife was a good woman – too good for me. Took to her heels some years back and my bairns with her...' He wafted a hand, as though scattering seed to the wind.

'I'm sorry.'

Frith raised his bushy eyebrows in surprise. 'Nothing for you to be sorry about, sir. Nothing at all.'

'Even so,' I said. Then in order to avoid awkwardness I patted the hamper. 'I've brought you some sustenance. Thought you might be hungry.'

'That's powerful kind of you, sir. And I won't deny that some wittles would be most welcome.'

I opened the hamper and told Frith to help himself. Before I could think about what I was saying, I added, 'There's plenty more where that came from.'

As soon as the words were out of my mouth I winced at the insinuation that my resources were bountiful when so many were starving, but Frith made no comment. After I'd watched him eat his fill, cramming the food into his mouth and swallowing almost without chewing, as if afraid I might suddenly withdraw the offer, I hesitantly offered him a nip of the brandy 'to keep out the cold'.

'I'd best not, sir, if you don't mind,' Frith said. 'Not if I desire to keep my wits.'

Once we'd wished each other goodnight, Frith blew out his lantern and melted back into the shadows. There were six men guarding the house, and I encountered them all as I performed my nightly circuit. They were all more or less like Frith – shabby and gruff, but polite, deferential. They were inordinately grateful for the food I'd brought, and they never ceased to be surprised by my concern for their welfare, though they tried not to show it. Their diffidence made me uncomfortable; this was one of the things I'd found hardest to come to terms with since arriving here. I wanted to tell them I was a fraud, that I was no more a gentleman than they were. But I didn't. I couldn't. The borders between the haves and the have-nots were too rigid. I knew if I'd tried to get closer to any of them, they would have regarded me with confusion and suspicion. The Victorian attitude, so alien to me, was that the rich and the poor held on to their pride by knowing their place in the scheme of things and sticking to it. There was little ambition among the working classes; the prevailing mood of aspiration, of attainment, hadn't yet filtered down to the lower stratas of society. There were exceptions, but based on my experience over the past three months the general consensus seemed to be that the poor and downtrodden were where they were simply because God had decided that was to be their lot in life.

None of the men had anything to report. All was quiet. I reached the last corner, having done almost a full circuit of the house, when something caught my eye. Across the white blanket of snow leading from the dark mass of the hedge at the front of the house to the now-dormant flowerbed beneath the drawing room's bay window, was a set of animal tracks. This wasn't unusual in itself, but it was the nature of the tracks that bothered me.

Placing the now almost empty hamper on the snowy ground, I approached the line of tracks cautiously, wary that whatever had made them might be lurking nearby. My hand crept again to the pistol in my jacket as I followed the tracks to their source, the hedge at the edge of my property.

The tracks by the hedge were those of a small bird, like a sparrow, with three toes at the front and a clawed spur at the back. These tracks made just enough of an impression to be picked out by the moonlight, a series of regular, icy-blue scratches on the otherwise pristine blanket of snow.

What was unusual was that as the tracks got closer to the house, they *changed*. The twig-like toes became thicker and less defined, and the tracks themselves deeper. Within the space of half a dozen steps, the markings altered shape completely, the toes becoming broader, more rounded, the rear spur expanding and flattening out.

It was as though a bird had landed on the lawn, and then, as it approached the house, had changed into a cat or a dog. The creature had walked up to the house, hung around by the bay window for a while (there was a mess of footprints here to indicate it had moved around a bit) and then had padded back towards the hedge, where its tracks had transformed once again into a bird's. The returning tracks then ended abruptly a few metres from the hedge, as if the bird had flown away.

Instinctively I peered into the moonlit winter sky, but saw nothing moving up there.

Nothing, that is, except a few random snowflakes spiralling lazily from the heavens to settle upon the earth.

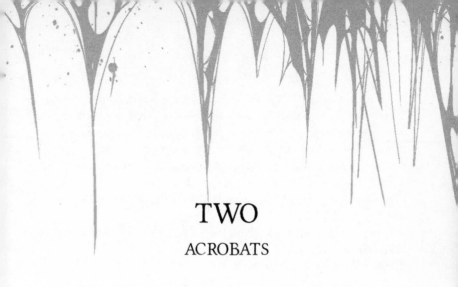

TWO
ACROBATS

'Good shot, sir.'

It was Boxing Day evening, creeping towards midnight, twenty-four hours since I'd found the tracks in the snow. Hawkins and I were in the snooker room on the second floor (I'd always loved the idea of a snooker room and now I had one!), potting a few balls, smoking fat cigars and demolishing another bottle of port. It should have been a relaxing, even mildly decadent end to the day, but as with almost everything I did here I felt like I was marking time. My overriding sense was one not of pleasure but of guilt. I carried it inside me like an ulcer. However much I rationalised it, however often I told myself the matter was in hand and there was nothing I could usefully do but wait, I couldn't help feeling I should be *out there*, scouring the streets, asking questions, tearing London apart in my search for the obsidian heart.

I took another gulp of port – I'd end up with bloody gout at this rate! – and watched the white ball roll sedately back down the table to nestle against the bottom cushion. I'd become pretty decent at snooker over the past three months – no doubt partly due to my misspent youth playing endless games of pool in seedy clubs and pubs as a teenager. It had been years since I'd picked up a cue, but since arriving here I'd found that knocking a few balls around at the end of the day was often a good way of untangling the turmoil in my head, helping me to think.

Squinting at Hawkins through ropy veils of blue smoke, I sighed and said, 'Are you *ever* going to call me by name, Hawkins?'

Hawkins paused, smiled. When he did so it transformed his austere, hook-nosed face. His smile was full of warmth, but there was sadness there too. I didn't know why. Although he was fiercely loyal to me, he was also proud, secretive; he revealed his true self only in increments. It was another characteristic of this age. It wasn't seemly to gush, to pour out your heart, to lay yourself open. Personal information had to be earned, eked out, like flecks of gold from hard rock.

'It wouldn't feel right, sir,' he said. 'You are the master of this house and I am the butler.'

I snorted. 'Come on, Hawkins, you know I don't hold with all that subservience crap. You know more about me than anyone here, except Clover. We're friends, aren't we?'

He inclined his head. 'I like to think so, sir.'

'Well, then.'

He regarded me a moment with his sky-blue eyes and then turned his attention back to the table. I'd partly snookered him behind the yellow. I could see him assessing the angles, wondering which red to go for. He strolled around the table, chalking his queue. He was around sixty, silver-haired, but he moved with the grace of a ballet dancer. Clover had a theory that he'd once been a cat burglar. 'He's *like* a cat,' she'd said. 'Or a panther. Silent and sort of sleek.'

He crouched, played the shot. A smooth, precise action. The white ball travelled up the table, kissing the side cushion, nudging the outermost red towards the top right-hand pocket. The angle wasn't quite right; the red wiped its feet, but didn't go in. But it was a speculative shot anyway. The white came back off the top cushion and rolled down the table unimpeded, stopping just short of the brown.

'Nice,' I said. 'Haven't left me much to go at there. You play a very cagey game, Hawkins.'

Once again a smile played on his lips. 'I'm a very cagey man, sir.'

I had no idea whether the word 'cagey' was an anachronism, though Hawkins spoke it as though it was. I matched his smile with a wider one of my own.

'I'll say. I've been here three months now and I still don't know all that much about you.'

'There isn't much *to* know,' he said, but the way his eyes slid away from me belied his words.

Before replying I took another sip of my drink, another puff on my cigar. Then I said, 'Oh, I think there is. I think you've got quite a story to tell.' I approached the table, chalking my cue. 'No pressure, of course, Hawkins, but you do realise that you'll have to spill the beans sooner or later? Otherwise how will I find you to employ you in the future?'

I bent to take my shot. Before I could, Hawkins murmured, 'It is a fair question, sir, to which the answer is that you would doubtless find the search a difficult one.'

'Oh?' I said. 'And why's that?'

'Because Hawkins is not my real name.'

I tried not to react in case it unsettled or embarrassed him, tried to pretend I was still focused on the table. 'Really?' I said airily.

'My real name is Abel Benczik.' He said this bluntly, as if it was something he didn't want to linger over, a bad tooth that needed to be extracted quickly to minimise the pain.

Still I took my time, my eyes fixed on the arrangement of balls on the table. I chalked my cue, then tilted the blue tip towards my mouth and blew off the excess dust. Crouching low, lining up my shot, I asked, 'What is that? Russian?'

'Hungarian.'

I played the shot, made a mess of it. Too much weight, not the right angle. Instead of potting the red that Hawkins had left close to the pocket and screwing back, the cue ball cannoned into it, sending it ricocheting around the table, before bouncing off the top pocket and smashing into the rest of the tightly packed triangle, scattering red balls over the green-baize surface.

'Bollocks,' I said. 'Made a pig's ear of that.'

I straightened up and glanced at Hawkins. His face was impassive, eyes fixed on the table.

'I wouldn't have guessed you were foreign,' I said. 'From your accent, I mean.'

His features barely flickered. 'I have endeavoured to conceal it.'

I didn't ask why. Having pried open the clam shell, I didn't want to force matters. If Hawkins wanted to explain himself he would do so in his own time. I drank more port and puffed on my cigar as I watched him pot a red, the pink, another red, the black, another red, the pink again, another red, before finally coming a cropper on the blue, which drifted away from its intended destination, the middle pocket.

'Mm,' he said contemplatively as he stepped back from the table. I had never seen him unruffled, had never seen him express anger or disappointment or disapproval. The only time he'd appeared even mildly shaken had been during his recollection of the horrors he'd seen in Tallarian's laboratory after he'd rescued me from the burning hospital. Even though I'd been known to describe Hawkins as uptight, he wasn't really – he was too open-minded for that – but he was certainly self-contained.

As I approached the table again, I was hyper aware of him behind me, lifting his port, taking a sip, setting the glass down with a gentle clink.

All at once he said, 'I am not ashamed of my homeland, sir. Far from it. Adopting a new identity was simply a matter of expediency. For your sake and my own it is best that I attract as little attention as possible whilst I remain in your employ. I have much to thank you for, not least of all my life, and I would never forgive myself if my... ah, *colourful* past were to become the beacon that brings your enemies flocking.'

'You don't have to worry about that, Hawkins,' I said, thinking of the tracks in the snow. 'I'm pretty sure my enemies are flocking already.'

'Even so.'

I played my shot, potting a red that was hanging over the top left-hand pocket. For a few seconds there was no sound in the room but the click of snooker balls, the gentle crackle of the fire and the muted ticking of the clock in its glass case on the mantelpiece. As I stepped back from potting the blue, Hawkins spoke again.

'My family and I were known as the Flying Bencziks. We were one of the foremost acrobatic troupes in the whole of Europe. Ours was a family tradition stretching back several centuries. Not only my immediate family – myself, my wife and my children – but also my parents, my grandparents and my great grandparents. We travelled many thousands of miles around the world, displaying our skills. Indeed, during the past two centuries members of my family have performed before most of the crowned heads of Europe.'

He broke off. This time I sensed he was eager to tell me more, to unburden himself.

'What happened?' I asked quietly.

He took a long, slow breath. 'A little over two years ago my family and I arrived in London as members of a prominent and sizeable travelling ensemble known as Langorini's Circus. Our one-week engagement in the city was to have been our first of a four-month tour, which would have seen us perform in over forty locations across the length and breadth of Great Britain. We had recently completed a similar and successful tour of France, and were feeling buoyant and optimistic. On our first day in the capital we set up camp in Bethnal Green and divided ourselves into small groups to traverse the local area and sell tickets prior to our first performance, which was to have taken place four days hence.'

Briefly he raised a hand and let it fall, a gesture of weary regret. 'Sadly we were ill-fated. Even now I am not fully conversant with what occurred, and I doubt that I ever shall be. All I know is that one of our groups, which included our strongman, a Danish fellow called Jakobsen, became involved in a fracas with a gang of local toughs after entering a tavern in the hope of drumming up business. At the time we regarded the incident as trivial – an unsavoury but minor disagreement. Such happenings, though not frequent, tended to be common enough.

'Unfortunately the local men did not view the incident so lightly. Or perhaps they simply took umbrage at our presence and would have acted whatever the provocation. The English, in general, are a tolerant race, though there are always exceptions to the rule. Whatever the reason, I was awoken in the early hours of the morning by a terrible uproar.

'A large mob of men had surrounded our camp and were shouting out threats and insults, using the most appalling language. My wife, Marta, and my children – I had four, sir, three daughters and a son...'

He faltered, his voice falling away, his face twitching, crumpling. Then he pulled himself together, his features smoothing out, becoming impassive once more.

'My apologies, sir. I am afraid—'

'No!' I said, raising a hand. 'I won't hear an apology, Hawkins. You've nothing to be sorry for.' I crossed the room, topped up his glass and carried it back to him. 'Drink this,' I ordered, 'and sit down.'

He hesitated a moment, then did as I suggested.

'You don't have to tell me any more if you don't want to,' I said. 'It can wait. Forever if needs be.'

Hawkins shook his head. 'No, sir. I have waited long enough to tell my story. I have carried it within me these past two years like... like Jacob Marley's chain.'

'I know the feeling. Tell me the rest of your story then, if you feel up to it.'

I leaned my snooker cue against the table and sat down opposite him, the fire crackling between us. I topped up our glasses and took another drag on my cigar as he continued.

'Marta, my wife, and my children were terrified. Even with the blinds covering the windows in our wagon, there was sufficient play of light and shadow in the gaps around the edges for us to ascertain that the men were armed with burning firebrands.

'Against Marta's wishes I pulled aside one of the blinds and looked out. There was a furious tumult of noise - banging and thumping - which reverberated like thunder, and I realised that the mob were striking the wagons with their fists in an attempt to goad the inhabitants to emerge.

'I am not a coward, sir, but concern for my family was uppermost in my mind. As such, I will admit that I prayed no one would rise to the provocation, that my fellows would sit tight in the hope that eventually the mob would become bored and disperse, or even that members of the constabulary would arrive to dispense justice.

'But it was not to be. Among our number was a small contingent of hotheads - not least the strongman, Jakobsen. He was a giant of a fellow, with long, flowing, yellow locks and a great beard to match.

'My heart sank when I saw Jakobsen's door fly open and the man emerge, roaring and swinging his fists. Some of the invaders, surprised by the attack and intimidated by Jakobsen's size and deportment, took to their heels - though many did not. Emboldened by their sheer numbers, and by the burning firebrands they held, these men advanced on Jakobsen, thrusting their flames into his face, driving him back.

'I saw his beard catch afire and then his clothing. The mob pressed forward, screaming with bloodlust - it was a terrible thing to see. Jakobsen fought like a bear, but eventually he fell, whereupon the mob, regardless of the flames that were rapidly consuming him, began to stamp and kick at his body, as well as to beat at him with clubs and lengths of metal.

'This was too much for many of the men of our company, myself included. Marta implored me to stay where I was, but I couldn't stand meekly by and watch one of our number be slaughtered like an animal. And so I ran outside, as did many of my friends and colleagues, and within moments battle was joined. Our company comprised a multitude of nationalities, but the mob, in its ignorance, began to chant anti-Semite slogans – which I suppose was their simplistic way of expressing their hatred for anyone born beyond these shores.

'The conflict was brutal and bloody. We were hopelessly outnumbered. We fought against the mob with all our strength, but we couldn't prevent them from...'

Hawkins' voice abruptly cracked again and I saw his head dip. I tensed, thinking he was about to slide from his chair on to the floor, but then he cleared his throat and carried on.

'...we could not prevent them from setting our camp afire. I was so intent on defending myself from the blows and kicks raining down on me that I didn't realise at first what was happening. I was only vaguely aware of flames leaping higher all around me, and of a ferocious roaring.

'I slipped, or perhaps I was pushed, and I fell down. I thought my time had come, but then I heard a cry, which I only realised afterwards must have been an order to the mob to retreat. All at once men were running past me, departing from the camp, disappearing into the shadows and the darkness beyond the flames like sewer rats.

'I was dazed and bleeding and bruised. I felt myself being hauled to my feet, and at first I thought my assailants had come again. But then I realised the hands belonged to my fellows, and that they were every bit as beaten as I was. But we had no time to dwell upon our injuries, because our homes were aflame. Every wagon within our camp was burning. And our families... our families...'

'Oh, God,' I breathed.

'I tried to fight the flames, sir. We all did. But it was hopeless. Insensible with fury and grief, I targeted the last of the mob, turning to confront those who had remained behind on the periphery of our camp to watch, perhaps to gloat. As I ran towards the men they scattered before me, but I pursued one of them along several streets and finally into an alleyway. The man was swift, but I was an acrobat, in the peak of condition, despite the beating I had suffered – added to which, the alleyway ended in a brick wall that was twice the man's height.

'I caught the fellow trying in vain to scale the wall, and I dragged him back to the ground. And then I... there is no pretty way to say this, sir... I put my hands around his neck and I strangled the life out of him. I was like a man possessed. I wanted nothing more than to make him suffer as my poor family had suffered... my wife, Marta, and my four children...

'When the deed was done, I felt the strength drain out of me. I cast the man's body aside, and I sat on the ground and wept. I had lost everything in a single night... my wife, my beautiful children... I felt as though my life was over just as surely as theirs was.

'I was still sitting beside my victim's body when the police found me. There is little more to tell. I was arrested, thrown into Newgate Prison, condemned to hang. It transpired that my victim was not a ruffian, but a more "superior" type of fellow – the son of an aristocrat no less!' He smiled grimly. 'I was resigned to my fate, sir. I cared not a jot for my own life. And then, the night before my execution, I awoke, and miraculously there you were, standing beside my cot in my stinking cell, the cockroaches and rats scuttling around your feet. At first I thought I was dreaming. Then I wondered whether you were an angel – or a devil. You were holding the obsidian heart, sir. And it was... moving in your fist, perhaps glowing... yes, I believe it was glowing...'

His voice had dropped to a murmur.

'You said, "You must come with me, Abel. It's time." Those were your exact words.'

I filed them away in my mind for future use. Later I would write them down.

'Before I could respond, you reached out and took my hand. And suddenly... here we were. And my life began anew.'

He fell silent. Lifted his glass and took a sip. His hand was completely steady. The story had been a hard one for him to tell, but he was calm again now, composed.

'Hawkins,' I said, leaning forward, elbows on knees, 'I'm so sorry, I had no idea...'

He turned his head aside to stare into the flames, raising a hand as I had done earlier.

'Please, sir,' he said quietly. 'Let us speak no more about it.'

It was hard, but I swallowed the sympathy, the compassion I was feeling, and leaned back in my chair, the leather creaking beneath me. 'All right,' I said, 'if that's what you want. But you'll have to give me the date I appeared in your cell, so that I can make it happen. You realise that, don't you?'

He nodded. 'I do, sir.'

The circularity of time. Cause and effect. The chicken and the egg. Hawkins was only able to tell me his story because two years ago a future version of me had rescued him from his condemned cell on the eve of his execution. But the only reason I was able to appear in his condemned cell, the only reason I knew of his plight, was because he was telling me this story now.

I snatched up my glass and threw more port down my throat. Dulling the senses with alcohol was sometimes the only way to cope with it. I was about to suggest we continue with our game when, from below, came the rat-tat-tat of the door knocker. I glanced at the clock on the mantel, then at Hawkins, my heart leaping.

A midnight caller! Surely that could mean only one thing?

As Conan Doyle might have said, the game was afoot!

THREE

BLACK DOG ALLEY

One thing (among many) that had surprised me about Victorian London was how many theatres and music halls there were. Even in the poorer areas you could barely walk three streets without stumbling across some establishment dedicated to providing entertainment for the masses.

Thinking about it, I suppose it was understandable. TV had yet to be invented, the rise of commercial cinema was still a few years around the corner, and there were only so many nights a family could sit indoors reading by candlelight or singing songs around the piano before going stark staring mad.

Our midnight caller was a messenger boy, shivering in the cold, his feet frozen and wet from the snow, which had soaked through the holes in his battered boots. Clover, alerted by his knock, astonished him by opening the door and greeting him with a warm smile. The boy was even more astonished when she exchanged the scrap of paper he was clutching for one of Mrs Peake's rabbit pies from the kitchen. Eyes alight with joy, he scampered off as if he'd just received the best Christmas present he'd ever had.

The message was from Horace Lacey, owner and manager of the Maybury Theatre, which was tucked down a narrow road colloquially known as Black Dog Alley, just off Brewer Street in Soho. Brewer Street was close to Piccadilly Circus and its relatively new addition, the Statue of Eros, around which flower-sellers displayed their wilting blooms by day and prostitutes offered passing gentlemen the chance of a 'threepenny upright' by night.

Although Christmas Night had been clear, a brown, choking smog had descended over the city on Boxing Day afternoon and showed no signs of shifting as the day drifted into evening. At this time of night, and in these conditions, it was almost impossible to find a hansom cab – which was why I'd paid to have one at our constant beck and call from a nearby stable yard. As Hawkins hurried off to rouse the owner, a muffler over his mouth and nose keeping out the worst of the acrid fumes, Clover and I bundled ourselves up against the elements. Waiting in the entrance hall, listening for the slow clatter of the approaching cab, I looked at Lacey's message again. In sloping, crabbed handwriting it read:

My dear Mr Locke

Apologies for the lateness of the hour, but I am responding to instructions to inform you without delay of any unusual occurrences within the vicinity of my establishment, The Maybury Theatre (address supplied above). One such, which you may wish to investigate – a singularly grisly murder, no less! – has taken place this very evening in the small courtyard behind this building. I shall await your arrival for two hours beyond the stroke of midnight, though please do not feel obliged to attend if you adjudge the incident to be beneath your consideration. I have sundry tasks to occupy me upon these premises, and so shall not be inconvenienced if you decide to forego this invitation and remain at your domicile.

Your faithful servant
Horace Lacey (esq)

A *singularly* grisly murder? What did that mean? Poverty and desperation ensured that murders were ten a penny on the streets of Victorian London, so what was so different about this one that it had prompted Lacey to call me out at such a late hour on Boxing Day?

Although I felt a tingle of anticipation I tried not to get my hopes up. I had followed enough dud leads in the past few months to last me a lifetime. Although my 'watchers', as I called them, came from all walks of life, I did employ a large number of the dissolute and the dispossessed – vagrants and vagabonds, mudlarks, prostitutes, even pickpockets and cut-throats. There were a couple of reasons for this. One, the majority of them spent most of their time on the streets, and therefore tended to be the first to know what was going on. And two, because they operated below the radar of 'normal' society, they could keep their eyes and ears open without attracting undue attention.

I paid each of my watchers a small stipend – as much as I could afford – for their services. But in order to motivate them to stay vigilant and pass on anything useful that came their way, I also promised a sizeable bonus to whoever might provide me with information that would ultimately lead to the recovery of the obsidian heart.

While this was a decent enough system, it did mean that, because many of my watchers were desperate for money, I received a lot of intel that was dubious at best and useless at worst. My problem, though, was that because I was paranoid of overlooking something that might turn out to be vital, I ended up following more of these leads than was probably good for me, which, as the weeks had turned into months, had become a demoralising and exhausting exercise.

What made me more hopeful about *this* particular lead, though, was not only that Lacey was one of the more affluent of my watchers, but also that, as far as I could remember, he hadn't contacted me before.

As if reading my mind, Clover put a hand on my arm and said, 'Try not to get your hopes up, Alex.'

I gave her a smile, which felt skewed and tight. 'I never do.'

'Yes you do. Every time. And it's eating you up.'

I knew she was right, but even so I couldn't prevent a hint of sharpness from creeping into my voice.

'Well, what do you expect?'

'Nothing less,' she said soothingly. 'But... look, I know it's pointless me saying this, but I'm going to say it anyway... try to stay calm. Focused. Try not to despair. We'll get there eventually. I honestly believe that.'

'Women's intuition?'

She locked my eyes with hers as if trying to instil some of her belief into me. 'I know we'll get the heart back because not getting it back is too horrible a prospect to contemplate.'

We'd talked about this already – about the implications of what might happen if we failed, of how things might unravel. I sometimes felt as though we talked about nothing else, as though our conversations just went round and round in a never-ending spiral, our own personal time loop.

I sighed wearily. 'Yeah, I know.'

We were saved from further conversation by the faint sound of the approaching carriage, the rumble of wheels and the clop of horse's hooves partly muffled by snow.

Clover briefly tightened her grip on my arm, giving me a reassuring squeeze, then she leaned forward and planted a kiss on my cheek. Her breath smelled warmly and sweetly of cloves, which I knew she chewed, along with mint, to keep her breath fresh.

'Once more unto the breach,' she said. 'You never know. Maybe you'll get a late Christmas present.'

'I thought you told me not to get my hopes up?'

'I also said I believed we'd find the heart sooner or later. Who's to say you won't get the breakthrough you've been looking for tonight?'

When we stepped outside we were met with a wall of smog. Instantly I felt it trying to crawl down my throat, and I pressed my scarf to my face as I trudged along the path of compacted snow towards the wrought-iron gate set into the high hedge. I knew the hansom was there only because we could hear the creak of its wooden frame and the snorting and shifting of the horse. The smog was so dense we couldn't even see the gates until we were almost upon them, beyond which the carriage was a vague patch of darkness in the murk. The soft clang of the gates as I closed them was answered with a creak as Hawkins pushed open the door of the hansom from within. I saw his hand emerge to help Clover climb aboard, then I stepped up into the carriage myself.

Hansom cabs were designed for two passengers, so it was a tight squeeze with three of us crammed in. What made it more uncomfortable was that, despite our best efforts, tendrils of smog continued to creep in through the crevices around the doors and windows, turning the air pungent. As the cab set off with a lurch, I thought of the poor driver on his sprung seat at the back of the vehicle, fully exposed to the elements. I thought too of the ever-present coterie of men watching the house (not that they'd be able to see more than a metre in front of their faces in these conditions), who were no doubt even now stamping their feet to ward off the cold and trying not to choke to death on the noxious fumes.

And they *were* noxious. That was no exaggeration. I'd known even before coming here that Victorian smog was basically a big ball of toxins – sulphur dioxide and soot particulates from the huge amount of coal that was burnt both domestically and industrially – that gathered together in the sky, became mixed in with low-lying clouds of water droplets, and were then squished back down onto the city as the air cooled, but I'd never realised quite *how* lethally pungent they were until I'd been given the dubious honour of experiencing them first-hand.

People died from inhaling London smog. Lots of people. In this age respiratory problems and cancers were rife – and here was I, putting lives at risk for my own selfish purposes. The driver of the hansom; the men guarding my house; every single person I employed as a watcher – they were all at risk because of me, for one reason or another. At risk from the elements; at risk from the Wolves of London...

Which made me what? A selfish bastard? Or something worse? Was I, in my own way, as ruthless as my enemies?

I continually told myself I was fighting the potential for chaos, that I was doing this for the greater good, that the end would justify the means – but did I really believe that? Was my battle *really* bigger than me? Would it *really* have far-reaching effects if I lost it? Or was it nothing but a personal skirmish? Something that would affect my timeline, but barely touch anyone else's?

Although it was less than three miles from my house in Kensington to the Maybury Theatre, the smog and snow meant that the horse could move at little more than a snail's pace. Yet even though the journey took well over an hour, we endured it mostly in silence. Admittedly the conversation was limited by the fact that we kept our mufflers over our faces, but I doubt we'd have talked much even if the air had been clear. I was too pensive to chat, Hawkins – never a big talker at the best of times – seemed lost in his own thoughts, and Clover, who was squashed between us and seemed to sense our joint mood, simply rested her head on my shoulder and took the opportunity to have a snooze.

Eventually we halted beneath the fuzzy orange glow of a street lamp. The driver rapped on the roof and we clambered out, Clover blinking sleepily. As Hawkins spoke to the cab driver, Clover and I, still holding our mufflers over our faces, climbed the short flight of wide, semicircular stone steps to the theatre's main entrance.

Although The Maybury was intended to be the proud centrepiece of a row of squat redbrick dwellings that stretched into the smog on either side, it wasn't a particularly impressive structure. The architecture was basic, devoid of elaboration, and the brickwork itself was blackened by a crust of soot. I rapped on the double doors, which were panelled in small, individual panes of glass – though they might as well have been painted black, so thick was the grime that coated them.

After a few seconds I heard the patter of approaching footsteps followed by the grating squeal of a key in a stiff lock. The right-hand door was plucked inwards, and a man all but leaped into the widening gap, brandishing a yellow-toothed scimitar grin.

It wasn't the grin that made me step back, however, but the smell that gusted from his body. It was eye-wateringly pungent – even more so than the yellow-brown smog, threads of which were now sliding around my feet, preceding me into the theatre's entrance lobby. I held my breath as the man's stench rolled over me like the first blast of heat from a steam room.

What he smelled of wasn't body odour, but perfume, which he obviously applied with wild abandon. Used sparingly it might have been pleasant – a welcome change from the sweaty stink that most people exuded – but his was a reek that clawed at the throat and stung the senses; it was like drowning in a vat of rotting lilies.

'Mr Locke, I presume!' the man exclaimed. 'This is a veritable honour, sir! Please! Come in! Come in!'

I cleared my throat and managed to croak, 'Thank you.' Then, bracing myself, I stepped past him, followed by Clover and Hawkins.

As the man turned his back on us to lock the door, I glanced at Clover. She responded by screwing her face into a squinty-eyed expression, like a dowager duchess presented with a dead mouse in a box. Trying to conceal a smile, I looked at Hawkins, who studiously avoided making eye contact with me.

Tugging the key from its lock and pocketing it with a theatrical flourish, the man swung to face us, side-swiping us with yet another waft of his cloying odour. Clover and I stepped back, and even Hawkins shuffled his feet. The man spread his arms, fingers extended as though he was cupping a pair of invisible crystal balls.

'Welcome to the Maybury Theatre!' he declared.

He was small and prissy, his black, wavy, slightly overlong hair and handlebar moustache carefully oiled and sculpted. He wore a red velvet tailcoat, floppy green cravat, silver waistcoat, striped trousers and gleaming, pointy-toed boots, complete with spats. He looked like Willy Wonka, or at least like someone trying too hard to be eccentric.

'Thank you,' I said again, and introduced my companions.

Once our host had finished simpering over her, Clover glanced around the gas-lit lobby. 'Charming place you've got here.'

It wasn't. It was shabby and grubby, the woodwork chipped, the carpet threadbare, the wallpaper, once ruby and cream, now dulled to sludge brown and urine yellow. Even the sagging red rope, which stretched across the bottom of the stairs between the newel posts, resembled a skinned snake.

The little man beamed at Clover. 'Thank you, my dear. It is too sweet of you to say so. I do confess that I regard the Maybury as my own little corner of paradise, though I expect you shall think me a fool for doing so.'

'Not at all,' said Clover silkily; she hated being called 'my dear'. 'I think the theatre suits you very well.'

As the little man simpered, I stepped forward and extended my hand, glad I was wearing gloves.

'You *are* Mr Lacey, the manager?'

'Manager *and* owner, sir,' he corrected me, grabbing my hand like a bulldog snapping at a morsel of food and shaking it vigorously. He puffed out his silvery chest. 'Manager and *owner*.'

As I nodded, Clover prompted, 'You mentioned a murder, Mr Lacey?'

Lacey released my hand so that he could wave dramatically. 'Indeed I did. Although...' He gave me a meaningful look.

'Is there a problem?' I asked.

Lacey glanced quickly at Clover, then back at me. 'Not a problem as such. No, no, I wouldn't call it a problem. Only...'

Clover frowned. 'Only what?'

'I'm sorry, my dear. Perhaps I'm a little old-fashioned; indeed, I'm certain that I am. But the fact is, the particulars of this matter may prove a little... distressing for delicate ears.'

Clover smiled, though her teeth were clenched.

'Oh, don't worry about me, Mr Lacey,' she muttered. 'I'm a lot tougher than I look.'

'She is, Mr Lacey,' I confirmed as he glanced at me dubiously. 'And the hour is late, and we're all eager for our beds. So if you could lead us to where the murder took place...?'

At once the theatre owner was all fluster and activity.

'Of course, of course! Please forgive me. This way...'

He skipped past us, liberating another waft of his nostril-stinging odour, and unhooked the rope barrier at the bottom of the stairs. He waved us through, re-hooked the rope, then darted ahead.

'This way, this way.'

He led us up the stairs and along a narrow corridor that skirted the left side of the auditorium. Evenly spaced arches along the right-hand wall led into the auditorium itself, which at this hour was nothing but a vast black space, whilst to our left were a series of doors, most of them marked: Private No Admittance.

Lacey ignored them all, stopping only when he reached the door at the far end. One of a set of keys was dangling from the lock. He grasped it and gave it a twist.

'This door allows one access to the back-stage area from the front of the theatre,' he explained breathlessly. 'One can also access the area via the stage, of course, not to mention through a door at the back of the theatre, which leads into the courtyard where tonight's deed occurred.'

'Is the victim's body still lying where it fell?' asked Hawkins.

Lacey looked shocked. 'Certainly not. I informed the local constabulary as soon as the matter was brought to my attention.'

'You intimated in your note that the murder was unusual, Mr Lacey?' I said.

'And so it was. Hideously so.'

'In what way?'

Lacey licked his lips and glanced worriedly at Clover, who said, 'It's all right, Mr Lacey. I'm a big girl.'

Nodding doubtfully, Lacey said, 'Although the unfortunate victim had been freshly despatched, her remains were... picked clean.'

'Picked clean?' I repeated.

'Of flesh, sir. The poor girl had been stripped to the bone. As if by an army of vermin. Or carrion.' He shuddered, causing fresh waves of perfume to waft over us. 'It was a singular sight. I wish never to view its like again.'

The way Clover looked at me I knew we were both thinking the same thing. Along with the tracks I had found last night, could this be evidence that the Wolves of London were nearby? Perhaps toying with us prior to closing in?

'How can you be certain that the murder was a recent one, Mr Lacey?' Hawkins asked. 'Is it not possible that the victim was slaughtered weeks or even months ago and her remains, for whatever reason, tonight transferred to the courtyard behind your premises?'

Lacey shook his head vigorously. 'No, no, it is quite impossible. There was blood, you see... a great deal of fresh blood... on the ground and... and on the wall beside the body.'

He slumped against the door. Recounting the experience was clearly taking it out of him. I could see his legs shaking, as if they were struggling to keep him upright.

Sweetly Clover asked, 'Are you all right, Mr Lacey? Would you like a chair?'

I shot her a warning look, but Lacey seemed unaware she was teasing him.

'No, no, my dear, thank you. It's very kind, but... I'm sure I shall be well in a moment.'

'Forgive me, Mr Lacey,' I said, 'but is it possible that Mr Hawkins could be right and that the corpse may have decomposed before being brought here? I mean, how do you know the blood found close to the body belonged to the victim?'

Lacey pulled a handkerchief from his pocket and dabbed at his forehead. 'She was recognised, sir.'

I raised my eyebrows. 'Recognised by who?'

Again Lacey glanced at Clover, as if unsure how much he should reveal in her presence. 'The truth is, sir, certain young ladies frequent the courtyard – against my wishes, you understand – to... er... consort with... that is to say, *entertain*–'

'Prostitutes, you mean?' said Clover bluntly.

Lacey blanched. 'Quite so.'

'And the victim was a prostitute?' I asked.

'Not only the victim, sir, but the... um... young lady who discovered her remains. She made quite a racket, I can tell you. I felt certain her screams would rouse the entire neighbourhood. Naturally her client took to his heels the instant she began her caterwauling, and so I failed to set eyes–'

'Sorry to interrupt, Mr Lacey,' I said, raising my hand, 'but didn't you say the corpse was picked clean?'

'I did, sir.'

'So how was the victim identified?'

'By her head, sir. Her face, I should say. That was left quite untouched – aside from the fact that her features were contorted in the most terrible agony.' His eyes swivelled again to Clover as his hand flew to his mouth. 'I beg your forgiveness, my dear.'

She waved away the apology with a flick of the wrist.

'And when was the victim last seen alive?' I asked.

'Earlier this evening, sir. The... er... young lady who named the deceased informed the constables that the victim had been present this afternoon in a tavern called The Black Jack – a most unsavoury establishment – and that she had subsequently been observed plying her trade in Piccadilly Circus.'

'I don't suppose the girl mentioned seeing the victim with any particular client?'

'I'm afraid not, sir.'

'Hmm. Well, thank you for the information, Mr Lacey. Now, if you could show us the scene of the crime?'

Lacey nodded and opened the door he'd been slumped against. He led us down a set of thinly carpeted steps to a long corridor at the back of the stage. This part of the theatre, out of bounds to paying customers, was even shabbier than the public areas. The corridor's only illumination, a pair of guttering oil lamps, above which greasy black stains fanned across the walls like coagulated shadows, was evidence that the Maybury Theatre was in decline. Electricity, though still in its infancy, was becoming more prevalent in public buildings, and yet the Maybury had not yet even graduated from oil to gas lighting. I looked up at the thick cobwebs clumped like balls of fog in the corners of the high ceilings, and winced as the uneven and possibly worm-eaten floorboards creaked alarmingly underfoot. We passed several doors, which Lacey told us were dressing rooms for the actors, or rather 'actors', his plummy voice emphasising the second syllable as if to impress us. Clover asked what was currently playing at the theatre, and Lacey told her that a travelling company were rehearsing a tragedy entitled *The Fall of Oedipus*, which was booked for a two-week run early in the New Year.

'But you must come and see the production, my dear,' he gushed. 'I shall send you tickets.'

'Thank you,' said Clover heavily. 'That would be lovely.'

The instant Lacey opened the door into the courtyard at the back of the building a thick brown wall of smog pressed in, wispy tendrils exuding from the main mass and reaching out like the long fingers of forlorn ghosts. Clover started to cough and pulled her muffler over her face. Pressing his handkerchief to his mouth, Lacey wafted at the encroaching murk, as if it could be discouraged like a flock of birds.

Lifting his arm and breathing into his sleeve, Hawkins asked, 'Where was the body found, Mr Lacey?'

The theatre owner pointed, the smog so thick it immediately enveloped his hand. 'Against the wall on the far side, almost directly opposite this door.' He lit a lantern from a small shelf beside the door and handed it to Hawkins. 'You had better take this.'

Hawkins took the lantern, gave a curt nod, then stepped into the smog without hesitation. He was swallowed up immediately, as was the lantern glow, though I could hear the soft crump of his footsteps on the snow-coated cobbles. I eyed the swirling brown cloud warily for a moment, then plunged after him.

Behind me I heard Lacey say weakly, 'I think I shall remain here if you don't mind?'

Clover said something in reply, but by now I was already half a dozen steps ahead of her, and heard only the tone of her voice – understanding, soothing – and not her actual words. It was as if the smog was cramming my senses like cotton wool, muffling my hearing, distorting my vision. I tried to breathe as shallowly as possible and squeezed my eyes into slits to prevent the pollutants from stinging them. The client of the doxy who had discovered the body must have been desperate for a shag to brave these toxic conditions. As for the girls themselves... well, they were just desperate. Prepared to risk their health, their lives, everything, for the sake of a few coins to buy food and gin.

It was impossible to tell how big the courtyard was, or what was in front of me. I used my left hand to hold my muffler over my face and my right to probe the way ahead. The smog swirled around the fingertips of my outstretched arm, forming fleeting spirals in the murk. In these conditions you would have to virtually trip over a body to find one – which was possibly what had happened. In which case it was no wonder the girl who'd found her friend had screamed the place down.

I'd advanced fifteen, maybe twenty steps through slushy, gritty snow when the dimness in front of me suddenly darkened and shifted. I jerked back as a shape loomed from the smog, its head glowing yellow – but it was only Hawkins holding up the lantern.

'Careful, sir,' he murmured, lowering the lantern to knee-level.

I looked down to where he was indicating. Through the thick brown veil I could see that the off-white ground had suddenly become darker, slicker. I lowered myself into a squat and in the glow of lantern light the oily blackness staining the snow turned red.

Blood. Lots of it. I wafted vigorously at the veils of smog, trying to disperse them.

Vaguely I saw that the wall of the courtyard was no more than a metre in front of me, just beyond the range of my outstretched arm. As Lacey had said, there was blood not only pooled among the cobbles, but spattered up and across the mouldering bricks in jagged streaks. It was clear that whatever had killed the girl must have done so swiftly and frenziedly for her blood to jet out like that. Most of the injuries must have been inflicted while her heart was still beating. But what could strip a human body to the bone with such manic efficiency? A school of piranhas that swam through smog as easily as they swam through water?

If I hadn't already seen the Wolves of London in action the idea would have been ludicrous. But I'd reached the stage where I was prepared to believe anything. This could even be the work of the shape-shifter. Though what puzzled me—

'Why was she killed, do you think?'

Clover, emerging from the gloom and squatting beside me, seemed to pluck the question from my mind. I shrugged.

'Perhaps she knew too much?'

'Do you think she might have been one of yours?'

It was something I'd considered, but if the girl had information why hadn't she reported it immediately? Given her profession it seemed odd that she would have held back when a potential payday was in the offing.

'Who knows?' I said. 'I'd need to speak to Cargill, find out who she was.'

Inspector Cargill was my senior police contact – and another of my watchers. I'd discovered that in this period the Metropolitan Police Force was more of a loose and baggy monster than a coherent and organised body, with many of the modern protocols and procedures I was used to still to be implemented. Its officers, in general, were not averse to earning a bit of extra money on the side, and indeed saw no conflict of interest in doing so. For that reason I could number several dozen serving officers among my network of watchers.

Clover tugged her muffler down and briefly sniffed the air. 'Can you smell something?'

I raised my eyebrows. 'Apart from the delicate bouquet of carcinogens, you mean? Or is a whiff of Lacey's Chanel No 666 drifting this way?'

She smiled. 'I'm serious, Alex. There's something else.' She lowered her head, as if to lap at the blood-spattered snow. 'It's a musty sort of odour. Weird.'

Since warning me about the blood, Hawkins had been silent, but now he too crouched down and lowered his left arm from his face long enough to sniff tentatively at the air.

'Miss Clover is right, sir. There *is* an unusual odour. It smells like...'

'Mouldy bread!' said Clover suddenly. 'Or like when you leave wet washing in the machine for too long.'

Hawkins nodded in agreement – though as he'd never set eyes on a washing machine, I assumed it was the mouldy bread reference he identified with.

'Quite so. It's the smell of decomposition.'

'But not meat,' said Clover. 'Something less... animal than that.'

I removed my muffler and twitched my nose. They were both right. Beneath the choking, smoky odour of the smog, there *was* something. Stale and heavy, it was *like* mouldy bread... and yet it had a uniqueness and unpleasantness all its own.

The smell disturbed me. It seemed to hover above the blood-slick ground like marsh gas. Turning my head I sniffed left and right, then rose to my feet and sniffed again. I took a few steps back towards the theatre and took another sniff, this time stifling a cough as I swallowed a lungful of freezing smog. Pulling my muffler over my face, I walked back to where Clover and Hawkins were still squatting.

'Can you do me a favour?' I said. 'Go back inside, get Lacey and take him into the lobby?'

Clover looked puzzled. 'Why?'

'Because I want to test something. I think that smell might lead back to the theatre. But if Lacey's there—'

'His smell will drown it out,' she said.

'Exactly.'

She nodded and straightened. 'I'll try. Though as I'm a mere woman I may have to punch him unconscious before he'll listen to me.'

I smiled. 'Hawkins, will you go with Clover?'

Hawkins glanced uneasily at the swirling smog.

'Are you certain you'll be all right, sir?'

'I'm armed,' I said, patting the bulge in my overcoat. 'I'll be fine.'

With another glance at the smog, Hawkins nodded, then he and Clover moved away. I listened to the slushy crump of their receding footsteps, aware as the lantern light faded of the damp, miasmic chill closing in around me.

Just you and me now, buddy, I imagined the smog – or whatever was *in* the smog – whispering. *So how about I show you what I'm really made of?*

I squinted. Was the smog solidifying to my left? Was a shape forming from it?

No. Course not. I was being stupid.

Even so, I shuddered and wrapped my arms around my body in a self-protective hug. No doubt bullets would be useless against a smog monster – although, to be honest, bullets would probably be useless against many of the Wolves of London.

I wished it were the heart I was carrying in my pocket instead of a gun. Unconsciously I cupped my hand, imagining the heart in my fist so vividly I could almost feel its contours beneath my fingers. I tried not to wonder when I'd next feel the weight of it in my palm – or if I ever would.

I gave Clover and Hawkins two minutes, forcing myself to count off the seconds slowly and steadily, and then retraced my steps. All that filled my vision was thick, brown, swirling smog above a ghostly pall of snow. I did as I had done before, edging forward with one hand outstretched and the other holding my muffler up to my face. When I judged that I was halfway across the courtyard I removed the muffler and cautiously sniffed the air. At first all I could smell was the smoky sharpness of the smog, but then, remembering the smell had been strongest near the ground, I squatted and sniffed again.

And there it was, faint but undeniably present. I felt like a bloodhound following a trail. Within seconds the smog started scratching at my throat, so I pulled the muffler back over my nose and mouth, and straightened up. My coughs, even stifled by the muffler, seemed both too loud and oddly flat in the shrouded atmosphere. I glanced around, worried that I was drawing attention to myself. But there was no sign of movement in the thick gloom, and no sound of anything moving nearby.

Less than a dozen shuffling steps later I reached the back door of the theatre and slipped into the building. Even though the corridor was dimly lit it was a relief to see my surroundings again. I locked the door and leaned against it for a moment, stamping snow from my boots and sniffing the air. As I'd hoped, Lacey's overpowering perfume had dispersed, but the mouldy bread smell, which was more subtle yet more persistent, was still detectable.

In fact, it was stronger in this enclosed space than it had been in the courtyard. Bending almost double, I moved forward, sniffing the air. After a bit of trial and error, I decided the smell was strongest around the door of dressing room five, the number of which was painted on the scuffed and battered wood in white paint that had glazed and partly flaked away.

I tapped on the door and got no reply. When I put my ear to the wood all I heard was silence. I tried the handle, expecting the door to be locked, but to my surprise, it opened. Still holding the handle I stepped into the room.

The space in front of me was dark, the flickering light from the corridor giving the room's contents only the most basic definition. The mouldy bread smell was stronger here than it had been in the corridor. Blinking into the darkness, my hand crept beneath my overcoat and closed over my gun.

If whatever had killed the girl was hiding here, it was lying low for now. Could it be lurking in the shadows, silent and motionless, watching me? I felt vulnerable in the doorway, framed by the light at my back, but I held my ground. I didn't want to retreat before investigating further, but neither did I want to step into the room before my eyes had adjusted to the dark.

Wishing the Victorians would hurry up and equip all their buildings with electric light, I peered into the blackest of the shadows. When I'd satisfied myself as much as I could that nothing was moving, I turned my attention to the parts of the room I *could* see. On the right-hand wall, close enough to the open door that its basic shape was sketched out in yellowish light, was a make-up table beneath a large mirror. There were items cluttering the table, including several candles in brass holders and a small rectangular box that I guessed held lucifers.

Glancing again at the most impenetrable patches of darkness, I crossed quickly to the make-up table and picked up the box of matches. I took one out, lit it and seconds later candlelight was pushing back the shadows. Slipping my finger through the metal loop of the holder, I turned, the candle flame flapping as I swept it from left to right.

The room was small, boxy, and contained only two possible hiding places. One was a squat, battered wardrobe in the corner beside the left-hand wall, and the other was a large trunk pushed against the back wall.

I drew my gun, and then, candle in one hand and pistol in the other, crossed to the trunk. Noting there was no padlock through the loop of the hasp, I used my left foot to nudge the lid open.

My first impression was of something shiny and shapeless, which entirely filled the trunk's interior, heaving itself upright. It took less than a second – during which my heart gave a single alarmed jolt – to realise that what I'd taken for movement was simply the trunk's tightly packed contents bulging under the release of pressure.

The trunk was full of costumes, most of which looked bulky and garish. The top one, which my brain had registered as something reptilian, was made of shimmering green satin edged with gold braid. Beneath it I could see something yellow, something pink, something patterned with bright harlequin diamonds. The costumes looked like ones that the cast of a Gilbert and Sullivan opera might wear. Perhaps that's what they were. As far as I could remember, Gilbert and Sullivan were still knocking about in this era.

Kneeling on the floor, I put the candle down and rummaged through the costumes with one hand to reassure myself there was nothing beneath the topmost layers of material. I didn't expect there to be, but I was cautious all the same. When I was happy the trunk contained no nasty surprises I straightened up and crossed to the wardrobe. The candle, which I'd left on the floor, didn't throw out much light, but there was enough for me to see by, even if the flickering flame did cause vast brown shadows to sway and lurch up the walls.

I listened at the door of the wardrobe, then pulled it open, stepping back and levelling my gun. But apart from a few more costumes on hangers, which jangled like unmusical wind chimes as they swayed from side to side, the wardrobe was empty.

I closed the wardrobe door and released a deep sigh, partly of relief. I might not have solved the mystery of the horrible smell, but neither had I had to defend myself against whatever had torn a girl to shreds out in the courtyard. Now I was convinced I was alone I realised I was shaking slightly; sweating too. I sniffed again. The mouldy bread smell still lingered; in fact, here in this room it had an almost muscular quality.

Wrinkling my nose, I took a last look round, blew out the candle, then exited the room, closing the door behind me. I hurried back to the foyer, slipping my gun back into my pocket so as not to alarm Lacey.

I smelled the theatre owner before I saw him. His overpowering scent curled along the corridor and clutched at my throat. Not for the first time I wished Victorian London didn't have to stink so much. If it wasn't the smog, it was the sewers or the people or the reek of horse sweat in the streets.

'Anything?' Clover asked as I appeared at the top of the stairs down to the foyer. From the way she jerked upright and took an eager step towards me, I could tell she'd been on tenterhooks.

'Maybe,' I said. 'Who's currently occupying dressing room five, Mr Lacey?'

Lacey looked puzzled. 'Five?'

'Yes.' I tried not to sound impatient. 'You told Mrs Locke earlier that a theatre company are rehearsing a play here. Is one of the actors using room five?'

'Why... yes,' Lacey said. 'That's my primary dressing room. It is currently at the disposal of my leading man, who also happens to be the head of the company.'

'I see. And what's his name?'

'Willoughby Willoughby,' replied Lacey, and then amended himself. '*Sir* Willoughby Willoughby.' He paled slightly. 'But why do you ask? There is nothing amiss, I hope.'

I forced a smile. 'I hope not too, Mr Lacey. In fact, I'm sure it's nothing. Tell me, what sort of man is Mr Willoughby?'

'Why, he's... cultured. Well bred. Well educated. He displays an enviable knowledge of the fine arts... and he is, of course, a consummate performer...'

'You don't like him, do you?' Clover said.

Lacey blanched. 'I beg your pardon?'

She gave him a conspiratorial smile. 'Come on, Mr Lacey, there's no need to be coy. You're among friends here. Naturally you're a gentlemen, and so you refuse to speak ill of your cast. But do I sense a certain... antipathy towards Mr Willoughby?'

Lacey smiled shakily, and I saw his body language change, his defences slipping as he succumbed to Clover's charms. In a hushed voice, as if afraid of being overheard, he said, 'I must admit, I do find Mr Willoughby's presence a little... disquieting.'

'Disquieting how?' I asked.

'There is... an aura about him that bothers me. Oh, admittedly he is pompous, perhaps one would even say overbearing, but it is not wholly that. There are... shadows about him.'

'Shadows?' Clover asked.

Lacey wafted a hand as though to dispel his own words.

'They are not literal shadows, they are...' he frowned. We waited silently for him to speak. Eventually he said, '...there is a darkness about the man. A sense of... danger.'

I'd heard and seen (and smelled) more than enough to set my spidey senses tingling.

'When are the company next rehearsing?'

'Tomorrow. They have been idle these past two days, celebrating the season, but tomorrow they shall be hard at it again.'

'Then we'll be back tomorrow to speak to Mr Willoughby. With your permission, of course.'

Lacey looked troubled, but nodded.

'You have it, sir. Gladly. I shall see you tomorrow.'

FOUR

NIGHT TERRORS

I was woken by screaming.

Almost before I was fully conscious I was throwing back my heavy blankets, grabbing my gun from the top drawer of the bedside cabinet, where I placed it every night, and leaping out of bed. Even when asleep my brain was on constant alert, half expecting an attack, and my reactions were both instant and instinctive.

As soon as my feet hit the floor I was running. The room was pitch black, but I knew its layout precisely, knew exactly how many paces it was to the door, how to grab the handle cleanly without fumbling in the dark.

The scream that had woken me bubbled and died. But the screamer was only drawing breath. As I wrenched the door open, only peripherally aware of freezing air washing over me from the unlit hallway, a second scream rose, louder and more piercing than before.

I now had enough of my wits about me to recognise who was screaming and where the sound was coming from. It was Hope. Her bedroom was at the far end of the long corridor, past the staircase on the left.

As I ran towards it a door opened in the right-hand wall ahead of me and a figure emerged. It was Clover in a long white nightdress, her hair hanging loose, her face a glowing, shocked mask, underlit by the candle in her hand. The bloom of light was welcome, coaxing the angles of the house to emerge dimly from the murk.

'Hope,' I gasped as she blinked at me, wide-eyed.

Her head jerked in acknowledgement. 'I know.'

Then I was past her, reaching the door at the end of the corridor, slamming into it, turning the handle. The door flew open and I catapulted into the room, raising my gun, not knowing what to expect.

By the dim glow of the nightlight burning on the desk beneath the window I saw Hope sitting up in bed, back pressed against the headboard, knees raised to her chest. Her hands – one flesh and blood, one mechanical – gripped the eiderdown, which she had drawn up to her chin. Her saucer eyes were fixed on something on the opposite side of the room.

I followed her gaze and saw nothing but shadows and furniture. I leaped across the room to the tall wardrobe – the only possible hiding place – and wrenched it open, aware that this was the second time I'd done this tonight.

And for the second time, thankfully, the wardrobe was empty of everything but clothing. Hope's dresses on hangers, her stockings and undergarments and petticoats neatly folded on shelves.

With a sense of déjà vu, I lowered my gun, breathed a sigh of relief, felt the tension leaving me. By the time I'd closed the wardrobe door and turned round, Clover was at Hope's bedside, wrapping her arms around the little girl, kissing the top of her head, murmuring soothing words.

A *nightmare*, I thought. *Just a nightmare.* Hope had suffered plenty when she'd first come to us, had woken in the night frequently, crying and confused. But in the last month or so the bad dreams had begun to subside, and for the last two weeks, she had slept relatively soundly. Even on the nights when the infection had flared up and the fever had gripped her, she had not screamed like this.

Maybe this one had been building up. An accumulation. A final explosion, like a boil bursting. Maybe now that she'd screamed it all out the bad memories would be expunged forever. It was cod philosophy, but I clung to it as I crossed the room and perched on the edge of the bed. Hope had her back to me, her arms wrapped tightly around Clover, who was on the other side. Clover glanced at me over Hope's tousled head and raised her eyebrows. I shrugged and stroked Hope's back gently. Her flannel nightdress was damp with sweat; her body radiated heat.

'Hey, sweetie,' I murmured, 'it's all right. There's no one here. You had a bad dream, that's all.'

Hope's breath hitched. Face still pressed against Clover's chest, she shook her head.

'Wasn't a dream.'

I tensed, glanced once more about the room. It was a nice room. Yellow wallpaper with a floral design; pictures on the walls; books on the shelves; a brightly painted toy box; the doll's house we'd bought for Christmas...

'What was it then, honey?' Clover asked.

Hope unpeeled herself from Clover's body, turned her head and stared again at the spot she'd been facing when I'd entered. Her face was red, flushed. She raised her good arm and pointed.

'He was there,' she whispered.

Her words, or perhaps the way she said them, sent a shiver down my spine. 'Who was?'

'The Sandman.'

Again Clover glanced at me, her eyes wider this time. 'The Sandman?'

Must be a story someone's read to her, I thought. *Polly or Mrs Peake*. I'd have words, tell them not to frighten the girl, impress upon them that she was still recovering...

'What did he look like? This Sandman?' asked Clover.

Hope's face crumpled. She buried it in Clover's bosom again.

'He was *horrible*.'

I didn't want to push her, but I had to know. Touching her back again, as if to anchor her somehow, I said, 'How do you know he was the Sandman?'

She didn't answer at first, and I began to think she wasn't going to. Then slowly she raised her head. She looked haunted.

'Because he told me,' she whispered.

FIVE

THE DEAR DEPARTED

Willoughby Willoughby's face reminded me of a sausage skin overstuffed with meat. I couldn't help thinking that if I pricked him with a pin he'd burst. Either that or a sticky, colourless fluid would ooze from him, like seepage from a blister. But despite his corpulence he didn't seem to sweat. The only wet parts of him were his eyes, so dark they looked almost black, which gleamed and squirmed in sockets made deep and shadowy by his bulging cheeks and overhanging brow.

Lacey had told us that Willoughby's company, the Guiding Light Players, would be rehearsing from ten a.m. until noon, and then again from two p.m. until five p.m. Clover and I turned up at the Maybury just after eleven, gritty-eyed and frayed around the edges after a night of broken sleep. We slipped into musty-smelling seats at the back of the auditorium and watched Willoughby and his colleagues strutting and fretting about the stage.

Willoughby was instantly recognisable from Lacey's description, though even if we hadn't been here specifically to see him he would have drawn our attention. With his intimidating bulk and stentorian voice he dominated proceedings. He was like a vast, dark planet around which lesser satellites orbited warily. He was clearly the driving force of the company, haranguing and bullying his fellow performers when they didn't meet his exacting standards, which seemed to be most of the time. After he'd reduced one trembling slip of a girl to tears for stumbling over a line, Clover leaned across and put her lips to my ear.

'When we talk to him, can I be the bad cop? I want to punch him right in the middle of his stupid, fat face.'

I smiled and stood up. 'I'm going to look around the yard again. You want to come along or stay here?'

'I'll come,' she said. 'If I stay here much longer I may not be responsible for my actions.'

We slipped out of our seats and went in search of Lacey, who we found trying to polish scratches out of the woodwork in the foyer. When I asked him if he could unlock the door into the yard, he scuttled to do our bidding as if we were on official business. Judging by the shabbiness of the Maybury, I guessed his obsequiousness was due to the fact that the money I was paying him was a lifeline he was terrified of losing. Added to which, like much of the Victorian middle class, he was probably a social climber, hoping to impress the 'gentlemen', as he no doubt assumed me to be (though in truth, the idea of me as a rich gentleman was something I was pretty sure I'd never get used to).

Although a haze lingered in the air, last night's smog had largely dissipated. The improved visibility, though, did the cobbled yard at the back of the Maybury no favours. The ground was slippery with muddy snow, which was rapidly turning to slush, and the crumbling brick walls were patched with green-black damp so slimy it looked gangrenous. In the twenty-first century the yard would have been closed off and a forensics team would be crawling over every square inch in their hunt for evidence. But in the nineteenth century, police interest in murder sites tended to be perfunctory. I knew from experience that once they'd taken the victim's body away, and spent half an hour grubbing listlessly around in the chilly murk, they invariably lost interest. In this case they hadn't even arranged for the gruesome evidence of last night's murder to be removed. Blood, blackened and congealing now, was still pooled around the area where the girl had died. And there was more blood spattered up and across the wall, the pattern of streaks it made so wild and jagged you could almost sense the violence that had liberated it from the victim's body.

I'd sent a message to Cargill first thing that morning, requesting as much information about the murder as he possessed, but so far had heard nothing back. Once again I stood with my toes a centimetre or two from the victim's spilled blood, and stared at the spatters on the wall as if they were a secret code I needed to decipher to identify the killer.

'The way I look at it there are two possibilities,' Clover said. 'Either this is a random killing or it was a calling card, maybe even a warning, aimed at you. Personally I favour the second option.'

I looked at her staring unflinchingly at a scene that many would have found distressing, and thought of how capable, how kick-ass, she'd become in the past few months. She'd never been a shrinking violet, of course, but even so it couldn't be denied that everything we'd been through, both in our own time and since we'd been here, had toughened her up.

'You think the girl *was* a watcher then?' I said.

'Not necessarily – but Lacey is. So if the killer knew that, he'd also know that Lacey would get word to you about this. So maybe this is just the Wolves' way of letting *you* know that *they* know about your network.'

'Yeah, but what would that achieve?'

She wrinkled her nose. 'Could just be mind games. Or maybe it's their way of telling you that you won't find out anything they don't want you to know.'

I thought about it. It was a depressing prospect, and one I was reluctant to accept. 'There's no way they could know about everyone. Besides, why not just kill Lacey? That would have got the message across just as effectively.'

She shrugged. 'Maybe because the girl was innocent? Make you feel doubly bad?'

It was a possibility, but my gut feeling was that Clover's theory was too vague, too woolly.

'I don't think I'm being manipulated,' I said. 'I think, if anything, this is proof that my system's working. I've got hundreds of watchers all over the city, primed to look out for stuff like this. It's been three months now. One of them was bound to come up trumps eventually.'

'So you think that's what's happened here?'

'Don't you?' I nodded again at the blood spatters. 'You really think this could be a straightforward murder?'

'I think...' She paused; I could almost see the cogs whirring in her head. 'I think we should take things one step at a time. I think we should keep an open mind.'

'I always do.'

It was almost noon and there was nothing more to learn in the yard. We re-entered the theatre and snuck into the back of the auditorium to watch the end of the rehearsal. Once it was over and the actors had left the stage we walked down to the dressing rooms and knocked on door five.

'Come!' called an imperious voice.

I pushed open the door and marched in, Clover at my shoulder. I had decided on a no-nonsense approach; there was no point being diffident with someone like Willoughby. He was the sort of man who would see politeness as a terrier would see a rabbit – as something to be pounced on and torn to shreds.

'Good afternoon, Mr Willoughby,' I said before the surprise on his face could turn to indignation. 'My name is Alex Locke and this is...' I'd been about to say 'my colleague, Miss Clover Monroe', but then remembered that Clover had been introduced to Lacey as my wife. Hoping that Willoughby wouldn't find my hesitation odd I said as smoothly as I could, '...Mrs Clover Locke, my wife. We're assisting the local constabulary with their investigation into the murder that took place here last night, and we'd be grateful if you would allow us to ask you a few questions.'

Willoughby's surprise *was* now turning to indignation – but that was fine. It was *de*fensive rather than *o*ffensive; we had him on the back foot.

'Me?' he spluttered. 'What could *I* possibly tell you? I was nowhere within this vicinity last night.'

I showed my teeth in a smile. 'I don't doubt it, Mr Willoughby. Even so, I'm sure you've been apprised of the details of the attack?'

The actor, wallowing in his chair before the mirror, looked suddenly wary, his currant eyes darting between Clover and me.

'Some of them,' he admitted.

'Then you'll know what a horrible crime it was,' Clover said. 'Brutal. Savage.' She paused. 'Cowardly.'

Willoughby's eyes fixed on her. 'Cowardly?'

'Very. The victim was a slip of a girl – young, helpless, innocent. She didn't stand a chance.'

Although he didn't sweat, a flush rose from Willoughby's collar, mottling his neck and cheeks.

'Innocent?' he scoffed. 'I was given to understand that this *unfortunate* was a mere drab?'

I felt Clover tense. 'Are you suggesting the girl deserved to die, Mr Willoughby?'

'I am suggesting, Mrs Locke, that the girl was fully cognisant of the dangers associated with her profession, and yet chose to defy them. I feel unable, therefore, to engender even the remotest scrap of sympathy for her.'

Clover said nothing to this. When I glanced at her I saw she was glaring at Willoughby, her lips pressed together.

Quickly I said, 'Have you set foot in the yard during your company's residency here, Mr Willoughby? Either before the murder or after it?'

'I have not.'

'Have any other members of your company been in the yard, to your knowledge?'

Willoughby scowled. 'I assure you that they too have not.'

'You seem very certain of that,' Clover muttered.

Willoughby's scowl curled into a sneer. 'My knowledge of my colleagues' movements within this establishment is absolute. It is my responsibility to ensure that decorum is maintained at all times.'

'Rule them with a rod of iron, do you?' she quipped.

Willoughby's black eyes receded to pinpricks. 'I am not sure I approve of your manner, Mrs Locke.'

If this had been the twenty-first century no doubt Willoughby would have been questioning our credentials, demanding documentation. There were times when I felt frustrated, even alarmed, by the flabby protocols and practices of the Victorian police force, yet there were other occasions, like now, when such flabbiness worked in our favour. Clover and I had found that if you *said* you were working with the police, most people tended to accept it without question.

'I'm sure Mrs Locke meant nothing by her query, Mr Willoughby,' I said smoothly. 'Isn't that right, my dear?'

Clover's smile couldn't have been sweeter. 'Of *course* no offence was intended. I *do* apologise, Mr Willoughby, for any misunderstanding which may have occurred.'

Willoughby glowered, but said nothing.

Briskly, as if the matter had been swept aside, I said, 'Were you aware,

Mr Willoughby, that the yard was being used for... *illicit* purposes?'

Willoughby remained silent for a moment. Then he huffed a bullish breath from his nostrils. 'I was not.'

I gave a short nod, as if I accepted his statement without question. 'Nevertheless you strike me as both a perceptive and observant man. Perhaps you can recall witnessing the recent presence of unsavoury or unusual characters within the vicinity?'

My attempt to butter him up made no impression. The chair beneath Willoughby creaked as he shifted to look pointedly at Clover.

'Present company excepted, you mean?'

Clover's response was a girlish laugh.

'Oh, you are a card, Mr Willoughby. Have you ever done comedy? You would be a wonder at it.'

Willoughby said nothing. I wondered if Clover's antipathy towards him was as obvious to him as it was to me. His stillness as he continued to regard her (and she continued to grin at him) was unnerving.

Could he be our killer? Could this heaving mountain of a man be one of the Wolves of London? If so, what was his aim? Had it been his intention to draw us here, as Clover had suggested? But for what reason?

What no one had mentioned since we had entered the dressing room was the mouldy bread smell, which I had tracked from the murder scene last night, and which was still detectable.

The elephant in the room, I thought, and had to stifle a smirk as the double meaning struck me. I cleared my throat and decided to plunge in.

'Mr Willoughby, have you been aware of a peculiar odour in the theatre these past few days? A smell reminiscent of... mould? Of damp perhaps?'

Willoughby's shiny red face was inscrutable. 'An odour?'

'Yes. It was prevalent around the murder scene – and in this corridor last night.'

Willoughby's round shoulders raised in a shrug.

'This is an old building, Mr Locke, and ill maintained. Such odours as you describe are commonplace. Rotting wood, damp plaster, burning oil, sweat-stained seats; even the malodorous breath of an attentive audience tends to linger... It is all part and parcel of the profession. If you find it offensive, I suggest you retire to your country parks and perfumed boudoirs, where the air is fresher, but perhaps less redolent of life.'

He spoke wearily, though the spikiness underlying his words was obvious.

Clover's response was just as measured – and just as spiky.

'Redolent of life? An unusual phrase for an odour that lingers around a murder site.'

Willoughby's eyebrows, as black and slick and carefully sculpted as his wavy hair, inched upwards.

'You think so? But violence and murder is the *stuff* of life, is it not? It is life lived on the edge. It is the threat of sudden death which gives life its danger, its thrill, its *flavour*. The meat of an animal that knows it is soon for the chop is said to be more succulent than one that has lived a life of indolence and meets its maker without fear.'

'People are not animals,' Clover muttered.

Willoughby's black eyes shone as he leaned forward.

'Oh, but they *are*, Mrs Locke. We are *all* animals. All of us ripe for the slaughter.'

'Including yourself?' I asked, wondering where this was leading.

'Of course. All actors are slaughtered by their audience at one time or another. Did you not know that, Mr Locke?'

I was startled to hear him chuckle. There was such an air of haughtiness and constrained hostility about him that he'd seemed incapable of humour. The laughter churned and rumbled inside him, and then, as the sound belched from his mouth, the air seemed to grow suddenly thicker with the stench of mouldy bread.

No, not mouldy bread, I thought now; not exactly. In hindsight the smell was more like mulch, or rotting fungi; it made me think of poisonous mushrooms tumescing in the dark. I felt an urge to gag; to run across the room, pull the door wide and gulp at the fresher air in the corridor. The building was draughty, unheated, the temperature outside hovering around zero, but even so I felt sweat beading my forehead.

I decided to call time on the interview, but Willoughby beat me to it. As his laughter dribbled into silence he consulted his pocket watch.

'And now if you'll excuse me, I have a prior engagement.'

I nodded, too nauseated to feel indignant.

'Of course, Mr Willoughby. Thank you for your time.'

He wafted a hand and turned away from us, the chair again creaking alarmingly beneath him. I would have loved it to break and spill him to the ground – though I didn't much love the image that accompanied the thought: of his clothes bursting open and his unrestrained flesh oozing out like barely set jelly.

As soon as the dressing-room door had closed behind us, the nausea I'd been keeping at bay rose up and I leaned against the wall, feeling sweaty and weak-kneed.

'You all right?' Clover asked – though she too looked a bit green.

'Did you smell that?'

'When he laughed, yes. It's him, I know it. And he *knows* we know. And he doesn't care.'

I glanced again at the door to Willoughby's dressing room and slowly straightened up. 'Come on, let's go. I don't want to still be here when he comes out.'

Our hansom was waiting outside the theatre. We climbed aboard, and I gave instructions to the driver to take us to the end of the road and conceal himself around the corner, out of sight of the Maybury. Less than a minute later, as soon as the cab was in position behind the high side wall of the house at the end of the terrace, Clover and I alighted and hurried towards the shelter of the low, snow-topped wall which enclosed the same house's front yard. From here we could keep watch on the front of the theatre, which was about two hundred metres away.

Although the neighbourhood was not exactly salubrious, it was quiet, tucked away like an afterthought. The redbrick buildings, edged with snow, looked festive despite their lack of Christmas decoration. The sharp, cold air was refreshing too, despite the hazy hint of smog that still softened the angles of walls and roofs.

'Wonder what the Maybury is back in our time?' Clover murmured.

It was a game we often played. Clover had lists of places and people she vowed to look up online once we got back to the twenty-first century.

I shrugged. 'Offices maybe. Or a phone shop.'

'Too big for a phone shop.'

'Carpet warehouse then.'

'My guess is this area was flattened in the Blitz.'

'Cheery soul, aren't you?'

She grinned and hummed the opening bars to Monty Python's

'Always Look on the Bright Side of Life'.

'Shh,' I said, putting a hand on her arm. 'This could be it.'

A brougham had rounded the corner and come to a stop outside the theatre. Seconds later one of the double doors opened and Willoughby appeared, his bulk swathed in a thick black overcoat, a stovepipe hat perched on his head. He reminded me of Dr Caligari from the silent film. He waddled down the steps and climbed aboard the brougham, his weight causing it to creak and tilt on its springs. We were too far away to hear the instructions he gave the driver, but as soon as the vehicle began to move with a wet clatter of wheels we scuttled back to our hansom and leaped aboard.

It wasn't hard to follow Willoughby's cab without being detected. Once on the main thoroughfares the thronging London streets provided plenty of cover. I'd never ceased to be amazed at how vibrant and varied Central London really was compared to Victorian street scenes reconstructed for TV dramas. The pavements were a constantly moving tide of people, the roads a clattering cacophony of omnibuses, hansoms, carts, broughams, trams, victorias... even the occasional early car chugged past, causing consternation and wonder. Small ragged boys weaved and dodged between the vehicles, scooping horse dung from the snow-slushy cobbles. Crammed together on street corners and against walls were stalls selling everything from candles and cloth to stewed eels and sheep's trotters. Here and there knots of people gathered around musicians and street performers, which caused other pedestrians to spill on to the roads, slowing the traffic.

What was perhaps most amazing was how multi-racial and multi-cultural the city was, even in this day and age. From the windows of the hansom, I saw Chinese men and women in brightly coloured silks, Indian gentlemen in turbans, straight-backed and beautiful African women whose dark skin contrasted with their white muslin gowns. In my business dealings I'd met Swedes, Russians, French, Germans and Spanish. Plus I'd encountered Malays and Lascars and Tartars, and once, at Hungerford Bridge pier, I'd even seen an American Indian in a dapper grey suit, feathers and beads woven into his long black hair.

We trailed Willoughby's cab north, through Camden – which at this time was nothing like the fashionable and bohemian enclave it would later become, but a grim little neighbourhood crammed with cheap lodging houses to serve the canal and railway workers. From there we moved into the more genteel commuter district of Stoke Newington, which, although the area had been absorbed into the seamless expansion of London in the past few decades, still retained something of the atmosphere of the village it had once been. With fewer people and less traffic to conceal our presence, I instructed our driver to fall back to avoid being detected, and was both relieved and intrigued when, at the top of Stoke Newington High Street, Willoughby's brougham came to a halt outside the pillared entrance of Abney Park Cemetery.

Judging by the black carriage and black, plumed horse waiting patiently on the snow-streaked cobbles outside the main gates, there was a funeral taking place inside. The carriage driver perched in his high seat, his top hat adorned with a silk mourning band, appeared to be snoozing, though behind him the drivers of a small procession of more conventional cabs were chatting quietly as they waited for their passengers – presumably the attendant mourners.

Was Willoughby a mourner too? If so, it looked as though he was late. Perhaps his lateness was deliberate to enable him to make a dramatic entrance? Although I'd only spent a short time in his company, he seemed the sort of man who would want to be the centre of attention even at someone else's funeral.

Shielding my face with my hand, and hoping that Willoughby wouldn't glance my way, I murmured to our driver to stop a little further along the road, out of sight of the main gates. This he did, whereupon Clover and I alighted from the cab and swiftly retraced our steps on foot.

By the time we arrived back at the gates, Willoughby was a couple of hundred metres ahead of us, still visible on the main path leading towards the chapel. I'd been afraid we might already have lost him – Abney Park is a big, rambling bone yard, comprising a nature reserve and arboretum, with dozens of routes sprawling across thirty acres – but the actor, although he appeared agile enough on stage, moved like a vast black slug through the snowy landscape, a cane gripped in his meaty right fist.

Due to the abundant cover – snow-draped trees and bushes, gravestones and other monuments edged in white – it was easy to keep out of sight as we sneaked along behind him. As it turned out, Clover and I need hardly have bothered trying to conceal ourselves; Willoughby didn't look round once.

Maybe it was my imagination, but even here in the open air and some two hundred metres downwind, I fancied I caught an occasional whiff of the mulchy smell that clung to him.

Perhaps he's ill, I thought. *Perhaps he's got some sort of infection – or worse.*

I swallowed and licked my lips, trying to put all thoughts of his fleshy bulk, of his unwashed folds and crevices, out of my mind.

Moving as silently as we could across the slushy ground, Clover and I tailed Willoughby for ten minutes, maybe longer, until eventually, just as I was beginning to think the funeral might be over before we got there, we arrived at our destination.

This was the first Victorian funeral I'd witnessed since arriving in 1890s London, but it was exactly the kind of thing I'd been expecting. It was, in fact, like watching the opening scene of a Hammer horror movie, or a Dickens' adaptation.

In a dip below us, within a natural amphitheatre surrounded by pine trees and studded with grey headstones, twenty or so black-clad mourners were clustered, heads bowed, around an open grave. The men wore black suits, gloves and tall hats; the women wore long dresses in black wool or silk, their heads covered in hoods or mourning bonnets. Standing at the edge of the grave in a central position, as if about to jump in, was a middle-aged woman wearing a voluminous black crepe dress and a widow's bonnet with a half-face veil. Weeping quietly, she was clinging to the arm of a young man, who I guessed must be her son. He wore a troubled but stoical expression beneath a bushy moustache that he might have grown in an attempt to look older and more authoritative than he really was.

At the head of the grave, swaying slightly like a small tree in a high wind, was a priest in black and white robes, strands of wispy grey hair twisting in cobwebby zigzags around his head. A prayer book bound in black leather was clutched in hands so gnarled they looked like pale roots, though it seemed the book was only for show; the priest's eyes were fixed on the black rectangle of the grave as he intoned what I presumed was the burial service in a muttering drone.

I expected Willoughby to trudge down the hill to join the mourners, and so was surprised when he first came to a halt, then shuffled sideways to take shelter behind a thick clump of pine trees bordering the burial area. I glanced back at Clover, who raised her eyebrows, and then gestured towards a patch of trees about thirty metres behind Willoughby that would enable us to observe him side-on and still see what was going on at the graveside.

As we crept towards our hiding place, I kept expecting Willoughby to turn and spot us, but he was intent on the funeral below. I wondered what it was that fascinated him – and more especially, why he was staying out of sight. Was the dead man a family member he was estranged from? An old enemy? A rival? Was Willoughby here to gloat? Or could this have something to do with the Wolves of London?

It was only when Clover and I had reached the cover of the clump of trees that I was able to see Willoughby's face for the first time. I was shocked. Though I could only see him in profile, he looked avid; no, more than that, he looked *lascivious*. His expression was almost sexual, his cheeks flushed and quivering, his eyes wide, his mouth open to release a wet, fat tongue, which roamed restlessly across his engorged lips. He looked like a man on the verge of orgasm. He looked as if he was eagerly drinking in the desolate scene below, as if he was getting off on the grief and misery of it.

What was going on? I glanced again at Clover and saw that she'd scrunched up her face in distaste. I turned my attention back to Willoughby, and then again to the funeral below, trying to make sense of what I was seeing. I peered at the mourners more closely, scanning each of their faces, searching for clues. And then suddenly I felt a shock go through me so fierce it felt like a spear of ice slicing down through my brain and heart and guts and shattering outwards, in cold shards, into my limbs.

I thought I'd frozen into immobility, that the shock I'd experienced was purely internal, but then Clover grabbed my arm, her fingers digging in.

I turned to face her. My body didn't feel quite like my own.

Her eyes, wide and fearful, darted across my face.

'What's wrong, Alex? You're shaking all over. You've gone as white as a sheet.'

I managed to move my lips, to dredge a voice up from somewhere. 'Look there,' I rasped.

She glanced at Willoughby, then back at me. 'Where?'

I swallowed, tried again. 'At the grave. The mourners. The young couple to the right of the widow.'

Clover looked across at where I had described, confusion on her face. 'What about them?'

'I know them.' Suddenly I felt a weird sort of laughter bubbling up inside me. I fought it down with an effort. 'They're the Sherwoods. Adam and Paula. My old next-door neighbours. They're the people who kidnapped Kate!'

SIX

STRATEGY

Clover gaped at me. 'They can't be!'

I felt anger born of impatience rising in me. Even though my instinct was to confront the couple, demand to know where my daughter was, there was still a rational part of me urging me to stay hidden, think this through, work out the most effective plan of action. I wanted to get Kate back more than anything, but I couldn't afford to let my heart rule my head. Even so, my reply to Clover's comment was a rasping snap.

'They *are*! I should know! I lived next door to them for a year! I spoke to them *every day*!'

Clover gritted her teeth and raised her hands in a placatory gesture. From the way she glanced anxiously at Willoughby it was clear my voice was too loud.

Luckily the actor was still engrossed in the funeral, his eyes now bulging as if about to pop from their sockets, his body heaving and writhing obscenely...

'Okay, okay,' she whispered, 'I believe you.' She bit her lip. 'Let's just think this through.'

I'd already thought it through - or at least my buzzing brain had done, independently of me.

'It's obvious what's happened. Whoever's got the heart has brought the Sherwoods back through time so no one can find them.'

'Or sent them forward - or is going to,' she countered.

I blinked at her, not understanding - and then suddenly realised what she meant. Despite all I'd been through it was still sometimes hard to think of time as anything but linear. But Clover was right. Just because I'd encountered the Sherwoods in my past didn't mean that had been the past for them too. Maybe their journey into the twenty-first century was in their future. Maybe they had yet to be corrupted – in which case, what I did now might have an impact on their forthcoming actions.

Oddly it was this that made me indecisive – that incapacitated me, in fact.

'What should I do?'

I felt as if I was about to cross a minefield with no idea where the mines were buried. However careful I was, there was no way of predicting whether my next step would seal my fate. What if it was only because of meeting me that the Sherwoods were targeted by the Wolves of London? It was horrible to think my own actions might somehow provide the catalyst for Kate's abduction – or rather, *have* somehow provided it, as it had already happened, as far as I was concerned.

'We,' Clover said.

I'd already lost the thread of our conversation. 'What?'

'It's what should *we* do, not what should *I* do. We're in this together, Alex. We work as a team, remember.'

I wafted a hand irritably. 'Whatever. I'm not quibbling over semantics.'

'It's not semantics. It's strategy.'

From the way she said it I knew she had something in mind.

'Go on,' I grunted, still struggling to stay calm. 'Tell me your plan.'

She glanced again at the mourners standing stoically in the cold, listening as the priest droned his way through the burial service.

'If the Sherwoods have already abducted Kate, then they'll know who you are. In which case, if you confront them and start throwing accusations about, they'll clam up, deny everything – added to which, the other mourners will be outraged by your intrusion. This *is* a funeral, after all.'

I nodded. I could already envisage the scene. I'd come across like a madman. And my antics would be deemed doubly unacceptable because of the occasion. No doubt I'd be pounced on by some of the more able-bodied male mourners, dragged away, perhaps even roughed up a bit, given the way friable emotions like grief can so easily find an outlet in anger if the right buttons are pressed. And in the confusion the Sherwoods would slip away, and all that would have been achieved would be that they would now be alerted to my presence, which would make them ultra-cautious, ultra-discreet – or might well prompt them to go into hiding, even leave London altogether.

All this flashed through my mind in the second or two it took for Clover to draw breath.

'So what I reckon,' she continued, 'is that I should handle the Sherwoods and you should stick with Willoughby, see what he does next. As far as I'm aware the Sherwoods have no idea who I am. I'll mingle with the mourners once the service is over, get the Sherwoods talking.'

I must have looked dubious, because she poked me in the chest.

'Don't worry. I'll work my magic on them. You don't spend three years as the owner-manager of a pole-dancing club without learning a bit of charm and diplomacy. I'm good at wheedling information out of people. I can be very persuasive when I put my mind to it.'

I held up my hands in surrender. 'You don't have to tell me.' I hesitated a moment longer, then said, 'Okay. I suppose that makes sense. Where shall we meet?'

'Is your mobile charged up?' She gave a cheeky smile at the face I pulled. 'Nah, mine either. So I guess we'll just have to meet back at the house. See you later.'

I touched her arm as she began to move away and she glanced back at me.

'Be careful.'

'Always am,' she replied, and cocked her head towards Willoughby, who was still crouched behind his clump of trees, shuddering in what appeared to be sexual ecstasy. 'You be carefuller. He looks frisky.'

SEVEN

HEART OF DARKNESS

Charles Dickens once described Victorian London as the 'magic lantern' which fired his imagination. It was a phrase that had stuck in my mind since I'd read it, and one I often recalled when I was clattering through the streets in a hansom, or weaving in and out of the ripe-smelling crowds on the pavements.

I'd always thought of Dickens' description as a positive, even joyous, one. Yet while it was true that the city was potent, colourful, clamorous, and driven by the twin engines of industry and prosperity, it was only after living here for a while that I began to truly appreciate the irony and darkness behind his words. Because under its brassy, gleaming surface, Victorian London was not just dirty and rundown; it was a stinking, black cesspool, an unbelievable Hell that you had to experience first-hand to truly believe in.

I realised that the real reason why Dickens had used the phrase was not because the city was full of wonders, but because to a writer as skilful and philanthropically minded as he was it was the perfect environment to foment ideas and hone opinions.

The Victorian London I knew was maybe ninety-five per cent poor. And when I say poor, I don't mean living-on-the-breadline-and-scrimping-to-pay-the-rent poor – I mean dying-from-malnutrition-and-freezing-to-death-in-the-streets poor. From my watchers I'd heard horrific tales about the bodies of children lying in gutters for days on end, being gradually eaten by rats or scrawny, wolfish dogs. I'd heard too, from my police contacts, of the rotting corpses – many of them babies – which washed up in their dozens on the banks of the Thames, day after day. My search for the heart had led me to filthy, reeking hovels in dilapidated rookeries, where I'd seen as many as thirty or forty people living, eating and sleeping in a single room no bigger than the average modern kitchen. In such neighbourhoods privies were often nothing but pits at the ends of narrow alleyways shared by up to four hundred people, where the air was often black with flies and gave off a reek so foul it could stun you into unconsciousness as effectively as a billy club. Or alternatively you might find houses clustered around a yard six inches deep in shit (or 'night soil'), into which bricks had been tossed as stepping stones.

I was surprised to find myself trailing Willoughby into just such a neighbourhood. Once Clover had slipped away to find a vantage point where she could 'casually' and 'accidentally' intercept the mourners as they filed from the graveside, I watched the actor writhing in orgasmic glee for a while longer, until eventually his body relaxed, the intensity left his face, and he began to look around sleepily, as if he'd just woken from an afternoon nap and was re-acquainting himself with his surroundings.

Leaving the mourners standing by the graveside, he turned and retraced his steps. Hidden behind my own clump of trees, I waited until he'd passed by and then followed him.

I tailed him all the way to the cemetery gates, then watched from the shelter of a stone angel as he climbed back into his brougham. As soon as he'd closed the door and the carriage had pulled ponderously away, I slipped out of the gates, using the other cab drivers as cover, and sprinted round the corner to where my hansom was waiting. I told the driver to follow Willoughby's carriage, and then for the next half hour or so we meandered back towards the city, our carriages rattling through the mean streets of Shacklewell, Hackney, and round the western edge of Bethnal Green, before eventually arriving in Spitalfields.

Like much of East London, Spitalfields was a labyrinth of rat-infested alleyways, narrow passages and cobbled yards, its sagging slums crammed with immigrants, sailors and destitute families. Because of its association with the tailoring industry, there were over a hundred thousand Jews here and in Whitechapel, many of whom lived in abject poverty and were shunned, often abused, by the native population.

Some of my watchers had told me that during the time of the Ripper murders the Jews had been targeted as scapegoats, as a result of which dozens had been kicked or beaten or hacked to death in the streets. If that was true, then the information had never been officially recorded.

Travelling through Spitalfields now, where the snow piled in the gutters and against the sides of the buildings was so black it looked like mounds of soil, I felt nervous, open to attack. Hansom cabs were an unusual sight here, and as we rattled deeper into the heart of darkness, I became increasingly aware of eyes glinting from the shadows of windows and doorways – though some who watched me pass were more blatant, more visible. A pack of skinny, ragged kids perched on a flight of crumbling stone steps turned their sharp, fox-like features in my direction; a fat woman with a red, bloated face, who was squatting on an upturned tub, shouted something incomprehensible around the short pipe clamped between her remaining teeth; at one point a spindly human scarecrow with long, uncombed hair stepped in front of the hansom and made a series of complex, esoteric gestures with his long, skinny fingers before scuttling back into the darkness from which he'd come.

I wondered whether Willoughby's brougham was getting the same level of scrutiny, the same kind of treatment. The streets soon became so short and narrow we found ourselves following the sound rather than the sight of it. When its clattering progress up ahead slowed and stopped, I told the driver of my cab to halt too. He did so reluctantly, his eyes darting back and forth, obviously scared of being ambushed. Taking a deep breath to steady my nerves – a bad idea, the air stank of sewage and decay – I disembarked from the hansom and stepped out on to filthy cobbles. I paid the driver, who snatched the money out of my hand and pocketed it in a flash, as if he was afraid the mere smell of it would bring the predators flocking.

'I 'ope yer not wanting me to await yer return, sir?' he muttered, his flickering eyes so wide I could see the whites around his pupils.

I shook my head. 'No, you get along. Thank you – and good luck.'

'It's you what'll need the luck I reckon, sir,' he said.

Before I could reply, he was hauling on the reins, forcing the horse to drag the cab around in a tight U-turn. I watched him go, but it wasn't until he'd turned the corner that I felt suddenly profoundly alone.

My hand slipped beneath my coat and closed around the handle of my howdah in its concealed pocket. Even in the daylight, places like Spitalfields, with their narrow streets and high, cramped, leaning buildings, seemed oppressive with shadows. I squared my shoulders and straightened my back to make myself look less of a victim. I thought of Benny Magee, the gangland boss who'd sold me out to the Wolves of London, and tried to channel some of his aggressive self-confidence.

Keeping a watchful eye on every side alley and gaping doorway, I hurried in the direction taken by Willoughby's brougham. The fact that I hadn't heard it move off suggested it was still parked no more than a street or two away. I imagined Willoughby engaged in the laborious process – for him – of clambering out and paying the driver. There was always the possibility the carriage might have been waylaid, that Willoughby might have come to harm, but I didn't think so. If that had happened I'd have heard some sort of commotion – shouts or screams, the sounds of a struggle.

Aware I was within spitting distance of what had once been Dorset Street (now demolished), where only a few years ago Jack the Ripper had murdered and mutilated Mary Kelly in her lodgings, I reached the intersection at the end of the street and peered around the corner. Beyond a soot-blackened, drab-fronted building that had the look of a workhouse or an abandoned factory, Willoughby's brougham was standing motionless. I could see Willoughby – or at least the dark, uncompromising bulk of him – speaking to the driver. I heard the faint chink of coins and then the brougham moved off, leaving Willoughby standing alone.

Feeling exposed, I drew back behind the corner of the wall, but Willoughby was already turning away. I watched him step on to the kerb and shuffle towards the doorway of a grime-coated tenement with cracked walls and windows so caked with soot (those few that had glass in them) they couldn't possibly admit more than a glimmer of light. A couple of skinny men in ragged clothes, one wearing a tall, crooked stovepipe hat that made me think of Dr Seuss's Cat in the Hat, were standing sentinel, one each side of the doorway. I watched with interest as Willoughby waddled towards them.

Even from thirty metres away I could hear Willoughby's wheezing breath, his cane tapping the ground. What was he doing in this neighbourhood? I wondered. Surely he didn't live here? The man with the stovepipe hat touched a finger to its brim and stepped back as Willoughby took a key from his overcoat pocket. Clearly then they knew him, were even showing him deference. I watched as the actor unlocked the door of the tenement and went inside.

Maybe he was the landlord, here to collect rent? But if so, why dismiss the brougham? And why come alone – or even at all? Surely men of means employed others to do their dirty work?

Perhaps he was visiting someone then? A friend or relative? Could the two men standing by the door be *related* to him in some way? It seemed inconceivable. Perhaps they worked for him then? Could they be his enforcers, his bodyguards?

I had plenty of questions, but no answers. And no way of *getting* answers either without approaching the two men and asking them directly.

I considered doing just that. After all, I had a gun, and it was unlikely that they'd be similarly armed. But what at this point would it achieve? I'd spoken to Willoughby already today. Turning up again here now would only make him more wary of me; it might even scare him off. If he *was* our killer, and if he *was* associated with the Wolves of London, then the priority had to be to get him to lead me to the heart and take it from there. Which meant playing it cool, not going in with all guns blazing. With a sigh, I made a mental note of the address and slipped away.

Moving quickly, head down, hand still clutching the howdah in my coat, I followed a meandering course along various side streets and back alleys. In my decent clobber I attracted plenty of scrutiny along the way, some of it clearly hostile, but I wasn't attacked or even challenged.

Eventually I reached Commercial Street, which was wider and more crowded than those around it, and headed north towards Shoreditch, ignoring the shouts of the doxies, who sounded both plaintive and aggressive as they touted for business. Prostitution was the most common profession among the women in this area, with many girls being put to work by their families as young as eleven or twelve – as a result of which they were more often than not riddled with syphilis by their teenage years.

It wasn't the prostitutes I was worried about, though, even if a lot of them did carry shivs on the off chance of sticking a rich client and stealing his purse. The real threat came from the gangs, which spilled like rats from the slums of 'Old Nichol', not far from here; or even the swarms of feral children known as 'little Arabs', who would slash a man to death if they thought there was something useful to be had from him.

I'd turned off Old Street, close to where the railway station would open for business in a few years' time, and was moving along yet another stinking, high-walled alleyway, when I sensed movement behind me. I turned, my fist tightening on the butt of the howdah – and saw a small, hunched, ragged figure silhouetted in the glimmer of murky light at the end of the alleyway.

I narrowed my eyes, trying to make out the figure more clearly. There was something wrong with the lower half of its face. It appeared almost exaggeratedly lantern-jawed, and above the filthy scarf wrapped around its neck, I detected a dull gleam of metal.

'Well, well, look who it is,' rasped a voice behind me. 'You're a bit far from 'ome, ain'tcha?'

I whirled round again. A man had appeared at the other end of the alley, more dark figures crowding behind him. In the murky December light they appeared almost simian, their hunched bodies bulked out by the layers of ragged clothing they wore to combat the winter cold.

The man who'd spoken walked forward slowly, his thick, scabby lips stretched wide in a grin that revealed a mouthful of black and rotten teeth. His face was craggy, its deep grooves ingrained with dirt, and one of his eyes was milky and bloodshot. He wore a battered bowler hat pushed back on his head and a long, grey, woollen coat that looked and smelled as if it had been trampled by pigs in a sty.

I knew this man. I'd first encountered him in my own time when he'd stepped from a newly formed cloud of yellow smog on the platform at Bank Tube Station and had cut the throat of the person I'd thought was Clover, but who'd turned out to be a shape-shifter working for the Wolves of London.

'Mr Hulse,' I said. 'I was on my way to see you.'

Hulse's grin widened. 'Oh, I knows it. Nothing escapes my notice round these parts. Me and the boys thought we'd come and meet yer, save yer shoe leather. Save yer throat too, more than likely. These are perilous streets fer gentlemen such as yerself. There are some shocking coves about.'

I chuckled. 'How goes it?'

'Oh, we has had a bountiful Christmas. Bountiful indeed. Ain't that right, boys?'

His cronies hooted and chortled.

'Glad to hear it,' I said, stepping forward to meet Hulse as he swaggered towards me, his hand outstretched.

The hand in question, scarred and filthy, the fingernails either black or missing entirely, was often to be seen wielding a vicious rusty-bladed knife. It was a hand which I knew had committed murder on more than one occasion – yet I grasped it now without hesitation and gave it a firm shake.

One of my first tasks after recovering from the smoke inhalation which had laid me low after arriving here had been to seek out Hulse and offer him a deal. It was a massive risk, but I'd thought about it a lot, and had spent hours talking it through with Clover and Hawkins, discussing all the angles and pitfalls.

I had a theory, you see; a theory to do with the mutability of time. As I've said, when I first encountered Hulse he appeared from a cloud of smog at Bank Tube Station and cut the throat of a shape-shifter which had been impersonating Clover, presumably in the hope of catching me unawares and stealing the obsidian heart. The second time I'd met him had been the first time I'd found myself in Victorian London, immediately after what I'd thought was Clover's murder. On that occasion I'd sought Hulse out, confronted him on his own turf, and received a beating for my troubles. The third time we'd met had been back in my own time, when Hulse had appeared in a police interview room and slashed DI Jensen's throat, minutes after I'd been forced to hand the heart over as evidence relating to the inquiry into the murder of its original owner, Barnaby McCallum...

Here was where it got complicated.

What if (I'd thought to myself) my first encounter with Hulse had not been *his* first encounter with me? What if *his* first encounter with me was my *second* encounter with him? I remembered how he'd denied all knowledge of Clover's murder, how he'd responded to my accusations as though he'd never seen or heard of either of us before. He and his cronies had chased me, and when they'd caught me they'd given me a pounding, and might even have killed me if the heart hadn't zapped me back to the twenty-first century.

But what if, on that occasion, they'd been acting on impulse rather than carrying out the orders of the Wolves of London? Hulse and his men were thieves and cut-throats, and to them my appearance would have instantly identified me as a fish out of water – and probably a rich one at that.

Perhaps, then, they'd merely seen me as easy pickings, and had acted accordingly. It was only because of 'Clover's' murder that I'd assumed they were working for the Wolves of London – but what if they weren't? What if the Hulse who had slashed the false Clover's throat was from a later time period?

And if *that* was the case, then who was to say that *I myself* hadn't sent him forward through time to kill the false Clover before she – or rather, *it* – could kill *me*? What if Hulse was *my* agent? On *my* payroll? His later murder of DI Jensen was harder to explain, but I had a few theories about that as well.

What if the Jensen who Hulse had killed was not the real Jensen? What if he too was a shape-shifter – or the *same* shape-shifter? I'd already seen evidence that the shape-shifter could survive the physical death of offshoots of itself without suffering any apparent ill effects. So what if the Jensen who had interviewed me (and the one I'd encountered in Jensen's office stealing the obsidian heart minutes later) had been an offshoot of the shape-shifter whose task had been to procure the heart? If so, then it was possible that Hulse was following *my* orders. After all, without his intervention I would have been too late to catch Jensen number two in the act of stealing the heart, and therefore wouldn't have leaped at him, grappled with him, crashed through the window, and ended up here.

The implications made my head spin, but ultimately it was all about cause and effect. It was also about making what I *did* know work for me as best I could.

'So what brings a refined gent like yerself to such a lowly quarter as this?' Hulse leered. 'Tired of living, is yer?'

Before I could reply I felt something nudge me from behind. I turned to find the figure that had followed me into the alley had now crept forward and was standing right behind me. He was bent over like a hunchbacked old man, gently bumping his head against my thigh.

Hulse laughed. 'Likes yer, does little Tom. One of his favourites, you are.'

I smiled and placed my hand on the boy's shoulder. His bones were as thin as a sparrow's beneath his ragged clothes.

'Hello, Tom,' I said.

Tom wasn't the name the boy had been given at birth, but it was as good as any. In fact, the boy hadn't been named at all – not as far as any of us knew. It was Hulse who had started calling him 'Tom' after Tom Thumb, on account of him being so scrawny.

Tom never spoke, but when he was happy he made a huffing noise that seemed to come from deep inside his lungs. He was making the noise now, and at the same time tilting his head up in little jerks to peer shyly at me. His eyes were a velvety black beneath his long, matted fringe, and I tried to focus my attention on them, even though my gaze, as always, was drawn to the lower half of his face.

Like Hope, Tom had been one of Tallarian's experiments – one of only two I'd managed to release from the doctor's laboratory before the place had gone up in smoke. Tallarian had removed Tom's lower jaw and replaced it with a large, ugly, hinged contraption inset with jagged metal teeth, like the scoop of a digger. The flesh, where the metal had fused into it, was horribly infected, though the same doctor who I'd employed to treat Hope had done his best – and was *still* doing his best – to keep the infection at bay.

Personally I would have preferred Tom, like Hope, to have moved permanently into my house in Ranskill Gardens, where it was clean and warm, and where he could have received round-the-clock care. But after finding him – thanks to my watchers – living rough in the East End, we'd tried that and it hadn't worked. The boy had been so unsettled that he'd refused point-blank to eat and had kept running away, despite the kindness shown him by Mrs Peake and her staff. In fact, he had been *so* unsettled (though never violent; despite my first encounter with him, Tom was a timid soul) that eventually, reluctantly, I'd had to let him return to the filthy streets of the East End, where he seemed happiest. I couldn't leave him to fend for himself, though, and so I'd paid Hulse to watch out for him and keep him safe. I'd also insisted he bring Tom to a pre-arranged rendezvous point for regular medical check-ups.

Hulse might not have been the ideal guardian and role model, but Tom seemed to be doing okay. He seemed to be thriving, in fact, despite his skinny frame and the infection eating away at his face. As he nuzzled into me, Hulse said, 'Scratch him behind the ears, mister. He likes that.'

Perhaps it was the way the men behind Hulse snickered that made me feel a sudden stab of anger. Looking at Hulse, I said coldly, 'He's a human being, not a dog.'

Instantly Hulse stiffened and his grin disappeared. Suddenly I was reminded that for all his rough-hewn amiability, this man could be volatile, unpredictable. I might be his current meal ticket, but I always got the impression that I had to tread carefully around him, that he was capable of lashing out on impulse if someone rubbed him up the wrong way.

'I knows that,' he said, his voice flat, 'and we treats him like one. Young Tom does well by us. Don't you worry yourself about that, mister.'

I raised a hand in apology. 'I know he does, Mr Hulse. And I'm grateful to you for taking care of him. I worry about him, that's all. I worry about...' I briefly patted my own jaw, not wanting Tom to see; I was never sure how much he understood of his condition.

Hulse gave a brief nod, but said. 'He does very well – don't you, Tom, my boy?'

Tom huffed happily in response.

Hulse's one good eye flickered from the boy and fixed its beady attention on me. 'Now, mister, what say you tells us why you're wandering these streets like a spring lamb in search of the butcher? Or is you just here to take tea and buttered muffins with your dearest chums?'

EIGHT

FINGERPRINTS

I went to bed shattered that night, but I couldn't sleep. My brain was like a nest full of angry wasps. After weeks of inactivity, during which, despite all the evidence to the contrary, I'd begun to worry I might *never* find the obsidian heart, suddenly things had started to move.

What was ironic was that it had come at a time when I'd least expected it. I'd more or less given up on Christmas week, had resigned myself to the fact that many of my watchers would be too preoccupied with the obligations of the season between Christmas and New Year, and that my best bet would be to start the search again, with a new impetus, at the start of January. But in the course of a breathtaking twenty-four hours we'd had the odd footprints outside the house, and the even odder murder behind the Maybury Theatre. And now our prime suspect for that murder had led us, unbelievably, to Kate's abductors.

Wheels within wheels. Cause and effect. I couldn't help but think it was because of my imminent contact with them that the Sherwoods had become (or were *about* to become) involved in the topsy-turvy craziness of my life. But how and why? And more importantly, was there any way of dissuading or preventing them from taking my daughter?

If I *did* dissuade or prevent them, though, how would that affect what, as far as I was concerned, had already happened? How much of my past would alter accordingly – or would it unravel altogether? Because if Kate had never been abducted, there would never have been a reason for me to get involved in *any* of this. I would never have had to steal the heart, which meant I would never have had to kill

McCallum, which meant I would never have ended up being pursued by the Wolves of London and living in a time that wasn't my own...

Which meant I would never have been in the position to dissuade or prevent the Sherwoods from abducting Kate.

As ever, the knot of complexities just seemed to get tighter the more I thought about them, to the point at which it became impossible to unpick the different strands. After giving up and going to bed, my limbs aching with tiredness, I lay sleepless for what seemed an eternity, my thoughts multiplying exponentially, questions branching into yet further questions, until eventually it seemed they were overflowing my head and filling the darkness around me, stifling and souring the air.

In the end, gasping for breath, I lit a candle and threw back my eiderdown. At first I was sweating, but then the sweat turned cold and I started to shake. Out of habit I got dressed – when I was awake I liked to be ready for immediate action – and then, holding the candle to light my way, I went downstairs.

Although the stairs creaked seemingly at every step, no one woke up. And that was fine, because I wanted to be alone. In the drawing room I stoked up the fire, lit a couple of lamps and sat in one of the leather armchairs, breathing in the calming Christmas scents of pine and orange and cloves. I realised there was a part of me that was almost *afraid* of going to sleep; afraid of losing the momentum gained over the past twenty-four hours; afraid of waking up to find that the previous day's promise had eluded me again, dissipated like a phantom.

It was a daft idea, but the early hours of the morning are a haven for daft ideas. The reason it was daft was because this afternoon Clover had returned to the house, arriving an hour or so after me, smiling like the cat that got the cream. She told me the Sherwoods were charming, that they were struggling to make ends meet, and that their son was three years old, which meant that – as she'd suggested – they were yet to travel into the future and move into the flat opposite mine. She also told me she'd used her 'womanly wiles', as she grinningly called them, to wangle us a dinner invitation for the following evening – which meant, as it was now something like 3:30 a.m., *this* evening.

It was all a bit surreal. I'd always got on well with Adam and Paula Sherwood – right up until the morning they'd kidnapped my youngest daughter. How I'd respond to them when I spoke to them again I couldn't say. Would the fact they weren't yet Kate's abductors make me feel differently towards them? As Victorians, would they even seem like the same people I'd known? Perhaps I'd feel guilty for imposing myself on their world – and possibly, therefore, drawing them into mine; perhaps I'd feel responsible for them in some way. All I knew for sure was that I'd prefer to meet them with my wits about me, but that the way things were going it was more likely that by this evening my brain would be like cement and I'd be all but dead on my feet.

Not even the thought I was potentially letting Kate down by not getting a proper night's sleep could make a difference. Maybe a whisky in front of the fire would relax me enough to allow me to slip into a state of unconsciousness? With a groan I hauled myself to my feet, crossed the room to the decanter and poured myself a healthy measure. I was raising the tumbler to my lips when I heard a soft pattering sound, like someone lightly drumming their fingers on the window.

I froze, then turned my head slowly to the left. The sound had come from behind the heavy damask drapes that covered the window closest to me. But had the noise been inside the room or outside? Having faced Tallarian's army of clockwork horrors and seen what the shape-shifter was capable of, I was primed to expect almost anything. It wouldn't have surprised me to find a spider the size of a cat perched on the windowsill behind the curtains. Or a squatting, red-eyed goblin. Or even a bubbling tide of green slime oozing its way through the hair-thin gaps around the frame.

I swallowed the whisky in one gulp, blinking at the alcohol burn in my belly. Grateful I was never complacent when it came to carrying my howdah, I put the tumbler down on the velvet cloth draped across the top of the piano and moved as silently as I could to the window. I stood beside the drapes for a moment, alert for the slightest sign of movement. Then, drawing my gun, I stretched out a hand and whipped the drape aside.

Instinctively I stepped to one side, my heart drumming. If this had been a horror movie a cat would have darted out from behind the curtain and gone yowling across the room – but there was nothing. Nothing on the windowsill; nothing attached to the inside of the tall sash window. But as I looked out at the snow-coated ground and the dark white-topped mass of trees and bushes beyond it, I suddenly realised that dotted and daubed on the lacy coating of frost on the outside of the glass were dozens of fingerprints.

I re-focused, staring at them. They reached from the bottom of the window to face height, and covered the area in a haphazard pattern, as if a child had dabbled its fingers over the frosty surface. In daylight such marks would simply have been curious, but now, in a silent house in the dead of night, they were eerie, and I felt a cold shudder ripple through me, negating the heat of the whisky.

What did the fingerprints mean? Were they a message? Or had something been trying – albeit feebly – to get into the house?

Before I had time to think I heard the same soft, rapid patter I'd heard moments earlier – only this time the sounds came from behind the drapes covering the *next* window.

Something was circling the house, tapping on the windows as it went. My already drumming heart leaped as a thrill of fear gripped me. But that didn't stop me from darting to the next window and yanking the drape back.

Nothing here either, except for more fingerprints. Whatever was making the marks had already moved on. I wondered what had happened to the men watching the house. Had this thing, whatever it was, slipped through their cordon unnoticed? Was it invisible? Insubstantial like a ghost?

The now-familiar tapping started at the next window. A rapid, flickering sound like a flurry of raindrops. This time I ran not to that window, but to the one beyond it. With a sense of triumph, mingled with a cold, sharp spasm of fear, I wrenched the drape back and stepped forward, raising my pistol.

And saw her.

She was standing in the snow, not close to the house as I'd expected, but further back, beside the hedge. She was wearing what she had worn every other time I'd seen her – a thin white nightshirt printed with a cherry design, the short sleeves edged in lace. Yet despite her lack of clothing she didn't seem cold; she was smiling at me, her soft blonde hair blowing in the wind, her delicate hands interlaced over her bulging belly. This was Lyn, my ex-partner, as I'd known her over five years ago when she'd been pregnant with Kate. She'd been beautiful then, and sane. Now she was not. Lyn was still alive – or at least, she had been on the day I'd left the twenty-first century. But this version of Lyn was a ghost of happier times.

It was only my reluctance to wake up the rest of the house that stopped me banging on the window, calling her name. I raised a hand – *Wait there!* – then ran out of the room and across the hallway to the front door.

My hands were all thumbs as I fumbled at the locks. As soon as the door was open I catapulted outside, the cold hitting me like a slap. My instinct was to veer immediately left and keep running, through the snow and around to where I hoped Lyn would be waiting. However, I knew I had to be careful. This might be a trick, designed to draw me out, or destabilise me into leaving the house open to attack.

Feverishly I tugged the door closed behind me, trying not to bang it, and twisted the key in the lock. Then, ignoring the instinct to sprint, I moved swiftly but cautiously around the side of the house, keeping close to the wall, my head darting back and forth as I peered in to the shadows that clustered around and beneath each clump of foliage, trying to cover every angle at once.

Reaching the corner of the house, I sidled around the wall, clutching my howdah. Although I was pointing the pistol at the ground – she might have been an apparition, but I didn't want Lyn to see me aiming a gun at her – I was more than prepared to jerk it into a shooting position if need be.

As soon as I rounded the corner, I looked across to where Lyn had been standing, and a plume of breath jetted from my mouth as I groaned in despair. She had gone, slipped away, before I could fully connect with her. It was as if she wasn't properly anchored to this world. As if she was an errant radio signal, elusive, easily lost.

But then, out of the corner of my eye, I saw a flash of movement, white against the grey-white of the snow. My head snapped round, and the lurch that my heart gave this time was one of joy, because there she was, drifting around the next corner like a winter spirit.

I hurried after her, half expecting one of the men watching the house to emerge from hiding to check I was okay. I wondered, if they did, whether they'd be able to see what I was seeing, or whether Lyn was visible only to me, my own personal phantom.

Again I wondered whether this was a trap. Since my first encounter with the shape-shifter I'd lived in a world of suspicion. I rounded the second corner, aware I was at the back of the house now, where it was darkest. The glow of the streetlamps, which filtered through the trees and bushes that bordered my property, was so dim it was almost negligible. For a moment I couldn't see anything but blurred grey shapes on a dark background. I narrowed my eyes, hoping it would bring things into focus, and partially it did.

Lyn was standing two-thirds along the length of the back wall, close to the house. Her head was a pale oval blur above the paler, more voluminous glimmer of her nightshirt. She was facing me, though her right arm seemed to be pointing at the house. Even though I was wary, even though I was clutching the howdah in an icy grip that made my hand ache, I felt a sudden, unexpected pang of longing. At that moment I wished more than anything that I could turn back time, return to that blissful period when Lyn had been sane and beautiful and radiant with life. Back then the two of us had been completely in love, completely happy, and our life together had seemed so simple, untroubled, full of promise.

And then *he* had come. The Dark Man. Lyn's personal demon. He had stepped into our perfect world and torn it apart.

Less than six years ago that had been. And yet from this vantage point it seemed like forever. Lyn wasn't dead, not physically, and yet the Lyn that *I* had known was dead. She'd been my one true chance of happiness, and she'd been taken from me. Everything else was damage limitation.

At once I felt angry, resentful. I stepped forward, more than prepared to fight, if a fight was what was coming.

'Why are you here?' I said gruffly. 'Why do you keep tormenting me?'

She said nothing. I couldn't see her face. After a moment she seemed to drift backwards, to melt into the darkness.

'No you don't,' I said, rushing forward, but it was already too late. I knew I was being rash. Hurtling onwards with no notion of what might be waiting for me.

Yet I kept going. Pushing through the darkness. Until eventually I was standing where she had stood moments before. There was no evidence she'd even been there. No footsteps in the snow, no lingering scent on the air. All was silent and still.

So *why* had she come?

Then I remembered how she had been standing, her right arm extended outwards from her body. I looked at the window she'd been standing beside – and my breath caught in my throat. There were not just fingerprints covering the rime of frost coating the glass this time, but words.

I tilted my head, trying to make them out in the gloom. The light that filtered through was the faintest of gleams, yet by moving my head back and forth, I could just make out what Lyn had etched into the frost with her finger.

Like a child learning to read I spelled out each letter, whispering to myself as I formed them into words.

'T... E... M... P...'

By the time I'd deciphered the entire message, I'd given up all hope of sleep.

NINE

THE SEVEN DIALS MYSTERY

'Tempting Treats,' I read, looking at the warped and peeling sign above the soot-blackened, mud-smeared window. 'Is that meant to be ironic, do you think?'

Hawkins grunted, his gaze flickering left and right. 'I wouldn't know, sir. But I suggest we enter the premises before our presence here attracts the attention of undesirables.'

The words Lyn had scratched in the frost on the window – or at least, that she'd drawn my attention to – had been not a message, but an address. I'd thought 'Tempting Treats' might turn out to be a coffee shop, or a place that sold sweets or cakes, but it was a narrow, filthy junk shop in the centre of a decrepit row of buildings.

The shop was in Seven Dials near Covent Garden, which in my day had evolved into a maze of quaint streets full of trendy retail outlets and buzzing with tourists, but which in this era was still part of the St Giles rookery, a notorious hive of appalling poverty and criminality, whose squalid, sagging buildings were studded with broken windows patched with wet paper and old rags. The residents of the area, who moved around us through streets coated with a slime of decomposing garbage, rotting food and human waste, looked more bestial than human, their bodies hunched and shuffling, their clothes ragged, their blank eyes staring from dirt-encrusted faces.

Although I knew Seven Dials had a reputation for occultism and strange practice, there was no evidence of that here – not unless you counted the fact that the place could have been mistaken for a reeking corner of Hell. Certainly it was hard to believe that these streets had been the birthplace for such grandiose and mysterious organisations as the Freemasons, the Swedenborg Society, the Theosophical Society and the Order of the Golden Dawn.

At Hawkins' words I glanced about and saw we were beginning to attract attention. There was a gin palace further down the street, shrieks and raucous laughter spilling from its shattered windows. When we'd arrived, a minute or two before, the crowd gathered around its doorway, squabbling and smoking and knocking back jars of gut-melting liquor, had numbered no more than a dozen. Now twice or maybe three times that many had drifted outside to gawp at us. Maybe most of it was curiosity. There might even have been a few of my watchers among the crowd. But it was just as likely several of the onlookers were sizing us up to have our noses slit and our purses pinched. Course, if they tried it they'd get a lot more than they bargained for, but even so it was advisable to avoid trouble wherever possible.

'Point taken,' I muttered to Hawkins, as I strode up to the black-painted door of 'Tempting Treats'. I was about to turn the handle when I noticed there wasn't one, so instead I put both hands on the door close to where the handle should have been and shoved. At first I thought the door was locked, but then it juddered inwards, as though scraping across a carpet of rubble. As soon as the gap was wide enough I slipped through it, at which point I noticed my hands and realised the door wasn't painted black, after all; it was simply coated in soot.

Hawkins followed me into the building, the door making the same juddering scrape as he pushed it closed behind him. As I wiped my sooty hands on a handkerchief, I peered into the gloom, trying to make sense of the shop's interior. The filth coating the bay window, which looked out on to the street, was as effective as a blackout curtain. Neither did it help that the darkness inside the shop was teeming with dust. I sneezed twice, and then, because my handkerchief was black with soot, wiped my nose on my sleeve.

'Look out, sir!' Hawkins shouted as I was lowering my arm.

I tensed, then something huge and black swooped at me out of the darkness. I flailed at it blindly, and was aware of Hawkins at my shoulder swinging his cane in a defensive arc above our heads. There was a passage of air, a faint musty smell, and then, with a raucous screech, our attacker – which I realised must have been a bird – was gone.

But where? Was it readying itself for another attack? In a half crouch, my arm held defensively in front of me, I peered around, searching for the creature in the gloom.

My vision was adjusting enough now for me to see that the room was long, narrow and very cluttered. Sideboards, chairs, tables, trunks, lamps, paintings, ornaments and other paraphernalia were stacked against the walls on both sides in tottering, seemingly haphazard piles. If there was any order to the place it was difficult to work out what it was because of the gloom, and the fact that the air was grainy with swirling dust motes.

At the far end of a narrow passage snaking between the room's stacked contents came a rasping chuckle. I flapped at the dust and narrowed my eyes to make sense of what I was seeing. Admittedly I wasn't at my best. Although I'd finally managed a couple of hours of pre-dawn sleep in the armchair before the fire, my eyes were gritty and I felt as though a tight steel band around my head was constraining my thoughts. The impression I had now was of staring through the wrong end of a telescope, of watching distant shapes at the end of a dark tunnel. I could see what looked like the glow of a lantern and a shadowy form half concealed by what might have been books stacked on a desk. I rubbed my face as though my tiredness was a brittle glaze that could be removed like old varnish.

Behind me, Hawkins called out, 'Who's there? Show yourself!'

The dry cackle came again, sharp-edged and mocking, before evolving into a voice. 'Show myself, is it? And who are you to give me orders in my own establishment?'

Hawkins stepped in front of me. 'This may be your establishment, sir, but when you attacked us you forfeited your entitlement to our respect.'

'I, attack?' said the voice in astonishment. 'I attacked no one.'

'Your creature then.'

'My "creature", as you call her, is old like me, and merely curious. Tell me, did she wound you?'

'She did not. Though she might have done, and my master too, had I not used my cane to deflect the possibility of such an outcome.'

The shop owner made a dismissive sound. 'You are a stranger here, are you not?'

'What has that to do with it?'

'Oh, a great deal, I should say. If you were from hereabouts, you would know of old Satan and her ways.'

'Satan?' I muttered.

'My crow, sir. Named for her plumage, not her demeanour. If I was to name her for her demeanour I would have to call her Saint, for she is the sweetest natured bird that ever took wing. The folk around these parts love her, sir, the nippers especially. Takes tit-bits out of their hands, she does, and never scratches nor pecks the skin. Gentle as a lamb is old Satan.'

The man's voice was getting closer, as was his bobbing lantern. I stepped up beside Hawkins and touched him briefly on the arm, tacitly instructing him to stand at ease.

Eventually the shop owner was close enough for us to make him out. They say that people grow to resemble their pets, which was certainly true in his case. Peering at us from behind the glow of his lantern was an old man. He was tall, scrawny, hunch-shouldered, his threadbare layers of clothing wrapped around him like a suit of matted black feathers. His hands, encased in fingerless black gloves, were long and talon-like, and his face was long too, the chin sharp, the cheeks hollow, the eyes a watery greyish yellow in the lantern light. His grey hair was sparse, straggling across a domed forehead that resembled a scaly egg, and drifting in cobwebby wisps about his narrow shoulders. The most remarkable thing about him was that his crow, Satan, was perched on top of his head like a bizarre hat.

The bird itself was large and sleek, though her feathers were tattered and dusty at the edges. The old man had described her as sweet natured, but she regarded us with arrogance, even hostility – which I suppose wasn't surprising, considering that Hawkins had tried to whack her with his cane.

I stepped forward. 'Good morning, Mr...'

The old man narrowed his eyes, as though weighing up the consequences of revealing the information. Then he muttered, 'The name's Hayles, sir.'

'Pleased to make your acquaintance, Mr Hayles. I apologise for the misunderstanding. My friend and I were startled, you see.'

The old man peered at us a moment longer, then his expression softened.

'I do see, sir,' he conceded. 'I see very well. I suppose it *is* queer to have a bird flying around the place, but the folks round here is used to her.'

'She's a fine specimen,' I said. 'Where did you get her?'

'I found her on my doorstep, sir,' said the old man. 'She was lying there, like a gift from the heavens. A mere scrap of a thing back then, she was. And her left wing was broke something grievous. I think it must have been a cat what done for her, sir. Vicious brutes they are round here. I took her in and fed her on beetles and grubs, and nursed her back to health. And she hasn't left my side since.'

I smiled. The shop and the old man might have been grotty, but it was a heart-warming story.

'Mr Hayles, my name is Alex Locke. Am I familiar to you in any way?'

The old man scratched the side of his head. 'Can't say you are, sir. *Should* you be?'

'I don't know,' I admitted. 'Your address was... given to me in unusual circumstances. May we look around?'

'Be my guests,' said Hayles. 'Everything here is for sale, and all of it the finest quality.' He threw up his left hand in a flourish that startled the crow and sent it flapping into the air with an indignant squawk. It circled the room and came to rest on a battered writing bureau perched atop a pile of other furniture, where it glared at us like the raven in Poe's poem.

For the next ten minutes Hawkins and I moved around the dim and dusty room, examining the haphazard stacks of furniture. We peered under and over and around the backs of things. We looked inside cupboards, and pulled open drawers, and rooted through boxes of depressing, worthless junk. We disturbed mice and spiders, one of the latter of which, swelled by a coating of dust, scuttled across my hand, making me jerk in fright. This startled Satan from her perch again and set her swooping and gliding around the room like a small, dark ghost.

It would have helped if Lyn could have told me what was so significant about this address before doing her vanishing act. Could it be that the heart was hidden somewhere amongst this clutter? Or was Hayles himself the focus? Perhaps the shop owner, or even his bird, were more than they appeared?

Eventually, coated in dust and dirt, I asked, 'Where do you come by your stock, Mr Hayles?'

The old man frowned suspiciously. 'Here and there.' He seemed to consider his own words for a moment. 'Yes, I would say here and there just about covers it.'

'And how often do you come by new items?' Looking around it wouldn't have surprised me to learn that the contents had not altered for the past ten, even twenty years.

'There is what I would call a "steady flow" coming in and going out. I buys 'em and sells 'em cheap, purely to keep things moving, you understand.'

'Though not without some profit for yourself, I'll be bound?' said Hawkins drily.

The old man, who had put the lantern down on a nearby table, spread his black-gloved hands. 'A small one, sir. Though it's barely a profit at all. Just enough to pay the rent and buy a few wittles for Satan and me. We has modest needs. But we all has to live, sir.'

'Indeed we do,' I said. I put my hand into the pocket of my trousers and jangled the coins in there.

The old man's head jerked round. His eyes fixed on my pocket like a bird of prey homing in on a scuttling mouse.

'What would you say to the chance of adding a bit more to your profit, Mr Hayles?'

Hayles licked his lips, but did his best to sound casual. 'I would say that I might be interested, sir, if the circumstances was favourable. Is it a business proposition you is offering?'

'I simply seek information,' I said. 'But it would have to come with a guarantee of loyalty. Is that something you think you can provide?'

Cautiously Hayles said, 'I am the soul of discretion if that is what you are asking, sir.'

'It is,' I said, and paused, to give him the impression I was deciding whether or not I could trust him. Eventually I said, 'The fact is, I'm looking for something. Something I want no one else to know about. Do you understand what I'm saying?'

I jangled the coins in my pocket again. Hayles nodded eagerly.

'I do, sir. You think I might have this... something you is looking for?'

'I think you might be well placed to find it for me. Or at least, to receive information as to its whereabouts. If that were the case I would expect you to tell me - me and no one else - immediately. Do you think you could do that?'

Hayles was still nodding. Above us the crow had settled again, its clawed toes gripping the ornately carved pediment of a mahogany wardrobe. It let out a single caw, as though sounding a note of caution.

'Oh, I think I *can*, sir. Yes, I surely do.' Once more the old man eyed my pocket. 'And... er... in return for providing this *exclusive* service, sir?'

'You would be paid handsomely. Very handsomely indeed if you find the item I'm after.'

Hayles flushed with excitement. He blinked rapidly and for the second time wet his lips with his tongue. 'May I be permitted to ask what the "item" is, sir?'

I glanced at Hawkins. He looked back at me steadily.

'It's a small human heart, about this size -' I showed him using my thumb and forefinger '- carved from obsidian.' I paused to gauge his reaction. If he had heard of the heart he gave no sign. 'You know what obsidian is?'

'It's a stone, sir, is it not?'

'It's a black rock.'

Hayles nodded hard, as if to convince me I'd come to the right man. 'Ah yes, sir. A black rock. I knows exactly what you mean.'

I doubted that, but it didn't matter. There can't be too many black stone hearts knocking around.

'So do I have your word, Mr Hayles, that if you receive any information pertaining to this item - or, indeed, if the item itself should come into your possession - you'll inform me immediately?'

Hayles nodded solemnly, his gaze sliding to my pocket again.

'You do and I will, sir.'

I took my hand out of my pocket.

He looked alarmed. 'Shall we shake on it, sir?' he asked hastily.

I smiled. 'In a moment. I thought I would pay you first. To cement your loyalty, as it were.'

I wondered if he would make a show of saying that immediate payment wasn't necessary, but he was clearly too desperate, too afraid I might take him at his word.

'Well, sir,' he mumbled, 'that's mighty generous of you, I'm sure.'

'And of course, you'll need to know *how* to contact me, should the need arise.'

He laughed nervously. 'You are right, sir. I was quite forgetting myself. My poor old brain must be addled by the excitement of our new business partnership.'

'Yes,' I said, reaching into the inside pocket of my overcoat. 'It must be.'

The way Hayles's eyes flickered once more into beady life and fastened on my wallet was almost like a physical sensation. I half expected to feel the wallet plucked from my hand by telekinesis; either that or Hayles would click his tongue and Satan would swoop down and snatch it from me.

Neither of those things happened, of course. I took three large white notes from my wallet – a ten and two fives – and a business card with my name and address on it. I expected Hayles to grab them from my hand, but he extricated them almost reverently, which reminded me of what he had said about Satan taking tit-bits from the fingers of local children. I glanced at the crow, still perched on top of the wardrobe, its head tilted as if observing the exchange with interest, its round eyes flashing like yellow gemstones in the gloom.

Twenty pounds wasn't a fortune – the average London labourer earned around a pound a week, maybe more – but it may have been the most money that a man like Hayles had ever earned in one go before. He gawped at the notes in disbelief, then raised them to his face with trembling hands to sniff them. Finally he rolled them deftly into a tube and concealed them somewhere within the ragged folds of his black clothing.

'That's what we call a down payment, Mr Hayles,' I said. 'I give you that money in the hope that you will serve me well and faithfully.'

'Oh, I will, sir,' Hayles replied, dipping his head and touching his forelock. 'You can count on that. I am a man of my word.'

'I'm glad to hear it,' I said, and extended my hand. 'Let's shake on it, as you suggested.'

He eyed my hand warily, as if afraid I might have a mousetrap concealed in my palm, then tugged the fingerless glove off his own right hand and stretched out his arm. I clasped his dirt-ingrained hand in my cleaner one, expecting his skin to be dry and cool like a snake's, but finding instead that it was warm and damp, perhaps with nerves. He gave my hand a perfunctory shake and tried to release it, but I held on for a moment, fractionally tightening my grip.

'A word of friendly warning before we depart, Mr Hayles,' I said. 'Not for my sake, but your own.' I smiled, but my voice was as cold and precise as I could make it. 'Please remember what I have said. It is imperative that you speak to no one about me, about the item I'm seeking, or about the deal that we've struck today. There may be others seeking the heart, and if they find out that you are helping me, they will show no mercy. Do you understand?'

Hayles swallowed. The gulp was loud in the dust-filled room.

'I do, sir.'

'Excellent.' I released his hand and stepped back towards the door. 'Then our business for now is concluded. We'll bid you a very good day.'

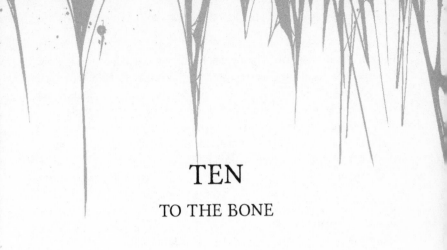

TEN

TO THE BONE

'What do you mean, she's gone to the theatre?'

It was barely noon, but the day had darkened so much it felt like dusk. Just when it seemed a thaw might be on the way, the air had turned even colder and new flakes of snow had begun to drift from the leaden sky. Hawkins and I arrived back at the house shivering and stamping our boots. I'd been looking forward to a bowl of soup and perhaps an afternoon snooze before dinner with the Sherwoods – but Hope's news had scuppered those plans.

She'd been playing with her doll's house in her room when I'd stuck my head round the door. She and her new toy had been inseparable since she'd unwrapped it on Christmas Day. She was so engrossed in her game she didn't notice me enter. I watched her for thirty seconds or so with a mixture of affection and concern. The way she played with the little wooden figures, creating individual voices for each character, I found so touching that tears welled in my eyes. A couple of months ago she'd have been incapable of this. Creative play would have been incomprehensible to her. She'd come on in leaps and bounds since then, but I was still reluctant to allow her to take that extra step of mixing with other children. It wasn't that I didn't think Hope wouldn't behave herself or know how to handle the situation; it was that I didn't trust other kids to accept her as we did. I didn't want her to be made fun of, or to be made to feel like a freak because of her mechanical arm. I didn't want her to feel she was something to be gossiped about, or feared, or stared at.

Eventually I cleared my throat, and she looked up. In the flat, dead light of the increasingly gloomy day her face looked grey and lifeless, her eyes a washed-out blue set deep in the hollows of their sockets. For a shocking instant I got the impression her skin had become translucent, that I could see the skull beneath it. I forced a smile.

'Having fun?'

She nodded and grinned, which, rather than dispelling the notion, made her face look even more skull-like.

Trying to push away the image, I sat on the bed and we chatted for a while. Just general stuff: how she was feeling, how she'd slept, what she'd been doing today. I asked her where Clover was, and felt my stomach clench when Hope told me she'd gone to the theatre. More sharply than I meant to, I asked her what she meant.

'What's the matter, Alex?' she asked in alarm, as if she felt she'd done something wrong.

I put a hand on her head to reassure her. Her hair felt damp, the skull beneath it radiating heat.

'Nothing,' I said. 'Sorry. I'm just... surprised, that's all.'

Ten minutes later Hawkins and I were again trundling through the snowy London streets in a hansom. It turned out a messenger boy had arrived forty minutes earlier, with a note from Horace Lacey saying that he wanted to see us as soon as possible.

The note had been waiting for us on the hall table when we'd come in, but I'd missed it. It was pinned beneath a glass paperweight, along with a scrawled note from Clover: *Thought I'd better pop along. See you there!* Once Mrs Peake had drawn Lacey's note to my attention, I compared it to the earlier one we'd received from the theatre manager. The handwriting was the same, but whereas the language in the first note was flamboyant, this second one was concise, even terse:

Dear Mr Locke
Please attend to me at the Maybury Theatre at your earliest convenience.
I have urgent news to impart.
Yours
Horace Lacey

'What do you think?' I'd asked Hawkins as we were waiting for the cab.

Hawkins had peered at the note as intently as if he was willing a hidden message to reveal itself beneath the one on the paper.

'In my opinion this was written in haste, sir. Perhaps in a state of excitement.'

'Or fear?'

Hawkins' steely grey eyes regarded me. I could imagine him wearing that same unflappable expression as he prepared to perform death-defying stunts with the Flying Bencziks every night. 'Possibly.'

Despite my anxiety, the rocking of the cab and the shushing of the wheels through the snowy streets lulled me to sleep. I was so exhausted it was like being anaesthetised. For a good thirty seconds after Hawkins shook me awake I had no idea where I was.

'We're here, sir,' he said as I blinked in confusion.

'Where?'

'The Maybury Theatre.'

I peered out of the cab window, but all I could see was a fresh layer of snow on the glass. As my senses returned I realised I could hear snow pattering on the roof above us.

'Is it night?' I asked.

'Early afternoon, sir,' replied Hawkins, pushing the door open. 'The weather is closing in again, I fear.'

He wasn't wrong. But at least the cold air and swirling snow helped blow the cobwebs away. Asking the cab driver to wait (he peered at us mournfully from beneath the brim of a hat topped with an inch-thick layer of snow), we ran up the snowy steps to the main doors.

'Should we knock, sir?' asked Hawkins, raising his cane.

Noting that the doors weren't quite flush with one another, I leaned my weight against the left-hand one and it opened immediately.

'No need.'

'Perhaps Miss Clover left it open to allow us easy access?'

'Perhaps,' I said. 'Though in my time we'd call that a best-case scenario.'

Despite my fluttering stomach, there was no immediate sign that anything bad had happened. The lobby with its threadbare carpet and wide steps looked the same as it had the last time I'd been here.

What *was* perhaps odd was that there was no sound coming from the auditorium. Shouldn't the Guiding Light Players be rehearsing? Wasn't their play due to start in a week or so? Then again, maybe this was their lunch break. Or maybe today's rehearsal had been postponed due to the snow.

There was no reason why we shouldn't have called out in the hope of attracting attention, but I was cautious. There was something not right about that note. If Lacey *had* written it out of fear – if he'd thought himself in danger, for instance – wouldn't he have vacated the premises, even jumped in a cab and come to see *us* rather than sitting tight and waiting for *us* to go to *him*? And if the situation wasn't urgent, why had his note been so curt? He was an obsequious man, he liked to make a good impression – so why had he dispensed with the sycophantic language he'd used previously?

'Let's take it slowly and quietly,' I murmured to Hawkins, and pointed to the left-hand turning at the top of the wide steps. 'We'll go round the outside of the auditorium to the back, check out the dressing rooms and the yard.'

'Understood, sir.'

I drew my howdah and led the way. I'd feel a fool if it turned out I was overreacting, and ended up scaring Lacey half to death, but better that than be caught unawares.

I ascended the stairs and edged through the arched opening. Only around half the wall lamps were lit along the curved corridor ahead, presumably to save money, which meant the interior of the theatre was gloomy. Patches of darkness quivered between the evenly spaced oases of light cast by the flickering gas flames. Most of the doors lining the left-hand wall were murky rectangles, whereas the openings on the right, leading into the main auditorium, resembled gaping black mouths.

I stopped at the first of these and peered through. The auditorium was dark and utterly silent. The stage at the far end was not visible at all. All I could see of the interior were the vague, shadowy outlines of seats in the two or three rows closest to where I was standing. I was aware that anything could be lurking in that darkness, no more than a few metres away, and I wouldn't be aware of it until it moved or made a sound. Gripping the howdah more tightly I moved on, Hawkins panther-silent behind me.

After a few more steps I halted and sniffed the air. 'Can you smell that?'

'I can, sir,' Hawkins replied. 'A stale odour, like old mushrooms.'

I nodded, my heart beating faster, and peered into the shadows. Was he here waiting for us? Willoughby? Was this a trap?

Maybe it wasn't only him. Maybe, despite the silence, we were surrounded by the Wolves of London. I tried to swallow, but my throat felt like it was filled with tissue paper. My muscles slowly tightened as I anticipated an eruption of movement, pictured nightmarish creatures swarming from every nook and crevice, every opening, every clot of darkness.

Should I shout? Call out a challenge? Bring them into the open?

At least I didn't feel tired any more. *Adrenaline overload*, I thought. I'd probably crash like a KO'd boxer later.

If there *was* a later.

There was nothing to do but keep moving forward. At each doorway I came to, each opening on my right, I paused, tensing, half anticipating an attack.

The theatre stayed silent. If there *was* anything here it was biding its time.

The mulchy smell grew stronger. My stomach coiled in response. I tried to breathe through my mouth, but that was almost as bad. It felt as though a bitter sort of dampness, a cluster of microscopic spoors or particles, was settling on my lips. Perhaps I was being poisoned.

'Sir?' Hawkins' voice was a hiss in the dimness.

I glanced at him, and saw that he was indicating a door on our left.

A door that was standing ajar.

Was it significant? An invitation? A challenge? I raised my left hand, urging caution, and steadied my right hand with the gun in it. I crept towards the door, and as I did so the mushroom stench grew stronger until it was almost overwhelming.

Blinking, hoping my eyes wouldn't water and blur my vision, I pushed the door slowly open.

Nothing moved. A wedge of feeble light crept into the room, dimly illuminating a small section of it. I stood on the threshold, peering, trying to make sense of what I could see. A table? No, a desk. Solid and heavy, like much of the furniture from this period. Probably mahogany.

But what was propped *behind* the desk? I got the impression of something spindly but top-heavy. A tangle of sticks? An effigy of some kind? A scarecrow?

'One moment, sir,' Hawkins whispered. 'I have a box of lucifers...'

He leaned his cane against the wall and reached into his pocket. Seconds later there came the scrape and flare of a match. The sharp, sulphurous tang of it was far preferable to the sour, mushroomy stench that hung heavily in the air. But sadly it was all too brief, quickly swamped by the more dominant odour.

Hawkins stepped up beside me and raised the match. Orange light swelled into the room, pushing back the dark, revealing what was slumped behind the desk...

'Fuck!' I blurted and took an instinctive step back, bumping into Hawkins. He dropped the match and the light winked out. As he fumbled for another, I bent double, pressing a hand to my stomach, and released a long gasp of air.

Although I'd only seen it for a split second, the terrible image of Horace Lacey lolling in the chair behind his desk was already branded on my mind. Even if I never saw it again – which wasn't likely, as already I could hear the soft rattling of matches as Hawkins extracted another from the box – I doubted I'd ever forget the sight. The theatre manager was dead, his glazed eyes staring out at different angles beneath half-closed lids, his mouth hanging open. But it wasn't this that had shocked me; it was the fact that beneath his head, which was intact, he had been nothing but a skeleton. His clothes and flesh – every layer of muscle and fat, every internal organ – had simply gone. Below the bloody stump of his neck Lacey had quite literally been stripped to the bone.

As a second match rasped and flared, I braced myself to look again. I vowed to examine the body as clinically as I could, to concentrate on the fact that Clover might need our help (I tried not to dwell on the fear that what had happened to Lacey might have happened to her too), and that any information we could arm ourselves with might prove useful.

I managed it... more or less. The most astonishing thing about Lacey's corpse was how thoroughly the meat had been removed. There were a few errant shreds of flesh clinging to the skeleton, but for the most part the bones were perfectly white, almost gleaming, as if they had been sucked clean.

There was also very little blood. That was the other surprising thing. In the split second before I'd knocked Hawkins' first match from his hand, my impression had been that there was blood everywhere. But when I looked again, I realised that although the walls and desk were spattered with it, there was nothing like the eight pints that the average human body contained.

So whatever had killed and presumably devoured Lacey had done so with astonishing speed and ferocity. We'd come to the same conclusion about the prostitute's death, of course, but in that instance we hadn't seen the body. *Witnessing* the damage rather than just being told about it was a whole different ball game. It made the impossible real – more so when it was likely the killer was still close.

Or killers. Because yet again what Lacey's corpse made me think of was a school of savage airborne piranhas. As the light from Hawkins' second Lucifer guttered out, I stepped back out of the room.

'There's nothing we can do for the poor sod,' I said. 'We need to find Clover.'

It was a relief to pull the door shut and trap some of that mushroomy stench inside. Not all of it, though. It trailed us down the corridor like tendrils of fog – or tenacious vines that had latched on to us and wouldn't let go. Its persistence made me wonder whether the stench itself, or some invisible thing within it, was the killer. If so, was it sentient or merely a weapon? Was it at this moment sizing us up, waiting for the right moment to attack, to unravel us in an instant? I imagined a kind of mutant Ebola, its power, its voracity, magnified to inconceivable proportions. If that was what we were up against there was nothing we could do. Our fate was sealed.

We reached the end of the curving corridor. In front of us was the door that led to the dingy, oil-lit area lined with dressing rooms. Was that where we'd find Clover? And maybe Willoughby too? Sprawled like some vast, gluttonous king on his throne, awaiting our arrival?

I tried the door. It was locked. I glanced at Hawkins, raising my eyebrows in surprise. If this *was* a trap, I would have expected our route to be unimpeded. I opened my mouth to speak – but just as I did so the dark openings on our right, which led into the auditorium, bloomed with light.

I jerked and spun round, pointing my howdah at the nearest

opening. I expected *things* to pour from them: Tallarian's nightmarish conglomerations of flesh and metal; flying piranhas with vast mouths and jagged teeth; monsters with tentacles and wings and too many eyes.

But nothing happened. Nothing but the fact that somewhere in the auditorium someone had turned on the lights.

From the angle and the subdued glow I guessed the illumination was coming from the stage. I moved silently towards the nearest opening, Hawkins behind me. Pressing myself against the wall beside the wide arch, I took a peek around the corner. The stage was down on my left, faced by sloping rows of seats. From here, with the rest of the auditorium in darkness, it reminded me of the mouth of a furnace fed by a wide conical chute.

There was a wooden chair in the centre of the stage and Clover was sitting in it, slumped forward. She wasn't moving. I hoped she was simply unconscious. The fact she hadn't fallen off the chair suggested she was tied to it, but from where I stood it was impossible to tell. I couldn't see anyone else, but the message was clear:

Come and get her if you dare.

My stomach clenched to see her so exposed and vulnerable, but I felt a measure of relief too. Although I couldn't say for certain whether she was alive, at least she hadn't suffered the same fate as Lacey, who had clearly been deemed surplus to requirements.

My prime suspect for Lacey's murder and Clover's capture was, of course, Willoughby, though perhaps I was jumping to conclusions and there was more to this situation than met the eye? Whoever he, she or it turned out to be, however, I wondered how effective my howdah would be against them.

Turning to Hawkins I said, 'We should approach the stage from opposite sides of the auditorium. I'll go in this side and crawl down using the seats for cover, and you can do the same from the other side. What do you think?'

Hawkins was as imperturbable as ever. Nodding slowly he said, 'I don't suppose that we've arrived here undetected, but it's as workable a plan as any. May I make one suggestion, though, sir?'

'Go for it.'

'Please allow me to draw the attention of our enemy while you remain concealed. With luck my presence will be sufficient to entice the blackguard from hiding, which may allow you to take a potshot at him.'

'You really think he'll be that gullible?'

'Frankly? No. But I still believe it's worth a try. Is it not better to make a heroic stand whilst endeavouring to rescue a maiden fair than to sneak away with one's tail between one's legs and leave said maiden to a grisly fate?'

There were times when I didn't know whether Hawkins was being entirely serious; times when his choice of words seemed a parody of the ultra-English persona he had adopted, and at the same time to hint at a gallows humour so black it was impenetrable. I looked at him quizzically.

'Are you *sure* you're Hungarian?'

He responded with a stream of guttural, Eastern European sounding words.

'That's easy for you to say,' I muttered. 'What does it mean?'

'It is the beginning of my country's national anthem. The poetic translation, as opposed to the literal one, is thus:

O, my God, the Magyar bless

With thy plenty and good cheer!

With thine aid his just cause press,

Where his foes to fight appear.'

'Very nice,' I said. 'Very appropriate.'

A thin smile appeared on his face. 'Ours is a just cause, sir. Let us hope that it is enough to win the day.'

He turned and hurried back along the corridor. I gave him a couple of minutes to get into position, then I bent low and slipped through the arched opening. I scuttled across to the seat closest to me – the last one on row R – and crouched beside it. As I paused, looking around, even craning my neck to peer into the shadows above to make sure nothing on the balcony or in one of the boxes was about to drop on me, I was suddenly struck by how totally and crazily my life had changed in the space of a few months. At the beginning of September I'd been gearing up for another year of teaching, of looking after my youngest daughter, of hoping I'd be able to juggle work and home and keep everyone I cared about happy. And now my life had flipped upside down and inside out, and I was a completely different person. I barely recognised the man I'd once been, and that saddened me more than I could say. *His* life, his simple ambitions, seemed unattainable to me now. Even though I was straining every sinew to become that man again, in my heart of hearts I doubted it would ever happen. How could it? I'd come too far, seen too much. I was a murderer, and a marked man, and however this whole crazy business worked out I would never be safe and normal again. Yet I still clung to that hope, because... well, because there wasn't anything else I *could* cling to. I had to believe I would get the obsidian heart back, and then Kate, and then my life. If I *didn't* believe that, then nothing would be worth anything ever again.

I shook the thought free and began to crawl towards the stage. I was pretty sure I was shielded by the rows of seats, but it was so quiet in the auditorium I had no guarantee my scuffling progress couldn't be heard from one end of the room to the other.

Although adrenaline was racing through my system, by the time I reached row H I was knackered. I was tense and scared, my heart was pounding, and even though the temperature inside the theatre wasn't much higher than it was in the streets, I was sweating, my skin crawling with an almost feverish heat.

I paused, took several deep breaths, and decided that perhaps now was a good time to raise my head above the parapet, check what was going on. When I did so, nothing seemed to have changed. Clover was still slumped on her chair and her attacker (Lacey's killer?) was still out of sight. I glanced to my right, along the row of seats to the other side of the auditorium, but there was no sign of Hawkins. Neither could I hear anything, which I told myself was a good thing – because if *I* couldn't hear Hawkins, then maybe our enemy couldn't hear *me*.

I knew if I was going to rescue Clover I'd have to venture into the open sooner or later, but I was determined to put that off for as long as possible. Or maybe I *wouldn't* need to show myself. Maybe Hawkins' plan would work and by using himself as a decoy we'd be able to turn the tables. I wondered, if the opportunity arose to pull the trigger, whether I'd actually be able to shoot someone, and what it would feel like if I did. I might only get a split second to think about it and do it – in which case, could I be decisive enough, clinical enough?

After a few moments I felt able to carry on. I crawled down to row A, and once I was there, facing the left-hand corner of the stage, I eased myself into as comfortable a position as I could and waited for Hawkins to make the first move. I pointed the gun vaguely at the stage, though not at Clover. Now that I was close enough, I was relieved to see that, although she was unconscious, she was definitely breathing.

A minute passed. I shifted position, my left foot starting to go numb. Had something happened to Hawkins? It sickened me to think he might have encountered Lacey's killer.

Shuffling back slightly, I peered along the narrow aisle between the first two rows, trying to make out any movement at the far end. I guessed that would be where Hawkins was hiding if he'd made it. *Could* I see something? The dark bulk of a figure, crouched out of sight as I was? Or was my mind playing tricks? Was I only seeing what I wanted to see?

'The game is up, Mr Locke. Please rise to your feet without delay, and then throw your weapon into the darkness behind you. If you fail to do so, your pretty wife will be slaughtered where she sits.'

Though I froze, it didn't surprise me that it was Willoughby's voice that rang out through the auditorium. Even though I was pressed into the shadows of the seats on my right, and there was no way I could be seen from the stage, I felt like a rabbit in the headlights. I was about to obey when it struck me that Willoughby might have spotted Hawkins and mistaken him for me - in which case, if Hawkins could keep his face concealed...

'Without delay, Mr Locke,' Willoughby repeated, his voice hardening. 'And the same goes for your companion. I shall count up to three, and if, by that time, you have not risen to your feet, Mrs Locke will die. One...'

I scrambled upright.

'Stop!'

On the far side of the auditorium, I was aware of another dark shape rising too.

'The weapon, Mr Locke,' Willoughby reminded me. I quickly scanned the stage, wondering if a quick shot fired in his direction might send him scrambling for cover, allowing us to grab Clover. But there was no sign of him. If he was standing in the wings he was taking care to remain out of sight. With a sinking heart I turned and flung the howdah into the dark mass of seats behind me. I heard it hit something with a thump and clatter to the floor.

'And *your* cane, sir,' Willoughby said.

Hawkins was still a dark blur on the far side of the auditorium. My eyes registered no more than a rapid suggestion of movement, which was followed by the hollow rattling clatter of his cane falling among the empty seats.

'Excellent. Now, gentlemen, if you would both take your places in the front row the performance can begin. Seats fifteen and sixteen will suffice, I think.'

Willoughby sounded confident and mocking – and why not? Feeling vulnerable, I stepped out in front of row A and walked along it until I found seat fifteen. I sat down, and a moment later Hawkins sat down beside me, a resigned almost weary look on his face.

For a few seconds nothing happened, and then Willoughby emerged from the wings on our right.

He appeared to be unarmed. Moving smoothly, even delicately, for a man of his bulk, he sauntered to the front of the stage and peered down at us. He looked smug and calculating. He looked like a performer in full command of his audience.

'Now, gentlemen,' he said, 'perhaps you will enlighten me as to who exactly you are, and why you are taking such a singular interest in my affairs?'

I tried to bluff it out. 'You know who we are. We're helping the police. We're investigating the murder that—'

'Poppycock!' boomed Willoughby. 'You are no more a peeler than I, Mr Locke. From our mutual friend Mr Lacey I gleaned that you may more accurately be termed a man of business, though it appears that even in this sphere you are little more than a lucky investor, who makes a comfortable living by skimming the cream of profit from an admittedly impressive array of providers. But who are you really? *What* are you? Why have you been paying our Mr Lacey to remain alert for, as he termed it, "unusual occurrences"?'

So Lacey *had* been interrogated before he died. And tortured too? I didn't want to know.

Sighing I said, 'There's no need to play games, Mr Willoughby. You know who I am.'

Willoughby was silent for a moment. Then, a little less confidently, he said, 'So it's true? The Society has tracked me down?'

I blinked. 'What Society?'

His face twisted in anger. '*Now* who is playing games, Mr Locke? Please do not provoke me. It is far too late to profess ignorance.'

He stepped across to Clover's chair, grabbed her hair in one meaty fist and yanked her head back. She groaned, but remained unconscious. I jumped to my feet.

'Leave her alone! There's no need for that!'

'*Sit down!*' screamed Willoughby. 'Sit down or I swear I shall snap this whore's neck and damn the consequences!'

I raised my hands and lowered myself back into my seat.

'All right, take it easy. Let's just talk like reasonable human beings.'

'Human beings!' he snorted. 'Is that what we still are?'

I wasn't sure how to respond to that, and he didn't look as though he expected me to. Flapping a hand dismissively, he said, 'So talk, Mr Locke. Talk for your lives and for my own. Tell me all that you know.'

I frowned. This wasn't working out the way I'd imagined. Willoughby wasn't behaving how I'd expect one of the Wolves of London to behave. He didn't sound as though he'd lured us into a trap on their behalf, but as though he was running scared. I wondered what this mysterious 'Society' was. A rival group to the Wolves of London? There was only one way to find out.

I started to talk. I told Willoughby I didn't want trouble; that all I wanted was to find the obsidian heart. I expected a reaction to that, but all he did was stare at me with bafflement and growing impatience on his face.

'What nonsense is this?' he growled, his fist tightening in Clover's hair.

'It's not nonsense, I promise you.' Choosing my words carefully, I said, 'I didn't come here looking for you, Mr Willoughby. I came because of what happened to the girl in the yard. Her death was... unusual. Impossible. The way she was killed was... beyond the means of any normal person.'

I held up my hands, as though pressing home my point.

'The group I'm looking for is the only one I'm aware of capable of such things. They call themselves the Wolves of London, and they have something I want... something I need...'

'This "obsidian heart" you spoke of?'

'Yes. It's the only thing that will allow me to find my daughter again. I've been scouring London for it, employing people to act as my eyes and ears. So you see, Mr Willoughby, I have nothing to do with this "Society" of yours. I've never even heard of them.'

'Why don't you tell us about them?' suggested Hawkins. 'Perhaps we can aid each other?'

Willoughby was silent, his eyes flickering from me to Hawkins and back again. I could tell he was wavering. I could tell that beneath his bluster and arrogance, he was scared shitless.

With a silent apology to Horace Lacey, and to the young girl slaughtered in the yard, I said, 'Hawkins is right, Mr Willoughby. Perhaps we *can* help each other. I can't believe that the Wolves and the Society are unrelated. So why don't we trade our information? You look as though you could do with someone to talk to.'

Willoughby licked his lips. Untangling his fist from Clover's hair, he took a couple of small, tottering steps backward. For a moment I thought we'd got through to him, thought that Hawkins and I had achieved – for the time being, at least – an uneasy truce.

I was shocked, therefore, when he muttered, 'No, I can't risk it. I will have to kill you – all of you. I will have to change my identity once more, start again elsewhere...'

With surprising spryness – or perhaps not so surprising, considering his background – Hawkins leaped to his feet.

'Kill us?' he scoffed. 'And how do you propose to do that, sir? You are not even armed. I suggest that your energy would be better served in flight.'

'Careful, Hawkins,' I said, jumping up too and putting a hand on his arm. 'I think there's more to him than meets the eye.'

But Willoughby seemed to be having problems. He tottered back a couple more steps, swaying slightly, as if about to faint. His mouth dropped open, his eyes rolled up in their sockets, and he started to shake violently. His face turned red and he began to make guttural, choking sounds. His huge body spasmed violently with each ratcheting bark. He sounded like a cat coughing up fur balls.

'He's having a seizure,' I said, thinking the stress must have been too much for him. 'Maybe even a heart attack.'

Grabbing our chance, Hawkins and I rushed forward and clambered on to the stage. Although he was a good twenty years older than me, my butler was a damn sight more agile than I was. While I was still hauling myself up and over the wooden lip, Hawkins, having vaulted past me, was rising smoothly to his feet and striding towards Clover. She was coming round now, groaning, trying to raise her head. Behind her, having retreated almost to the back of the stage, Willoughby was shaking like a volcano about to erupt, his head a crimson balloon, his mouth yawning open.

Hawkins reached Clover at the same moment that something oozed from between Willoughby's widely stretched jaws and hit the stage with a splat. I was clambering to my feet, and so only caught a glimpse of the thing as it emerged, but when it hit the wooden boards my head snapped up.

What the hell was it? My first thought was that Willoughby had coughed up one of his internal organs. I stared at him, expecting to see blood on his chin and waistcoat, his body crumpling to the floor like a downed zeppelin.

But he was still standing, his eyes rolled back so that only the whites showed. He was still making that awful furball noise too, his body heaving with each retching expulsion.

I looked at the thing that had come out of him. Hawkins had frozen in the process of untying the rope that secured Clover to the chair and was staring at it too. It was blue-grey and as smooth, wet and gleaming as a fresh liver. About the size of a clenched fist, it was roughly spherical in shape. At first it was inert – and then it moved! I felt a jolt go through me; I might even have cried out.

I guess what the thing really looked like was an ocean creature, a sea slug or something, but in that moment I thought of it only as a living, breathing tumour. Something nasty, poisonous, that might invade a human body and make its host ill, and have to be cut out before it could grow and spread.

It moved again, its gelid mass giving a weird lurching spasm, like a newborn taking its first gulp of air. Then it began to pulse and shudder, its blue-grey flesh rippling as thick, dark veins bulged on its surface.

And then, as if that wasn't repulsive enough, a mass of spines suddenly sprang from its slick flesh like porcupine quills.

'Fuck!' I blurted, and even Hawkins cried out in surprise.

At the back of the stage Willoughby gave another choking heave, and a second blue-grey lump surged out of his mouth. Even as this one plopped wetly to the ground like a puppy in a placental sac, he heaved again, disgorging a third creature, and then, in quick succession, a fourth and a fifth.

I thought of the heart, of the way it could change form, become fluid. I thought of the spike that had extruded from its surface like the eyestalk of a snail, but which had turned instantly hard enough to puncture Barnaby McCallum's skull as easily as if it were an egg.

Were these... *things* akin to that? Or were they the heart's antitheses? Its nemeses even?

And then I thought of Horace Lacey and my original notion of airborne piranhas.

'Fuck!' I shouted again, stumbling forward and grabbing Hawkins' arm. 'It's them! They're the things that killed Lacey!'

Maybe I should have made the connection immediately, but connections are easy to spot when you're observing events from afar. When you're in the thick of it, with no time to do anything but react, it's different. The obvious isn't so obvious then.

Clawing at the knots securing Clover to the chair, and despairing that there were so fucking many of them, I yelled, 'We've got to get her free! We've got to get out of here!'

I heard Willoughby cough up another of the creatures, and then another. My fingers were starting to bleed from my attempts to pick the knots apart. Beside me, Hawkins was working just as urgently, but with less panic. I heard another wet splat, then two more. I stole a quick glance at Willoughby. What I saw yanked a gasp out of me.

He had *deflated*. He'd become thin. But it wasn't a healthy thinness. It was not only his clothes that now hung grotesquely loose on his bones, but his skin. His face looked as though it was melting, wattles and dewlaps of flesh swinging pendulously from his jawline, his mouth and eyes sagging at the corners. He looked like a waxwork under a heat lamp, or a child clothed in the flesh of an adult.

Appalling as this was, it didn't horrify me as much as the creatures milling around his feet. There must have been two dozen of them now, maybe thirty. They were quivering and pulsing, as if girding themselves for action. Around half were bristling with porcupine-like spines; the rest still seemed to be acclimatising.

I renewed my attempts to untie Clover, but the knots were tight and many. I tried to focus on my task, but I was aware that half a dozen metres away the things that had killed Lacey and the girl in the yard were massing for attack.

Several possible courses of action spiralled through my head. Should Hawkins and I pick up Clover, chair and all, and carry her out between us? No, we'd be too slow, too hampered by our burden. Should we attack the creatures then? But how? By kicking them? Stamping on them? But what if that just invigorated them? Goaded them into retaliation?

Perhaps my best option was to look for my gun? I knew roughly where it had landed – or thought I did.

But no, I couldn't abandon Hawkins and Clover, not even temporarily. If they were attacked while I was poking about in the dark, I'd never forgive myself.

The only thing to do, therefore, was stand shoulder to shoulder with my friends against whatever horror we were about to face. Whether we lived or died, the three of us would do it together.

Then another possibility occurred to me: what if I attacked Willoughby? Punched him senseless? Maybe the creatures were mentally linked to him in some way, and maybe, by knocking him out, it would neutralise them?

Much as the prospect of approaching the spiny, pulsing monstrosities repulsed me I decided it had to be worth a try. I blurted my intentions to Hawkins, but he shook his head.

'Let me do it, sir. I'm more dispensable than you.'

'Bollocks! Besides, it was me who got you into this. I should be the one to try and put it right.'

'I wouldn't be here at all if you hadn't rescued me, sir. I owe you my life.'

'No, you don't!' I said, appalled. 'Don't ever—'

'Too late!'

The cry, shrill but slurred, came from Clover. Though still groggy, she was recovering quickly now. I glanced at her and saw her looking in Willoughby's direction. I followed her gaze.

'Oh, shit!'

While Hawkins and I had been arguing – swinging our dicks at each other, Clover would have said – Willoughby's army of spiny, man-eating tumours had continued to rally themselves. Now, bristling with spines, they were turning in our direction. Or, considering they had no faces, they at least gave the impression they were.

'Leave me,' Clover muttered. 'Just go.'

'No way,' I said.

She shoved at me angrily. 'Don't be a dick, Alex. There's no point us all dying.'

'We're not leaving,' I said. 'We'll fucking carry you if we have to.'

But then there was no more time to debate. With a horrible slithering sound Willoughby's creatures surged towards us.

'*Call them off!*'

The voice, harsh and rasping, echoed round the auditorium. At first I had no idea where it had come from, and then, as the advancing mass came to a sudden halt, I realised that Willoughby had the point of a large rusty knife pressed into his baggy-skinned throat. Standing behind him, holding the knife, his other hand clamped around the actor's now bony shoulder, was a filthy figure in a ragged overcoat and battered bowler hat.

'Mr Hulse,' I said, almost laughing with relief. 'Where did you spring from?'

'Come in round the back, didn't I? Been keeping my beady eye on him, just like you told me. I followed him here, then waited outside to see if he come out again. When he didn't I took myself off for a pie; the snow was coming down fierce, and I was in need of something hot to keep me tripes from perishing. I got back in time to see you arrive in yer hansom. The way you run up them steps I thought: aye-aye. So instead of following through the front, I decides to go round the back. That way, I thought, if it comes to it, we can attack the problem from two sides, maybe catch our little fishy unawares.' He winked. 'And there you has it. Worked a treat.'

Although we weren't out of the woods, I couldn't help but grin. 'Mr Hulse, you may have just saved our lives.'

'Worth a bonus, I reckon.'

'A big bonus,' I agreed.

Hawkins was still working at Clover's ropes. With a sudden yank he finally succeeded in loosening what must have been a major knot. The rope sagged around her middle, allowing her to tug her arms free. Moments later she manoeuvred her way out of the chair and stood up, then immediately staggered to one side. I grabbed her before she could fall.

'Whoa,' she said, clutching at Hawkins and me for support. 'Still a bit punch drunk. The bastard chloroformed me just after I found Lacey. Caught me with my pants down. Not literally.'

Now that Clover was free, Hawkins had turned his attention to the mass of spiny tumour-creatures, which had flowed halfway across the stage and then stopped. They were poised, quivering, as though awaiting further instructions.

'Clearly the creatures are beholden to Mr Willoughby,' he muttered.

'Which makes *him* the murderer,' I said.

'Please,' Willoughby's voice was almost as rusty as the knife at his throat, 'let me explain.'

'Explain murder? This'll be good,' said Clover.

'Not murder,' protested Willoughby. 'Survival.'

Perhaps it was simply the knife, but along with his corpulence had gone the bluster and arrogance we'd become used to. The transformation from the man we'd seen bullying his fellow actors at yesterday's rehearsal to the pitiful wreck before us now was startling. I wondered whether the creatures had something to do with that, whether they acted as storehouses for Willoughby's viciousness – or, more to the point, whether they were living, breathing distillations of the more vile aspects of his character.

'The Society did this to me,' he wheedled. 'In fear of my life, I joined their number, and was transformed into a... a ghoul, forced to gorge on misery, grief and terror, base emotions which in turn manifest as these vile forms that feed on human flesh. It is the only way I can be provided with the sustenance I need, the only way I can survive. It's a miserable existence, but don't you see? I have no option but to kill, and to keep on killing. I don't *wish* to do it, but I *must!*'

He looked abject, but Clover sneered. 'Oh, boo hoo! My heart bleeds. Who are you to think your life is worth more than the lives of the people you've killed? Of *course* you've got another option, you selfish bastard. You've *always* had another option. You should have killed *yourself*!'

Livid with fury, she took a lurching step towards him, as if intending to take a swing at him. I grabbed her arm.

'Careful. Don't get too close to those things.'

She glared at me – then almost instantly nodded and I felt her muscles relax.

'Sorry, it's just... he makes me sick.'

'I know,' I said. 'Me too.'

Although I shared Clover's revulsion, I didn't want this to turn into a slanging match. All I wanted was information that might give us a possible route back to the heart and Kate.

'Tell me about the Society, Mr Willoughby,' I said. 'Who are they? Where do they come from?'

Willoughby looked drained; his voice rose barely above a mumble. 'I know precious little about them – and that, I swear, is true. Their full title is the Society of Blood. They are a clandestine organisation, and an itinerant one. They have no meeting house, no set location in which to conduct their affairs.'

'How did you encounter them?' asked Hawkins.

Willoughby began to shake his head, and then, with Hulse's knife jabbing his throat, thought better of it.

'I remember nothing of the encounter. I regret to say I was drunk and high on opium. Before becoming an actor I lived the life of a libertine, a lotus eater. Mine was a debauched existence. I sought no goal but my own gratification...'

'So what's new?' muttered Clover.

'There is an opium den in Limehouse, the Thousand Sorrows in Floral Court. It was there that I made the acquaintance of a man named Darnley, who spoke of the Society as if it were a paradise on Earth – a place in which a man might discover all the sinful pleasures he could imagine, as well as many that he could not. It was Darnley who enticed me to accompany him to one of the Society's gatherings, which was where I encountered an individual known as the Dark Man, who transformed me into the lowly creature I am now.'

I gasped as if punched in the stomach.

'The Dark Man? Who is he? What did he look like?'

Willoughby – as well as he was able with Hulse's hand on his shoulder – shrugged.

'I recall nothing of the encounter, nor of the process by which he changed me.' His voice, already a mumble, became even more hushed. 'But some claim he is the very Devil.'

Thrown by Willoughby's mention of the Dark Man, who I had only ever previously heard referred to by Kate's mother, Lyn, and who I had always assumed was simply her way of personalising her own psychosis, I tried to keep on track.

'A while ago you accused Hawkins and me of being members of the Society. You said you were worried they had finally tracked you down. So does that mean you're on the run from them, that you and the Dark Man don't see eye to eye?'

Willoughby sighed. 'The reason that the Dark Man altered me – the reason he alters anybody – was to make me an acolyte, one of a group whose numbers grow by the day. But I did not wish for that to become my fate, Mr Locke. I may be wicked, but I am not half so wicked as my pursuers.'

My mind was racing. The Society of Blood and the Wolves of London. Were they one and the same, a slippery, ever-shifting organisation with as many names as the Devil? And the Dark Man: who or what was he? Their leader? The spider at the centre of their web? Or were there many 'dark men'? Was it simply a nominal title, a catch-all term?

'What else can you tell me?'

Willoughby spread his hands, the skin on them wrinkled, ill fitting. 'Nothing. That is all I know.'

'What shall we do with him, Alex?' Clover said.

Why ask me? I wanted to snap. *I'm not your boss!* But that would have been unfair.

'He's a murderer. We should hand him over to the police.'

'No! I beg of you!' Willoughby made a half-hearted attempt to pull away from Hulse, then squawked in pain as Hulse jabbed the knife harder into his scrawny throat, drawing blood.

Trying to stay calm, Willoughby said, 'If I am in custody the Dark Man will find me. I beg you to let me go. If you do, I will disappear, go about my business quietly. You will never hear from me again, I sw—'

125

He was still speaking when Hulse slashed his throat. The cut was deep and swift and savage, and made a noise like serrated metal tearing through cardboard. Blood sprayed everywhere, jetting over the wooden boards of the stage and over Willoughby's creatures, which instantly began to shrivel, to dissolve into powder, giving off a high, sickening, mushroomy stench. In less than the time it took for Willoughby's emaciated body to hit the floor with all the grace of a sack of rocks, the creatures had become nothing but blue decay.

Shocked by the suddenness of Willoughby's death, I could only stare at Hulse, who sniffed.

'Pardon me,' he said, 'but it struck me that a feller like him ought not to be out and about in this world. Unnatural, he is. Fierce unnatural.' He leaned over and wiped his blood-smeared knife on Willoughby's jacket. 'Besides which, my poor old ears had had enough of his whining. Getting on my nerves something rotten he was.'

ELEVEN

GOOSE AND BACON PIE

The snow fell steadily through the afternoon, settling on the ground like a pristine carpet laid directly over one that was old and filthy. Although it had stopped by the time Clover and I arrived at the Sherwoods' modest terrace in Gloucester Square, the air was still dense with ice crystals and wraith-like tendrils of freezing fog.

I wouldn't exactly say I'd *recovered* from the events earlier that day, but a couple of hours' solid sleep when I arrived home at least meant I wouldn't spend the evening acting like a zombie. Despite the hum of exhaustion in my muscles and guts, my brain had been so wired with stress and trauma that when I'd lowered my head to the pillow I'd thought there was no way I'd ever sleep again. But as soon as I shut my eyes my head felt like a boulder sinking into the depths of a deep, dark sea. The sensation was so blissful I felt my muscles instantly relax. I inhaled the darkness, happy to drown.

Perhaps I wouldn't have slept so easily if I hadn't known that the information Willoughby had given us wasn't already being acted upon. There had been a part of me – a *big* part – that had wanted to rush over to Limehouse immediately, even though I was almost dead on my feet, but Hawkins, Clover and even Hulse had persuaded me not to. They'd said the wisest thing to do would be not only to re-charge my batteries first, but also to arm myself with as much information as possible before rushing anywhere.

I knew they were talking sense, and yet I *also* knew (and I'm pretty sure *they* did too) that even if I gleaned a whole *dossier* of information about the Society of Blood and the Thousand Sorrows, chances are the outcome – whether good or bad – would ultimately be the same. Because the simple fact was that now the heart was no longer in my possession, I had nothing to fight my enemies with. All I could rely on was my gun and my wits, but I doubted whether either of them would be much use if the Wolves' (or the Society's) only intention was to squash me like a troublesome bug.

I was kind of relying on the fact that it wasn't, though; that the reason they hadn't already killed me was because I was somehow important to them. Although nothing was certain, including my enemies' motives, they seemed to have gone to a lot of trouble to draw me into their world, inveigle me into their affairs. So maybe I was as wrapped up in *their* destiny as they were in *mine*?

In the end I agreed to hold off visiting the Thousand Sorrows until later that night – specifically, until after Clover and I had fulfilled our dinner invitation with the Sherwoods. The clincher came when Hulse promised me he'd employ a couple of men to keep an eye on the place until then. And in truth, dinner with the Sherwoods might turn out to be equally important, if not more so, than my proposed visit to Limehouse. Whatever transpired, it looked as though it was going to be a busy evening, and an interesting one.

Our knock on the Sherwoods' door was answered by a stout, grey-haired woman wearing a neat, black pinafore dress. From what Clover had told me about the Sherwoods, I guessed she was their only servant – a combination butler, housekeeper, nursemaid and cook. Adam Sherwood (if that was his real name) was a clerk, one of thousands who, due to the new businesses springing up almost daily in London, either lived in modest accommodation in the city or commuted from the suburbs. Clerks were generally young, either single or recently married, and they earned an average wage of around one-fifty, two hundred pounds a year. This placed them in the relatively new social strata of what was increasingly being called the 'lower middle class' – though in the social-climbing environment of Victorian London it didn't stop them from trying to impress their friends and neighbours by living as grandly as they could.

The grey-haired woman appraised us coolly, then inclined her head. 'Good evening, sir, madam.'

'Good evening,' I said, handing her my card. 'Mr and Mrs Alex Locke. I believe Mr and Mrs Sherwood are expecting us?'

She glanced at the card. 'They are, sir. Won't you come in?'

'Thank you.'

I deferred to Clover – the polite thing to do – then stamped the snow off my shoes and stepped into the house behind her. As we took off our coats and hats, I looked around, thinking of the Sherwoods' flat in twenty-first century London and wondering if I'd see anything I recognised.

I didn't. The only similarity between that flat and this house was that they both had a narrow hallway. But whereas the flat's had been carpeted and made even narrower with a slim, Ikea-style bookcase, this one was tiled and tastefully, if sparsely, furnished. I draped my coat over the servant's outstretched arms and was about to put my hat on top when I said, 'Oh, I almost forgot.'

I slipped my hand into the pocket of the now-dangling coat and pulled out a package wrapped in patterned paper and tied with a red ribbon.

'A little Christmas present,' I said. 'For... Master Sherwood.'

I'd been about to say 'Hamish', but I had no idea whether that was his actual name or the name the Sherwoods had adopted for him (or *would* adopt) for their twenty-first century personas.

The servant nodded, her face deadpan. 'Very kind, sir, I'm sure.'

She hung our coats and hats on a set of hooks by the front door, then padded up the hall to a door on the left.

'Mr and Mrs Sherwood will receive you in the drawing room,' she said, reaching for a knob fashioned in honey-coloured glass. She opened the door and stepped aside to let us enter.

Clover went first. She usually wore skirts and jackets, but tonight she was wearing a mint-coloured satin evening gown with lacy ruffles on the sleeves and bodice and a darker green sash around her waist. She'd pulled her hair up into an elaborate mass of braids and curls, which showed off her long neck, and had topped the whole thing off with a little jewelled tiara. With her wide-set eyes and generous, smiling mouth she looked stunning, and with her straight back and natural grace, she had an almost regal air. When she stepped into the Sherwoods' drawing room, she seemed to shimmer and flow like liquid, the light catching her jewellery, making her sparkle.

Adam Sherwood was standing by the mantelpiece, facing the door, side-on to a fire that was crackling in the grate. He was smoking a cigarette, and although he had clearly been awaiting our arrival, he jerked as if startled when the door opened. He seemed to freeze when he saw us, and my first thought was that he was so captivated by Clover's beauty that he couldn't move. Then I glanced at Paula, sitting stiffly behind her husband in a mauve evening dress with puffed sleeves, and noticed that she too looked pensive, almost fearful.

My God! I thought. *They know me! They know who I am!*

Despite what Clover had said – that the Sherwoods' son was only three, whereas when I'd known them he'd been the same age as Kate – for a few seconds I felt sure I was right. I braced myself, half expecting them to... I don't know, try to escape through a window, or attack us, or collapse into a gibbering heap and confess all.

But then Adam Sherwood seemed to collect himself. Planting a smile on his face, he flicked his cigarette into the fire and stepped smartly forward, thrusting out a hand.

'Mr and Mrs Locke! Welcome! Welcome!' He grasped my hand and shook it warmly. 'This is an honour, sir! A veritable honour! You do my wife and I a great service by gracing us with your presence – and on such a night too! I only hope we can repay you with a passable meal and a... a warm fire.'

As he stuttered and reddened, I realised he didn't recognise me, after all. He was nervous not because he was scared of confronting the man whose daughter he'd abducted in the twenty-first century, but because of my social standing in this one.

It was another example of the obsequiousness of the Victorian 'lower' classes towards their 'betters', and as ever my instinct was to break down the barriers, treat Adam as an equal. I knew, though, that that would have only freaked him out. Even so, considering what the Sherwoods were destined to become, I knew I had to play this one carefully. I had to make them view me, if not as a friend, than certainly as a positive influence, a benefactor.

'Not at all,' I said, offering what I hoped was a friendly but not over-familiar smile. 'Thank you for the invitation.'

From his flushed expression and fixed grin I could see he was beginning to realise how much he'd overdone his welcome. He released my hand and stepped back.

'Please,' he babbled, gesturing a little wildly, 'come inside, sit down.'

Like the hallway, the Sherwoods' drawing room was tastefully furnished. For the Victorian era it was fairly modern, relying not on rich, dark colours and heavy fabrics, but on lighter shades – pale grey, sage, delicate olive greens. A tall mirror above the mantelpiece made the room seem larger than it was, as did the fact that it was less cluttered than your average Victorian drawing room.

'What a lovely tree!' Clover said, as if matching Adam's gushing enthusiasm with her own. Eyes sparkling wickedly, she dabbled the tips of her fingers on the lapel of my dinner jacket. 'And don't you just adore the decoration on the mantelpiece, Alex? Isn't it wonderfully festive?'

The Christmas tree in the corner was small but pretty, and the 'decoration' she'd referred to was an interwoven tangle of thin branches, pine cones and holly leaves with red berries, which stretched from one side of the marble mantelpiece to the other. The pine cones had been painted white and green, and the whole thing smelled as if it had been infused with cloves or cinnamon.

'It's charming,' I said, and waved a hand. 'This entire room is charming.'

'A little smaller than you're used to, I expect, Mr Locke?' Adam said. Out of the corner of my eye I noticed Paula wince.

Mischievously Clover said, 'Size isn't everything, Mr Sherwood.'

'Oh, I quite agree, Mrs Locke,' Adam said hastily. 'I hope you don't think I'm bemoaning my lot in life. No, Maude and I are very happy here – for the time being, at least. My wife is an excellent homemaker, and I – oh! But I'm forgetting! You haven't been formally introduced! Please forgive me!'

'There's nothing to forgive,' I said, thinking: *Maude?* Moving across to where she (*Maude?*) was sitting I said, 'I'm not a man who likes to stand on ceremony. Formality is tedious, don't you agree?'

'Er... yes!' Adam said, sounding both surprised and pleased. 'Yes, I *do* agree!'

I reached Paula (*Maude*) and bowed, holding out my hand. She put her hand in mine and I kissed the back of it.

'I'm very pleased to meet you, Mrs Sherwood. Thank you for inviting us to your lovely home. I hope you don't mind, but I took the liberty of purchasing a small Christmas gift for your son. He's three, I believe?'

I handed her the present. She seemed genuinely touched. 'He is, Mr Locke. Thank you. This is most generous.'

'Not at all. It's nothing much – just a small tin drum, which I thought would amuse him. Small boys do enjoy hitting things, don't they?'

Paula's (*Maude's*) lips twitched in a wry smile, and for a split-second I caught a flash of the woman I would get to know and like, and who would eventually betray me.

'I can't speak for all small boys, Mr Locke, but the one who lives here certainly does.'

We all laughed, and Adam started to thank me again. Perhaps to ward off a second wave of enthusiasm, Clover said, 'Give it a day or two, Mr Sherwood, and you'll be cursing us for bringing your son such a noisy gift.'

Formalities over, we sat down and the Sherwoods offered us sherry. Normally I didn't touch the stuff, but I accepted the glass that Adam handed to me with a show of enthusiasm. For the next twenty minutes the four of us chatted politely. Though Clover had become pretty adept at the weird formality of Victorian conversation – everyone deferring to everyone else, listening intently to what was being said and never butting in – I still found that I had to concentrate to stop myself speaking out of turn. Whenever I found myself in a social gathering like this one (which wasn't often; I tried to avoid them like the plague), I felt as if I was playing a role in some genteel drawing-room drama. The fact that this particular conversation involved the Sherwoods, who I'd known in the twenty-first century, only emphasised that feeling, to the extent that I kept half expecting someone to crack, to break out of character.

As we were talking I kept trying to equate *these* Sherwoods, the Victorian Sherwoods (Paula/Maude referred to her husband not as Adam but as 'Linley') with the Sherwoods I'd known in my old life. They had the same faces, even some of the same characteristics, but they were so different in character I couldn't imagine the amount of training that would be needed to turn them into a convincing twenty-first century couple.

How long would such a process take? Six months? A year? It might even be longer, in which case were the Sherwoods on the brink of being snatched away to begin their 'programming'? Could it be that the Wolves, or the Society, were watching the house at this moment?

I wondered again whether the Sherwoods were being targeted purely because of me. If so, then I was currently contributing to my own destiny. Was this how the Wolves operated? Did they undermine you by taking your friends (or potential friends) and turning them into your enemies?

The Sherwoods might have been financially stretched, but they'd certainly put on a good spread for us. I felt guilty watching their servant, Mrs Mackeson, heaping enough food on the table to feed a large family. Although I knew these people would eventually abduct my daughter, at this point I couldn't help thinking of them as victims, and hoped they weren't planning on going hungry for the rest of the week just to push the boat out for us tonight. We were served hare soup and oyster patties as a starter, followed by a main course of goose and bacon pie, pork chops, two different types of potatoes, a savoury rice dish, devilled eggs, various cheeses and a huge steaming tureen of vegetables.

Like most Victorian meals, the food was meaty, starchy and filling. We ate slowly, and washed it down with a red wine that was eye-wateringly acidic. As the drink flowed and the Sherwoods became more relaxed, I gently probed them for information. I asked about their backgrounds, and gathered – though neither of them admitted it outright – that Maude's family were more well-to-do than Linley's, and that there had been some resistance to the marriage from her parents.

The fact that the marriage had gone ahead regardless showed a strength and depth of character to Maude that she kept relatively well hidden. On the surface she seemed a typical young Victorian wife – demure, reserved, naïve – but there was clearly steel behind her long-lashed, pale grey eyes. Although Linley did most of the talking she was the one I found most interesting. In the twenty-first century she'd been the more outgoing of the pair, whereas Linley, although pleasant enough, had always struck me as shy and quiet – even, in retrospect, a bit uncertain.

Perhaps, then, she'd become the driving force, the one who would jump at the opportunity, when it came along, to cast off her Victorian shackles and adopt a newer, freer persona. But how far would she go to acquire her freedom? Was she so corruptible she would be prepared to abduct a child for her new... what? Employers? Guardians? Allies? Captors? Or would she and Linley become victims of a force too powerful to resist? Were they fated to be tricked, or threatened, or brainwashed in some way? When I'd first met them, the Sherwoods had seemed a normal, friendly, happy couple – but had that all been a sham? Had they just been puppets? Had they had any free will of their own or were they – despite appearances – completely under the control of their new masters?

As usual, there were more questions than answers. All I could do was gently prod and poke in the hope of unearthing some clue.

Wondering whether the Wolves might use subtle means to ingratiate themselves with the Sherwoods, rather than launching a full-scale attack, I asked, 'Who do you work for, Linley – if you don't mind me asking?'

Linley flushed, though whether that was because he felt embarrassed by my question or had just had too much wine, I wasn't sure. In a tone that fell somewhere between pride and justification he said, 'I am employed by Masterson and Company. Their offices are based at St Katharine's Dock by Tower Bridge. They import foodstuffs from overseas – in particular, sugar from the Americas. Perhaps you have heard of them?'

He asked this with a wheedling sort of hope. I nodded encouragingly. 'I'm certain that I have.' I paused, wondering how to phrase the next question. 'Tell me, have you made any acquaintances of an... unusual nature in the course of your work?'

He frowned. 'Unusual?'

'What I mean is... have you been approached, or perhaps targeted for friendship, by a... work colleague or business associate? Have you been invited to join any clubs or societies? Has anyone made a request that you consider... out of the ordinary?'

To my own ears I sounded like a concerned parent trying to quiz a child about a dodgy character seen hanging around the schoolyard.

Sure enough, Linley looked puzzled.

'I don't believe so, sir. Why do you ask?'

I took a sip of wine, wondering how best to climb out of the hole I'd dug for myself. Before I could speak, Clover asked, 'Have you ever heard the phrase "headhunting", Mr Sherwood?'

He blinked, more baffled than ever. 'In relation to African savages, do you mean?'

Clover laughed. 'That is the more grisly connotation. But no, my meaning is different. It's a modern business phrase meaning to seek out promising recruits from rival companies for potential employment. A headhunter's job is to identify those recruits and either inform his employer about them or approach them directly.'

'I see,' said Linley, who clearly didn't. He looked from Clover to me, hoping for enlightenment.

Maude, though, had clearly twigged what Clover was getting at.

'I think...' she said, and paused, either because she didn't want to presume or because she was hoping her husband would grab the baton and run with it.

He looked at her, still bemused. 'What, my dear? What do you think?'

She took a deep breath, then shook her head.

'It doesn't matter. I am being presumptuous.'

'Oh, I don't think you are, Mrs Sherwood,' Clover said, and looked pointedly at me. 'Is she, Alex?'

I knew what Clover was getting at, even if Linley didn't, and thanked her silently for it.

What was that old phrase? Keep your friends close and your enemies closer?

'No,' I said, 'she isn't. In fact, she is being very perceptive.' I placed my knife and fork either side of my plate, laced the fingers of my hands together and fixed Linley with an unblinking stare. 'I hope you won't think me impertinent, Linley,' I said, playing the 'Victorian benefactor' for all I was worth, 'but what is your current weekly wage?'

'My...' Linley blanched and swallowed. 'I'm not sure I... that is to say...'

'Just answer Mr Locke's question, my dear,' said Maude quietly.

Linley glanced at her, and then, as if taking strength from her calm resolve, sat up a little straighter in his seat. With almost defiant pride he said, 'I earn three pounds and ten shillings a week, sir. It is not a fortune, I grant you, but—'

'How would you like to earn double that amount?'

He froze, his mouth still open. Then he made a little choking noise. 'I beg your pardon?'

I smiled benignly. 'I admit to a little subterfuge, Linley. You may have wondered why my wife was so insistent on procuring a dinner invitation when she met you in the cemetery yesterday?'

Linley still looked shell-shocked. 'Well, no... I...' but his wife cut across him.

'I must admit, we *were* surprised by Mrs Locke's friendliness, sir. But we simply assumed her to be possessed of a warm and generous disposition.'

'As indeed she is!' added Linley hastily.

'Just so,' I replied, 'although I readily admit to you now that her intentions – *our* intentions, I should say – were a little... underhand. You see, I have recently been receiving very good reports about you, Linley. *Exceptional* reports, in fact.'

Linley looked flabbergasted. 'You have?'

'I have. Indeed, the reports have been *so* good that I am prepared to double your wages in order to procure your services.' I paused to let this sink in, then I leaned towards him.

'So, what do you think? How would you like to come and work for me?'

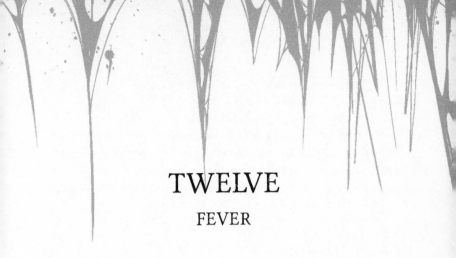

TWELVE

FEVER

'Eviscerated?' I exclaimed.

The man who'd delivered the news twirled his cap in his hands, looking as shame-faced as if he'd done the deed himself. His face was so lumpy and bleached of colour it looked as though a child had moulded it from clay. The reek of his body odour, which rolled over us in waves, made me want to throw open the windows.

It was 11:40 p.m. and Clover and I had been home for less than twenty minutes. The man, his shapeless layers of clothing coated in a crust of icy snow, had arrived ten minutes later with a message from Hulse. When I invited him in to warm himself by the drawing-room fire he looked at me with wary alarm, as if he thought I was leading him into a trap.

For a few moments he'd been able to do nothing but gape at the grandeur around him. It was Hawkins who'd snapped him from his stupor by coldly reminding him why he was here. The man's message was grim: one of the two watchers who'd been assigned to keep tabs on the Thousand Sorrows had been found in the Thames, his body hacked open and his innards removed, and the other was missing. Hulse's messenger had said the word 'eviscerated' with great care, pronouncing it with a hard 'c' instead of a silent one.

'That was what Mr 'ulse said to tell you, sir,' he mumbled now, staring at the cap in his hands. 'Them's were his exact words.'

'I see,' I said. 'Well... thank you for letting me know. Here's something for your trouble.' I blindly handed him a couple of coins.

'Perhaps you'd like a cup of beef tea before you go,' said Clover, 'to warm you on your way?'

The man's muddy eyes lit up. 'I wouldn't say no, madam. Thank you kindly. Only there is one more thing...'

'Then tell us quickly,' growled Hawkins.

'It's more by way of an askin' than a tellin'. Mr 'ulse wanted to know whether he should send two more fellows to keep watch in Floral Court, then two more after 'em, if needs be.'

I shuddered. It was bad enough having the blood of even one man on my hands, never mind a steady stream of them.

'On no account. Please tell Mr Hulse that I'll be taking direct charge of the situation from now on.'

The man nodded. 'Very good, sir.'

As soon as he'd gone Clover said, 'Don't tell me you're still planning on your little excursion to Limehouse after this?'

I looked at her, surprised. 'Why not? I don't see that it changes anything. In fact, it just confirms that we're getting closer.'

'Closer to the grave maybe.'

I scowled. 'We always knew what we were doing was dangerous. What did you think? That once we tracked down the Wolves they'd meekly hand the heart over?'

'No, of course not. It's just...'

'Just what?'

'Well, is it wise facing them in these circumstances? On their own territory? On their own terms?'

Frustration made me snappish. 'We've waited three months for a lead like this, Clover. We can't afford to let it slip through our fingers now. Or I can't, at least.'

Clover looked at me, then at Hawkins. She sighed. 'So what's the plan?'

I shrugged. 'There isn't one. Apart from the fact that I go there and play it by ear.'

'*We* go there, you mean.' She gestured at all three of us. Hawkins nodded.

I shook my head. 'No, just me. I'm not risking your lives as well as my own.'

Clover scowled. 'Bollocks to that! Those fuckers destroyed my club! They killed Mary, and half my customers, and maybe even some of my girls! This is just as personal for me as it is for you, Alex. Those bastards deserve some payback.'

I laughed bitterly. 'And how are we going to give that to them? I'm prepared to go along because... well, because I'm not convinced that they want me dead. And because you've given me faith.'

'I have?' said Clover, surprised.

'Well, not you personally. But the fact that you've seen me when I'm older – and that you wouldn't be here, *couldn't* be here, if I hadn't survived. You've seen me with the heart. You've seen me *controlling* the heart. That must count for something?'

She looked uneasy. 'I don't know if it proves anything. And neither do you. We've talked about this, remember? We've talked about it until we're blue in the face. What if history *can* be changed?'

'Yeah, but what if it can't?'

As Clover had said, we'd had this conversation, or variations on it, many times before, and as such I knew full well that I was on very shaky ground.

Angrily she said, 'So what you're saying now is that you're impervious to harm just because I've seen you in the future? You're saying that if I were to put a bullet through your head at this moment nothing would happen?'

I shrugged. 'Not in so many words. But you've got to admit, evidence of an older me is at least *kind* of reassuring. And it goes without saying that we won't get anywhere by running away from danger whenever it rears its head. He who dares and all that.'

Clover rolled her eyes. 'For fuck's sake! Who do—'

Then, from upstairs, Hope screamed, and our conversation ended instantly.

A look flashed between us. I guessed we were all thinking the same thing: *What if they're here? What if they've got in?*

Clover jumped to her feet. 'It'll just be another bad dream,' she said, as if trying to convince herself. 'I'll go.'

'I'm coming too.'

'Perhaps we should all go,' suggested Hawkins, but Clover shook her head.

'We don't want to terrify the poor mite by crowding her. She'll be confused enough as it is.' She touched Hawkins on the arm. 'We'll call you if we need you.'

Like a heroine in a Gothic melodrama, she swept from the room, across the hallway and up the stairs in her satin gown. I followed, but as we reached the upper landing I put a warning hand on her arm and moved ahead. Hurrying along the corridor, I noticed that Hope's door was ajar and leaking a line of flickering light.

Clover and I entered the room more or less simultaneously, my gaze immediately drawn to the wardrobe opposite the bed against the far wall. I'm not sure what I expected to see: the door hanging open, something monstrous and spindly emerging from it – or perhaps even dragging Hope through the rack of clothes into some dark Narnia beyond?

But the wardrobe doors were firmly shut, so my head snapped in the other direction, fixing on the bed towards which Clover was already moving. Her gown was so voluminous it all but blotted out the lamp on the bedside table, throwing the bed into shadow. My first impression was of something bulky, back humped like a huge caterpillar, at the end of the bed. Above that a dim figure seemed not only to be oddly twisted, but to have two heads and too many limbs.

Then my perception shifted, and I realised I was looking at Mrs Peake, in a long white nightgown, leaning over Hope, her back so arched that her grey head and Hope's blond one seemed almost to be touching. Hope was on her back, shuddering with cold or shock. She had kicked her eiderdown off, so it was hunched at her feet. Mrs Peake was gently stroking Hope's arms and making shushing noises to try and calm her.

'Oh, Mr Locke, Miss Monroe,' she said, turning towards us as we entered, 'thank goodness you're here. I was shocked awake by the poor girl's scream. I had no idea what time it was.'

Mrs Peake was a slim, rangy Irish woman in her late fifties, with flat feet and big hands. I'd always secretly thought she resembled a startled tortoise: she had deep bags under protuberant eyes, a wrinkled little mouth and virtually no chin. Despite her naturally dour expression, though, she possessed a heart of gold and bags of patience, and she doted on Hope.

She shuffled aside to let Clover kneel at the bedside. Placing a hand on Hope's forehead, Clover said, 'She's burning up.'

I moved to the other side of the bed. Hope, flushed and sweaty despite the chilly night air, was wriggling and moaning.

'It's that bloody infection,' I said, ignoring Mrs Peake's frown of disapproval at my potty-mouth. 'If only we had some antibiotics.'

'I have my Beecham's Pills, Mr Locke,' Mrs Peake said. 'Shall I fetch one?'

I shook my head. Knowing how much Mrs Peake swore by her Beecham's Pills I'd asked the doctor who regularly attended Hope what was in them and he'd told me they contained little more than aloes, ginger and soap. What this meant was that they made you sweat and they made you vomit, which to the average Victorian was as good a cure as you could expect from modern medicine. If you were ill and you couldn't puke it up or sweat it out you were buggered.

'I don't think they'll do any good,' I said, anxiety making me more blunt than I'd intended.

Mrs Peake looked offended, as if I'd insulted a cherished family recipe. 'A bread poultice then? To draw the poison out?'

Clover touched Mrs Peake gently on the arm. 'You're a darling, Mrs Peake, but why don't you go back to bed and let Alex and I deal with this? It's not fair depriving you of sleep when you have to be up so early.'

Mrs Peake slid a glance at Hope, still shivering and twitching on the bed. 'But I do so worry about the poor scrap.'

'As do we all. But really, Alex and I will attend to her. We'll sit up all night if we have to.'

'Well, if you're sure...'

'I am. Goodnight, Mrs Peake.'

We didn't sit up with Hope all night, but we sat up with her for the best part of the next hour. Clover wiped her face with a damp cloth to bring her fever down, while I examined her arm as best I could by lamplight.

The flesh around the metal graft was discoloured and leaking a trickle of foul-smelling discharge, but it looked no worse than it had on previous occasions. There was no doubt, though, that Hope's condition was deteriorating. Whether that would continue as a gradual decline or whether the infection would suddenly take hold and irreparably poison her system was impossible to say. Dr Pasco, who had given me the lowdown on Mrs Peake's Beecham's Pills, thought that Hope's only chance of survival was through immediate surgery – a suggestion I'd so far resisted. Without surgery, Pasco believed, Hope would die within months, if not weeks, whereas if he were to amputate the infected limb she would have a twenty per cent chance of surviving the operation and making a full recovery.

I had no doubt that Pasco knew his stuff – he was an experienced police pathologist with an excellent reputation – but Clover and I had decided the odds were unacceptable. We knew we were playing Russian roulette with a little girl's life (and if she died we'd never forgive ourselves), but we also knew that if we could find the heart and get Hope treated in the twenty-first century, her survival chances would leap from twenty per cent to near one hundred per cent.

At last we managed to get her fever down and she started to settle. I lifted her out of bed and into an armchair so that I could change her damp bedding. While I was doing that Clover carefully peeled Hope's sweat-soaked nightie over her head and replaced it with a fresh one. Hope stayed asleep and compliant throughout the process, but as Clover lifted her back into bed she opened her eyes.

'Hey, sweetie,' Clover murmured, kissing her forehead while I pulled the eiderdown back over her.

Hope blinked sleepily, and for a moment I wondered whether she was properly awake. Then she asked, 'Has he gone?'

'Who, honey?'

'The Sandman. I don't like him. He frightens me.'

Clover and I exchanged a glance. The Sandman again. Something crawled in my gut.

'There's no one here,' I said. 'It was just a dream.'

'No.' She raised her good arm and pointed into the far corner of the room, to the left of the wardrobe. 'He was there. Sand came out of his eyes. Then he opened his mouth and sand came out of that too. Then I screamed and Mrs Peake came in and he went away.'

I felt so unsettled I had to fight down an urge to argue with her, to get her to admit she'd been dreaming.

Softly Clover said, 'And he's not coming back, I promise. Now close your eyes and go to sleep.'

'That's what he wants me to do...' But Hope's voice was drowsy; she was already drifting away.

Clover smoothed the ruckled edges of the eiderdown over Hope's chest and gently pushed away a few errant strands of hair.

'Don't make promises you might not be able to keep,' I whispered.

Clover looked at me, surprised. 'What do you mean?'

I crossed to the corner Hope had pointed at and knelt down. I was disturbed enough to want to prove to myself that she *had* been dreaming. But when I touched the carpet my fingers came into contact with something gritty. I clenched my hand into a fist and stood up.

Clover rose slowly from the bed when I turned towards her. A little fearfully she asked, 'What have you got there?'

I crossed to the lamp that Mrs Peake had left on the bedside table. Slowly I opened my hand.

Clover gasped as she saw what I'd picked up, and what was now trickling through my fingers.

Grains of fine black sand.

THIRTEEN
THE THOUSAND SORROWS

It wasn't quite a 'London Particular', but the fog that rolled in from the Thames in billows and swags, bringing the stink of effluvia with it, was clammy and dense. Combined with the snow, it spared us the foulest details of Limehouse's mean streets, transforming the area – packed with sailors' lodging houses, pubs, marine stores, oyster shops and shipyards – into a maze that you might encounter in a dream. The fog blurred every outline, smeared every surface, muffled and distorted every sound. It seemed to turn our surroundings into a realm of ghosts, a place where time had slipped its moorings, and echoes from the past haemorrhaged into the present.

Although the fog compromised our senses, I had to admit I was grateful for it. Not only did it keep the majority of people indoors, but it also meant Hawkins and I could go about our business shrouded in a blanket of invisibility.

That worked both ways, of course. We might have been able to use the fog to cloak ourselves, but then so could our enemies – or any other threat that might come our way.

We stumbled across the gamblers just as we were beginning to lose our bearings; just as the fog was beginning to seem less a boon and more a hindrance.

We heard what was happening a few minutes before we saw it. Drifting from the fog came the high, crazed squealing of animals, the guttural cries and low, nasty laughter of men. Reverberating through the thick, white soup that swirled around us, the sound seemed – quite literally – hellish.

I halted and grabbed the sleeve of Hawkins' overcoat.

'Christ! What's that?'

Unflappable as ever, Hawkins cocked his head one way and then the other, trying to tune in.

'Something to be avoided,' he murmured.

The sounds rose and fell again like a bad radio signal.

'Where's it coming from?'

It was impossible to tell. One moment the cries seemed to swoop down from above, the next they seemed to sneak up from behind. It was as if the billows of fog formed a series of reflective surfaces that bounced noise in all directions.

We had no option but to keep moving cautiously forward, keeping close to the walls, looking out for street signs. Even so, we were still surprised when we rounded a corner and suddenly a dozen men manifested in front of us, hunched forward, facing the wall in a rough semicircle. Their voices – all at once shockingly clear – barked encouragement or brayed laughter at something which the dark wall of their bodies concealed from view, but which squealed like an animal, or several, maddened with rage and pain.

Hawkins, a few paces in front of me, came to an abrupt stop, stretching a warning arm out across the front of my body. I stopped too, the snow crunching and scuffing beneath my feet. But it was too late. We'd been spotted.

The wall of bodies broke apart as the men turned towards us. Through the gap, dimly, I saw what their attention had been focused upon. Within a makeshift arena of wooden fruit boxes, a pair of rats had been set against one another. Squealing and thrashing, they were still locked together, claws and teeth sunk in one another's flesh. On the ground by the men's feet coins were dull, brassy pockmarks in the snow.

'Well, well,' one of the gamblers said. 'And who might you fine gentlemen be?'

'No one who need concern you,' Hawkins replied, his voice considerably more cultured than the man who'd asked the question. 'We wish only to pass along this street. Return to your sport.'

'*This* street?' said the man in mock surprise. He was a bulky silhouette threaded with tendrils of white fog. 'Why, this street is *our* street. And there's a fee to be paid for setting foot upon it.'

'Then we'll find an alternate route,' Hawkins said, but before we could turn away the man sprang forward, arm upraised, the dull gleam of a blade in his hand.

'I'm afraid the damage is already done, gentlemen.' His cronies grunted assent behind him. 'So I suggest you hand over your purses without further ado.'

I drew my howdah from my pocket and pointed it at the man's head. 'And *I* suggest you put that knife back in your pocket, chum, unless you want to be paid in bullets.'

Immediately the crowd of men shrank back, muttering. Their leader froze, then slowly lowered the knife.

'No need for that, shipmate,' he said. 'We was only joshing with yer.'

Behind him the rats, ignored now, continued to tear one another apart. I kept my gun trained on the man's head as he put the knife away, then raised his hands in a placatory gesture.

'As you seem to know these streets so well, perhaps you can help us find our way through them,' I said.

The man dipped his head in a half-bow. 'I'm sure nothing would give me greater pleasure.'

'We're looking for an establishment somewhere near here – the Thousand Sorrows. Have you heard of it?'

The man's head snapped up. His cronies froze, as if playing Statues.

'I can see you have,' I murmured.

'Tell us what you know of the place,' ordered Hawkins. 'Quickly now!'

Despite Hawkins' tone the knifeman chose his words carefully. 'I'm not familiar with the establishment in person, you understand, and I have no interest in the business what's conducted there – but if it's the pleasures of the pipe you're after I'd advise you to seek them under a different roof.'

'Why do you say that?' I asked. 'What have you heard about the Thousand Sorrows?'

'Stories. Rumours. No more than that.'

'What stories?'

I could almost hear the man's grim smile in his reply. 'Stories that would make your flesh creep, shipmate. Stories that would turn your hair white.'

'Don't be obtuse, man,' snapped Hawkins. 'Give us particulars.'

The knifeman paused. Then he said, 'Neither I nor the good fellows you see here would go within a mile of that place at night, and we're not what you would call lily-livered. We shrink from no man, but it's said there's more than men walk the streets around the Thousand Sorrows after dark. People I know – reliable people – have heard things, seen things.'

'Like what?' I asked.

'As for the hearing – clanks and groans and creaks; voices speaking in ways that ain't human. And as for the seeing – nightmares come to life: machines that walk; rats as big as horses; men that turn into shadows; a beast that moves from roof to roof, stalking its prey.'

I looked at Hawkins, who returned my gaze steadily. We were definitely on the right track.

'We'll take our chances,' I said. 'So if you'll just point us in the right direction, we'll leave you to your amusements.'

The knifeman shrugged, as if to say, *It's your funeral*, then gave me the information I asked for. I thanked him curtly, then Hawkins and I went on our way, though I kept my gun trained on the dark, motionless shapes of the gamblers until the fog had swallowed them up. Bit by bit the shrieks of the rats grew fainter. We were about to turn the corner at the end of the street when the knifeman's parting shot drifted out of the fog. Now he was no longer staring down the barrel of my gun his voice was again full of bravado.

'May your God go with you, gentlemen, 'cos it's a stone-cold certainty you'll bleedin' well need him before this night is out.'

His cackling laughter, and that of the other men, pursued us for the next twenty paces before dwindling to silence. When the only sound was again the soft crunch of our footsteps in the snow, I stopped and turned to Hawkins.

'I really think I should go on alone. Like I said earlier, I have a feeling the Wolves want me alive for some reason – if they didn't they'd have killed me by now. But I can't say the same about you.'

Hawkins' raised eyebrow was like a teacher's response to a tiresome pupil.

'Forgive my insubordination, sir, but the only way you'll force me to leave your side would be if you were to shoot me.'

I was touched by his loyalty, but frustrated too.

'That's not fair, Hawkins. I don't want your death on my conscience.'

Hawkins pursed his lips – another teacherly expression.

'I believe I'm currently outside the contracted hours of my employment, am I not, sir?'

I sighed. 'Yes you are.'

'In that case, there is no reason why your conscience should be troubled. I am a responsible adult, and am accompanying you of my own free will. If I choose to place myself in danger, surely it is my own concern?'

'You're incorrigible,' I said. 'You're as bad as Clover.'

The twitch of a smile appeared briefly on Hawkins' beaky-nosed face.

'Thank you, sir. I shall take that as a compliment.'

It had been a hell of a struggle getting Clover to stay behind. The only way I'd been able to dissuade her from coming with us was by convincing her that after what had happened that night there was no way we should leave Hope with only Mrs Peake and the girls to protect her.

Clover hadn't been happy, but she had seen the logic of my argument. As we'd left the house she'd put her hands on my shoulders, thrust her face into mine and said fiercely, 'Don't go getting yourself killed, you prat. If you do I'll never speak to you again.'

The knifeman's directions proved accurate, and twenty minutes after leaving him and his cronies behind us in the fog, Hawkins and I were standing across the street from what I guessed was the Thousand Sorrows. It was exactly as the knifeman had described it: the last house on the left at the end of a narrow dead-end street, opposite a Chinese restaurant with a lantern-festooned display window, whose brick facade had been painted white and emblazoned with red Chinese characters beside a black and gold dragon design.

It was the gaudiness of the restaurant – now closed and dark – which drew the attention. The small doorway in the scabrous brick wall on the opposite side of the street, illuminated by a single yellow lantern, was hardly noticeable by comparison. There was no sign above the door, and no number painted on the brickwork. Hawkins and I scrunched up to it through the snow. Even up close it was impossible to tell what colour the door was in the foggy darkness: grey maybe, or muddy brown.

Standing there made me think of the first time I'd stood in front of the door of Incognito, the pole-dancing club which Clover had owned in Soho before the Wolves of London had burned it down. Remembering what the knifeman had told us, I looked up, half expecting to glimpse a vast dark shape leaping silently from one rooftop to another.

But there was nothing. Nothing to see, nothing to hear. The fog was like soundproofing, the silence so dense that the only sounds I *could* hear were internal: the crackle of my neck muscles when I turned my head, the faint rush of blood in my ears. Reluctant to break the silence, I looked at Hawkins and raised my eyebrows in an unspoken question: *ready?*

He nodded and I tapped on the door.

It opened immediately, as if whoever was on the other side had been expecting my knock. A hollow-cheeked Chinese man in his seventies or eighties peered out of the three-inch gap between door and frame, his thin, drooping moustache giving him a mournful expression. He wore a traditional Chinese-style shirt in blue silk over a pair of black silk trousers and slippers, a black satin beanie hat perched on his head. I wondered if he'd adopted the clichéd appearance purely for the benefit of the punters who came here. His gaze fixed on me, but he said nothing. Was he waiting for a password?

'We're looking for the Dark Man,' I said.

There was no flicker of reaction on the Chinese man's face, but after a moment he stepped back, pulling the door open behind him. Was he letting us in because I'd spoken the magic words, or because he'd assessed us and found us acceptable?

He turned and ambled away along a narrow, dimly lit corridor, whose walls, floor and ceiling were painted black. It was almost as if he'd forgotten about us, or as if, by opening the door, he'd done his job and couldn't care less what happened next. I wondered what he'd do if we didn't follow him, though as the only alternative was to hang around in the hallway, that wasn't really much of an option. At the end of the corridor was a flimsy barrier, made of thin cloth or perhaps even paper, behind which burned a red light. As we followed the Chinese man, who I wasn't surprised to see had a tightly knotted pigtail dangling down his back, the impression was of being inside a vast throat.

The smell of opium, sweet and pungent, grew stronger as we approached what I could now see was a thin curtain of white cloth. When the Chinese man pushed the curtain aside, his shirt turning a shimmering purple as he was bathed in red light, a smoky haze drifted out towards us.

I didn't want to stick around long if we could help it, didn't want to breathe in too much opium smoke and become too lethargic to do what we'd come here to do. Grabbing the flimsy cloth barrier as it swung back into place behind the Chinese man, I ducked into the next room, my hand reaching for the howdah in my pocket as I looked around.

The room was larger than I'd expected, and my initial impression was of people moving and breathing and moaning around me. Apart from the Chinese man, no one was standing up. They were lying on a haphazard arrangement of thin, low, cot-like beds, separated by diaphanous and slightly ragged drapes, which gave the place the look of a makeshift hospital ward – although lit like a bordello.

Almost at once I realised two things: one was that the occupants of the beds offered no immediate threat, and two was that they were moaning not in pain but satisfaction. My gun hand drifted to my side as I saw that each of them was either smoking an opium pipe or had one on a tray of paraphernalia beside them. Most of the men – all of whom, although they were in their shirtsleeves, looked reasonably well-to-do – were out of it, their eyes glazed, their mouths half open, though a couple were propped up by cushions, groggily drinking black tea out of delicate china cups.

The Chinese man halted beside an unoccupied bed and turned to face us. He looked at me and indicated the bed, and although he didn't speak the gesture was obvious: *you take this one.*

I stepped towards him, shaking my head, my hand slipping inside my overcoat once more. I wasn't reaching for my howdah this time, but my wallet. I opened it and took out a ten-pound note. The Chinese man looked at the money, his thin dark eyebrows coming together in a frown.

Aware that Hawkins was standing behind me, watching my back, I said, 'We don't want opium. We want information.'

The Chinese man's face hardened. Did he understand me or was he just reacting to my refusal to take the bed? I held the money out to him. He stared at it, but didn't reach for it.

'We're looking for the Dark Man,' I said. 'The Society of Blood. You understand?'

No reaction, though I sensed hostility coming off him in waves. The opium eaters around us seemed oblivious. Even the tea drinkers just stared into space, locked in their own worlds.

'Sir,' Hawkins murmured, and gave my left elbow a tap to indicate I should turn that way. When I did I saw that two more Chinese men, one in red, the other in black, had appeared from behind a set of filmy, overlapping drapes in a shadowy area on the far side of the room. They carried no weapons – in fact, they had their hands crossed almost demurely in front of them – but from the way they stood, legs apart like policemen, and the intensity with which they regarded us, their intentions were clear.

I held up both hands, the big white ten-pound note still clutched in my right like a flag of surrender.

'We don't want trouble. We just want to know where we can find the Dark Man. I can pay you for the information. Even more than this, if you like.'

I extended the note towards the man in the blue shirt, but he scowled and wafted his hands at me: *go, go.*

As if my gesture had been provocative, the two men on the far side of the room began to move towards us, weaving almost casually between the maze of beds.

I briefly considered drawing my howdah, forcing them to talk to me – but I rejected the idea just as quickly. I had no argument with these men. They weren't my enemies. I wasn't even sure whether they understood what I was here for. Maybe they just thought I was a troublemaker who needed ejecting as swiftly and efficiently as possible.

'All right,' I said, 'all right.' I held out my palms to the two men and wondered whether it was too late to take the empty bed that the Chinese man had offered me, whether sticking around and indulging in the 'pipe of poppy' was the price I ought to pay for getting what I wanted.

No. Desperate as I was to get Kate back, I wasn't prepared to put myself in such a vulnerable position. I was already feeling lightheaded. If I fell under the spell of the opium who knows where I'd end up? Okay, so maybe by coming here I was willingly, even foolishly, walking into the lions' den, but at least I was doing it with my wits about me, and I wanted things to stay that way.

Hawkins was obviously thinking along similar lines.

'I believe our wisest course of action might be to make a dignified exit, sir.'

I nodded and we backed away, me with my hands still raised. The Chinese men came to a halt, their arms folded; they clearly wanted nothing more than for us to leave with as little fuss as possible.

I wondered what our next move should be. We'd learned nothing here. Despite looking promising, it seemed this lead might now peter out like all the others I'd followed in the past three months. I felt the familiar despair creeping over me. I thought about making one last plea, calling out to the room in general, asking whether anyone had heard of the Dark Man or the Society of Blood. I was still thinking about it when I felt my trouser leg snag on something. I looked down, expecting to see a stray jag of wood or metal sticking out of some low item of furniture – but instead I saw a hand had snaked out from the bed I was passing and had clutched the material of my left trouser leg just above the knee.

The hand was attached to an arm, which belonged to a sweaty-haired man with a plump, shiny face. The man was staring at me avidly with bloodshot eyes. Beads of sweat glittered in his rust-coloured moustache.

'Outside. Ten minutes,' he hissed.

Before I could reply, he released my trouser leg and rolled away from me. Was he aware of what he had said or had it been the drugs talking? There was only one way to find out.

Hawkins and I were standing in the doorway of the Chinese restaurant, stamping our feet against the cold, when the door of the Thousand Sorrows opened ten minutes later. The top-hatted figure that emerged, blurred by the fog, was clothed entirely in black: astrakhan coat, sharply creased trousers, boots with spats. Once the door had closed behind him, he paused to light a cigarette with his black-gloved hands and then he looked around. It was only when we moved out of the shadows of the restaurant doorway that he spotted us. He stiffened warily, then relaxed.

'Fifty pounds,' he said. His voice was husky, but with a clipped, upper-class accent.

Sometimes you only need a moment to form an opinion about someone. The instant this man spoke I detected a sneering arrogance about him, an untrustworthiness, which made my skin crawl. It was there not only in his voice, but in his glittering bloodshot eyes, in his plump whiskery cheeks, in the curve of his fleshy lips. It was there in his bearing – the set of his shoulders, the position of his feet, the lazy, almost dismissive way he held his cigarette.

'What do you know?' I asked.

He waggled his fingers. 'The money first.'

I paused, held his gaze. He looked raddled with over-indulgence, his face pockmarked and pouchy. I'd have guessed him to be an unhealthy forty, but he might have been even younger than that.

'How do I know you won't run off with it?' I said – a joke but with a hard edge.

He rolled his eyes. 'Please! Do I look like a common footpad?'

'More to the point, how can we be sure the information you possess is worth such an amount?' Hawkins asked.

His tone was mild, courteous, but I'd known Hawkins long enough to detect the undercurrent of distaste in his voice. I wondered if the man could detect it too. He appraised Hawkins with guarded disdain.

'You're looking for the Society of Blood, are you not?'

'What do you know of them?' I asked.

The man smiled. Instead of improving his appearance it made him look even more repellent.

'I know where they are. I can take you to them.'

'If this is true, Mr...'

'No names,' said the man. 'It's less complicated that way.'

'All right. That suits me very well.'

The man took a drag of his cigarette and blew smoke out the side of his mouth.

'So? Do we have a deal?'

'Perhaps. But first answer me this: how do you know about the Society? Are you one of their number?'

The man barked a contemptuous laugh. 'If I was, do you think I'd be speaking to you?'

'Perhaps,' said Hawkins. 'If the Society wished to bait a hook with a wriggling maggot.'

The man glared at Hawkins, then at me. 'I'm not sure I like your *retainer's* tone.'

I shrugged. 'It was just a turn of phrase. I'm sure he meant nothing by it.'

Hawkins said nothing.

The man scowled. Now he looked like the sulky, pouting schoolboy he must once have been.

'If you don't trust me, then don't accept my offer. I really couldn't care less. It means little to me one way or the other.'

'It means fifty pounds to you,' Hawkins said drily.

'Fifty pounds?' The man snorted. 'Loose change to a man in my position.'

But the way his gaze flickered away belied his words.

My guess was that he was a young man from a good family who had fallen into bad company, or perhaps simply bad habits, and was now struggling to make ends meet. Perhaps he'd been disinherited by a disappointed father. Or maybe he'd already inherited the family fortune, and then had promptly pissed it away on opium, gambling, women and booze. There might already be no way back for him; he might be hopelessly addicted, or crippled by debt, or riddled with syphilis – or all three. I'd seen desperation in that eye flicker; desperation and hopelessness. Our new friend might *claim* that fifty pounds was nothing but loose change, but I doubted that very much. What I reckoned was that, to him, fifty pounds constituted a much-needed lifeline.

Did that make him less or more trustworthy, though? Impossible to say. It certainly made him someone to be wary of – but I'd already decided that about him anyway.

'Let's stop fannying about, shall we?' I said and handed him thirty pounds.

He took it from me, but curled his lip. 'What's this? I said fifty.'

'You get the other twenty when we reach our destination.'

He looked about to argue, but then with a childish 'hmpf' he turned and stomped away. In the fog and the snow, which was beginning to swirl lazily around us again, his back view made me think of old Jack the Ripper movies: the looming, top-hatted silhouette.

For the next ten minutes no one spoke. Our nameless guide trudged ahead of us through the deepening snow and Hawkins and I followed. I tried to keep track of where we were, but the snow, coming down more thickly with each passing second, blew in our faces, obscuring our surroundings and making it impossible to memorise the route.

After a while, beneath the polystyrene creak of our feet in the freshly fallen snow and the whistling moan of the wind, I started to hear another sound, faint at first but gradually getting louder. Feeling uneasy, I strained my ears. Was it breathing? The deep, liquid respiration of something vast and inhuman?

Then I almost laughed out loud. Of *course* not; it was *water*. Waves slapping gently against what I guessed was a harbour wall. Which meant we were close to the Thames.

Over the next couple of minutes the gradual thickening of the fog, rolling in with the chill from the river, confirmed that fact, as did the garbage, oil and briny mud stink of the river itself.

The ground beneath our feet changed, the pavements giving way to cobbles, the bumpiness of which I could feel beneath their covering of snow. I looked around uneasily, but could make out even less of my surroundings now than ever. Even so, I got the impression the buildings around us were vast and, at this time of night, unoccupied. I guessed they must be factories or warehouses. One of them we trudged past seemed to possess a huge set of gates barring its entrance; another stank of fish.

We passed through a stone tunnel beneath a bridge or viaduct, the slimy walls, half obscured by fog, giving us a couple of minutes' shelter from the snow. When we emerged from the other end the slapping of waves and the stink of the Thames ambushed us. But despite being close to the river, we still couldn't see it. Ahead of us was simply a solid wall of fog, across which swirling snow twitched and flickered like static.

Halfway between us and the river our guide came to a halt and started peering about. There was a crust of snow on his shoulders and the brim of his top hat.

'Where are we?' I asked.

He answered without looking at me. 'Blyth's Wharf.'

I was none the wiser. This wasn't an area of London I knew well, not even in my own time.

'For what purpose?'

He turned and strode back towards me, holding out his hand.

'The rest of my money, if you please.'

I scoffed at him. 'For what? You've brought us to the middle of nowhere. You said you'd lead us to the Society of Blood. So where are they? In a secret base beneath the Thames?'

'They're here,' he said. 'This is where they... congregate.' He glanced about nervously.

'Have a caution, sir,' Hawkins said, making no attempt to lower his voice. 'I smell a rat.'

Agitated now, the man pointed to his left.

'Twenty paces that way you will come upon a docking bay, from which a ramp ascends to a manufacturing warehouse. Ascend that ramp and you will find what you are looking for.'

I shook my head, as much in pity as denial.

'You expect us to believe that?'

'It's true!'

'Then lead the way.'

Our guide looked not just nervous now, but scared.

'Why should I? I have no wish to become involved in your dispute.'

'Who said anything about a dispute? For all you know, we and the Society are the best of friends.'

'Clearly he knows we are not,' Hawkins said conversationally, then he turned to fix the man with one of his penetrating stares. 'How much did they pay you to bring us here?'

A few moments ago Hawkins had said he smelt a rat; now the man looked like a trapped one. His eyes darted about as if looking for an escape route. Then he changed tactics, gave a sudden cringing smile.

'I'm sure I don't know what you mean.'

Hawkins sighed. 'Then the opium must have addled your brain. Did you believe we didn't mark you as a wolf in the fold from the outset? And know that you were leading us into a trap?'

For a moment our guide seemed caught out; then he began to bluster.

'If you suspected a trap, why did you follow so willingly?'

'Because sometimes,' I said, 'to get what you want you have to take risks.'

I gave him the biggest, craziest grin I could muster. I'm a tall, thin, moody-looking bloke, and I've been told in the past that when I flash my teeth in a smile it can sometimes be alarming. The man standing in front of us certainly seemed to think it was. He took a couple of stumbling steps back, his expression suggesting it was starting to dawn on him that maybe he was out of his depth.

'You're mad,' he muttered. 'Stark staring mad. I want no further part in this.' He rooted in his pocket, pulled out the three ten pound notes I'd given him and tossed them on the snowy ground. 'Keep your money. I don't want it. I don't n–'

The attack came without warning. It was so brutal, so swift, it was nothing but a blur.

What I saw – what I *thought* I saw – was a huge black tentacle, attached to something above and behind us, come lashing out of the murky sky with the speed and ferocity of a whip. It must have been ten or fifteen metres long, and thick too – thicker than a man; too thick for my hands to have met if I'd wrapped my arms around it. Although I only caught a glimpse of it, I got the impression the tentacle was tipped by a flat diamond-shaped appendage edged with long, curved spines. Before our guide could finish what he was saying, even before he could scream or widen his eyes in alarm, the razored appendage had sliced him clean through.

The top half of his body, his hat still attached to his head, was scooped into the air by the force of the blow and flung to one side, trailing a streamer of blood and innards and the tattered remains of the astrakhan coat.

Even after the fog had swallowed the top half of the body, the lower half, the legs, remained standing for a moment, as if startled to find themselves left behind. Then they folded at the knees and collapsed like a faulty deckchair, a bright red froth of blood and guts spilling from the waist and fanning out across the virgin white snow.

I was so stunned by the abrupt, savage death of a man I'd been speaking to only a moment before, that for maybe ten seconds I couldn't move, think, even breathe. All I could do was gape at the grotesque sight in front of me while my mind replayed what I'd just seen. If I'd had to defend myself at that moment I wouldn't have been able to do it. I was like a bird I'd once seen on a garden wall with a cat stalking towards it, so immobilised by terror it looked like it had been frozen into place.

I don't remember seeing the tentacle retract; don't remember anything else until Hawkins touched my arm and said, 'Sir.'

It was his touch and his voice that snapped me back to myself. I turned my head to blink at him, and that was when I heard *them*.

All at once I realised they were all around us, closing in, clicking and whirring and buzzing, slithering and scuttling and blowing out steam.

I whirled, looking around, but I couldn't see them in the fog and the snow, not clearly anyway. They were smears of approaching darkness, suggestions of nightmarish forms. They were coming from all directions; there was no escape.

Surely, though, this was what I'd wanted? To find the Wolves, confront them? It's ironic, isn't it? I spend all my time and energy trying to track my enemies down, and when I do finally manage it my shock and horror kicks in, and my only instinct is to turn tail and run. Maybe it would have been different if I hadn't seen a man killed in front of me as casually as anyone else might kill a fly. Or maybe it's just human nature to blunder blindly into a potentially lethal situation and not think about the possible consequences until it's too late.

Although I'd previously convinced myself that, for whatever reason, the Wolves, or the Society, or whatever they called themselves, wanted me alive, right now, with the guts of a dead man steaming in the snow at my feet and monsters coming at me out of the fog, that theory seemed as flimsy as tissue paper.

It was for this reason that instead of waiting to confront the Wolves I grabbed Hawkins' sleeve and screamed, 'Run!' It was for this reason too that I ran in the only direction it was possible *to* run – towards the impenetrable blanket of fog on the far side of the quay, from beyond which came the rhythmic slap of water against stone.

With Hawkins beside me, I ran as fast as I could, until suddenly, sickeningly, the ground was no longer beneath my feet. Arms and legs pedalling frantically, I felt myself plunging into fog and blackness. If I hadn't known primal terror before that moment, I knew it then: the sense of being out of control, of feeling I might fall forever – or worse, that my fall might be broken not by water, but by stone or steel, by something that might smash and rip my body apart.

But my fall wasn't broken; it was simply cancelled, mid-plunge. I was plucked from the air like a cricket ball – though at first, when the vine-like tentacles curled around my chest and limbs like a dozen writhing fingers, I thought it was the tightness and coldness of my own fear; thought it was my nerves, my thoughts, my consciousness, shrivelling inwards, retreating into themselves, bracing themselves for impact, for pain.

Then I was rising, going backwards, and I realised with a new horror that something – presumably the same monstrous creature that had killed our guide – had snatched me from the sky, and I was now being pulled back into the nightmare.

However much I writhed and screamed, there was no escape. I had been captured by the Wolves of London, by the Society of Blood, and nothing and no one could save me.

Even as I was being reeled in, I spared a thought for Hawkins, my friend and companion – and faintly (although it might have been my imagination) I heard a distant splash. Then the air was rushing past me with such speed and force I couldn't breathe. And the next thing I knew I was lying on the hard, cold, wet ground, and the tentacles around me were loosening, retracting, snaking away.

So they did want me alive.

But for what?

I was aware of movement around me. Sound. I had a vague, horrifying sense of being in the middle of a web as monstrous creatures scuttled around me. Then my jangling senses started to stabilise. I realised snow was falling into my eyes. I blinked it away and looked up.

A face loomed over me. Long and white, puckered with scar tissue, its hair burned away. Its eyes were glass discs that seemed to reflect nothing but fog. Its lipless mouth was wide and red and wet.

Tallarian.

The doctor who'd given Hope her metal arm; who'd created a menagerie of sickening horrors in his basement. As a man he'd held me captive three months ago, until, with Hawkins' help, I'd managed to overcome him. And as a part man, part machine – perhaps a product of his own hideous experiments – I'd encountered him twice in the future, once in Incognito, and once in Queens Road Cemetery, when Benny Magee had betrayed me and Frank Martin had rescued me from his clutches.

This was a different Tallarian again now, though. This was a Tallarian who was partway between the two. He'd clearly been rescued from the fire that had destroyed his laboratory, although not without cost.

We can rebuild him, I thought crazily. *We have the technology.*

I heard a ratcheting whirr and something moved into my field of vision. It bisected Tallarian's ruin of a face as he held it up to show me.

I realised it was one of his fingers, from the tip of which projected a syringe full of some yellowy-orange liquid.

'You see what I've become, thanks to you?' he said, a hissing buzz underpinning his voice, as though it was a recording on an answerphone.

'Fuck you,' I said – or tried to. I'm not sure the words actually left my mouth.

Before I could say it again I felt a sharp, quick pain in the side of my neck, and that was the last I knew for a while.

FOURTEEN

THE SANDMAN

I'm somewhere in the room watching, though I have no sense of myself. It's as if I'm paralysed. As if I exist as consciousness only.

Clover's sitting beside Hope on the bed, reading a storybook. It's a big one with a bright cloth cover, but I can't make out the title or image. The room's lit by yellow light from the lamp on Hope's bedside table. It's a shadowy scene, but cosy. The light gives the impression of warmth, and the girls look relaxed.

Clover's sitting on top of the eiderdown, her stockinged feet crossed at the ankles, whilst the lower half of Hope's body is under the covers. They're both propped up by plump white pillows, which are stacked against the headboard behind them. I can hear Clover's voice, but I can't hear what she's saying. Her voice is a soft, soothing burr.

I want to speak to them, attract their attention, but I can't. Even though I'm in the room - or feel I am - I'm as distant from them as if I'm watching them on TV. Despite the domesticity of the scene, I have a sense of foreboding. When the wardrobe door on the other side of the room creaks open I feel dread, and also guilt, as if just by being here I've caused what's about to occur.

Hope presses into Clover's side, looking scared, and points at the wardrobe with her good arm. Clover pauses in her reading and follows Hope's pointing finger. I see her smile and tilt her head towards the girl. She speaks to her, and even though I can't tell what she's saying I know from her tone and the expression on her face that she's offering words of reassurance.

Hope's voice when she replies is jagged, slightly shrill, but I still can't make out what she's saying. Clover redoubles her efforts to soothe Hope's fears. She strokes her hair gently, then leans to the side and plants a kiss on the top of Hope's head. There's a quick exchange of conversation, then Clover closes the book and lays it aside. When she stands up and walks over to the wardrobe I follow her progress as if I'm turning my head, or at least swivelling my eyes. I feel tense as she reaches the wardrobe, grabs the handle and pulls the door wide. But the wardrobe is empty, and my tension eases.

Then Hope screams, and as Clover turns, so my vision swivels back to the bed. Sliding out from the shadows beneath it, its movements nightmarishly fluid, as if I'm watching a film in reverse, is a figure in a patchy, dusty harlequin costume. Streams of black sand pour from the empty sockets in its withered grey face and from between the long, rotted teeth in its gaping mouth. As Clover cries out and moves towards the figure, it cups a skeletal hand beneath its chin and then with a flick of its arm hurls the sand it has caught into Clover's face.

She staggers, chokes, throws up a hand as a belated defence. Then her eyes widen in horror as her body starts to stiffen. Within seconds she is paralysed.

Hope is still screaming, but the harlequin figure, the Sandman, throws a handful of sand into her face too. Her screams become splutters and then dwindle to silence, as she too stiffens with paralysis. Unchallenged now, the Sandman moves across to Clover and examines her, tilting his head this way and that, the bells on his three-pointed hat tinkling. From the way Clover's eyes bulge and glare I know she's straining every sinew in an effort to move.

The Sandman raises his hand and I see he's holding a large needle, through the eye of which trails a line of thick black thread. He pushes the point of the needle into Clover's flesh just beneath her bottom lip and, as blood trickles down her chin and tears of agony leak from her eyes, unhurriedly sews her lips together.

When he's done he admires his handiwork, nodding in satisfaction, then turns back to Hope. Although she can't move, her terror of the Sandman, her overwhelming desire to shrink away from him, to run, to scream, is evident on her face. The Sandman slides up the length of the bed until he's standing right beside her, leaving a trail of black sand in his wake. Once again he holds up his right hand, except this time it's not a needle and thread pinched between his twig-like fingers but a scalpel, the blade dull and dirty.

I want to scream, to fly at him, to stop him, but I'm as immobile, as helpless, as the two girls.

I can only watch as the Sandman uses the scalpel to cut deep into the flesh around Hope's eye.

FIFTEEN

BROKEN HEART

My scream of denial ripped me out of there and back into my body. I was aware of my eyelids tearing apart, of the taste of blood, coppery and raw, at the back of my throat. I was breathing too fast, hyperventilating; I squeezed my eyes shut again to stop my vision from spinning, and tried to calm myself, to regulate my breathing. After ten or fifteen seconds my heartbeat, which had been pounding in my ears, began to slow, to quieten. This, though, only made me realise I was surrounded by a mass of stealthy clicks and rustlings. Once again, more cautiously this time, I opened my eyes.

The darkness that enveloped me was bone-chillingly cold and stank of the river. Although I couldn't see anything, I could tell by the acoustics that I was in a large, empty, high-ceilinged room. For a moment my mind was filled with the terrible images from my... premonition? Dream? Vision? Then I remembered Tallarian and his syringe and I reached instinctively for my gun.

Or I tried to. Because it was only when my shoulder muscles twinged as my arm failed to obey what my brain was telling it that I realised I'd been sat in a chair and hog-tied, my arms pulled behind me and my wrists and ankles lashed together with the same rope. I moaned in pain, suddenly aware that my back was aching, and that the muscles in my arms and legs were so taut they were on the verge of cramping. I tried to relax, to fight down the panic that threatened to rise up out of my gut like bile. There was a part of me that wanted to call out, but there was a greater part too scared to draw attention to myself.

I couldn't decide what was worse – seeing or not seeing the room's occupants. The prospect of Tallarian's army emerging from the shadows and revealing themselves in all their grotesque and horrifying detail was terrifying, but so too were the workings of my imagination as it tried, almost against my will, to give form to the insectile whirrings and clickings around me. Even the fact I'd encountered Tallarian's army twice before didn't help; if anything it increased my apprehension. Tallarian's creations were an affront to nature, and the thought of confronting them again was like the prospect of having the still-tender scar of an old wound reopened.

How long I sat there I don't know, but it was long enough for the collective gaze of the unseen things around me to feel like a physical sensation, as if beetles were crawling over my skin. Although I was terrified, I was nevertheless almost grateful when something stirred in the darkness in front of me.

When the darkness suddenly gave voice to a tortured, metallic creak, though, my balls tightened and goosebumps broke out on my arms and back. The first creak was followed by another, and then another, each new sound accompanied by a clank that made me think of Frankenstein's monster taking its first steps, its weighted boots thumping the floor.

The creaks and thumps were accompanied by other sounds too, none I could easily identify, but which gave me the impression of a kind of metallic shifting. I imagined some long-disused machine slowly stirring into life. A machine that for now was still hidden in the darkness, but that was creeping inexorably closer.

My eyes ached as I stared into the black. Was it my imagination or could I now see movement: a shape blacker and more solid than the darkness around it? I was staring so hard my eyes started to water. I blinked to clear them, and through the swimming blur of tears I saw the approaching shape suddenly pull free of the shadows, acquire a more definite form.

It was a huge metal spider – or at least that was my first impression. Its legs, jointed at the knees, resembled curved, upside-down Vs. The creature's main 'body', centred in its mass of clanking, creaking limbs, seemed to ripple and shimmer, as if made of some glossy, net-like material.

The thing came closer, its legs moving slowly. As it did so I realised it was less a mechanical insect and more a sort of self-propelling sedan chair. Its occupant, perched on a kind of dais in the centre, was draped in what looked like a mosquito net – maybe for protection, or maybe simply because he or she wanted to remain anonymous.

The machine came to a halt about five metres in front of my chair, and for a few seconds the shrouded figure regarded me – or at least that's what I imagined it was doing. I stared back, trying to look defiant. Tension brimmed in the air like strange, dark energy. There was a part of me that wanted to jabber to fill the silence, but I kept my mouth shut. As a kid I'd been conditioned not to tell the enemy – which back then had mostly been the police – anything more than I needed to.

The net-like shroud rustled as the occupant of what I already thought of as the 'spider-chair' tilted its head to one side. The movement made me think of a quizzical cat confronted with something new.

Finally the figure spoke, its voice an ancient rasp, like the whisper of withered leaves blowing across a dusty stone floor.

'Do you know me?'

My throat felt almost as parched as the figure's sounded. The croak I dredged from it made me sound like I was trying to imitate it.

'Should I?'

The thing in the chair paused. I wondered whether it was offended or just gathering strength to speak. Certainly every syllable it uttered sounded like an effort to produce.

'You've been... looking for me... for a long time.'

My heart jolted into thumping life again.

'You're the Dark Man?'

The creature sighed; a rattling breath of what sounded like satisfaction. Could this really be him? The man, the creature, which had sent Lyn mad? That had been behind the abduction of Kate?

Perilous situation or not, rage rushed through me.

'If you're him... if you...' I was so furious I could hardly speak. I took a couple of deep breaths and tried again. 'You ruined my life! What fucking right have you got... what possible fucking motive...?'

The emotion flowing through me, combined with my dry throat, overwhelmed me again and I began to cough, great hacking barks that doubled me over, wrenching at the muscles in my bound arms and legs, sending hot threads of agony through me. I clenched my teeth, trying to feed on the fury pulsing like hot coals in my head. When I next looked up I felt feverish, as if my skin was sizzling. The dryness in my throat had gone, and suddenly I was all bile and phlegm.

'Answer me!' I shouted. 'Fucking answer me, you bastard!' I remembered the dream (the vision) I'd had just before waking up. My saliva sprayed the air as I screamed at him. '*What have you done to Clover and Hope? If you've hurt them, I'll fucking kill you!*'

I was in no position to make threats, but I made them all the same – and I meant them too. I *would* kill this cunt. Somehow I'd find a way.

I realised the Dark Man was speaking. I tried to still the pounding in my head so I could listen.

'What you saw... was one possible future... a future you can prevent...'

Despite the rage I felt hope leap inside me.

'Prevent? So Clover and Hope are still safe? Unharmed?'

'For the moment...'

Fuck your moment! I wanted to scream it at him, but instead I gulped down my rage with an effort. The Dark Man's words had suggested not only a way out for Clover and Hope, but me too.

'How?' I asked. 'How can I change the future?'

The net-like shroud rustled. For a moment I wondered whether the Dark Man was about to reveal himself. What would I see if he did? The Devil? But what did the Devil look like? Would he have horns and a pointy beard? Perhaps his face would be so terrible that seeing it would drive me mad? Almost unconsciously I found myself gritting my teeth, narrowing my eyes, like a child watching a scary movie, bracing itself for a shock.

But the Dark Man didn't reveal himself. Instead his arms rose up behind the veil, his hands coming together. As the net-like material slid away from them I saw that the arms, though human, were as thin as twigs, and that the hands were hideously claw-like, the skin stretched tightly over the bones, the fingernails dark as bruises. In fact, the flesh of the Dark Man's arms and hands, yellow and wrinkled, was livid with either bruises or patches of rot. Hideous wart-like tumours clung to them like fungi, black and seeping.

It wasn't the hands, though, but what was cupped in them that drew my attention. It seemed to be a fossilised egg, black and dusty and scored with countless cracks, ash-like flakes sloughing away from its brittle surface.

The 'spider-chair' creaked a couple of steps closer, the Dark Man extending his scrawny, cancerous arms as though presenting the egg to me like an offering. I wondered if he expected me to dip my head and kiss it. My instinct was to do the opposite: rear back, turn my face aside, like a child refusing a spoonful of food. I was about to tell him to get the filthy thing away from me – and then I saw that the object wasn't an egg but a carving. My stomach gave a sickening, weighty lurch.

'Oh fuck. Please tell me that's not...'

But it was. There was no mistaking it. Cupped in the Dark Man's hands were the crumbling remains of the obsidian heart.

I wanted to cry; I wanted to be sick. This couldn't be happening. It *couldn't*!

I tore my gaze from the decaying husk in the Dark Man's hands and stared at where I estimated his eyes would be underneath the shroud.

'That isn't real. It's a trick. Tell me it's a trick. It *can't* be real...'

Even as I pleaded, an inner voice was yammering in my head. Of *course* it wasn't real. If the heart was dead, there was no way that Clover and Hawkins could be here. They were here because of a future me – a me who had had the heart. And what about Frank? How could he have rescued me from Tallarian's army back at Queens Road Cemetery? I hadn't met him yet, hadn't brought him back from the dead. So how could he have appeared in my life if I'd never been in his?

A rasp came from beneath the shroud. 'No trick.'

'Fuck off!' I shouted. 'Of *course* it's a trick! I get the heart back! I *know* I do!'

But I knew no such thing. I had no idea how time worked. Perhaps we jumped parallel tracks all the time without knowing it. Perhaps, while I'd been unconscious, I'd lurched into a world where Clover was still in the twenty-first century, where Hawkins had been executed for murder, where Private Frank Martin was destined to become one of thousands of white gravestones in a French field. Perhaps my memories of them were false. Perhaps the only reason I still retained those memories was because of my proximity to the heart, or of my previous contact with it.

Perhaps I'd never see Kate again. Perhaps she was lost forever.

Bitterness welled up in me. I spat it out in words.

'What the fuck have you done? Why are you showing me this?'

The Dark Man took a long, rattling breath.

'This heart... was taken from you... centuries ago. There was a policeman... Jensen... my soldier took his form...'

'Your soldier? The shape-shifter?'

'The heart brought you both here... it fell into my possession...'

I scowled. 'But that was only three months ago. Not centuries.'

And then it clicked. If my hands hadn't been tied behind my back I might even have slapped my forehead in realisation.

'Oh, shit. You've been using it to time travel, haven't you? You've used it and used it and now you've worn it out. So all the time I was looking for it, it wasn't here, because you were off on your travels.' I recalled the effect the heart had had on me on the few occasions that *I'd* used it. With bitter satisfaction I said, 'And not only have you worn *it* out, but it's worn *you* out. Well, *good*. I hope it's really fucked you up. I hope you're suffering.'

'I'm dying...' the Dark Man hissed.

'Even better.'

Another long, rasping breath. 'But you will help me...'

I laughed. I meant it to sound derisory, but it came out shrill, almost hysterical.

'Help you? How *can* I help you? Why would I even *want* to? You've fucked things up for both of us! Maybe for everyone! God only knows what'll happen now!'

I *was* becoming hysterical. I controlled myself with an effort. The Dark Man waited until I'd slumped into silence, and then he spoke again.

'Somewhere here, in London... is an earlier heart... a younger heart... it is your destiny to find it...'

An earlier heart? Did he mean another heart? A prototype? And then, as before, I realised what he meant.

'You mean the same heart as that one?' I nodded at the crumbling thing in his hands. 'You mean a version of the heart that existed before you stole it? Before McCallum owned it even?'

I remembered how the old man, McCallum, had appeared to me after his death, having used the heart to travel forward in time from a point before I'd murdered him. On that day he'd been in possession of a heart and so had I. But it had been the same heart. Two versions of the same object existing simultaneously.

'Yes,' rasped the Dark Man. 'You will find it...'

I had a horrible suspicion where this was leading.

'And if I do? *When* I do? What then?'

'You will bring it to me... and all will be restored...'

'All?' I said. 'What do you mean, *all?*'

'*All*...' he repeated, emphasising the word. 'Your life will be restored to you... you and your companion will be returned to your own time... you will be reunited with your daughter...'

'And Lyn?' I said. 'What about Lyn? You drove her mad, you corrupted her mind!'

'She will also be returned just as she was...'

'Before you fucked her up, you mean?'

Again the Dark Man gave a single nod beneath the veil.

'I will go back through the timelines... withdraw my influence from your lives...'

'Well, that's fucking big of you. But why did you have to fuck up my life – all our lives – in the first place?'

'It was necessary...'

'*Not for me it wasn't!*'

My voice rang in the vast room. In the shadows around me I heard things creaking and rustling, as though disturbed by my outburst. Again I tried to put a lid on my fury, to clamp it inside myself. What the Dark Man was offering was a golden ticket, a chance to erase the misery and heartbreak of my past. But could it really be that easy? Wouldn't such an action have consequences? And even if it *were* that easy, could I trust the Dark Man? He'd already proved himself to be ruthless, murderous. What was to stop him killing me once I'd fulfilled my part of the deal?

'How do I know you're telling the truth?'

'You don't...'

'So why should I do what you say?'

'Because you have no choice...'

Something stung the back of my neck. I hissed in pain. An insect? Then I thought of Tallarian, the fire-ravaged muscles and sinews in his limbs enhanced by cogs and levers, by mechanics. I imagined his elongated body folded into the shadows behind me, stretching out an arm, his fingertip peeling back like the petals of a flower, releasing a hypodermic needle.

All at once I felt woozy, as if I was leaving my physical body behind, drifting away. *Hey, no, wait* I wanted to say, but I no longer had a mouth or a tongue. And then it didn't matter; nothing mattered; anxiety, pain, fear, regret, anger, it all sloughed away from me like dead skin.

The Dark Man shimmered, smeared, was reclaimed by the dark.

An instant later so was I.

SIXTEEN

PRIMAL SOURCES

I'm walking in the desert. The pure white sun in the heat-bleached sky is so intense it will burn out my eyes if I gaze at it. I'm an insect under the concentrated glare of a magnifying lens. If the rippling, colourless sand beneath my feet were any hotter, it would liquefy to glass.

I stop and peer about me, turning in a slow circle, but there's nothing to see for miles. The desert is flat – no wind, and therefore no dunes. I feel as if I'm the only man in the world, and maybe I am, but the thought doesn't alarm me. On the contrary, I feel calm, unburdened. My mind, for once, is unfettered.

Even the fact that the sun is beating down mercilessly, and that I have no food or water, is not a problem. I can leave here whenever I like. I don't know how I know this, but the knowledge reassures me all the same. Although the landscape is featureless, I seem to be walking *towards* something, though I don't know what it is. Perhaps I'll know it when I find it, but for now I'm simply enjoying the tightening and relaxing of muscles in my legs as I walk, the sense of freedom. My shadow stretches out long and dark in front of me. Does that mean it's morning or afternoon? I don't know, and I don't really care.

Then I'm on my knees and I get the feeling I've found what I'm looking for. I push my hands into the sand, forcing my fingers in all the way up to the third knuckle – and then deeper still, until both of my hands are engulfed to the wrist.

I close my eyes and concentrate. Like a plug in a socket, I'm connected to the earth, drawing out its energy. Primal sources are

175

involved here; you might even call it magic, if magic wasn't simply a power source that we don't understand, and therefore can't explain.

My fingers wiggle beneath the earth, like bait to attract prey. Eventually I have what I need and I grasp it and begin to pull at it, hauling it from the ground.

It's wet, and at first it writhes, but as the sun hits it, it transforms, adapting to its surroundings, becoming clay and stone and root matter. But that's fine, because its energy is in my hands now, and I can forge it, shape it to my will. My fingers move deftly as the heart takes shape beneath them, each valve, each vein rendered in the minutest detail. Once I've finished, the heart responds, feeding off my energy and its own, which are now one and the same, adopting yet another disguise, forming a shell around itself.

A shell of blackest obsidian.

There's a gap then, a sense not of time passing, but of nothingness, of oblivion. When I next become aware I'm drifting upwards, or at least I get the impression that I am. There's a world beyond the surface and I'm rising towards it, I'm being reborn. I feel... regret.

Someone speaks my name, and I open my eyes.

I see blurs of light and dark, which my brain tells me is a face. But isn't that always the way? Aren't our brains conditioned to – what's the word? – anthropomorphise the random patterns in trees and clouds and rocks? I remember the curtains in the room in my gran's house that I sometimes slept in as a kid, whose pattern was a busy psychedelic riot of leaves and flowers, stalks and vines. My mind conjured so many faces from those brightly coloured swirls and shapes that after a while the curtains began to scare me so much I couldn't look at them. Lying in bed I'd sense all the secret faces peering out, all the eyes staring at me. Sometimes I'd cover my ears to block out the sound of breathing from the faces in the curtains.

The dark blur of the mouth in the face hovering above me widens, grows blacker, as it speaks my name again. I blink and suddenly the face comes into focus, and I'm surprised to discover it's one I recognise.

'Clover,' I say.

She smiles. 'Back with us, are you?'

SEVENTEEN

BESIDE MYSELF

As soon as I heard Clover speak it was as if a line had been drawn, as if all at once I'd been rooted back into a world of rigid rules, hard edges. I stared up at her, trying to put the past few hours together. Where had I been? What had I done? My mind was a fug, my thoughts disconnected.

'Where am I?' My voice sounded mushy in my ears; the inside of my mouth, my tongue, felt weirdly soft, misshapen. I had the alarming sensation that I was dissolving, melting. I gripped the edges of the bed to anchor myself.

Clover frowned. 'What's the matter, Alex?'

'Coming apart,' I said, or tried to. 'Got to hold myself together.'

She put a hand on my forehead. I flinched, thinking her fingers would sink into doughy flesh, leaving circular depressions.

'You're fine, Alex,' she said. 'They gave you a drug, which is fucking with your perceptions. The Wolves must have brought you home, although nobody saw a thing. All that security and... nothing. Talk about taking the piss. First thing we knew there was a knock on the door, and when we answered it we found you unconscious on the doorstep. You've been asleep now for... five hours? Six maybe? What do you remember?'

I thought about the Dark Man, the crumbling heart, the proposition he had presented to me.

Maybe the connections took longer than they seemed to, or maybe I looked bewildered, because Clover's face receded from me as she straightened up.

'Never mind, you can tell me later. For now, I think, you need to rest.'

Her words were like a hypnotist's suggestion. I closed my eyes and within seconds I was gone again.

The next thing I remember is feeling uncomfortably hot, pushing my bedclothes away with arms that felt too weak for the task. I heard someone say, 'He's burning up,' in a booming, hollow voice. Then some more time must have passed, because when I next bobbed to the surface I was aware of something soft and cool and damp on my cheeks and forehead. I put my hand up to see what it was, and another hand intercepted my own, squeezing gently.

'He's coming round,' someone said.

Clover? No, it was a male voice this time.

Suddenly I realised who the voice belonged to, and felt a lurch of excitement, which gave me the impetus to open my eyes.

And there he was, as austere and immaculate as ever.

'Hawkins!' I croaked.

Hawkins' lips twitched in a smile. 'Correct, sir. I'm relieved to find that you appear to be in full possession of your faculties.'

I struggled to sit up. Clover, on the other side of the bed, who had been dabbing my face with a cold cloth, leaned forward to help. She supported my back with one hand while plumping up the cushions behind me with the other.

'I was worried,' I said. 'I didn't know what had happened to you.'

The words, coming in a rush, were scratchy in my throat and ended in a coughing fit. Clover passed me a glass of water, before hurrying out on to the landing to find one of the maids and ask her to bring me something more substantial. When my coughing had subsided Hawkins told me his story.

'The instant I leaped from the Wharf, the Society's interest in me, such as it was, ended. It was you they wanted, sir, and you only. When I landed in the river – a somewhat bracing experience, I must admit – I had no inkling of your whereabouts. I called out your name, but, receiving no reply and knowing that remaining in the water and searching for you would be a futile exercise, I struck out immediately for shore. I reached the harbour wall, but it was too sheer and slippery to ascend. I therefore made my way along it until I came to a set of stone steps, whereupon I climbed out and hurried back to Blyth's Wharf.

'By the time I arrived, the place was deserted. Even the remains of our unfortunate guide had gone. Still unsure whether you had been captured or lost in the river, I searched the surrounding premises as best I could, by which time my wet clothes and the inclement weather were beginning to take their toll. Much as it pained me to abandon my search, I made my way back to where I hoped I might find a cab, but collapsed in the street, overcome with the cold. I was fortunate that within a very short time I was discovered by a Chinese lady, who was on her way home after completing her nightly toil waiting tables in a nearby restaurant. She ran to fetch her husband, and together the two of them carried me back to their living quarters, where they kindly revived me with a warm brazier and a bowl of excellent fish soup.

'As soon as I was well enough and dry enough to take my leave I thanked them for their hospitality and made my way back here, hoping that you might somehow have preceded me. It was not to be, of course – but then, not half an hour after my return, a knock came on the door, whereupon you were discovered lying on the doorstep, deeply unconscious but otherwise none the worse for your ordeal.'

Clover, who had come back halfway through Hawkins' story, leaned forward when he had finished and murmured in my ear, 'As usual Mr Hawkins is doing his stiff upper lip routine. Fact is, he thought you were dead. He was very upset.'

Hawkins frowned. 'Well, naturally I was concerned—'

'*Very* upset,' Clover repeated. Looking at me meaningfully, she pulled a sad face and trailed a finger from the corner of her eye down her cheek.

Hawkins harrumphed and flared his nostrils. It was such a haughty gesture that Clover giggled.

'I hardly think this is the time for flippancy, Miss Monroe,' he said, which only made her giggle all the more. Dismissing her with a toss of the head, he turned back to me. 'As I said, sir, I *was* concerned. I still am. What happened to you after we lost touch with one another? I assume you fell into the Society's clutches?'

'I did,' I said, and told them my story. Clover's laughter dwindled into a smile, which, by the time I'd finished, had hardened into a frown.

'Well, he can fuck right off for a start,' she said, referring to the Dark Man's proposition. 'There's no way he'd ever honour that agreement.'

I shrugged. Clover's frown deepened into a scowl.

'Come on, Alex, don't tell me you're actually giving this load of bollocks some serious consideration?'

I was saved from having to answer by the arrival of Hattie carrying a tray loaded with tea things, a couple of boiled eggs in eggcups, and a plate stacked high with hot buttered toast.

'Hattie, you're a life saver,' I said.

She blushed and muttered her thanks.

Clover took the tray and placed it across my lap, before transferring the teapot, milk jug and cup and saucer to the washstand beside the door, where she could pour the tea on a more stable surface. I bit into a slice of toast, then lopped the top off an egg with a knife.

'Well?' said Clover, putting one cup down with a rattle of china on my bedside cabinet and handing another to Hawkins.

I shot her a sidelong look. 'Delicious.'

'You know what I'm talking about!'

I sighed and rested my head back against the pillows, still chewing.

'I haven't really had time to think about it. But I'm not sure I've got much of a choice.'

She scowled. 'You've always got a choice.'

'Do I, though?'

'Of course you do! I mean, all right, without the heart you've got nothing to fight the Wolves with – your gun and all this security are just so much window dressing – but, and this is a big "but", Alex, we now know that the Wolves think you're the only person who can find the heart for them, which means they definitely want you alive.'

I pulled an expression of general agreement, but she hadn't yet finished.

'The way I see it, that means it's a pretty dodgy game they're playing. Because the heart makes you strong. And as soon as you *do* find it, you've got a weapon to fight them with. At the very least you've got a way of getting out of here.'

I raised my right hand, which now held a knife smeared with butter and egg yolk.

'Correction: I would have if I knew how to use it properly. Plus you're forgetting, they've still got Kate. I'm not going to put her at risk by defying them.'

'I'm not forgetting,' she said. 'It's just... well, the heart is your only asset. Your only weapon. Your only bargaining chip. What's to stop the Dark Man from killing you when you hand it over?'

'Nothing,' I said. 'But if I don't hand it over he'll kill Kate – or at least hurt her.'

'But will he? Isn't she *his* only bargaining chip?'

'Are you suggesting I take a risk with my daughter's life?'

She threw up her hands. 'No! I don't know! Oh, for fuck's sake, there must be *some* way we can turn this situation to our advantage!'

Silence fell in the room. I took a sip of tea and stared into the fire.

'What do *you* think, Hawkins?' I asked.

'I think we should do as we *have* done, sir. We should continue to concentrate our efforts on finding the heart. Once it is back in your hands, perhaps a solution will present itself.'

'It'll be too late then,' Clover said.

'Maybe so,' I said, 'but I don't know what else we *can* do.'

Once I'd eaten, Clover and Hawkins left me alone to get some rest. I lay back, still groggy after last night's ordeal. I wondered what I'd been injected with: laudanum? Opium? Of course, it needn't have been a contemporary sedative. Tallarian had turned up in my own time too. Then again the Tallarian I'd seen last night, though his body had been modified, had been fire-scarred, which presumably meant he was still healing from the burns he'd suffered three months ago.

Exhausted, I closed my eyes, and immediately my thoughts began to spin away like water down a plughole. I didn't realise I'd swirled with them, back into sleep, until I felt myself jolting awake again.

For a moment I couldn't work out why the room was dark, why the fire had guttered down to glowing embers. I felt so disorientated I wasn't sure whether I'd been shaken awake or shocked from a dream. Then someone on the other side of me spoke my name.

I twisted round, but before I could turn all the way, a hand grabbed my shoulder.

'Brace yourself,' said a voice that sent an immediate thrill of fear through me. 'This is going to be a shock.'

The hand on my shoulder relaxed and I spun all the way round, my heart pumping.

The man sitting beside my bed, illuminated by the fire's glow, was myself.

He looked – *I* looked – done in: haggard, haunted, hair tousled, eyes dark-rimmed in a pale, waxen face. It was one thing seeing yourself in a mirror, but being confronted with a physical, three-dimensional representation – no, not just a representation, but an *exact* double, and one that you instinctively knew wasn't *just* a double, but was actually *you* – was... well, there are no words that can do justice to the experience.

The phrase that immediately occurs to me is 'mind-bending'. And yes, although the experience *was* mind-bending, it was also much, much more. Would it sound strange to say that I was scared? Because I was. Deeply and profoundly. In fact, I wasn't *just* scared, I was bloody terrified.

It wasn't that I thought I'd hurt myself, or that the other me was some kind of evil twin, or anything like that. The whole experience just felt deeply, intrinsically *wrong*. It felt as if what was happening was against the laws of nature and time and... well, everything. It felt, at that moment, as if two mes being in the same room together – the same person occupying twice as much space as they should, possessing two brains, two hearts – was enough to make everything fall apart, to make reality shatter. I know that sounds stupid, and I know it's difficult to grasp, but I could almost sense chaos trying to push its way in through the rift we'd created – *I'd* created. I could almost hear the approaching howl of the void.

For this reason – because I was so taken aback, so affronted – my first response was angry, almost petulant:

'What are *you* doing here?'

The other me leaned forward. His face was etched with anguish, with horror. His eyes widened, and I waited for him to say something.

But then he turned his head to one side, leaned over and puked.

It was as he was puking, filling the room with the hot stink of vomit, that I noticed what the simple shock of seeing myself had stopped me from registering immediately. Firstly the other me was wearing trousers and a jacket which he had pulled on over the very nightshirt I was currently wearing. And secondly, and far more importantly, I noticed that clutched in the other me's right hand was the obsidian heart!

I gaped at it, dumbstruck. Slowly I raised a hand and pointed at the heart like a very small child pointing at a toy it wanted. As the other me straightened up, looking wretched (*using the heart made me sick again*, I thought, and felt a wriggle of concern at the potential damage being done on my future body), I rediscovered my voice.

'Where did you find it?'

The other me scowled and flapped a dismissive hand.

'It doesn't matter. The only thing that matters is what I'm here to say. Are you listening?'

I nodded, wondering whether the other me was remembering my responses and thoughts from his own past. 'Go on.'

'I'm you about... five minutes from now. You're just about to get the heart back. And when you do – *as soon as you do* – the Dark Man will arrive and he'll ask you for it.'

The other me suddenly clutched my arm and I realised he was trembling.

'As soon as he does you have to give it to him. Don't think about it, don't hesitate. Just give it to him, okay?'

As I frowned, I saw an expression cross his face. Perhaps it was a realisation of how weird and intense he was being, or maybe a memory of how he'd felt at this precise moment, just a few minutes earlier. He let go of my arm, muttering an apology.

'Why *should* I give it to him?' I asked.

I could see he was traumatised, trying to hold himself together long enough to explain.

'Because if you don't he'll kill Kate.'

I jerked, as if he'd suddenly grabbed my balls. Now it was my turn to shoot out a hand and grip *his* arm.

'What do you mean? Where *is* Kate?'

'She's with the Dark Man. He'll have her with him. And if you hesitate, even for a second, he'll kill her. I know! I've seen it! He did it right in front of me...' His voice suddenly broke into sobs; with an almighty effort he pulled himself together. He leaned forward, wild-eyed and distraught. I could smell the vomit on his breath.

'Promise me! Promise me you'll do what I say!'

I had no idea how to respond. My thoughts were pinballing inside my head. As well as the sheer shock of meeting myself, I felt horrified at the prospect of seeing Kate killed in front of me. Yet at the same time I also felt a wriggle of suspicion.

I'd seen the shape-shifter turn itself into perfect replicas of Clover and McCallum and DI Jensen, so how did I know this really *was* me five minutes from now? Instinctively I *felt* as though it was – but could I trust my instincts? This *was* an extraordinary situation, after all.

Was it another of the Dark Man's tricks? Was he just trying to panic me into doing what he wanted? But how could I make a decision one way or the other? I couldn't gamble on Kate's life.

Stalling simply because I didn't know what else to do, I said, 'But won't that change the future?'

The other Alex stared at me, astounded and furious. *Why is he angry?* I thought. *Why didn't he know I'd ask this question when he must have asked it himself five minutes ago? Then again, if he was also visited by his future self, why didn't he obey his own instructions and hand the heart over before Kate could be killed?*

Before I had chance to even *begin* to think this through, the other me barked, 'Fuck the future! Who wants a future where Kate's dead? Anything would be better than that!' The anger slipped, became desperation again. 'Say you'll do it, Alex! Promise me! For both our sakes!'

Still I hesitated.

'*Please!*' he wailed. 'Believe me, you don't want to see what I've seen. You don't want to feel what I'm feeling right now!'

From below there came a frantic pounding on the front door. I leaped in shock, my nerves already stretched to breaking point, my head snapping round, as if I expected the bedroom door to burst open.

'What's–' I said breathlessly, turning back to the other me – but the words died in my throat.

The chair beside my bed was empty. The other me had gone.

EIGHTEEN

A SHADOW ACROSS THE MOON

My initial thought on hearing the pounding downstairs had been that the Wolves were at the door. But then I realised how unlikely that was: firstly because I didn't think the Wolves would knock; and secondly because how could I give the obsidian heart to the Dark Man if I didn't yet have it?

Clearly, though, if the future me had given an accurate account of what was about to happen, things were coming to a head. In which case, I didn't want to have to face the Wolves barefoot, unarmed and wearing only a nightshirt. It wasn't a question of vanity, but practicality – what if we had to leave the house at a moment's notice? For this reason, instead of racing immediately downstairs, I decided to prepare myself.

Yanking open the top drawer of my bedside cabinet, I reached in to grab my gun – and then remembered that the last time I'd seen it had been when I'd pulled it on the knifeman in Limehouse. For a moment I thought it wasn't going to be there, and felt relief wash through me when my hand closed around its familiar shape. It must have still been in my jacket when I'd been dumped unconscious on the doorstep, and Hawkins, knowing my habits, must have transferred it to the drawer – though probably not before drying and cleaning it first. I checked the weapon was loaded, then threw back the blankets and leaped out of bed, taking care not to step in the puke that the future me had left on the carpet and that was now stinking out the room. I ran across to the wardrobe, grabbed a jacket and trousers and pulled them on over my nightshirt (I assumed they were the same ones the future me had been wearing), then I pulled my boots on over my bare feet and swiftly laced them up.

By the time I reached the top of the staircase, which overlooked the hall, Clover had already answered the door. The girl who'd entered looked agitated, scared. She had skin like polished mahogany, a thin face, big dark eyes and masses of curly black hair. I suspected the rest of her was thin too, though it was hard to tell; like many of the poor she kept as warm as she could by wearing as many threadbare layers of clothing as possible. I knew this girl. She was a prostitute, who lived and worked around Covent Garden. She was also one of my watchers. She had an exotic name, something like Mayla, and on the few occasions she'd seen me she'd been cheerful, even cheeky.

She wasn't cheerful or cheeky now, though. Her fear was making her aggressive. I heard her voice - strident and weirdly accented, somewhere between Cockney and African - insisting she'd speak to no one but me.

Clover, facing the girl, was holding up her hands as if to placate a dangerous animal.

'I've told you, Mr Locke is sleeping. Can't you just—'

'No, I'm not,' I called, whereupon Mayla, Clover and Hawkins, who was hovering silently at Clover's shoulder, all swivelled their heads in my direction.

It was only as I descended the stairs that I realised Mrs Peake and the girls were there too, lurking in the shadows further back along the corridor to the left of the staircase. All of them were staring in wonder and trepidation (and in Mrs Peake's case, disapproval) at the new arrival. Hattie in particular was gaping at Mayla as if she was some rare and exotic creature.

As soon as she saw me, Mayla rushed forward, and was only prevented from ascending the stairs by Hawkins, who stepped in front of her and raised a hand. Tilting her head to peer around him she said, 'I got something for you, Mr Locke. And mighty glad I'll be to get rid of it too.'

I saw Hawkins tense, even take a half step forward, as she lifted the outer layer of her voluminous skirts and began to root among the folds.

'It's all right, Hawkins,' I said, knowing what she was going to produce and thinking how ironic it was that, having looked for the heart for so long, all I could feel at this moment was anxiety, trepidation.

As expected, Mayla's hand emerged clutching the obsidian heart. Clover gasped and I saw Hawkins' shoulders stiffen in surprise. As if she couldn't bear to possess it any longer than she had to, Mayla gave a flick of her wrist and suddenly the heart was arcing through the air towards me.

I knew I would catch it, and I did. In fact, I'm pretty sure I could have done it with my eyes closed. The heart smacked snugly into my palm as if connected to me by a length of elastic. The instant I closed my fingers around it I felt something I hadn't felt for the past three months, but which all the same was as familiar and comfortable and natural to me as breathing. It was a sense of completeness, affinity. It was the unshakable notion that I was part of the heart, and it was part of me.

My drug, I thought, and wondered if the feeling was unique to me or whether *anyone* with a prolonged connection to the heart would feel the same. Did it exude an influence, maybe even a chemical, which linked you to it? Was this, for the heart, a symbiosis of convenience? Maybe the thing was just a kind of vampire that intoxicated its chosen victim and created dependence within them?

All I knew for sure was that as soon as the heart was back in my possession I felt strong again, full of energy. Descending the last few steps into the hallway I held up the object as though it was a holy relic.

'Where did you get this?'

Hawkins moved aside so that Mayla and I were face to face. Eyeing the heart warily, she said, 'Mr Hulse gave it to me.'

'Hulse?' said Clover. 'And where did *he* get it from?'

All at once it came to me. 'The crowman's shop,' I said. 'Tempting Treats. My guess is that it's just come into his possession. Am I right?'

Mayla nodded.

Clover looked at me curiously. 'How did you know that?'

'Stands to reason. What would have been the point of Lyn drawing the place to my attention otherwise?'

The face that Clover pulled showed she didn't know how to even *begin* to answer that question. I could hardly blame her. None of us knew who or what the version of Lyn that sometimes appeared to me was. She couldn't be a ghost, because the real Lyn was still alive. All I could say for sure was that she was some kind of guide, one who occasionally popped up to point me where I needed to go.

I wondered how the heart had found its way to Hayles' shop, and from where and who it had come. Had it simply turned up in a load of house-clearance junk, or could it be that a future version of me had left it there knowing that that was where I'd find it?

Could that even work? It seemed like an impossible loop. A chain of events in which the heart was basically conjured into being from nothing, or at least from not much more than the mind-boggling machinations of time. And even if such a thing *could* work, where did that leave my future self? Wouldn't leaving the heart in Tempting Treats for me to find mean that the future me would be stranded in this time period?

'Why didn't Mr Hulse deliver the heart to Mr Locke in person?' asked Hawkins, breaking in on my thoughts.

Mayla was still looking at me, as if I was the only one who was speaking. 'He said there were dogs on his tail, but that he'd try to draw them off.'

'Dogs?' said Clover, alarmed.

Hawkins' voice was stern. 'Were you followed here, girl?'

For the first time Mayla looked away from me, her dark eyes fixing on Hawkins. 'Maybe. I don't know. There was a shadow...'

'What shadow?' said Hawkins irritably. 'What do you mean?'

Mayla gave an almost sulky shrug. 'A half-dozen times on my way here I thought there was someone behind me. But when I turned to look all I saw was the moon above the rooftops. Twice, though... I don't expect you'll believe me, but twice I saw a shadow pass across the face of it.'

Clover and I glanced at each other, but Hawkins, still scowling, said, 'A cloud, you mean?'

The look that Mayla flashed him was impudent and contemptuous. 'Weren't no cloud. I know what a bleedin' cloud looks like, don't I?'

One of the girls – Florence, I think – gave a gasp at Mayla's language.

Keeping my voice low so that neither Mrs Peake nor the girls could hear, I said, 'The Wolves are coming. We need to get the innocent out of harm's way.'

The innocent. Although I'd never used it before, the phrase slipped easily off my tongue. It spoke volumes about what I thought of myself. I wasn't 'innocent'. On the contrary, I was riven with guilt. Some might have said I was a victim of circumstance, but I couldn't forgive myself quite so easily. Not only was I guilty of killing McCallum, for all that he'd engineered his own demise, but I also had the blood of others on my hands: Horace Lacey; all those who'd been in Incognito on the night of Tallarian's attack; the two men who Hulse had assigned to keep watch on the Thousand Sorrows – all of them people whose lives wouldn't have been cut so brutally short if they hadn't intersected with mine.

I didn't want Mrs Peake, the girls and Mayla to likewise become collateral damage. And neither did I want anything to happen to Clover and Hawkins, for all that they saw this as their battle too.

Mayla's eyes narrowed at my words.

'The Wolves?' she repeated. 'Who the bleedin' hell are they?'

'Bad people,' I said shortly, and turned to the group huddled in the corridor. 'Mrs Peake, will you take Mayla and the girls to the kitchen and give Mayla a hot meal? Lock yourselves in and don't come out until I tell you it's safe.'

Mrs Peake opened her mouth to protest, but I held up a hand.

'Please don't argue, there isn't time. Just believe me when I tell you that this is for your own good.'

Mrs Peake pursed her lips, then nodded. Stepping forward she beckoned Mayla with a crooked finger.

'Come along, girl.'

Mayla, though, stood firm. Tossing her head contemptuously, making her black curls tumble and ripple about her shoulders, she said, 'Don't "come along" me, missis. I ain't one of your serving girls.' She jabbed a finger in the direction of the heart. 'That thing attracts trouble, I know it. And I ain't sticking around to face it when it comes.'

'It's a bit late for that,' I said. 'Step out of this house and you'll be dead for sure.'

Mayla looked defiant, but I saw fear in her eyes.

'And if I stay here I'll live. Is that it?'

I hesitated, then lowered my voice so that only she could hear.

'I can't promise anything. But if you stay out of sight and keep quiet, you've got more of a chance. Please, Mayla.'

She looked me in the eyes for a long moment, and then nodded. It was a relief to watch Mrs Peake and her entourage disappear along the corridor. I could only hope that by staying out of sight they'd be beneath the Wolves' consideration and would therefore remain safe.

I also hoped, although with less confidence, that I'd likewise be able to persuade Clover and Hawkins to make themselves scarce before the Wolves arrived. Predictably, though, as soon as I suggested to Clover that she take Hope up to the attic and hide there, she shook her head.

'No way. I'm not leaving you and Hawkins to face them alone. Look what a mess you got into when you went off to Limehouse without me. This time we'll do it together. We're a team.'

'You really think they'll give a shit about that?' I said. 'Besides, I'm not suggesting that Hawkins and I face them without you. I want you *both* to be out of the way when they arrive. They've come for the heart and I'm going to give it to them – I'm not going to fight them.'

Their protests were immediate and loud – or at least Clover's were. Hawkins made his point with a shake of the head and a curt refusal to leave my side.

I told them, as briefly as I could, what had happened upstairs, and tried to convince them yet again that I was the only one the Wolves might not kill. Clover, though, argued that the second the Wolves had the heart they'd have no further use for me.

'All the more reason to keep casualties to a minimum,' I said in frustration, but Clover shook her head.

'Why do you think I was brought to this time period?' She jabbed a finger at me. 'It was to help you, you idiot, not to hide as soon as the going got tough.'

Before I could reply, Hawkins added, 'Miss Clover is right, sir. I can't believe that your future self rescued me from the gallows for no reason.'

'But maybe that reason was just to look after me when I got here,' I said. 'To rescue me from the fire, install me here, nurse me back to health. Or maybe he did it – *I* did it – just because I had you in my memory and didn't want to risk changing the past.'

Clover scowled almost aggressively. 'It doesn't matter what you say, Alex. You can't get rid of us. Whatever happens, we're staying right by your side.'

Under other circumstances I might have laughed, but at that moment I just felt pissed off. 'You're being childish. Not to mention selfish.'

Her eyes widened. 'Selfish? How do you work *that* out?'

'What if the Wolves turn up and Hope hears them and comes down and walks right into the middle of... whatever it is?'

She was silent for a moment, clearly deciding how to respond. Finally she conceded, 'Okay, fair point. But what if I—'

But all at once the time for discussion was over. Before she could finish her sentence there was an almighty thud and a sharp, splintering crack from the direction of the drawing room.

A split-second glance ricocheted between us, then we were running towards the source of the sound, me in the lead, Clover and Hawkins just behind me. As I entered the drawing room, I subconsciously raised the heart as though it was a shield or a weapon, my eyes darting this way and that as I tried to cover every corner, every angle.

All seemed normal and undisturbed: the Christmas tree untouched in the corner, the ornaments intact on the shelves and tables, the pictures still hanging on the walls. My brain was already replaying the sound I'd heard – it had reminded me of something, and as I glanced towards the thick red curtains I realised what.

One Saturday morning, a year or so ago, a bird had flown into the glass doors of the balcony of my Chiswick flat. It hadn't broken the glass, but it had made a hell of a bang – loud enough to make me jump and Kate to burst into spontaneous tears. The bird hadn't injured itself (when I investigated, expecting to find it dead or stunned, there was no sign of it), but it had left a ghostly smear of itself on the glass. The noise I'd heard half a minute ago had sounded like that – except whatever had hit the window this time had been much heavier than a bird.

I crossed the room quickly, aware of how vulnerable Victorian houses were compared to their twenty-first century counterparts. There was no double glazing here, no elaborate locking systems, no burglar alarms. I knew such things wouldn't have proved a barrier to the Wolves of London in any case, but that was hardly a comfort.

Choosing a window at random – it was one of the central ones – I grabbed one of the heavy damask drapes that kept out the cold, and yanked it aside. The snow that blanketed the land glowed a deep minty blue in the moonlight. There was no fog this evening; in fact, I couldn't remember when I had last seen the sky so clear.

I'd chosen the right window. The glass was bisected top to bottom by a crack that looked as if it had been drawn on by a black marker pen. In the centre of the crack was a silvery star ringed with concentric circles, where the glass, absorbing the impact of whatever had hit it, had splintered along myriad tiny fissures, but held.

I leaned over the windowsill, looking out. Clover, beside me, did the same. Lying on the snowy ground under the window was a dark spherical object, like an out-of-shape football. I realised what it was just as Clover gasped.

It was a human head, the mouth open in a slack yawn, the eyes like grey, glazed marbles. The face, thin and bony, was that of an old man or woman – death had rendered it sexless, and the sparse hair, clumped with snow, which straggled across the features, made it even more difficult to identify. Although I couldn't see it clearly, one side of the face looked dented and discoloured, I guessed by its impact with the window. As my stomach curdled in shock and revulsion, I found myself wondering if the head belonged to one of the men who were supposed to be watching the house, and who were conspicuous by their absence. And then Hawkins, who had ghosted in to stand on my right, murmured, 'Poor Mr Hayles.'

As soon as he said the name I recognised the dead face, and felt ashamed I hadn't done so straight away. Of course! This was the old man from Tempting Treats, who Hawkins and I had visited only a couple of days before. Although I wasn't the one who had killed him, I couldn't help feeling that his death was yet another I was responsible for, another splash of blood on my hands.

'Bastards,' I muttered, reeling away from the window and letting the drape fall back into place. Cutting off the man's head and using it as a projectile was a barbaric act, one designed to intimidate and destabilise us. Although it was hard, I knew I had to try and detach myself from my own guilt and horror. I had to focus my mind and be ready for whatever might happen next.

What *did* happen was that we heard a scratching sound, like claws on stone, from somewhere above us. I went cold, my eyes turning instinctively up to the ceiling.

Had the fuckers got inside while our attention was diverted? Were they in Hope's room even now? Was the Sandman looming over her bed, sand pouring from his mouth and eye sockets as she gaped up at him, too terrified to scream?

I could see that Clover had had the same idea. Her eyes widened and she went rigid, like a deer in the forest sensing danger, then she swung towards the door.

Hawkins, though, turned the other way. I saw him take a step towards the fireplace, tilting his head. We could still hear the scratching, echoing and ghostly. Then there came a softer sound and the fire crackled as soot trickled into it from above.

'It's in the chimney,' Hawkins said.

It was true. The scratching wasn't above our heads – it was coming from behind the wall above the fireplace. It was getting louder and closer as it descended. And accompanying it was a gentler but no less ominous sound: a beating or fluttering.

I jerked forward towards the metal fireguard that stood loosely on the hearth as a barrier against sparks or chunks of dislodged coal.

'We need to block—'

But before I could act, or even finish my sentence, a wild, flapping shape burst out of the chimney in a cloudy cascade of soot and erupted into the room like a phoenix rising from the flames.

The new arrival was no radiant mythological creature, though. It was a ragged, tattered, squawking thing, black and trailing soot as if moulded from the grime of London itself. It was a crow, I realised. But was it *the* crow? Satan? The one that had belonged to the old man? Was it so attached to its owner that it had followed his killers all the way here? And if so, what did it want? Revenge? Help?

If I'd been thinking rationally, I'd have realised how ridiculous those questions were. But I wasn't. I was reacting to the situation, my thoughts pinging randomly in my head. The crow rose above us, screeching and darting. Each time it flapped its wings more soot sifted down like fine black snow. I'd never been scared of birds, but it struck me, even more than it had in the old man's shop, how much bigger and more primal a crow seemed in a confined space; how you couldn't help but flinch whenever it came near you; how much more wary you were of its stabbing beak and sharp claws.

Maybe I should have put two and two together. Maybe I should have realised there was more to this than met the eye. But the bird's appearance had caught me off guard – had caught *all* of us off guard – and it never occurred to me that the bloody thing was anything but what it appeared until Hawkins reached up towards it, as though to snatch it out of thin air, and it *changed*.

The transformation was lightning quick – *so* quick it was more an impression than anything; a vague after-image that lingered in the memory like an imprint of a childhood nightmare.

When I recall the incident now, what I 'see' is the bird expanding, stretching like a piece of elastic. But that makes the creature, and the shape it became, sound more solid than it actually was. Because what it *really* seemed like was an *absence*, as if reality had suddenly become two-dimensional; as if it had become nothing but a screen with an image of the room on it, and someone had slit that screen open and allowed the blackness behind it to come pouring through.

The microsecond it took for the slit to change again and to converge, to descend, on Hawkins, is even more of a blur in my memory. Trying to access it now is like trying to make sense of a distorted image in an out-of-focus photograph. What I 'see' in my mind's eye is the slit becoming a huge, black, guillotine-like blade, which sweeps down across Hawkins' body and then just as quickly withdraws from him. The next thing I'm aware of is Hawkins lying on the ground, several feet away from his right arm, which has somehow, impossibly, become detached from his body.

For several seconds after the attack I could do nothing but stare down at my friend in disbelief. Although his mouth was open and twisted in agony, his eyes bulging, his face so drained of colour he looked monochrome, he made no sound whatsoever. I can only suppose it was the enormity of what had happened that had silenced him. The pain and shock must have been so great they had overwhelmed his senses, his ability to think.

Blood gushed from the stump of his shoulder and spread across the carpet with such force it was like a living thing. Like some gelid, shimmering organism that seemed desperate to reach the limb lying inert several feet away, in the mistaken belief it might somehow find a way to reattach it to the host body.

Clover screamed and dropped to her knees beside Hawkins as if her legs had been cut from under her. She looked wildly around for a moment, then grabbed a cushion from the nearest armchair and pressed it against the gushing wound.

Whether at the pressure of the cushion or not, Hawkins' body went rigid, his back arcing like a bow, his heels digging into the carpet. He let out a gurgling gasp and his legs began to kick. Then his bulging eyes rolled back in his head and his chalk-white face went slack.

The black shape, meanwhile, flowed across the room like smoke or oil, shrinking and solidifying as it went. Tearing my gaze from Hawkins' body and Clover's frantic efforts to staunch the blood, I turned to see it compact down into a roughly human shape. When it moved to the half-open door of the drawing room and slid out into the hallway, panic spiked inside me, breaking through the numbness that had caused me to freeze and finally enabling me to move. I imagined the thing slithering like a vast black slug up the stairs to Hope's room, oozing under her door. Although I was desperate to help Hawkins, I knew my priority was to protect Hope, and so, after giving my friend one last agonised glance, I turned and ran after the creature.

Stumbling across the room, I tried to draw strength and comfort from the heart in my hand. I wondered if it would spring to life to defend Hope if the creature (and I could only imagine this was the shape-shifter I'd encountered in my own time) attacked her. Still half a dozen steps from the door into the hallway, I heard the familiar groan and creak of another door opening, and instantly I realised what the shape-shifter was doing. It hadn't left the room to find and threaten Hope at all. It had left the room in order to open the front door and let the other Wolves into the house.

I came to a halt, suddenly unsure what to do. I knew if I followed the shape-shifter into the hallway, the likelihood was that the Dark Man would demand I hand over the heart immediately. However, if I stayed here and waited for them to come to me, might there first be time to use the heart to somehow save Hawkins' life, as it had apparently saved Frank Martin after he was shot during the battle of Passchendaele – or would the delay put Kate at risk?

I may well have stood there like an idiot until the Wolves entered the room, unable to decide, if Clover hadn't barked my name. I turned to see her kneeling in Hawkins' blood, which now covered not only the bottom of her dress, but also gloved her hands and arms in slick, drooling redness almost up to her elbows. There were further smears and spatters on her white blouse, plus she had a blob on her chin and a thick streak on her forehead where she must have pushed a strand of hair out of her face. The cushion she'd been using was now so saturated it looked like an engorged and dripping internal organ.

As for Hawkins, he looked worse than ever, grey and limp, his mouth hanging open. It was hard to believe he wasn't already dead.

Perhaps he was, but even so, Clover scowled and barked, 'Help me!'

I ran over and dropped to my knees beside her.

'Use the heart!' she shouted, letting go of the cushion with one hand to jab at it, flecks of blood flying from the tip of her finger.

'I don't know how,' I said.

'Just try!'

Before I could the door flew back, and with a grinding creak the Dark Man's spider-like conveyance edged sideways into the room.

I jumped to my feet and turned to face him, stepping in front of Clover and Hawkins to shield them. As the spider-chair advanced, it knocked over a small table, home to a Chinese vase, which toppled to the floor, breaking into pieces.

A couple of metres from me the spider-chair came to a halt, its limbs settling with a pneumatic wheeze. The thing sitting upright beneath the shroud of dark netting stirred feebly, like a sickly, newborn creature unable to break free of its placental sac.

I had no idea how the Dark Man had got here, but he hadn't come alone. As well as the oily, vaguely humanoid form of the shape-shifter, which oozed into the room behind him, he'd also brought Tallarian, who had to dip low to fold himself through the doorway, and whose fire-scarred flesh resembled a wax mask that had partly melted, then solidified.

It was none of these three, though, that grabbed my attention. It was the smallest, most ordinary-looking member of the group that made me gasp.

It was Kate. My Kate. My little girl. Looking just as she had on the day she'd disappeared. She was even wearing the same clothes: green and red duffel coat buttoned up to her throat, jeans, white trainers with pink flashes. And of course she was also wearing her pink-framed spectacles – although her eyes, behind the lenses, were wide and teary with fear.

I fell to my knees, all strength, all resistance, draining out of me. I felt as though I was crumbling, as though my heart was melting. Tears shimmered in my eyes and I blinked them away, desperate not to lose sight of her even for a second.

'Kate,' I whispered. 'Kate.'

She was standing in front of Tallarian, whose long-fingered hand was clamped over her shoulder. It was this that prevented her from running to me when I raised my arms towards her; this and the fact that Tallarian's other hand was poised above her, glinting hypodermic needles projecting from the tips of his fingers.

I could see that my daughter's bottom lip was trembling. I could see that her fear and bewilderment were far outweighing any joy she might have felt at seeing me. I wondered how long it had been for her since her abduction. Months? Weeks? Days? Hours? The fact that she looked no older, no different, suggested the latter.

'Daddy,' she whispered. 'I don't like these people. I'm scared.'

Fury rushed through me then. Fury combined with an aching, overwhelming love, and an instinctive, primal desire to protect my beautiful daughter.

I wanted to rage at the Dark Man. Wanted to turn the full, destructive force of the heart upon him. But I couldn't let Kate see that. It would terrify her, scar her. I forced myself to smile, to speak softly.

'It's all right, sweetheart,' I said. 'There's no need to be scared. It'll all be over soon.'

The thing beneath the shroud stirred. The front of the black, net-like material bulged outwards, forming a point, and then the material slid away with a whisper from the Dark Man's blackened, mummy-like hand.

'Give it to me,' the creature rasped.

'No, Alex!' Clover said, but the future me's voice was louder and more compelling. Somehow, in some alternate future, this had already happened, and I had hesitated and Kate had died.

Perhaps she still would. Perhaps, once the Dark Man had the heart, he would simply kill us all. But it was a risk I had to take.

Stepping forward I placed the heart in his outstretched hand.

He gave a long, gurgling gasp of satisfaction and his fingers closed around the heart. He grasped it tightly as if he expected it to squirm and wriggle and try to escape. Behind me I heard Clover groan in despair. My eyes flickered towards Tallarian. He hadn't moved. Was he waiting for an order from his master? In my mind I heard the Dark Man hiss, *Kill her. Kill them all.*

'Now fulfil your side of the bargain,' I shouted. 'Give me back my daughter!'

I waited, breath held. What would he do?

His hand, still curled around the heart like a bird's claw, snaked back beneath the shroud, the black netting closing over it. Even now, with Kate only an arm's length away, I felt a pang of dismay at the knowledge that the heart was again slipping from my grasp.

And then, beneath the Dark Man's shroud, the heart came alive.

Without warning there was a sudden blaze of light – or maybe, more accurately, of energy that my mind interpreted as light. Certainly it wasn't light as you'd normally define it, but a kind of... purple-black effulgence. An eruption of unearthly, blistering power.

I staggered back from it. Felt it buffeting me, changing the air around me. This was the first time since I'd come into contact with the heart that it had acted independently of me, and oddly, mixed in with the wonder, the terror, even the exhilaration at what was happening, was a sliver of... envy, of jealousy. In that moment, stupidly and inappropriately, a tiny part of me felt like a husband who has just watched his wife kiss another man on the lips.

Even the fact that the heart was *attacking* the Dark Man rather than obeying him didn't entirely temper the feeling. And there was no doubt that it *was* attacking him, because the instant it came to life he released an appalling, piteous scream.

I had no reason to feel anything but hatred for the Dark Man, yet the sound he made was so gut-wrenchingly awful I found it almost unbearable to listen to. My instinct was to try to intervene, to implore the heart to stop, to show its victim some mercy.

But I didn't. Fists and teeth clenched, I stood by and endured it, and watched.

After bursting into life, the energy emanating from the heart didn't continue to radiate outwards, but instead seemed to turn back in on itself – or rather, back in on the Dark Man. It engulfed him like a swarm of devouring insects. His screams grew shriller, more inhuman, as the dark energy of the heart lit the shroud from within, turning it semi-transparent. Beneath it I could see his emaciated form, already twisted by age or illness, writhing and thrashing in agony.

Tearing my eyes away, I looked at Tallarian, alarmed by the prospect of how he might respond to the torture being inflicted on his master. Would he panic and kill Kate? Would he be distracted enough for me to snatch her from him? But even if I *could* snatch her, how would I be able to defend her and myself if he lunged at us, syringe fingers extended?

Within seconds I realised my questions were irrelevant. Horrified, I saw that both the Surgeon and my daughter were becoming indistinct, losing shape, their outlines blurring and running together like a watercolour left in the rain. What was this? Some visual distortion caused by the energy pulsing from the heart? Or was leakage from the heart affecting them even as it destroyed the Dark Man?

'No!' I shouted, and leaped forward, intent on yanking Kate out of harm's way. Clover, though, grabbed the jacket I'd put on over my nightshirt and pulled me back.

'No, Alex!' she yelled. 'Don't! It's not her!'

My impulse was to swing round, lash out, try to break free of her grip – then I realised what she was saying. I froze, took another look at Tallarian and Kate. Clover took advantage of my indecision and wrapped her bloody arms tightly around me.

'It's a trick, Alex,' she said. 'Don't you see? That's not Kate, it's the shape-shifter. In fact, it's not even the real Tallarian. They're both part of the same thing.'

At once I realised what Clover was telling me was true. Exposed to the heart energy the two forms were losing integrity, running into one another like melting tallow. It was like watching a detailed waxwork display exposed to the heat of a blast furnace. Kate and Tallarian were losing texture, colour, reducing to a kind of black, primordial gloop, which in turn was shuddering, squirming, as it became increasingly shapeless, like a salted slug in its death-throes.

I didn't know whether to feel relieved that this wasn't Kate or dismayed that she was as far away from me as ever. I didn't know how to feel about the Dark Man's plight either. Subject to the full force of the heart's power, the death of this creature, who for whatever reason had invaded my life and picked it apart piece by piece, now seemed imminent, inevitable.

Given all he had put me through, it hardly seemed possible. Was I *really* watching his last moments, or could this be a trick too? The Dark Man had been my (often anonymous) nemesis for so long it was hard to believe I was watching him die. And yet here he was, his screams having dwindled to gasps and whimpers, his body beneath the illuminated shroud crumbling, collapsing like ancient bones.

Less than ten seconds later he was even less than that. The shroud sunk in on his ashen remains as the dark and terrible effulgence from the heart, having done its work, faded and died.

The gloop on the floor, like a patch of oil given rudimentary life, continued to shudder and spasm as if in pain, or in a vain attempt to reform itself. There was no sign whatsoever now of the black, almost primordial form of whatever off-shoot of the shape-shifter had let the Dark Man into the house and that had been standing on the other side of the spider-chair. Distracted by everything else that had been going on in the last few minutes I'd lost sight of it. Perhaps it had broken down more quickly than the more elaborate forms of Tallarian and Kate, and been absorbed into the larger form?

Clover's arms around me loosened, but they tightened again as I took a step forward.

'Careful, Alex,' she said. 'It might still be dangerous.'

I realised she thought I was about to tackle what remained of the shape-shifter, though what she expected me to do to it I have no idea.

'It's all right,' I said. 'I'm not going near that thing. I've seen what it can do.'

The shape-shifter shuddered again, as though it had heard me, then its body suddenly elongated, stretching out like a snake. Clover yelled in surprise and jumped back, almost pulling me off balance, as the thing flexed, then shot past us. I caught a glimpse of it flowing across the floor, past Hawkins' motionless body, up the wall and into the flue of the chimney above the still crackling fire. Then it was gone.

'Shitting thing,' Clover said. 'Good riddance.'

Although her words were defiant, her voice was shaky. Feeling shaky myself, I stepped forward, grabbed the edge of the Dark Man's shroud, and, wary of the possibility that he may have one last, unpleasant surprise for me (maybe the spider-chair was booby-trapped?) I pulled it away.

Nothing happened. The Dark Man was nothing but ash and a few brittle, grey bones, in the middle of which, like a black bomb, sat the heart. Grimacing, I reached across and picked it up, holding it gingerly between my thumb and forefinger as I wiped the dust of its latest victim, which dulled its surface, on my jacket sleeve.

'Alex,' Clover said from behind me, her voice urgent but still shaky.

I turned. She was kneeling beside Hawkins again, one hand resting lightly on his chest.

'Use the heart. Now that they're gone.'

'How?'

'I don't know.'

I dropped down beside her, my knees squelching in blood.

'Is he dead?' I asked, looking into Hawkins' face, into his glazed, half-open eyes.

'I don't know. I think so. But you can bring him back, can't you? You brought Frank back. He told me.'

I had no idea what to do, but I had to try. Tentatively I put the heart against Hawkins' chest, against his own heart. Nothing happened. Both hearts remained silent, inactive.

'Come on,' I muttered. 'Come on.'

'Hit him with it,' suggested Clover.

'What?'

'Hit him with it. Like you're giving him CPR. Like you're trying to get his heart started again.'

'I can't hit him with this. I'll break his ribs.'

Her voice splintered. 'What does it matter? He's dead. You have to try, Alex. You have to fucking *try!*'

I tried. I hit Hawkins in the chest. Then I did it again. Again. Something cracked.

'Come on,' I muttered. 'Come on.'

I tried again. Again. Again.

'Come on.' I started to chant it. 'Come on. Come on. Come on.'

Bitter tears of rage, frustration and grief welled up in me, spilled out of my eyes, down my cheeks.

'Come on. Come on. Come on.'

Clover was crying now too, her face wet and red, her body hitching.

'Come on. Come on. Come on.'

I don't know how long I tried for. Twenty minutes. Half an hour. But nothing happened. The heart didn't respond. Hawkins stayed dead.

In the end, the strength draining out of me, I slumped forward over my friend, the man whose life I had once saved, and who had saved mine in return. I opened my hand and the heart, nothing but a black stone now, heavy and inert, rolled out of it and into Hawkins' blood on the floor.

'You can't give up,' Clover said, but I could tell by her voice that she knew it was hopeless. 'Alex, you *can't*!'

'It's too late, Clover,' I said. 'He's dead. We've lost him.'

She reached for me, and, clinging together, we wept.

NINETEEN
HEART TO HEART

Hawkins' funeral was a small affair. To reduce the risk of being identified in public as a convicted murderer who'd mysteriously absconded from a condemned cell the night before his execution, he was a man who had kept a low profile, and so for that reason the only mourners gathered around his graveside five days into the New Year were me, Clover, Hope, Mrs Peake and the three girls. Mrs Peake surprised me by weeping bitterly throughout the ceremony. After it was over we trundled silently back to the house in a couple of carriages through wet, muddy streets still streaked with dwindling patches of grey snow.

The house had been like a mausoleum since Hawkins had died, cold and mostly silent, the adults drifting around one another like ghosts. For the first few days I'd busied myself by examining and then – with the aid of Frith and a couple of others, all of whom had been paid a handsome bonus to keep schtum – dismantling the Dark Man's spider-chair. I'd hoped to learn something of his nature, something that might give me an advantage over the existing Wolves, or an insight into Kate's true whereabouts, but the conveyance turned out to be simply a machine composed of steel and pistons and cogs. Ingenious, yes, but nothing that couldn't have been conceived and knocked up by a forward-thinking engineer or mechanic.

Once the spider-chair had been broken down and taken away I'd had the carpet – which had been saturated with Hawkins' blood right through to the floorboards – ripped up and replaced. Though even after the floorboards had been scrubbed and the new carpet laid I'd still caught the occasional coppery whiff of blood on the air.

It was all in my imagination, of course. What I was really smelling was my own guilt. I felt wretched about the fact that I'd been unable to save Hawkins, or bring him back. I blamed myself, told myself he was dead because I hadn't cared enough about him. Clover, during one of our rare murmured exchanges, told me that that was bollocks, said that maybe nothing had been able to save Hawkins, and that maybe it was simply his time. I couldn't be swayed, though. I was haunted by the thought that he was dead because of me. And the fact that a future version of me had rescued him from his condemned cell and gifted him a few extra years of life did sod all to ease that conviction.

Foregoing the tea and sandwiches and little cakes that Mrs Peake had laid on for after the funeral, I sloped away and installed myself in the armchair before the fire in the drawing room. It was here where I'd been spending most of my time, brooding and thinking, since all trace of the Dark Man's visit had been eradicated. The Christmas tree in the corner was like a mockery of happier times; it turned my stomach just to look at it. But we'd left it up for Hope's benefit, thinking, rightly or wrongly, that if it had disappeared along with Hawkins, she might subsequently associate Christmas with death – assuming, of course, she was still with us twelve months from now.

After stoking up the fire I sat back, staring into the flames. Now and then my eyes strayed to where the shape-shifter had slithered around the upper lip of the fireplace and up the flue like an oily snake. Several times over the past few days I'd wondered whether the thing was still up there, licking its wounds, biding its time. I'd become so obsessed by the idea that yesterday I'd got down on my hands and knees, lit a match and stuck my head up the chimney. As I'd done it I'd thought about how people in horror films always seemed such dicks when they did stuff like this. If I was a viewer I'm sure I'd feel I *deserved* to have some monstrous, tentacled thing rush at me out of the darkness, piranha jaws stretched wide to devour my face.

In my defence I did grip the heart tight in my left hand while raising the match in my right, hoping that if the shape-shifter *was* up there, either it would sense the heart's proximity and keep its distance or it would attack and the heart would protect me. As it happened, the chimney seemed empty of everything but soot – not that I found that reassuring. What if the shape-shifter was higher up than I could see, hidden in the darkness? Or what if it had crawled back out of the fireplace while the room was empty and was now somewhere else in the house, disguised as a lamp or a pot plant or one of Hope's dolls?

Obsessive thoughts, I know, but I couldn't help myself. The irony that the Dark Man's death had made me more paranoid than ever wasn't lost on me. Slumped and introspective in front of the fireplace by day I'd taken to prowling the house by night. I carried the heart with me at all times, in the hope it would alert me to danger. Although I'd known the Wolves had been capable of it, the ease with which they'd invaded my home and killed Hawkins had shaken me to the core. And the fact that their leader (I *assumed* he was their leader) was dead – or at least, the decrepit version I'd met in *this* timeline, which didn't mean there couldn't be younger, more vigorous versions in other timelines – proved to be no consolation at all. In fact, it made me more afraid for Kate's welfare than ever. If the Wolves were leaderless, in disarray, would that improve her chances of being released or put her into greater danger? What if the Wolves wanted revenge for the Dark Man's death? Or what if his immolation had finally proved to them that they and the heart were incompatible, that any further attempt to seize ownership of it was futile, and that Kate was no longer of any use to them?

I wasn't exactly a stranger to dark thoughts, but the ones that swirled in my head in the days after Hawkins' death were among the blackest I'd ever known. I felt rudderless, unsure what to do next. I felt as if I was becoming obsessed by my own fears, and as a result was isolating myself from the world around me.

There was a knock on the drawing-room door. I scowled into the fire, hoping that if I ignored it, whoever was there would get the hint and go away.

The door opened and I sighed, but still I didn't look up. Footsteps came towards me, soft on the carpet. I hunched down further into my armchair, focusing on the dancing flames. Then I pictured the shape-shifter in its most basic form – black and oily and vaguely humanoid – moving across the room towards me, intent on revenge, and that was enough to make me turn and look up.

'I come bearing gifts,' said Clover.

She had a cup of tea in one hand and a slice of cake in the other.

'I'm not hungry.'

Undeterred, she crossed the rest of the distance between us and placed the tea and cake, with a tinkle of bone china, on the hearth. Then she lowered herself with a rustle of bombazine (she was still wearing her floor-length mourning dress) into the armchair opposite me and gave a dismissive flap of her hand.

'Whatever. I'm not really here to feed you. We need to talk, Alex.'

'I'm not in the mood.'

'So you've given up on finding Kate, have you?'

She paused, and when I didn't reply she said airily, 'Yeah, you're right, it's probably a waste of time. Might as well just forget about her and get on with your life.'

That stung. I gripped the arms of the armchair, digging my fingers in.

'Fuck off! Do you honestly believe I don't think about her every minute of the day? But I can't see a way forward. Can't see a way of finding out where she is.'

'You could use the heart.'

'How?'

'I don't know, do I? I'm not its keeper. But we know that in certain circumstances it responds to you. Maybe you should be putting your energies into trying to... I don't know... communicate with it, get it to show you the way.'

'It didn't respond to me when I wanted it to save Hawkins.'

'No,' she conceded. 'But like I said, maybe it couldn't. Maybe Hawkins is no longer part of the story.'

'Story?' I scoffed. 'This isn't a story, Clover. These are *lives*. Messy, complicated, unpredictable lives.'

'But everyone's life is a story. Everyone has a beginning, a middle and an end.'

I grunted.

Leaning forward, she fixed me with an intent look, as if she was trying to hypnotise me, impose her will on mine.

'I would have thought you, of all people, would concede to the notion of destiny, Alex. Don't you think it's at least possible our lives are mapped out for us?'

I stared back at her. 'If they are, then who's to say it isn't the will of God, or Allah, or old Father Time, or whoever, that I sit here and...'

'Sulk?' she said.

I scowled. 'Don't try to goad me, Clover. My point is that, going by your argument, we can do no wrong, because whatever we do is only what we're *meant* to do. According to that way of thinking, our thoughts, our decisions, our mistakes, aren't *ours* – they're just planted there by... by fate, or a higher force.'

Now it was me who wafted a hand dismissively.

'But seeing as you're asking, then no, I *don't* believe that. I don't believe in destiny. Maybe once I might have considered it as a possibility, but not any more. Life is too much of a fuck up. Which means this conversation is irrelevant.'

She responded with a half-smile, as though pleased with herself for drawing even this much out of me.

'Go on.'

'Go on where?'

'Let's talk about this properly. Destiny versus free will.'

'Why?'

'Because I think it's important.'

I sighed, though in truth it was something I'd been thinking about a lot over the past few days. Although we'd discussed the circularity and inconsistency of time travel numerous times before, most of our previous conversations on the subject had been sketchy, guarded, hypothetical. For various reasons we hadn't yet discussed the circumstances surrounding Hawkins' death – partly because we were too shell-shocked by what had happened; partly because I hadn't been willing to externalise what I saw as my guilt (despite Clover's insistence that I was blameless) any more than I had to... and partly, I admit, because, purely and simply, I was scared of digging too deep.

The fear I had of voicing the wildly veering thoughts in my head was almost superstitious. I had the notion that if I could keep those thoughts contained, all would be fine, but that once I started to give vent to them, to bring them into the open, it would be like... I don't know... like unleashing a swarm of voracious insects or a deadly virus.

I know how crazy that sounds, but what you have to grasp is that whereas time travel is a fun and exciting idea in books and movies, in reality it's terrifying. It shouldn't work. It *can't* work. It's impossible. And yet the fact that, regardless of that, it *did* work meant that I either had to accept and try to come to terms with a concept no human mind was designed and equipped to cope with, or go completely insane.

'All right,' I said, and promptly passed the buck to Clover. 'You first.'

I saw her draw herself in, saw her adopt the focused expression of a sportswoman about to run a race, or throw a javelin, or perform a high dive.

'Okay,' she said carefully. 'Well, we know, don't we, from what happened the other night, that small things can be changed? We know that a reality existed in which the Dark Man asked for the heart, and when you hesitated, or refused to give it to him, he had what you thought was Kate killed, which then created the... the emotional charge, I suppose, that the future you needed to travel back in time and warn the you of a few minutes earlier not to make the same mistake. But because you – the you that's sitting here now – was given that information, you *didn't* hesitate, and so the future was changed. You gave the Dark Man the heart and it killed him – and here we are.'

She paused, looking breathless, even fearful, which made me suspect, despite her goading, that she was also wary of stirring up whatever might be lurking in the pool of time. Already I felt as if my mind was bending and hurting, as I contemplated how, by changing the future, I'd created a paradox, an impossible situation, whereby, because the events that had forced the future me to travel back in time had subsequently been altered due to the future me's warning, it meant that the future me had no longer experienced them, and therefore had no reason to travel back in time to warn his/my past self to change them.

'So,' Clover continued, 'let's think about what this means. Is this reality now the *only* reality, or is there a reality running parallel to this one where you *don't* hand over the heart to the dark man and he carries on living?

'Or are there not just two realities, but lots of them? Are there, in fact, a multiverse of possibilities, where circumstances are constantly changing? Is reality like a tree, branching off in all directions, infinitely splitting into smaller and smaller shoots?'

Almost grudgingly I said, 'Even with what we know it sounds mad to say it, but... yeah, maybe. But that's not even the question we should be asking. What we *should* be asking is whether, because of what the heart can do, it's possible to travel *between* these alternate realities, if they exist, skip from one to the next like... like moving between lanes on a motorway.'

Both of us were silent for a moment, digesting the concept.

Then I said, 'Personally I think we can. Or at least I think whoever has the heart can.'

'Because of the crumbling heart that the Dark Man showed you, you mean?'

I nodded. 'Unless the Dark Man stole the heart from a future version of me, and was lying about owning it ever since the shape-shifter took it from me at the police station, he must be from an alternate timeline, one where I never got the heart back after ending up here and probably spent the rest of my life looking for it. In that timeline I might even have died in Tallarian's laboratory because Hawkins wasn't there to rescue me. But if that's true, then I'd never have *been* in Tallarian's laboratory in the first place, would I, because the future me would never have been able to resurrect Frank Martin, who would never have rescued me from the crypt in Queens Road Cemetery that Benny took me to? And so it goes. Take away the future and the past collapses like a pack of cards. *Unless*, as you say, there are a ton of alternate realities – what did you call them?'

'A multiverse.'

'Multiverse, yeah. If there's a multiverse, and if whoever has the heart can jump between them, then literally anything is possible, isn't it? It'd mean that different versions of this story could be played out over an infinite number of timelines, each of which could affect any of the others.'

I paused, my mind again boggled by the concept. Was this really the only way to make sense of things, to fit all the misshapen pieces of the puzzle together?

Certainly it was the only explanation *I* could think of, crazy though it seemed. The idea of an infinite number of mes living an infinite number of separate but interrelated lives was almost too massive an idea for me to get my head round. Yet at the same time it was an explanation, of sorts, for the impossible and contradictory tangle that my life had become. It was something, at least, to cling to.

Clover looked as though she was clinging to it too. Face pale above her high-necked mourning dress, she said, 'So where does that leave us?'

I shrugged. 'I don't see that it changes anything. However many versions of us there might be, it doesn't alter the fact that *we're* still us, and that here, now, in this reality, we still have to do whatever we can to get Kate back and put things right.'

Clover turned away, staring into the fire.

'Or we could just mooch around and do nothing, let all the other versions of us from all the other realities, if they exist, take responsibility and do all the stuff the future you has set up.'

Frowning, I said, 'But if all the different versions of us thought the same way, nothing would get done anywhere, would it?' Then I realised she was having another dig at me for spending the last few days brooding, and gave her a wry smile. 'All right, point taken.'

She smiled back, then looked thoughtful again.

'If the multiverse *does* exist, do you think all the other versions of us are as clueless as we are?' Before I could respond she amended her question. 'Well, not clueless. Maybe that's a bit harsh. But do you think they're all winging it like we are? Or do you think there are other Alexes out there, future Alexes maybe, who've cracked how the heart works, and who can use it at will, zipping from one reality to another, shoring things up, papering over the cracks?'

I took the heart out of my pocket and hefted it in my palm. It was an interesting question. I'd always assumed *I'd* be the one to pay off Candice's debt, and buy this house, and rescue Hawkins, and befriend and resurrect Frank (I even carried a notebook with me in which I kept a To Do list of all the things I needed to set in motion in the future) – but what if it wasn't me? Or rather, what if it was a *version* of me from an alternate reality? Did that mean that all bets were off where not only my future actions but also my personal safety were concerned? Might that mean I could die here without it adversely affecting what had already happened, because an alternate version of me would take up the slack?

I didn't know. Again it was too mind-boggling a concept to take in.

Shrugging I said, 'I think we have to assume that we're *it*, because if we assume anything else we'll start to believe in superhero versions of ourselves who can cross realities at will, clearing up anomalies and righting wrongs, and that'll make us complacent.'

Clover narrowed her eyes and nodded slowly.

'Agreed. Because even if there *are* versions of you who are more adept with the heart than you are, it doesn't necessarily mean they've got an overview of the multiverse, and that they can hop about through time, from one reality to another, changing things at will, does it? Because if they *are* constantly changing things, then they become part of the reality, don't they? So they can't have an overview of something that's constantly in flux, because the particular timelines they're setting out to change won't actually exist until they go in there and change them...' She paused. 'Does that make any sense? It kind of did when I was thinking about it, but now I've said out loud what was in my head, I feel like it's kind of got away from me.'

I laughed. It was the first time I'd laughed since... well, since before Hawkins and I had set out to investigate the Thousand Sorrows in Limehouse over a week ago. I can't exactly say it felt good to laugh, but it was a step forward, I suppose.

'Tell me about it,' I said, jabbing at the fire with a poker and stirring the smouldering logs into life. 'Talking about this stuff feels like opening a safety valve and releasing the pressure that's been building in our heads. Now the pressure's *been* released I reckon our best bet is to shut the valve off again and just concentrate on our immediate problems, and on how to move forward.'

Clover gave me an appraising look.

'So you're ready for that now? To move forward?'

I felt a bit ashamed under her scrutiny.

'Yeah, I think so... Sorry for being such a selfish prick these past few days...'

She raised her hands. 'We all need a bit of space now and again. I haven't exactly been proactive myself.' She grimaced. 'There is one thing we've been neglectful of, though. Or one person rather.'

I felt another pang of shame. 'Hope?'

She nodded.

'Yeah, you're right. I need to spend more time with her. I'll take her to the park this afternoon. A walk in the fresh air will do both of us the world of good.'

Clover shook her head. 'I'm not sure she'll be up to that, Alex.'

'Why not? What's wrong with her?'

'Didn't you see her at the funeral? How sick and weak she was? She's getting worse. If she doesn't get proper treatment soon...'

She let the sentence hang, but it was obvious what she meant. If she didn't get proper treatment soon we'd lose her.

'I'll *have* to get the heart operational then, won't I?' I said, aware that I was speaking as though the task was achievable through application alone; as though the heart was nothing but an old jalopy I was doing up for a trip to the coast.

'Do you think you'll be able to?'

'I *have* to. I've got no choice. I've already lost Hawkins. There's no way I'm going to lose Hope as well.'

TWENTY
SICK GIRL

Sitting at Hope's bedside I said, 'Do you remember when I told you about science, Hope? About what it was?'

Lying in bed, her eyes almost cartoonishly big in her hollow-cheeked face, she wrinkled her nose. Clover was right – her health *had* deteriorated. I hated myself for having taken my eye off the ball after Hawkins' death, for not having noticed that Hope had become increasingly listless and feverish. She had no energy to play with her toys, and no appetite, and though she bore it well she was clearly in pain. The flesh around the stump where the metal arm had been grafted on to her body was now looking not only red and inflamed, but alarmingly discoloured. The wound itself was crusted with a dried seepage that was part blood, part pus, and that had to be carefully cleaned several times a day. The seepage had a bad smell, which made me fear that gangrene might be setting in. I desperately hoped that we weren't already too late.

Hope's voice was weak and slightly husky. 'Yes. Science is when men find out things.'

I smiled and gently pushed aside several strands of her damp fringe, which were stuck to her forehead.

'That's more or less right. Though it's not just men, it's women too. Science is all about discovery, about the advancement of human knowledge. For instance, inventing new machines to make it easier for us to do things – that's science. And inventing new medicines, and new ways of making us better if we're poorly – that's science too.'

She shifted in bed, trying to get comfortable, and I caught another whiff of the rotten odour emanating from her wound.

Quietly I said, 'For instance, if we could find a place where there were lots of men and lady doctors who had done so much science they could make your arm better, would you like to go there?'

Her eyes sparkled with eagerness or fever. 'Yes please.'

I felt a pang of disquiet, but tried not to let it show on my face. The reason I had given this little girl, who I had rescued from Tallarian's laboratory, the name Hope was because she had been the most positive thing to come out of that awful experience. The last thing I wanted, therefore, was to build her hopes up only to dash them again. But the truth was, I had no idea whether the heart would do my bidding or whether it would simply ignore me. *If*, however, I could get it to take us back to the twenty-first century, I wanted Hope to be as ready as she could be for the brave new world she would suddenly find herself thrown into.

'Good girl,' I said. 'I knew you'd be brave. So even if the place was very different to what you're used to, even if it was full of really bright lights and lots of strange and sometimes scary-looking machines that made funny noises, do you think that would be all right?'

Uncertainly she nodded. 'Of course. If the machines made me better.'

I held her hand. It was like a warm, damp rag full of fragile twigs.

'They *will* make you better, I promise.'

Trying to ignore the yammering voice telling me I had no right to make such a promise, I continued, 'Now, is there anything *you* want to ask *me* about this place before we go there? Anything you'd like to know?'

Her voice was tiny. 'Will you and Clover be there with me? I'm not sure I'd like to go on my own.'

I squeezed her hand as hard as I dared.

'Of *course* we will. We'll be there whenever you need us.'

Clover and I had briefly discussed whether to explain the concept of time travel to Hope, and had almost immediately discarded the idea. It would be hard enough for the girl to get her head round the dazzling and terrifying new environment she would suddenly find herself in, without having to take on board the fact that she'd travelled over a century forward in time as well.

Before coming to us, Hope had had no concept of numbers whatsoever, and bright, curious and quick though she was to latch on, it had taken her a good while to grasp the concept of time – of how seconds led to minutes, minutes to hours, hours to days, days to weeks, weeks to months, months to years. She'd been unable to understand how each month had a name, and how each day within that month had a name *and* a number that was unique to itself, and that, once it was over, would never reoccur.

It had been two days since Hawkins' funeral, two days since Clover and I had had our fireside chat. Since then I'd been locked away with the heart; I'd been, for want of a better word, *communing* with it. Not sure how else to go about it, I'd sat with the heart cupped in my palms and tried to impose my will on it, to let it know what I wanted, what I needed it to do.

Had it responded? I'm not sure. If it had it hadn't done so overtly. It hadn't burst into life, or changed shape, or communicated with me telepathically. On the other hand I'd been so intent on trying to communicate my desires that on a few occasions – and more often as time had gone on – I'd found myself slipping into a meditative, even trance-like state.

And on those occasions I'd dreamed.

I say 'dreamed', though in truth the experiences had felt more like visions. Maybe some of them had just been wish-fulfilment fantasies. It could even be that they'd all come from my subconscious, and not from the heart at all – but it had been encouraging, even so. If nothing else, it had at least *felt* like progress.

In some of the dreams (or visions) I'd found myself back in the desert. The heart, the one I'd forged – or dreamed I'd forged – with my hands from the vital stuff of the earth, from life and energy and something so primal, so unknowable, that the only word I can think of for it is 'magic', was a black speck on the white sand, an object so tiny that it seemed destined to sink back under the ground from where it had come, to be overlooked, ignored, even less than forgotten, having never been owned and treasured and lost and remembered in the first place.

In these dreams, or visions, I'd observed the heart, but I'd also *been* the heart. I was its spirit, linked to it eternally. I was aware of the centuries passing, of the world turning. I was aware of life evolving, adapting, of simple organisms becoming more complex and diverse with each generation. I was aware of life spreading from the sea on to the land, expanding to populate the planet. I was aware of the rise and fall of the reptiles, of cataclysmic climatic change, of continual death and rebirth.

And throughout it all I was aware of the heart, of how impervious and constant and infinitely patient it was, as it waited to be discovered.

Then finally, inevitably, it *was* discovered, and I was aware of it passing from hand to hand, of time slipping across it like a breath, like a soft breeze, impregnating it but never eroding or destroying it. Indeed, it was time that *strengthened* the heart, that stirred up the stuff it was made from and bonded with it. And I was aware that time was not set, not linear, not constant, that it was not a single fixed point across which events shifted constantly and evenly.

No, time was mutable, ever-changing; it was a world unto itself. A world in which the heart and its dependents could travel at will.

Oddly, I emerged from these dreams, or visions, both reassured and terrified. Reassured because they gave the heart a context of sorts, a history, something solid to cling to. But terrified because they suggested the heart was the most ancient, incredible, dangerous artefact ever created; even more, that it was a dispassionate and primal force, which attracted acolytes as a planet's orbit might attract minute particles of space dust.

But was *any* of this stuff actually true? I had no way of knowing. It could be that the heart was giving me an insight into its nature, as it had given a similar insight to million of guardians, or acolytes, that had gone before me. Or it could be that the whole thing was a load of flannel dredged up by my subconscious as a way of trying to come to terms with all the crazy, impossible things I'd seen and heard these past few months.

Whatever the answer, it didn't change the fact that the most important aspect, as far as I was concerned, was how the heart affected me – and *could* affect me – here and now.

Hope was still holding my hand, and now she squeezed it with all her strength, which admittedly wasn't much.

'I'll never be scared of anything ever again if you and Clover are with me. Not even the Sandman. When can we go to the place?'

I smiled to hide the nervousness, even the dread, I was feeling.

'There's no time like the present. Wait here and I'll get Clover.'

As I slipped my hand from hers and rose from the bed with a squeak of springs, I felt as if I was leaving my stomach behind. Would this work? And if it did work, how would it affect me? Using the heart had never failed to fuck me up physically; in fact, the effect had been accumulative. How many more times could I link myself to the heart before it killed me? Before it sucked so much out of me that my brain ruptured or my heart gave out?

Anxious as I was, I tried to console myself with the thought that *if* the 'evidence' was to be believed, and *if* the me that would later buy this house, rescue Hawkins, meet Frank Martin and pay off Candice's debts *was* actually me and not a visitor from the multiverse, then I'd still be around to use the heart in the future, and not just once or twice but lots of times. So did that mean I'd eventually get used to the heart's power? That it only made you sick until you'd acclimatised to it? Might it even mean that maybe, like a drug, you started to crave the buzz of it after a while?

As well as being worried for myself, I was also worried about whether Hope, in her weakened state, would be able to survive the trip. Again, though, I consoled myself with the apparent evidence I'd received so far that it only seemed to be the person directly linked to the heart, the 'driver' if you like, that was affected by its power. The last time the heart had brought me here, when I'd been clinging to the shape-shifter in the form of DI Jensen as the two of us had smashed out of the police station window, I'd lost consciousness, but hadn't suffered the same ill-effects I'd suffered on previous occasions. I could only guess this was because in this instance the shape-shifter had been the 'driver', whereas I'd just been along for the ride. As to *why* the heart had obeyed the shape-shifter and not me – and then later, presumably, the Dark Man – when, by killing McCallum, I'd apparently taken on the role of its new guardian, I had no idea. But that wasn't a question that concerned me right now.

I opened the door and stepped out into the darkened corridor, to find Clover sitting on the floor a few feet away, her back against the wall, her apprehensive face glowing with yellow light from the wall-lamp above her.

'We all set?'

I gave a brief nod.

She rose to her feet and puffed out a quick, hard breath, as though bracing herself for the ordeal to come. She was wearing jeans and a blue short-sleeved top beneath a black, hooded jacket – after all this time it was weird to see her in modern clothes again.

She reached out and clasped my hand. 'Okay, let's do this thing. Let's make like Marty McFly and head back to the future.'

There was stuff we were leaving behind, loose ends left dangling – my various business concerns; the Sherwoods – and at first that had bothered me. With Hawkins dead, who would look after things while I was away? Who would keep the Sherwoods out of the clutches of the Wolves? How would I build my relationship with them?

But then I realised that with the heart I needn't worry about such things. Because once I learned how to use it, and to control or even allay the side effects, I would have mastery over time. Time wouldn't carry on without me. My life wouldn't unravel while I was gone. Because I *wouldn't* be gone. As long as I made a note of the date I could travel back here whenever I liked, simply pick up where I had left off.

Forcing my facial muscles into a smile, I led the way back into Hope's room. I saw Clover flinch at the smell, then she became brisk, business-like.

'Right then. Where do you want us?'

I sat on the bed beside Hope, who was looking at me with dulled, unquestioning eyes, and clasped her limp left hand in my right one.

'I want you to hold on to my hand as tightly as you can, Hope, okay?' I said – though I had no intention of relinquishing my grip on her if I could help it. 'Hold tight, and whatever happens, don't let go.'

I half expected her to ask why, but even in the minute or so I'd been out of the room she seemed to have become too sleepy or feverish to care. She gave a woozy nod and I felt the pressure of her hand increase a tiny bit in mine, which at least showed she understood what I'd told her.

As I drew the heart from my pocket I told Clover to sit on the bed to my left and hold on to my arm. She did so, pressing herself tightly against me and wrapping both of her arms around my upper arm, as if we were about to take a ride on a roller coaster.

'Now what?' she said.

'Now I need you to be quiet so I can concentrate.'

Nervousness made my response more brusque than I'd intended, but she didn't take offence. She nodded and closed her eyes and pressed her face into my shoulder.

The light in the room was dim. The house was silent. Beyond it, faintly, I could hear the static-like ebb and flow of wind through the upper branches of the leafless trees in the garden. The sound was not distracting but soothing; it helped my concentration rather than disturbing it. It made me think of a mother's blood coursing through her body, of nutrients rushing through her system, feeding the baby in the womb. But who was the baby? Me or the heart? Or were the two of us entwined, indistinguishable from one another?

I held the heart loosely in my palm and stared at it. I stared until my eyes became unfocused, until the black object seemed to lose solidity, to become a mass of darkness, its edges blurring into shadow, its surface swirling like oil. As my concentration deepened, turned inward, I became aware of my breathing, slow and steady, and of the weighty, sonorous thump of my pulse in my arm, my hand, my eyes. As I continued to stare at the obsidian heart, it seemed not only to pulse in time with my own heart, but to become warm in my hand.

I communicated my thoughts to it, told it what I wanted, what I needed. I ordered it to obey me; I begged it to obey me; I pleaded with it to help me. My surroundings darkened. I narrowed my eyes to close out everything but the heart. I hunched forward, aware of nothing but the pulsing mass of darkness in my hand. The heart seemed to be drawing shadows to it as a flue draws smoke. I hunched over until I was bent almost double, losing myself in the darkness. If Hope and Clover were still beside me, still connected to me, I wasn't aware of them. I closed my eyes, pressed my forehead against the heart.

Please, I thought. I might even have whispered it. *Please. Please.*

There was no sense of displacement. No sense of the world shimmering or shifting around me. The first indication that things had changed was when I heard Clover gasp. I was still hunched forward, my eyes tightly shut. When I eased them open, they became flooded with red – the effect of sunlight shining through my eyelids, illuminating the blood vessels. The next thing I knew, my mobile phone, which I'd retrieved from beneath a pile of underwear in my chest of drawers, where it had been lying inert for the past three months, came alive in my inside jacket pocket, vibrating like crazy as messages started to come through.

'We're back,' Clover breathed, her grip on my arm tightening. Her voice became louder, more excitable. 'Oh my God, we're back! You've done it, Alex!'

I could hear traffic now, coming from outside. Slowly I felt my senses returning, my body settling back into itself. I tried to fully open my eyes, but the light was too harsh. I squinted, trying to acclimatise.

'Back?' I said, and felt a spasm of alarm. 'What about Hope? Is she—?'

'She's here too! We're all here!' Clover laughed. 'I think you've cracked it, Alex! How are you feeling?'

How *was* I feeling? I was feeling... okay. No, better than okay. I felt euphoric. Triumphant.

My phone stopped vibrating. I opened my eyes, saw Clover's face shimmering in the sudden daylight.

I grinned at her. 'I feel—' I said – and that's when it hit me.

A colossal, crushing force of sickness and pain. It smashed down on me like a wave, engulfing me completely.

Somewhere within it I was vaguely aware of falling, of Clover screaming my name.

Then the world convulsed, as if the ground had given way, and I was swallowed by blackness.

TWENTY-ONE

THE VISITOR

I came to suddenly, as if I'd been switched back on. The period between the crushing pain that had caused me to pass out and the moment when I'd snapped back awake was nothing, a void; it was like I'd been cut from reality for a while, then pasted back in. Even so, I woke gripped by a sense of urgency, and with a name on my lips, as if my subconscious had been beavering away behind the scenes while I'd been gone.

'Kate.'

My voice was clogged and muddy, as if dredged from my throat by metal hooks. The pain made me grimace, made my body shift slightly as my muscles tensed. This in turn gave me a sense of where I was – lying on a firm mattress, my head supported by pillows – and also made me realise it wasn't just my throat that hurt; it was all of me.

I winced and groaned as multiple aches awakened in my body. I felt as if I'd been through an almighty workout; there wasn't a bit of me that wasn't affected. My throbbing head felt like a boulder I couldn't raise. My chest ached as if I'd been punched repeatedly in the sternum and ribs.

I became aware of movement to my left: a rustle of fabric, a shifting of light.

I tried to turn my head, but pain crackled in my neck and lanced up through the back of my skull. When the pale blandness of the ceiling above me was obscured by a creeping smear of shadow, I at first thought it was unconsciousness reaching for me again. If it wasn't for my anxiety about Kate, I might have welcomed it. But not only did I remain fully aware, my mind actually grew sharper as the dark smear became a solid, clear-edged oval. As I continued to stare my vision adjusted, like the contrast and brightness dials on my mum's old TV, and the oval resolved itself into a face arranged into an expression of relief and concern.

'Back with us, are you?' the face said, and offered a shaky laugh. 'You gave us a right shock, you bastard. We thought we'd lost you.'

'Kate,' I repeated, but speaking was so difficult that my throat spasmed with pain again, preventing me from saying more.

The face widened, then narrowed its eyes. The alarm that appeared on it made me realise its owner must be thinking I'd woken up with brain damage or something.

'I'm Clover. Not Kate,' the face said carefully. 'Do you remember what happened?'

I swallowed, clenched my fists and braced myself, determined this time to get the words out.

'Yes,' I croaked. 'I know... you're Clover. Where's Kate?'

The coolness of Clover's hand on my arm – as if she was trying to anchor me, stop my thoughts from drifting – made me realise how hot I was.

Still in that same careful voice, enunciating each word as though I was hard of hearing, she said, 'We haven't found her yet. But we will. What's the last thing *you* remember, Alex?'

I couldn't answer immediately. After forcing out over a dozen words my throat was burning.

'Water,' I rasped, then realised this might only baffle her. 'Need drink.'

'Oh,' she said. 'Yeah, course.'

She moved out of my range of vision and I got the impression she was twisting around, reaching for something. A moment later I felt something pressing gently against my bottom lip. When I tried to open my mouth my lips resisted for a moment, then peeled apart. As soon as the thing slipped between them, I tasted soft plastic and realised that it was a straw.

I sucked and cool water flooded my mouth. I grunted in near ecstasy. In that moment I swear it was the greatest physical sensation I'd ever experienced. Swallowing was even better. It was like a downpour of much-needed rain on a parched desert. I imagined it flooding through the desiccated channels of my body, soothing my internal wounds like a balm, restoring me to life.

'Careful,' Clover said. 'Not too much.' Pinching the straw between thumb and forefinger she tugged it from between my lips. I groaned in complaint, puckering my lips like a child offering a kiss.

'I know you're thirsty,' she said. 'The nurse said you would be. But she also said you'd be sick if you drank too much. So let that settle and you can have a bit more.'

Nurse. My eyes flickered to look beyond her, but all I could see was a white ceiling, a patch of white wall.

'Am I in hospital?'

'Private hospital,' Clover confirmed. 'Very posh.'

Private? I realised I had a lot to catch up on. The water had smoothed over the rough edges in my throat. It was still sore, but at least I could talk without feeling as though I was coughing up barbed wire.

'What happened?'

'We got back four days ago. That's how long you've been out. You were spot on with the date, by the way, or the heart was. We arrived back only a day after we left, all those months ago. From where I was sitting it seemed like a really smooth transition. One moment we were in 1896 and the next we were back in our own time. You seemed fine for about thirty seconds, then suddenly – wham! You keeled over and started having some sort of fit. It was horrible, Alex. Your arms and legs were jerking, your face went blue; I thought you'd had it. I got my phone out to call an ambulance, but before I could, one had already arrived. I thought it was a trick at first – something the Dark Man had maybe set up – but then I realised it could have been you – a future you, I mean, or an alternate one, who knew this would happen. The thing is, we had nothing to lose, or you didn't. If I hadn't let the paramedics in, if they hadn't treated you straight away, stabilised you, you'd have died. Me and Hope came with you in the ambulance, and they brought us straight here. As soon as we walked in they knew who you were, who Hope was. Everything was organised, and it's all been paid for.'

'By me?' I said, trying to get my head round it all.

Clover shrugged. 'Maybe. I'm guessing so.' She glanced at her wrist. 'But we'll know soon enough. One of the doctors told me this morning that someone was coming to see us – me and you – at 1 p.m. I said you were still unconscious, but the doctor said that whoever had given him the message had said that everything would be fine.' She pulled a face. 'So I guess whoever's coming knew you'd be awake by then.'

I stared at her. Could it be true? Could a future version of me really be coming to speak to us? In which case, what would he do? Give me instructions? A pep talk? Make sure I knew enough about what was ahead of me to fulfil my obligations?

Again the impossible circularity of time, its apparently infinite recursion of events, made my head reel. Had I really survived because a future version of me had provided immediate medical assistance, which had saved my life? A future version who had presumably himself once been in my situation and had been saved by the actions of *his* future self, who had in turn been saved by *his*, and so on?

'What time is it?' I asked, more to anchor myself in the here and now than anything else.

'Twenty past eleven.'

A hundred minutes. Just enough time to get my head together, to be brought fully up to date on everything that had happened since my collapse. I remembered what Clover had said about the staff here knowing who Hope and I were when we arrived.

'So what about Hope? How's she? Is she okay?'

I clenched my fists, dreading the expression that might appear on Clover's face, knowing that within a split-second I'd know Hope's fate.

Relief flooded through me when Clover smiled.

'She is! She's fighting fit and bright as a button. They operated on her the day we got here. They took off that horrible metal arm, cleaned up the area around it and dosed her up with so many antibiotics they pretty much killed the infection stone dead. The wound itself was a bit of a state, but there was no gangrene, which is a massive relief. She spent most of the day after the op asleep, but now she's bouncing all over the place, driving the nurses crazy – though I think they love her really. You should see her, Alex – in fact, you *will* see her soon. She's been to visit you a few times, and each time she's come in she's given you a kiss on the forehead and told you to wake up. The surgeon who did her op, Dr Shah, has been talking to her about getting a prosthetic arm, which she's really excited about. Oh, and she's taken to the twenty-first century like a duck to water. One of the nurses has been showing her how to use a computer, and she's gone mad for it! God knows what'll happen when she discovers Facebook and Twitter.'

I've never considered myself a particularly sentimental bloke, but as Clover talked about how much Hope was thriving, I felt myself welling up – my sore throat thickening, my eyes growing hot and stuffy. At least, I thought, *something* good has come out of this. Despite the blood on my hands, at least I'd made *one* person's life better.

The fact I'd nearly killed myself doing it made me even prouder in a way. On the other hand it worried the hell out of me too. If I'd only just escaped death this time, what would happen *next* time I used the heart? I couldn't imagine being able to do it without it killing me for sure. So what about all the future mes who kept popping up? How would I do all the things I was still supposed to do, all the things I'd benefited from? Even if the other mes *were* from alternate futures – from the multiverse as Clover had called it – the question remained as to why the heart hadn't had the same effect on *them* as it had had on me. Did it have different properties in each separate dimension? No, that didn't make sense. Then again, did *any* of this make sense? Was it even a problem that could be approached logically?

I sniffed and blinked away the tears in my eyes and tried to speak, but I still felt too emotional to force any words out. Clover could see how affected I'd been by her news, but she didn't make a thing of it. She just smiled and gave my arm a brief, vigorous rub.

'You did good, Alex. Brilliant, in fact. I'll tell the nurses you're awake.'

She went out – more to give me a few moments alone than anything else, I guessed – and came back a minute or so later with a tall, broad-shouldered, smiling nurse, whose rust-coloured, corkscrew-curly hair had been pulled back in a loose ponytail.

'Back in the land of the living, are you, Mr Locke?' she said cheerfully. She took some readings – blood pressure, heart rate – and then, at my request, she and Clover took an arm each and helped me sit up, an ordeal of back-crackling, teeth-clenching agony, which I was determined to endure if it meant ending up with a more interesting view than a ceiling and a section of wall.

Once I was in position and pillows had been bunched up behind me, the pain in my spine receded to a dull throb. I had more water and a couple of painkillers, and properly took in my surroundings for the first time. The room I was in was spacious, nicely furnished and occupied by no one but me. To be honest, it didn't look like a hospital room at all; it looked like a hotel room with a few added extras. Although the autumnal sky beyond the tall, rain-speckled windows was murky, the view was a restful one. From where I sat I could see a rising green bank covered by bushes and topped with a row of slim trees whose largely leafless branches grasped at the sky.

Not only did the place not look like a hospital, it didn't sound like one either. There was no clanking of trolleys, no echo of footsteps or voices from the corridors. It was quiet – and not *just* quiet, but quiet in that plush, refined, dignified way you only seem to get in exclusive (by which I mean expensive) establishments.

Now that I was sitting upright and properly conscious, it was only just dawning on me how thoroughly I ached and how exhausted I was. I was hungry too, and told the nurse so.

'I'll bring you some soup,' she said. 'Throat's still a bit sore for solids, I expect?'

It turned out the reason my throat was sore was because I'd had a plastic tube down it to keep my airways open. I'd also been catheterised, had cannulas inserted into both arms and another into the back of my right hand – for medication, and also to take constant readings – and I had suction pads on my chest, attached to leads which were hooked up to a heart monitor. The staff had been feeding me intravenously, and for the first couple of days they'd been giving me oxygen too because I'd been unable to breathe properly. When I asked the nurse what exactly had happened to me, she told me a doctor would be along soon to explain everything.

Sure enough, the doctor arrived as I was finishing my soup. He wore a dark grey suit and a blue bow tie, and with his large, wide, bespectacled eyes, pert mouth and white tufts of hair sprouting from the sides of his freckled, bald head, he looked like a tanned owl.

'Ah ha! The sleeper awakes!' he said, and approached my bed, holding out his hand. 'Good afternoon, Mr Locke, I'm Dr Wheeler.'

He held my hand lightly as he shook it, so as to cause me the minimum discomfort from the cannula. 'How are you feeling?'

'Tired,' I said. 'A bit rough. What happened to me?'

'Don't you remember?'

I glanced at Clover. 'I remember collapsing. It came out of the blue.'

Wheeler's big eyes appraised me and he nodded. 'Of course.'

Maybe it was the way he said it, or the expression on his face, but all at once I understood. There wouldn't be any awkward questions from him, or from any of the staff here. Not about me, and not about Hope, whose metal arm must have raised some eyebrows. Whoever our benefactor was, he, she or they had paid handsomely to ensure complete discretion.

'So what's the damage, Doctor? To my body, I mean.'

Wheeler puffed out his cheeks and raised his hands, moving them as if weighing up two objects of equal weight.

'The exact cause of the episode is still a mystery,' he said. 'I can tell you *what* happened, but not *why* it did. Have you heard of anaphylaxis?'

I frowned. 'I've heard of anaphylactic shock. It's what happens when you suffer an extreme allergic reaction, isn't it?'

He nodded, pursing his lips in a half smile as if pleased with me.

'Precisely. What you suffered appears to be a form of anaphylaxis – or at least, your condition shared many common factors with it. But at the same time you appear to have been hit by a series of transient ischemic attacks – or mini-strokes, as they're more commonly known. We're still not entirely sure whether one of these conditions led to the other, though at this stage we have to say that's a strong possibility. At any rate these two factors, in turn, appear to have caused a further series of chain reactions within your body –' he swirled his hands around to indicate a maelstrom of symptoms '– to the extent that for a while there it looked as though your system was about to go into complete shutdown. Frankly, Mr Locke, we genuinely feared we might lose you.'

'Shit,' I said. 'So what does that mean in the long term?' I thought of how exhausted I felt, how immobile. 'Am I an invalid? Will there be permanent damage?'

Wheeler cocked his head to one side, downturning the edges of his little mouth as if pulling a sad clown face. I couldn't help thinking he was acting pretty nonchalant about what sounded to me like a drastic health scare.

'It's a happy no to your first question. Though as to the second, only time will tell. The prompt treatment given to you at the scene will certainly work in your favour, and it goes without saying that the care you've received since you've been with us has been second to none. Your system has received an almighty shake-up, Mr Locke, but you've responded well to treatment, and your heart, at least, appears to be sound. We'll continue to monitor your progress, of course, and at some point in the next day or two, when you feel up to it, I'd like to send you for a full body scan. But for now it's simply a case of plenty of rest, plenty of fluids and keep taking the medication.'

He beamed, as if it were really that simple. All I could think of was Kate, of the fact that while I was stuck here in bed she was still out there somewhere.

'How long will I have to stay here?'

Wheeler pulled the sad clown face again. 'How long is a piece of string? It entirely depends on how your body responds to the trauma it's been subjected to, and how you respond to the treatment we're administering *for* that trauma. Think of the attack like an earthquake. The whole frightening episode may be over in one fell swoop – and let us all sincerely hope that it is – but we mustn't discount the possibility that there may be one or two aftershocks to contend with. Personally I would recommend a minimum of ten to fourteen days complete bed rest, after which we'll reassess your situation.' He brought his hands together in a soundless slow motion clap. 'And now I understand that you are to receive a visitor very soon. In which case, I shall take my leave and allow you to titivate yourself.'

When he was gone Clover said, 'I'm not sure he's entirely human.'

I tensed, reawakening the gnarly aches in my shoulders, limbs and chest.

'You think he's one of them? One of the Wolves?'

She laughed. 'No. Sorry. Joke. I just meant... he's an oddball.'

'Oh, right.' I relaxed back into my pillows. 'I must have had a sense of humour bypass along with everything else.'

Neither of us spoke for a moment, then Clover said, 'You know you can't risk using the heart again?'

I frowned. She was only voicing what I'd been thinking, but I felt myself bridling all the same.

'What's the point of me having it if I can't use it?'

She answered my frown with an even fiercer one.

'Alex, you *can't*! It'll kill you!'

'But if I don't use it, what'll happen to all this?' I waved my hand around the well-appointed room. 'If I don't set up all the stuff I'm supposed to set up in the future, who's to say it won't collapse about our ears?'

She raised her hands. 'I know, I know. It's a conundrum.'

If I hadn't felt so miserable and frustrated I might have smiled at her choice of language.

'It's more than a conundrum, it's a fucking... disaster. There must be *some* way round it. Something we haven't thought about.'

'Maybe we *have* thought about it.'

'The multiverse, you mean?' I shook my head. 'Fuck that. I'm not going to lie back and let those other mes do all the work – if the buggers even exist, that is. Why should *I* be the weak link in the chain? Why hasn't the heart affected them like it's affected me?'

'Maybe you were just unlucky. Maybe...'

'Maybe what?'

She shrugged. 'I don't know. Maybe life's a lottery.'

I snorted softly. 'Look at us. We're just as much in the dark as we ever were. We're just prawns in the game.'

'Pawns, you mean.'

'No, prawns. Little, pink, wriggling things that could get eaten at any moment.'

She laughed, but the humour was hollow, a bit desperate. I looked out of the window at the gently waving trees, black against the dingy sky.

'Where are you, Kate?' I muttered. Then I looked at Clover, surprised I hadn't thought of it before now. 'And where's the heart, for that matter?'

She held up a hand as if to stop me leaping out of bed.

'Don't worry, it's safe.'

'Safe where?'

Her eyes flickered to the door, and her voice dropped an octave.

'It's back at the house. It's well hidden.' She leaned forward, put her mouth to my ear. 'There's a box of muesli in the kitchen cupboard. It's at the bottom of that.'

I had to concede it was a pretty good hiding place, but now that I'd finally got the heart back I felt nervous being so far away from it. Even if I couldn't use it, it still remained a bargaining tool – though how useful was that in reality? Surely whoever was holding Kate held the *real* winning hand? I'd give up the heart for her like a shot, and I'm sure my enemies knew that.

In which case why didn't they just come right out and offer me a straight swap? Kate for the heart? No strings attached, no messing about, just a clean transaction. Despite what I'd said about the world collapsing around our ears if I didn't set up all I was supposed to, I was pretty sure that if push came to shove I'd be more than willing to risk everything if it meant the resumption of a quiet, normal life with my daughter.

Not that our life *would* be quiet and normal, of course. There would still be loose ends to tie up. Including...

'Oh shit.'

'What?' asked Clover, alarmed.

'I've just remembered – Jensen. Hulse cut his throat. But the police'll think I did it. They'll be after me for murder. And they found the heart on me, so they must already suspect me of killing McCallum.'

Although the door was closed, Clover again glanced towards it, putting a finger to her lips.

'You don't have to worry about that. You're in the clear.'

'What? What do you mean? How do you know?'

'I checked your phone after you collapsed – well, not *straight* after, obviously, but, y'know, once you were here and they'd got you stabilised – and there was a voicemail message from Jensen asking where the hell you were, where you'd disappeared to.'

I gaped at her, the implications of this whirling through my head.

'You're sure it was Jensen?'

'Yep. I called him back. Spoke to him.'

'What did he say? What did *you* say?'

'Like I said, he wanted to know where you were. He wanted to know how you'd managed to walk out of a locked interview room, and how and why you'd absconded from police custody. I told him you were in hospital. I said you'd collapsed with stress and that you weren't to be disturbed. I said I didn't know anything about you absconding from police custody. All I knew was that you'd been found wandering in the street not far from the police station in a distressed and confused state.'

'Fuck,' I started to grin. 'And what did *he* say?'

'He wanted to know if you had any physical injuries, and when I said no and asked him why he said it didn't matter.'

'It must be because of the broken window in his office. Christ, did he honestly think I'd jumped through that, landed on the ground in one piece and walked away?'

'Well, you *did* jump through it,' Clover said.

She started to smile, and I smiled along with her, though it was more out of relief than anything. Did this mean I was in the clear – at least as far as Jensen was concerned? That it wasn't Jensen that Hulse had killed in the interview room but simply another manifestation of the shape-shifter? Presumably this meant that when the real Jensen had eventually turned up to speak to me he'd found no body, no blood – nothing but an empty room. It also meant that if *both* Jensens I'd seen at the police station were the shape-shifter, then the real Jensen had no knowledge of the obsidian heart.

Unless, of course, the Jensen who Clover had spoken to had been the shape-shifter and the real Jensen *was* dead, after all. I asked her whether this was possible, but she shook her head.

'There would have been something on the news. Your face would have been all over the papers. But there's been nothing. You're off the hook, Alex – well, apart from the fact that Jensen is very cross with you for doing a runner.'

'So did you tell him where I was?'

She gave me a look, clearly disappointed with the dumbness of my question.

'What do *you* think? Admittedly he did start to get quite insistent, so I'm afraid I had to cut the poor lamb off in his prime.'

I hooted, and then regretted it as pain crackled through me.

'He's not going to like that.'

'He *doesn't* like it. He's left several messages expressing that very fact.'

Despite the fact that Jensen was angry with me, and no doubt still suspicious of my part in Kate's disappearance, I felt a weight had been lifted off my shoulders. Maybe things *did* have a way of sorting themselves out. Maybe, if the future we'd been led to believe was ahead of us was compromised, time had a way of compensating, of shifting the pieces around, papering over the cracks.

'You look tired,' Clover said. 'Too much brain overload.'

'Thanks,' I said. 'I love you too.'

She smiled and glanced at her watch. 'It's half twelve. Why don't you get some rest, recharge your batteries in preparation for this mysterious visitor at one o'clock? I'll check up on Hope and be back here at five to.'

My instinct was to protest that I was fine, that I didn't need to rest, but in truth, ridiculous though it was, I felt zapped.

'Yes, nurse,' I said, and closed my eyes. For a moment my head was full of everything we'd talked about, and then it wasn't. Next thing I knew Clover was prodding my arm.

'Come on, sleepy head. It's nearly time.'

She helped me shuffle upright and for the next few minutes we sat, barely speaking, as we waited for our visitor. Though I tried to give the impression I was relaxed, I felt increasingly apprehensive. My eyes kept straying to the watch on Clover's wrist, which I couldn't quite see. Was I really about to meet myself again? An older version this time? If I was, how much would the future me reveal about what was ahead? Presumably as much as he remembered *his* future self revealing when *he* was *me*?

What I'd really want to know, of course, was whether he had any news of Kate. And also whether he could tell me the secret of how to keep using the heart without it killing me. But what if he was ten or twenty years older than I am now and he *still* hadn't found Kate? The prospect of that – the *fear* of that – made my stomach curl into itself like a snail retreating into its shell.

Clover glanced at her watch.

'What time is it?'

'Two minutes past.'

Maybe he's not coming, I thought, and felt a surge of hope, of impending relief, rather than disappointment.

There was a knock on the door.

Clover and I looked at each other. She seemed pensive. My guts were doing slow cartwheels. I imagined our visitor entering the room and me greeting him by abruptly and spectacularly throwing up. I cleared my throat.

'Come in,' I called, my voice wavering slightly.

The door opened and a man in a pale grey suit entered. I stared at him, surprised by the sense of anticlimax. It wasn't me. It wasn't anyone I knew. The man looked at us and his smile of greeting became stiff and a little uncertain, I guess because of the intensity with which we were staring at him.

'Mr Locke?' he ventured. He was young and wiry with prematurely thinning hair cropped close to his skull, and a neatly trimmed stubble of beard. He looked as though he ran marathons or went on very long bike rides at the weekend.

'Yes,' I said warily.

He turned his attention to Clover. 'And Miss Monroe?'

She nodded.

Suddenly I had an impression of this neat, young, unassuming man unravelling, erupting into a maelstrom of birds or bats or snakes or deadly insects. The Wolves of London, the Society of Blood: they could be anywhere; they could include anyone among their number. The shape-shifter could adopt whatever form it chose to gain access to wherever it wished, to bypass even the most stringent security. And even though we had seen the Dark Man die, that didn't necessarily mean he was dead *now*. In one timeline he had apparently owned and used the heart for centuries. So who was to say a younger version of him wasn't still running things here in the twenty-first century?

'My name is Daniel Worth,' the man said, approaching the bed. 'I work for Coulthard, Harvey and Glenn. We represent Mr Barnaby McCallum's estate.'

All I heard – or registered at that moment – was the name of the man I'd murdered, and debilitated though I was I immediately felt my defensive hackles rising. Bracing myself to deny whatever accusation the visitor might be about to throw at me, I only vaguely heard Clover say, 'You're a solicitor?'

The young man nodded. 'I am.' He held up the case he was carrying and beamed at me. 'And I have good news for you, Mr Locke.'

'For me?' I said, surprised.

'Indeed. May I?'

He indicated that he'd like to put his case down on the end of the bed. I nodded and he laid the case flat just below where my feet made hummocks in the bedclothes, and clicked the catches aside with his thumbs.

The lid of the case sprang open and he reached inside. Another little mind movie danced through my head: his hand would emerge brandishing a gun with a silencer, which he would use to shoot first Clover, then me.

From the case he pulled out a sheaf of papers.

'Mr Locke,' he said, still beaming, 'it is my happy duty to inform you that you have been named as a major beneficiary in Mr McCallum's will. Specifically, Mr McCallum has set up a private bank account in your name, into which will be paid a monthly sum of £10,000 for the first year, starting on the first day of next month, with this sum then rising by a further ten per cent at the beginning of each subsequent calendar year. What this means in practice is that next year's monthly sum will total £11,000, the following year it will rise to £12,100 and so on and so forth. This sum, with its annual adjustments, will be paid into the account each month for as long as you live. I have all the paperwork here, including a copy of the original will. All I require from you is your signature on several documents.'

I gaped at him. For a moment I couldn't take in what he'd said.

'I... don't know what to say,' I muttered.

A smiling Clover said, 'You could try "thank you".'

'Yes. I mean... wow!' I fixed my attention on the young man and tried to pull my thoughts together. 'Why me? I mean... did Mr McCallum give a reason?'

Daniel Worth was beaming with satisfaction. He was clearly delighted to be the bearer of good news. Cheerfully he said, 'The motives of our clients are not our concern, Mr Locke. Our job is simply to carry out their wishes and instructions.'

'Yes,' I said. 'Of course. Sorry.'

Why was I apologising? I guess because I wasn't thinking straight. The fact is, I knew why McCallum was giving me the money. It was because I was now the heart's guardian, and because McCallum felt, rightly or wrongly, that the least he could do to ease my burden was to provide for me, enable me to live comfortably while the heart was in my possession.

The question was, was McCallum doing this for my benefit, for his own (by which I mean was it his way of assuaging his guilt for passing his burden on to me?) or for the heart's, which he perhaps mistakenly thought could be protected, at least to some extent, by wealth?

The fact I'd been named in McCallum's will again made me wonder *why*, and also *when*, he'd picked me. Had I been carefully or randomly selected? Or had the heart itself, and not McCallum, made the choice? Had McCallum merely used the heart to travel into the future and suss things out, after which he'd carefully manipulated events to ensure that the pieces fell into place as he clearly thought they were supposed to? But what had motivated him? Duty? The fear that some catastrophe might occur if things didn't happen exactly as he'd been shown they would? And what about *my* future? Would I have to do the same thing when my time came? But how would I know? Would the heart somehow inform me? And what if I refused to do what it wanted? Would it find a way of making me? Or would it seek an alternate route, go off at a tangent in order to reach the same destination?

Questions, questions, more fucking questions. And really, at the end of the day, they all boiled down to *one* big question, to that same circling 'conundrum', as Clover had called it:

Were our actions the result of free will, or was everything we did preordained and therefore inescapable?

Incredible though the heart was, it was also a burden, a poisoned chalice. It might be the dream of many to hop about in time like *Doctor Who*, but if there was one thing I'd learned since all this had begun it was that time was a trap, a sticky, clinging web that tightened around you the more you tried to struggle against it.

TWENTY-TWO

A WHOLE NEW WORLD

'Knock, knock,' I said, sticking my head round the door.

The room was in semi-darkness, though Hope, sitting cross-legged on the bed, was not. Her face and yellow pyjamas were illuminated by flickering light from the little TV on the wheeled trolley beside her. Her lips were stretched back in a grin of wonder, and her eyes were wide and shone like liquid. Even before entering the room I'd recognised the soundtrack of what she was watching: Disney's *Aladdin*, with Robin Williams giving it his all as the genie.

Hope's head turned slowly and with obvious reluctance towards me. I could hardly blame her. Moving images on a glass screen must genuinely seem like magic to her, cartoons even more so. The difficulty she had tearing herself away from them gave me time to see that the right sleeve of her pyjama top was empty, and that it had been pinned up to stop it trailing loosely by her side. When she finally focused on me her face wore a stupefied expression. Then her smile reappeared, wider than before.

'Alex!' she yelled.

She leaped off the bed and ran towards me. 'Oof!' I said as she threw her left arm around my waist and turned her head to thump her cheek into my belly. It hadn't exactly been a full body slam, but even the impact of her slight frame sent shockwaves through my aching bones and muscles. I'd needed a stick, which I was clutching in my right hand, to hobble here along the two corridors I'd negotiated to and from the lift, so we were both effectively one-armed. I wrapped my own left arm around her and bent forward with a teeth-gritted wince of pain to kiss the top of her head.

She smelled... modern. That was the only way I could think of to describe it. The Victorian odour of carbolic soap and rose water, which partially masked the faint sooty sourness that clung to even the most scrupulously clean inhabitant of the nineteenth century, was gone, and in its place was the fresh fruity-floral smell of bath gel, shampoo and talcum powder.

She was a new girl, facing a new life, a new beginning. Despite the fact that she had no official identity – which would be someone else's problem, not hers – the vista of possibility before her was breathtaking. If she'd been older, even by six or seven years, she might have found the twenty-first century bewildering to the point of being overwhelmed, even traumatised by it. But she was young and infinitely adaptable. Based on what I'd heard about how she'd coped so far, and judging by the enthusiasm with which she'd greeted me, I had a feeling she'd be fine.

She stepped back from me, took my big left hand in her smaller, daintier one and gave it a tug.

'Come and look at this.'

I allowed her to lead me to the bed. When we got there, she let go of my hand, scrabbled up on to the mattress, shuffled over and half twisted to pat the space beside her.

'Sit here, Alex.'

I grinned at her confidence, her new-found energy. Even in the dimly lit room I could see how pink and rosy her skin was now; I'd never seen her so healthy.

I plonked myself on the bed beside her, grunting with relief. It was frustrating to be so lacking in energy. Even walking forty or fifty steps up a couple of hospital corridors had knackered me.

'Look!' she said, pointing at the screen.

I nodded. 'It's called a cartoon. Great, isn't it?'

She looked at me as though I was deluded.

'It's called *Aladdin*. He's a boy and he loves Princess Jasmine. He has a lamp, which has a genie in it, and he's blue and funny. And there are *songs!*' Her eyes lit up, and the joy on her face was so pure, so unadulterated, that I felt my heart clench.

'And look, Alex! Jackie brought me these.'

'Who's Jackie?' I asked, but she had already leaped forward on to all fours and scrambled across the bed to the TV. Despite her missing arm she was as swift and agile as a monkey. She dropped on to her stomach and leaned forward, her upper half hanging over the edge of the bed, her left arm reaching out to grab something from the lower shelf of the wheeled trolley supporting the TV.

Her voice muffled, she said, 'Jackie's a nurse. She's really nice. She's got a boy called Ed, who's eight, and a dog called Jasper, and she likes swimming and she comes to work on a bicycle.'

She re-emerged, her hair awry and her face flushed, clutching a handful of DVD cases.

'Look at these, Alex. They've got silver circles inside.' She dropped them on the bed and pointed at the slim black DVD player tucked into its own little slot beneath the TV. 'You press that button there and a drawer comes out and you put the circle in and then you press that other button with the little triangle on it and the story comes up on there.' She pointed at the screen. 'That's called a *Tee Vee*,' she added proudly, emphasising each letter. 'It stands for t-t–' she wrinkled her nose, trying to remember. 'Taller Vision?'

'Television,' I said softly.

'Yes,' she said with a happy grin. 'It's like a story book that moves. And look, I've got all these stories to choose from.'

She scooped up the DVDs in her left hand and dropped them in my lap. I started to browse through them – *Cinderella*, *The Jungle Book*, *Madagascar* – and then I froze.

Toy Story 2. Kate's favourite. I glanced at Hope, and suddenly, for a split second, it was as though Kate was back with me, as though the last three months had been nothing but a strange and vivid dream.

Then the moment passed, and it took part of me with it. I felt suddenly hollow, empty, and into that emptiness, like poison into an abscess, came a fresh surge of anguish and sorrow and loss.

Hope looked up at me, her little face etched with concern.

'What's the matter, Alex?'

I hadn't realised I was so transparent. I tried to smile. 'Nothing.'

'Then why are you crying?'

'I'm not crying.' I swiped at my cheek and realised that I was.

'They're happy tears, that's all. I'm happy that you're happy. I'm happy that you're better.'

But she was too bright to be fobbed off so easily.

'You're not happy, you're sad. Are you sad about Kate? Because you don't know where she is?'

'A little bit,' I admitted, trying to stop my voice from cracking.

'You'll find her,' Hope said confidently. 'I know you will.' She twitched her right shoulder to draw attention to her missing arm.

'It's because you were so brave and clever that I'm going to get better, and I'm going to get a new arm. I know because Clover told me.' With a curiously adult gesture she reached out with her left hand and wiped my tears from my stubbled cheek. 'Don't worry, Alex. You can do anything.'

TWENTY-THREE

DIRTY MONEY

'Let me speak to him first,' Clover said. 'We don't know how he'll react.'

Ten to fourteen days' bed rest, Dr Wheeler had said, but less than a week after his recommendation I discharged myself from Oak Hill Hospital. During the short time I'd been there I'd discovered it was a former stately home in the Hampshire countryside, not far from Farnborough. I'd also discovered that my stay and treatment, and that of Hope's, was being paid for out of McCallum's estate.

When the solicitor, Daniel Worth, had first appeared and told me about the bank account that McCallum had arranged for me, and about the monthly allowance that would be paid into it for as long as I lived, I'd been gobsmacked. My overwhelming emotion had been relief at the knowledge that I wouldn't have to worry about money while I continued my search for Kate.

Once Worth had gone, though, and I'd started to think more deeply about the implications of McCallum's gesture, my attitude had changed. I'd started to feel uneasy, and then increasingly angry and resentful. And the more I thought about it, the more I realised that the wheels McCallum had set in motion to ease my task as the heart's new guardian were not for my benefit, but the heart's. My wishes were irrelevant; my life was irrelevant. I existed simply to be moulded, manipulated, and if my loved ones happened to suffer because of that, then tough luck.

Whether McCallum himself had chosen me as the heart's guardian or whether it had been determined by the heart, or even by a greater power – Fate maybe – was irrelevant. The point was, I felt belittled, beholden. I felt like calling up Daniel Worth and telling him to stuff the money, to donate the lot to charity.

I didn't, though. Because of Kate. McCallum's money might have been dirty money, blood money – or at least that was what it felt like to me – but so what, fuck it. Principles were all very well, but the only thing that *really* mattered was getting my daughter back, and at the end of the day the more resources I had to do that the better.

Sitting around for a week with nothing to do but think about my daughter damn near drove me mental. However, I didn't have much choice in the matter. Physically I was fucked, and as desperate as I was to be out there, continuing the search, I was warned that trying to do too much too soon would almost certainly have resulted in a relapse, setting me back even further. Even so, I might still have been pig-headed enough to take the risk if Clover hadn't been there to stop me. She helped me with my exercises, she encouraged me and monitored my progress, but she also reined me in when I reached my limit. Most importantly she kept me from going completely insane by convincing me that we needed a proper plan of action, and that we should use this period of enforced inactivity to concoct one.

'I mean, what are you going to do if they let you out right this minute, Alex?' she said. 'You'll run around like a headless chicken and get nowhere.'

She was probably right, but it was tough all the same. Aside from Clover and my eldest daughter Candice, who I chatted with on the phone a few times, the only other person who made that week bearable was Hope. She was a bundle of energy and enthusiasm. In contrast to me, each day was a new adventure to her. On the evening of the day when I'd decided I was going to discharge myself (Clover had tried to persuade me to stay for the full ten days, but I'd been adamant), I'd dreaded telling Hope I wouldn't be around to play board games or watch cartoons with her any more. But she was fine about it, especially once I promised we'd still be visiting regularly. In fact, as soon as I told her I'd be heading back to London, her eyes lit up and she said, 'Alex, do you have a mobile phone?'

I smiled. She was steadily breaking out of her Victorian cocoon and adopting the mannerisms and speech patterns of the twenty-first century.

'I have,' I said.

'Jackie's got one too,' she said innocently. 'And so has Ed. He was showing me how to use it. It's cool.'

Clover's favourite nurse, Jackie, had brought her son Ed in for a visit, thinking Hope might be bored with no one of her own age to talk to. Hope hadn't been bored, but she and Ed had hit it off nonetheless.

'Is that so?' I said, trying to keep a straight face.

'Mm,' she said, 'and I was thinking, well if I had one too I could ring you up and talk to you on the days when you might be too busy to visit me. And did you also know that you can use a mobile phone to write messages to people? You just press a button and the message flies through the air to the other person's mobile phone? And then they can read your message and send you one back?'

'Really?' I said. 'Fancy that!'

'So *could* I have a mobile phone, Alex?' she asked. 'I know you bought me lots of presents for Christmas, but it would be ever so useful, wouldn't it?'

I thought of those presents, and of how unreachable they were now. I smiled again.

'We'll see.'

The next day, after kissing Hope goodbye after breakfast, Clover and I put the first part of our plan into action.

I say 'plan', though 'strategy' might be a better word for it. The first part had been to get ourselves mobile and hire a car, which Clover had done the previous day from a place in Farnborough. With me strapped into the passenger seat, she'd then driven the fifteen miles or so from Oak Hill to Guildford. Pulling up to the kerb outside Benny Magee's house, Clover had asked me to let her go ahead, speak to Benny first.

'No way,' I said, fumbling with my seatbelt. 'I'm not letting you put your neck on the chopping block. We'll go together.'

She rolled her eyes. 'Lord save me from working-class chivalry.'

I must have looked stung, because her gaze immediately softened.

'I don't need protection from Benny, Alex – never have, never will. Whatever's happened in the past between the two of you, there's no way he'd ever harm a hair on my head.'

'Yeah, but what if he's been got at?' I said. 'The last time I saw him he was surrounded by Tallarian and his freaks. What if he's become one of them? Or what if what looks like him answers the door, but it's really the shape-shifter?'

'What if, what if,' she said. 'We can't base everything we do on what ifs. What if *I'm* the shape-shifter? After all, I was once, wasn't I? What if I'm leading you into a trap?'

I scowled. 'I'm just saying we should be careful, that's all.'

'But that's exactly what I *am* doing by suggesting that I speak to Benny first, before you show your ugly mug. Or do you still think Benny and I might be in cahoots?'

'Course not,' I said, thinking back to the last time I'd been here, when I'd been unsure how much I could trust the woman I'd ended up on the run with. A lot of filthy water had flowed under London Bridge since then. 'It's just... oh, all right, go ahead. I suppose you're right. I don't suppose it'll make much difference in the long run. I mean I haven't even got the heart on me to protect us if we *do* get attacked.'

'Exactly,' she said cheerfully. 'So we'd be buggered whatever happens.' She unclipped her seatbelt and opened the car door. 'I'll tell Benny to leave the gate open, if that makes you feel better. That way I can make a quick getaway if I need to.'

'If you get into trouble, just holler and I'll come hobbling.'

'No you bloody well won't. You'll start the engine and hightail it out of here. No point both of us getting got.'

She jumped out of the car, shutting the door firmly behind her, then strode up to the black iron gates in the high wall fronting Benny's house. Wearing skinny black jeans, black high-heeled boots and a black fur-trimmed jacket she reminded me of Emma Peel from *The Avengers*. She was certainly a different proposition from the girl I'd met over three months before, who'd been too nervous to get directly involved in the burglary of McCallum's house.

She took out her phone, made a call, and a minute later the gates opened. Once she'd gone through, I got out of the car on my side, grunting and wincing with effort. I felt much better than I had when I'd woken up in Oak Hill a week ago, but I was still nowhere near fighting fit. At least I didn't need a stick any more, though. Those first few days in hospital had given me an insight into what it must be like to be eighty. Where would I be when I reached that age, *if* I reached that age, I wondered. Hopefully sitting in front of a blazing fire with my slippers on and Kate bringing me cups of tea.

I moved round the front of the car to the driver's side and leaned against the door with my arms folded. From here, even at hobbling pace, I was close enough to the gates to slip between them if they started to close. The street was quiet and peaceful, the big houses tucked away behind high hedges and tall trees, as if politely but firmly discouraging visitors. I wondered how many of Benny's neighbours knew about his background. I wondered how many of them had equally dodgy pasts. It was a cold autumn morning, the air so brittle it felt as though you could reach out and snap it with your fingers. The sky was the colour of despondency and the ground was covered in withered brown leaves.

Clover must have gone into the house. I certainly couldn't hear the sound of voices from beyond the hedge. The big reunion must have come when I was struggling to get out of the car, my own wheezing and grunting having drowned out the ringing of the doorbell and Benny's surprised exclamation at seeing Clover standing there. As I waited I breathed in air so icily sharp it stung my sinuses, then blew it out in long white plumes. Glimpsing movement high to my left I twisted round so quickly that my aching ribs and stomach muscles sang briefly with pain, but it was only a squirrel, slipping with quicksilver swiftness from branch to branch.

'It's okay,' said a voice, as if assuring me that the squirrel was no threat. 'You can come in now.'

I turned to face front again, twisting my body more cautiously this time. Clover had reappeared in the gap between the open gates and was looking at me. I couldn't tell from her face what sort of encounter she'd had with Benny; I got the feeling she was keeping her expression deliberately neutral.

Jerking my head in the direction of the house, I asked, 'How is he?'

'Come and see for yourself.'

I followed her up to the house. The door into the front porch stood ajar. I felt annoyed for being nervous, but that didn't stop the fluttering in my stomach. I couldn't work out whether it was the prospect of seeing Benny again that unsettled me or the possibility that he might have been got at by the Wolves. How many times could I walk knowingly into danger and escape with my life? Then again, what other choice did I have if I wanted to see Kate again?

Entering the porch, I heard a whirr and a faint rattle behind me, and turned to see the gates in the high wall sliding slowly closed. There was nothing sinister in that, I told myself. Benny simply valued his privacy; besides which, with his background, he couldn't be too careful when it came to security. I pulled the porch door closed behind me as Clover opened the one that led into the hallway. I followed her through and there was Benny, standing with his arms folded in the centre of his sumptuous domain, slight but somehow solid, indomitable. The hallway was just as I remembered it – the grandfather clock, the artwork on the walls. There was no sign of his wife, Lesley, or their little dog. Benny was staring at me, his expression as unreadable as Clover's had been at the gate.

'Alex,' he said.

I gave a nod of greeting. 'Hello, Benny.'

Now that I was in his presence I realised how little the wariness I was feeling had to do with Benny himself. The awe he'd previously inspired in me, the dark glamour that had seemed to cling to him, had now largely vanished, and not only because he had betrayed me. Since meeting up with Benny in the Hair of the Dog (months ago for me, only a week or two for him), I'd seen such wonders and terrors, had had my horizons expanded to such an extent, that he and his concerns now seemed petty in comparison. For the first time he seemed to me like a little man who wanted to be a big one. A man with delusions of grandeur who couldn't see beyond the high walls he'd built around himself.

He narrowed his eyes, as if he knew what I was thinking. In a cagey voice he said, 'You look different.'

'I'm older,' I said with a shrug, but he shook his head.

'That's not it. It's something else.' For a moment we stood, appraising each other. Then he said, 'Never mind. Monroe said you wanted to talk, so let's talk. Come through.'

He turned and stalked away, leading us not left to the conservatory at the back of the house – which I guessed was either too cold to sit in now that the weather had turned chilly or was still in a state of disrepair after being partially crushed by the sinewy darkness that Frank had unleashed upon it – but along a corridor to the right of the staircase. He stopped at the first door, glanced back to ensure we were still following (or perhaps to check I hadn't pulled a gun on him), then pushed the door open and entered the room.

The decor of the spacious sitting room beyond was cream coloured and made me think of desserts – meringues and white-chocolate parfaits and swirls of white icing on wedding cakes. There were cream rugs on a blonde wood floor, three white leather sofas so pristine they looked as if they'd been carved out of fresh snow and a gleaming white grand piano in the corner. My instinct was to squint against the glare, even though the light filtering through the long, narrow windows that overlooked the front drive was murky.

As he turned towards a sideboard crowded with bottles of spirits on the back wall, Benny swept a hand towards the bulky sofas, which surrounded a glass coffee table like a trio of school bullies closing in on a smaller, weaker victim.

'Take a seat,' he said, making it sound like an order. 'Drink?'

'Whatever you're having,' Clover said, and I nodded.

'Same here.'

Two minutes later he handed each of us a thick glass tumbler full of Scotch and soda, the latter having come from a siphon that resembled a mini fire extinguisher. Instinctively I'd seated myself on the right-hand sofa so that I could keep him in my sights while he was preparing the drinks.

Benny perched on the sofa directly opposite me (Clover was sitting back, apparently relaxed, on the one between us and at right angles to us both, like the bottom bar of a squared-off 'U') and after taking a sip of his Scotch, leaned forward to place his tumbler on the table with a glassy clunk. He stared at me for a moment and I stared back unflinchingly. Although I'd been aware of how much Clover had been changed by her recent experiences, of how much tougher and more resourceful she'd become, I hadn't been particularly aware of any significant change in my own attitude and capabilities until now. But confronting Benny like this, realising I no longer felt even remotely intimidated by him, was a revealing yardstick, to me at least.

Eventually he spoke.

'Who the fuck *are* you, Alex?'

I took a sip of my drink as I considered his question. Who was I? I was the guardian of the obsidian heart. But what did that even mean?

Snorting with quiet humour, I said, 'I'm not anyone. I'm just a normal bloke who's been caught up in... extraordinary circumstances. I'm just a dad who wants his daughter back.'

Now it was Benny's turn to sip his drink and look thoughtful. It struck me that the conversation was like a chess game, each player contemplating the board before making his next move. I was so focused on his pale blue eyes staring into mine that when Clover flapped a hand in front of her face I jerked in surprise, thinking for a moment there was a bird in the room, remembering how the shape-shifter had burst from the chimney in a cloud of soot.

'Whew,' she said, 'I can hardly breathe for the testosterone in here.'

I smiled, but Benny frowned in irritation. Gesturing at me with his glass, he said, 'Don't give me that. If you're no one how come so many people are interested in your welfare? And when I say people, I mean powerful people, people with money.' I saw him grimace, almost shudder. 'People who aren't even people at all.'

'You know why,' I said. 'It's because of the heart, the one I stole from Barnaby McCallum. It's not me they want, it's—'

But Benny was wagging a finger rapidly from side to side, as if erasing my words as they emerged.

'No, that isn't it. I don't buy that. It's not just the heart. It's you *and* the heart. I've been giving this plenty of thought since that... since what happened in that fucking crypt. And you and that fucking thing are tied together somehow. I don't know how, but you are.'

I suddenly realised that what had happened in the crypt (and also, presumably, before that, in this very house, when Frank's darkness had engulfed us) had shaken Benny to the core. He'd tried to maintain his tough exterior, was trying even now to keep his fear contained, but the more his mouth ran away with him, the more the cracks in his façade widened. His drink clattered against the table when he put it down, a sign of how much his hand was shaking. I almost felt sorry for him. But there was a part of me too that felt a secret satisfaction at the way his hubris had been punctured.

Before I could speak, Clover said coldly, 'I hope you got your blood money, Benny, for trying to turn Alex in. I hope it was worth it.'

He slid her a glance, and for a moment I felt sure she'd been mistaken when she'd told me that Benny would never harm her.

Then he sighed and looked down at his glass. In a softer voice he said, 'Tell you the truth, I was just glad to get out of that place in one piece. Once those things turned up, money was the last thing on my mind.'

'How *did* you get out?' I asked him.

Benny shook his head. 'You tell me. One minute I was surrounded by those things, the next – nothing. I guess I must have blacked out. When I came to I was alone. I tried to tell myself I was going mad, that I'd imagined the whole thing.' He barked a laugh. 'Believe me, that felt like the preferable option.'

'You were so insignificant they didn't even bother to kill you,' Clover said spitefully.

Benny shrugged off the jibe. 'I'll take that any day of the week if it means I get to carry on breathing.' He spread his hands. 'Look, I fucking admit it. I got into something I couldn't handle. Does that make you feel better?'

'A bit,' Clover said, and scowled at him. 'How could you, Benny? Betraying your friends? That's beneath even you. That's *really* low.'

His head snapped up and for a moment I thought he was actually going to snarl at her like a dog. But I detected a suggestion of shame in his expression too.

'Don't give me that! You know who I am, *what* I am. I was offered a fucking big payday to hand him over – and he's no friend of mine, I don't owe him a fucking thing. It's no skin off my nose what happens to him.'

'What a charmer you are,' Clover said.

'What do you want me to say? Grow up, girl. I've got nothing against the boy – at least I didn't until he pulled that weird voodoo shit in my house – but I'm a businessman.'

'You're a crook.'

I thought that might sting a reaction out of him, but he just laughed.

'We all know that, don't we? That's not even an insult. In fact, it's justification for what I did. But, you know, the money wasn't the only reason I handed him over. I also did it for you.'

Clover recoiled. 'Oh, *pur-leeze!*'

'Think what you like. But I'm telling the truth. When that... thing came to my house, when *he* brought it here, I wanted him out of it. Gone. I wanted him to fuck off and never come back. But when you went with him it nearly broke my heart.'

'Yeah, right. I'd believe you if I thought you had a heart to break.'

'Like I say, believe what you like. I don't care. But when I got that phone call, asking me to deliver Alex to that crypt... well, it wasn't a hard decision to make.'

He went silent, as if simply mentioning the crypt had brought the full horror of what we'd encountered there rushing back into his mind. Clover stared at him with grim satisfaction.

'Except you got a bit more than you bargained for, didn't you?'

He took another gulp of his drink. He had a haunted look in his eyes. He tried to tough it out with a smile, but it flickered and didn't catch. At last in a low rumble he said, 'What were those things, Alex? I mean, what the fuck...'

He shook his head, his words drying up.

He wasn't quite broken, but it was clear he'd never view the world in the same way again.

Quietly I said, 'Believe it or not, Benny, they were the Wolves of London.'

A flash of anger. 'Don't take the piss, boy.'

'I'm not. That's not what I'm here for.'

'So why *are* you here?' All at once on his guard, his eyes danced quickly from me, to Clover, then back again. 'Revenge? Is that it?'

Clover gave a snort of disgust. 'Don't judge us by your standards, Benny.'

'So what then?'

'Believe it or not,' I said, 'I'm here because I want your help.'

He stared at me for five, ten seconds.

At last he said, 'You're bullshitting me, right?'

'No,' I said. 'I'm just trying to find my daughter, and I want you to use your connections to help me do it. It's a business proposition, that's all. Whatever the Wolves of London offered to pay you to hand me over, I'll pay you more to keep you on my side. I'm not asking you to put yourself at risk for me. You can do what I'm asking from the comfort of your armchair. All I want is for you to put the word out, set up an information network. I just want people to keep their ears to the ground, and if anyone hears anything, anything at all, I want to know about it.'

'And that's it?'

'That's it.'

'And what if I don't help you find her? What if she's never found?'

'At least I'll know people are looking, keeping their ears and eyes open, and that's the important thing.'

Benny looked thoughtful. 'So where's this money coming from?'

'Inheritance,' I said. 'It's not something you have to worry about.'

He shrugged. 'Fair enough.'

'So are you in?' asked Clover.

'I'm prepared to discuss terms.'

'One more thing,' I said. 'If the Wolves contact you, I want to know about it. Whatever they might offer you to do the dirty on me, I'll give you more. Okay?'

Benny nodded. 'Sounds reasonable.'

'I *would* like to say that by making you this offer we're giving you a chance to redeem yourself,' Clover said, 'but we all know that's idealistic bullshit. If you really *do* care about me, though, you'll help Alex as much as you can. No more throwing him to the Wolves, okay?'

Benny slid his lizard-like gaze in her direction. 'I've *said* the offer's a reasonable one. What more do you want from me? Blood?'

'A handshake'll do,' I said, standing up and extending my hand across the glass table. 'To seal the agreement.'

For a moment I thought Benny was going to leave me standing there like a lemon, but then he rose to his feet and offered his hand in return. The moment our palms touched it was as though an electrical connection had been made – or perhaps broken. There was a sense of... *shifting*. As though I'd inadvertently stumbled. Or as if the walls of the building were re-aligning themselves around me.

And all of a sudden I was somewhere else.

It wasn't far away, though. I came to in another room in the house. I recognised it immediately. It was the conservatory. I felt as though I'd fallen asleep without realising it, then had sleepwalked in here and jerked awake.

Except suddenly it was night. So what had happened? Had I fallen asleep or passed out? Had I been unconscious for hours? Perhaps Benny had put something in my drink? And where was Clover?

Even as I asked myself this last question I realised there were two other people in the room. With relief I saw that the closest, sitting in an armchair to my left, illuminated by the rosy glow of a table lamp with a red shade, was Clover. She was wearing a long white nightshirt, which she'd pulled down over her bare legs, having tucked her feet underneath her. In the lamplight her glossy hair seemed to be the deep maroon colour it had been when I'd first met her.

Looking beyond her, I focused on the person she was talking to, who was standing with his back to the glass wall of the conservatory that overlooked the garden - not that a single detail of the outside world could be seen through the glass. The panes were nothing but a series of black screens imprinted with a faint reflection of the room.

The second person raised a mug to his mouth and took a sip. I froze. I'd assumed it would be Benny, but it wasn't.

It was me.

Suddenly I knew not only where I was, but *when*. This was the night when Frank had first appeared, when his darkness had enveloped Benny's house before eventually breaking in and smothering us. He'd done it not to harm us, but to drive us out before our real enemies, the Dark Man and his cohorts, showed up. I'd saved Frank's life and he'd returned the favour - though, of course, I hadn't known that until later.

But what was I doing back here now? Had I somehow slipped through a gap in time as easily as I might slip on a wet pavement? But I didn't have the heart with me. I hadn't yet been back to the house to retrieve it from its hiding place. Could it be that I didn't need it now, that I had absorbed enough of its power to operate without it? Or perhaps it was influencing me from afar?

Clover was talking, telling the other me about her family, about how Benny had helped her buy Incognito so she could set herself up in business. Neither past Clover nor past me seemed aware that I was there. I was clearly a ghostly observer, invisible and undetectable.

'He thought it would be a nice little starter business for me,' Clover was saying.

I heard myself ask, 'And has it been?'

Curled in the armchair she shrugged. 'I was doing all right - until all this stuff with McCallum and the heart. I wish I'd never got involved now.'

Over by the window I saw myself give a stiff smile. 'Crime doesn't pay.'

'Benny doesn't seem to have done too badly out of it,' Clover said, wafting a hand, her brow furrowed in a frown.

I saw myself glance around the room, shrug, pull a laconic face. 'Suppose so. Unless you count the fifteen, twenty years he's spent in prison. Not sure I'd consider that a worthy trade-off. Even for this little lot.'

Hang on. Had I really said that? Maybe, at the time, I'd been thinking it, but I'm pretty sure the words hadn't left my mouth.

Baffled, I saw Clover stretch, yawn. 'Horses for courses. I'm sure Benny's prison experiences were a lot different to yours.'

The other me snorted. 'I'm sure they were. When I was in Pentonville he ran that place like it was his own personal hotel. He even had the governor and the screws in his back pocket.'

'Screws,' she said with a mischievous smirk. 'You still speak the lingo then, Alex? Once a lag always a lag? Is that it?'

The me that was standing by the window laughed, and she laughed along with me. The me that was standing apart and undetected, however, was feeling uneasy. Wasn't it before now that the conversation had been interrupted by the darkness that Frank carried within him? Hadn't Clover's eyes widened just after her remark about Benny having done okay out of crime, and hadn't I turned to see blackness squirming across the outside of the glass like a mass of writhing black snakes made of smoke or oil?

I was certain I had. So where *was* Frank? Why wasn't he here? My sense of unease grew as I watched the past versions of Clover and me obliviously conducting a conversation I was sure we'd never had. She asked the other me about *my* background, and I then proceeded to tell her more than I'd told her previously about Kate and Lyn. Standing apart, I listened, incredulous (it was like watching a deleted scene from my own life), and as the conversation wore on, continuing for another five minutes, then ten, then fifteen, and still Frank failed to appear, my unease slowly blossomed into fear, and then into a heart-clenching sense of dread so awful that I found I could no longer take in what Clover and the other me were saying.

I wanted to scream at them, tell them to run, but all I could do was observe. The fact that they continued to chat blithely away, with no inkling that anything was wrong, was agonising. Even the fact that one of these two people was me, and that I knew this was not what had happened, made no difference to how I was feeling. The terror I felt was like being tied to a railway track with a train advancing through the darkness.

I heard a sound behind me – a fumbling at the door, a scuff of movement. My heart leaped. The fact that I was nothing but an invisible observer seemed at that moment irrelevant. I swung round. Benny was standing in the doorway. He was wearing a black, silky dressing gown, black leather slippers on his bare feet. He looked past me, at Clover in the armchair, at the other me still standing by the glass wall of the conservatory.

'What's this then?' he growled. 'Mothers' meeting?'

The other me raised an apologetic hand. 'Sorry, Benny, my fault. I couldn't sleep, came down to make myself a cuppa. I didn't mean to disturb anyone.'

Benny sniffed. He looked sceptical. 'That right?' He nodded at Clover. 'What about you, Monroe? You suffering from insomnia too?'

Before Clover could answer the other me said, 'That's my fault again. She heard me moving about and woke up.'

Benny shot the other me a sharp look. I expected him to say he'd been speaking to Clover, not me. But instead he said, 'Not sure how I feel about people sneaking round my house in the middle of the night.'

'Oh, come on, Benny,' said Clover. 'You're not serious? You honestly expect us to stay in our rooms during the hours of darkness?'

Benny moved into the room, all but brushing against me as he passed by. I didn't know why, but I was starting to get a very bad vibe about this situation; you might even have called it presentiment. But surely Benny wasn't the danger here? He was volatile, unpredictable even, but he wouldn't seriously do anything to endanger either of us, would he? Not at this point anyway.

He approached Clover, came to a halt beside her chair. Watching him I tensed, but Clover seemed relaxed in his presence.

'When people are in my house, I expect them to observe my rules,' he said quietly.

Clover gave him a quizzical look. 'I wasn't aware that there *were* any rules.'

'There are now,' Benny said, whereupon his hand shot out with incredible speed and grabbed her throat.

The other me by the window sprang forward, but almost immediately came to an abrupt halt, a look of horror on his face. It wasn't because Benny had barked, 'I wouldn't do that, Alex.' No, it was because Benny was changing.

The hand he'd used to grab Clover was transforming into a black, ropey tentacle. It was winding round and round her throat, stretching her neck, forcing her chin higher. Her face was already puffing up, turning red; her eyes were bulging. Awful choking sounds were coming from her mouth; her swollen tongue twitched.

'Let her go!' the other me roared, and suddenly the obsidian heart was in his (my) hand. He (I) brandished it like a grenade.

The shape-shifter in the guise of Benny merely smiled.

'Well done, Alex. You've saved me the bother of asking you to take that out of your pocket. Now look behind you.'

I could see something coming out of the darkness on the other side of the glass. Not Frank, but a huge, spider-like shape: the Dark Man's mechanical conveyance.

The other me ignored the shape-shifter's words. He refused to turn to see what was creeping up behind him.

'Let her go now or I'll fucking use this!' he (I) shouted.

The shape-shifter sniggered. 'I don't think you will. Because first, you don't really know how to. And second, I'll kill her the instant you try anything. How confident are you that the heart will stop me before I end her life?'

Clover's face was turning purple. Her eyes were flickering. The other me cast an agonised glance from the shape-shifter to Clover, torn by indecision.

The shape-shifter smiled. It was a warm smile. Friendly. It looked completely alien on Benny's face. It transformed his features into a grotesque mask.

'Sensible boy,' the shape-shifter said. 'Now, as I was saying, if you turn and look behind you, you'll see–'

And that was when Clover struck.

I thought she was on the verge of unconsciousness. Maybe she was. Maybe her action was instinctive, a final desperate attempt to survive before blackness claimed her.

The sequence of events happened quickly. It took everyone by surprise, including the shape-shifter. One moment Clover's hands were hanging limply by her side, the next she'd grabbed the red-shaded table lamp from beside her and had thrust it like a glowing red sword directly into the shape-shifter's face.

The red lampshade crumpled, the bulb beneath it exploded. There was a bang and a white flash and the shape-shifter let out a roar of pain or rage.

Almost simultaneously, as the shape-shifter lurched backwards, there was a crack sound, like a whiplash, and suddenly Clover's head separated from her body. It seemed to leap upwards from her shoulders as though on a spring, to spin through the air, trailing a flowing ripple of hair and a scatter of droplets that looked black in the sudden murk. I saw her headless body slump to one side, saw the other me's face expand with horror, eyes and mouth opening wide.

Was it me or the other me who screamed? Or did we scream together? All I know is that the jolting shock pulled me out of the moment. This time there was a sense not of shifting, but of being wrenched, physically and spiritually, from an intolerable situation. I felt momentarily like a bungee jumper who, having reached the end of his elasticated rope, is snapped back up into the air again.

The world rushed by. Dark became light. I was disorientated. Was I shouting or was someone shouting at me? I struggled, felt a weight on me, holding me down.

My body was stinging all over. When I moved, something crunched.

Then I heard Clover's voice: 'Hold still, Alex. Stop wriggling. You'll make it worse.'

I was so overjoyed to hear her, to know she was alive, that I obeyed without question. I stopped struggling. I opened my eyes.

There were two faces above me. In between them was part of a white ceiling. The faces belonged to Benny and Clover. Benny was scowling; Clover looked scared.

'Back with us, are you?' Benny said.

I blinked up at him. 'What happened?'

It was Clover who answered. 'You fell, Alex. You just collapsed.'

'Right on to my glass table,' Benny growled. 'Smashed it to fucking bits.'

TWENTY-FOUR

HEALING

I stood by the window, my left hand resting on one of the three horizontal bars that prevented suicidal residents from diving through the glass on to the gravel below. I could see beads of moisture, reflecting the autumn sunlight, glittering on the huge, wet expanse of lawn, creating a gentle green shimmer that soothed my busy mind and gave me a rare and welcome moment of calm. It was so peaceful here, but then I suppose it had to be to counteract the frantic chatter of agitated minds contained within these walls. I'd always thought that being crazy must be like living inside your own private hell – unless, of course, you were too crazy to realise that that's where you were.

Eventually I turned from the window and looked across the room at Lyn. She was sitting in the chair by the dressing table, cupping the obsidian heart in her hands. She was motionless, her eyes half closed, a blissful expression on her face.

'Are you all right?' I asked her.

Without looking at me she murmured, 'I'm more than all right. I can feel myself healing.'

I didn't know if that was true, though I couldn't deny that the improvement in her since the last time I'd seen her was amazing. She still did everything slowly, cautiously, as if afraid of upsetting some delicate internal balance, but there was a brightness about her, a spark of understanding, of intelligence, that I hadn't seen in... years.

When I'd first walked into her room that morning, she'd not only smiled and said, 'Hello, Alex,' but had stood up from her chair and crossed the carpet to greet me, even reaching out to take both of my hands in hers. The genuine warmth she'd shown had made me so immediately choked up I'd been unable to speak. It had been a long time since Lyn had been so self-aware, since she'd truly been able to read and respond to the emotions of others. When she saw the way I was gaping at her she laughed.

'I know what you're thinking,' she said, 'and I can't believe it either. I've been drowning for such a long time, Alex. Drowning in the dark. I've been so scared. I didn't know where I was. But since you sent the Dark Man away I've been much better.'

I'd glanced at Dr Bruce, who was eyeing me watchfully, waiting for my reaction.

'Could you give us some privacy?' I asked her, smiling.

She hadn't liked it, but she'd nodded curtly and left. It was Dr Bruce who'd told me of Lyn's dramatic and continuing improvement when I'd arrived, but hearing about it second-hand and actually witnessing it were two different things.

As soon as Dr Bruce had gone, Lyn asked me, 'Did you bring it?'

I nodded.

She gave a sort of shudder. 'Can I hold it? I won't damage it. I know how important it is. But just knowing it's contained, that it's trapped...' she shuddered again '...you can't know how happy, how *free*, that makes me feel.'

So I gave the heart to her, and immediately she let out a deep sigh and sank back into her chair, half closing her eyes. I watched her for a moment, wondering whether I should talk to her, ask her the questions I'd come to ask, wondering how responsive she'd be. But after a few seconds I decided to leave it until she'd finished her meditations and had handed the heart back to me, and I went and stood by the window and looked out over the rolling lawns and gardens that surrounded Darby Hall.

It was two days since I'd collapsed in Benny's house and demolished his glass coffee table. Miraculously, apart from a couple of minor nicks and a bruise on my hip, I hadn't been injured in the fall. Clover had driven me straight back to Oak Hill, where I'd been checked over by Dr Wheeler, who'd pronounced me fit and well but still very much in need of rest. If it had been up to me I'd have made the trip down to Brighton to see Lyn the next day, but Clover had insisted I put my feet up and take it easy for another twenty-four hours. So I'd sat in the house at Ranskill Gardens swaddled in blankets and watching an old Gary Cooper Western on TV. It had been weird sitting in the room where Hawkins had died, and still feeling raw over his death, even though, in linear terms, it had happened over a century before.

Although the decor and contents of the room had altered drastically since the 1890s, one thing that had survived was the fireplace from which the shape-shifter had emerged, complete with its original tiled surround – though the tiles were now crazed and faded. Even though the house now had central heating I'd insisted on building a real fire, which I'd spent a good portion of the rest of the day alternately gazing in to and dozing in front of. At one point I'd seen Kate's face in the flames, only to jerk forward so violently I'd woken myself up. I'd wondered what would happen if I simply dropped the heart into the fire and had done with it. I'd wondered too, watching the smoke spiral up the flue, whether the shape-shifter, or a piece of it, was still up there somewhere, embedded in the fabric of the house, biding its time.

Although what had happened to me at Benny's house had disturbed me I kept it to myself. I don't know why. Perhaps because I didn't want to risk Clover using it as proof that I wasn't yet well enough to press on with our strategy. Or perhaps because I was worried about what it might signify and didn't want to hear her put it into words – not yet anyway.

Strategy. It was a highfalutin word for what we were really doing, which was simply clearing the decks and setting out our stall. Visiting Lyn had been my idea, but Clover had been wary about it. It wasn't the fact that I wanted to see Lyn and gauge her progress that bothered her; it was that by 'interrogating' Lyn (her word, not mine), Clover thought I might be on a hiding to nothing.

'I can't see anything coming of it, Alex,' she'd said. 'Added to which you might only end up upsetting her even more.'

'How do *you* know nothing will come of it?' I retorted.

'Because if something *does*, then it already would have, and we wouldn't be having this conversation. I just don't think it's possible to change the past to such an extent. I think it might be dangerous to even try.'

I was silent for a moment, then I said, 'You think, but you don't know. Neither of us knows.'

'No, I *don't* know. But that's my theory all the same. Since Hawkins died, I've started to think that...' she paused, trying to order her thoughts '...well, that small changes might be possible, but not big ones. I think big ones might disrupt the... the *time stream*, or whatever you want to call it, too much.'

'But what about the multiverse?' I said. 'All those alternate pasts and futures?'

At which point she'd thrown up her hands in exasperation.

'Oh, I don't know! I just... don't know!'

That had settled it. We'd agreed – or at least, sort of agreed – that if something *couldn't* be changed then maybe it *wouldn't* be; that Time or Fate or whatever would simply intervene and disallow it. But we'd also agreed that there was no harm in trying – or rather, we hadn't agreed, but I'd argued the toss until Clover had become ground down enough to accept that I was going to try regardless. Secretly I knew as well as she did that we didn't know enough about the possible consequences of our actions, and that there might, therefore, actually be a *great deal* of harm in trying. But from where *I* was standing, I felt it was worth the risk.

When Lyn said she could feel herself healing I crossed the room and perched myself on the edge of the bed, facing her.

'That's the best news I've heard all year.' Without thinking I added, 'I'd give anything in the world to get the old you back.'

She cast her eyes downwards, and there followed a moment not only of awkwardness between us, but of sadness, of regret, for the years we'd lost.

'Don't raise your hopes too much, Alex,' she said quietly. 'I'm not sure *that's* going to happen.'

I tried to be encouraging, but it ended up sounding like empty bluster – to my ears anyway. 'You never know. I mean, I know a lot's changed, and that we're both different people now. And I know there's still a long way to go before we could even think of—'

'Stop. Just... stop.'

I did. She was frowning, breathing hard, her eyes still staring down at the heart in her hand. For a moment I thought I'd pushed it too hard, that because of me the dark clouds were going to move in again and blot out the light of what was still a very fragile sun.

When she next spoke, though, I was relieved to hear that her voice was calm. A little trembly, but calm.

'I can't even begin to think of anything beyond getting better just now. It's just... it's too much. Sorry, Alex.'

'Hey,' I said gently. 'No need to apologise. I'm the one who should be saying sorry. I'm an idiot.'

'Let's neither of us say it,' she said. 'Let's just... relish what we've got right now.'

'Suits me.'

She held out the heart. 'Here, take it. Keep it safe. Keep it *contained*.'

'I will. I promise.'

She raised her eyes and looked at me. 'How's our daughter, Alex? How's Kate?'

To say the question was like a punch in the face was an understatement, though perhaps I should have expected it. In fact, I definitely should have. I should have realised that once Lyn's mind started to clear, Kate's welfare would be one of the first things she'd think about. She was the child's mother, after all. It was only natural. Yet for a second or two after she asked me the question, I felt she already knew everything, and was accusing me, or trying to catch me out. I felt an urge to throw myself on her mercy, apologise for letting her down, for not looking after our daughter well enough.

Then she frowned, and I realised she knew nothing at all.

'What's the matter?' she asked, alarm creeping into her voice. 'Kate *is* all right, isn't she?'

I laughed. Probably too brashly, but it seemed to undo the knot of concern forming between her eyes.

'Course she is,' I said. 'She's fine. She's flourishing.' It killed me to keep smiling. 'I was just surprised, that's all. To hear you ask about her, I mean.'

'I've been thinking about her a lot. Since I last saw you, I've been thinking about a lot of things I haven't thought about in...' She wafted a hand.

Terrified she might suggest I could bring Kate along with me next time I came for a visit, I asked quickly, 'Do you know how long you've been in here, Lyn?'

She looked at me even more searchingly, a trace of fearful wonder in her eyes.

'They tell me... they tell me it's been five years.' I could see she wanted me to laugh, to poo-poo the idea. Her voice dropped to a murmur. 'It hasn't been *that* long, has it, Alex? It *can't* have been that long.'

Her hands, empty of the heart, were now resting limply in her lap. After a moment's hesitation I reached out and took them. They were cold.

'How long do *you* feel it's been?'

She shook her head. 'A day? Forever? I honestly don't know.' She looked out of the window, as if she could gauge time by the clouds, the sky. 'How old is Kate now, Alex? Is she all grown up?'

'Of course not,' I said. 'She's five.'

'Five,' she repeated, a whispering echo. 'So it's true.'

I squeezed her hands tighter, as if to keep her with me.

'What would you say if I told you I'd found a way of turning back time? What if I said I could change all of this, everything that's happened since you met the Dark Man, by going back and stopping him from ever meeting you? What if I said I could get our future, the future we were meant to have together, back for us?'

She was looking at me as if I was some strange and wonderful creature she had never seen before. When she smiled I saw the old Lyn appear behind her ravaged features – just for an instant. A fleeting glimpse, and then gone.

'I'd say you were as mad as me,' she replied, her voice warm with affection and humour. 'I'd say you needed to book yourself a room here.'

I smiled along with her. 'Ordinarily you'd be right. But I vanquished the Dark Man, didn't I? I took his darkness.'

'What are you saying?'

I gave her hands another squeeze. 'I'm saying you should never give up hope. I'm saying that miracles happen. There's something I need you to do for me, Lyn. It may be the most important thing you've *ever* done.'

'What is it?' she whispered.

'I need you to think back to when you first met the Dark Man. I need you to remember the exact date.'

TWENTY-FIVE
WHAT MIGHT HAVE HAPPENED

Over the next couple of days I had three more visions. That's to say, I had three more episodes like the one I'd had in Benny's house. Given that I found myself revisiting specific events in my past rather than having premonitions of the future, I'm not sure 'visions' is the right word to describe the experiences – but that's what they felt like all the same. I'd be going about my business when all of a sudden that weird sensation of *shifting* would wash over me, and the next moment I'd find myself in another place, another time.

Although the vision I'd had in Benny's house had started off by tallying with the exact memory of the conversation I'd had with Clover in the conservatory, only one of the subsequent visions (the second of the three) followed the same pattern. In the first I *did* find myself in familiar surroundings, though my memory of what had happened there deviated pretty much from the get-go. In the most recent – which was also the most disorientating, and in some ways the most horrible – I found myself in a place and a situation I'd never been in before, and never wanted to be in again. I emerged from this one not just shocked and horrified, but shaking and crying.

One factor that each vision *did* share was that I was never part of the action, but merely an observer. In the first I found myself back in my cell in Pentonville with my twenty-year-old self. The past me was sitting cross-legged on his (my) bunk, head bowed over a book, which was open in his (my) lap, forefingers pressed into his (my) ears to muffle the ever-present prison din. The current me had a strong feeling that the book, a thick and hefty tome, was *Psychology of Behaviour*, which I'd been reading when Benny had first paid me a visit.

So was this the same day? Was I about to witness a reenactment of that meeting? I stared at my past self in the familiar grey prison sweatshirt and marvelled at how skinny and callow I looked, even whilst feeling a sense of deep apprehension at what might be about to happen. The past me was engrossed in the book, and the present me was engrossed in the sight of my past self, narcissistic though that might sound. Both our heads snapped up when the cell door closed with a bang.

The present me, standing with my back to the wall opposite the door, saw that three men had entered the cell. In my split-second assessment of them I registered that they were big, meaty, mean looking. One had slick black hair and dark stubble and one was a squat, round-shouldered skinhead with blue tattoos on the backs of his hands and up the sides of his neck. The third man didn't make much of an impression except as a threatening presence, the reason being that what happened next happened so quickly, without any words being exchanged, that it seemed hardly more than a blur.

As I might have said before, violence in prison is swift, shocking and brutal. There's rarely any preamble, rarely any name-calling or squaring up. It's almost a functional thing, a way of subduing and incapacitating your opponent as quickly and efficiently as possible. Before the past me could move, except to look up from his book, the three men had crossed the cell.

The past me was still sitting cross-legged when the first man - the skinhead - swung a haymaker into the side of his (my) face. The blow connected with such a sickening crunch I felt sure my cheekbone must have shattered. I watched my past self fall back, the book sliding from his lap and hitting the floor. One of the other assailants - the one whose appearance had barely registered - swept the book up and started battering him about the head and body with it. I saw his (my) hands flapping ineffectually in an attempt to fight the men off. The guy with the slick black hair grabbed my past self's feet and ran backwards a few steps, yanking him off his bunk. The present me winced as the past me landed with a thump, cracking his skull on the stone floor. Immediately the men started to kick and punch and stamp on him (me). There was the meaty crack of flesh impacting on flesh. There was the sound of crunching bone. There was a lot of blood.

Throughout the attack, which lasted maybe a minute but seemed much longer, my past self – barely conscious now – just lay there. Now and again, through the melee, I saw his (my) head and feet jerk up, in the way the opposite ends of a cushion will jerk up if you hit it in the middle. My past self looked less like a person than a thing, a punch bag that was being pummelled even though it had snapped from its supports and was now prone on the floor.

Finally one of the men – the skinhead, I think – spoke the only three words I heard any of them use during the attack: 'Roll him over.'

Mercifully I jerked from the scene just as they were yanking down my trousers and underpants.

In the second vision I *shifted* from sitting at the kitchen table in Ranskill Gardens, where I was eating a tuna salad sandwich and talking to Clover, to standing beneath an arch looking out on what appeared to be a candlelit stone cavern. At first my mind reeled as I tried to work out how Clover had gone from emptying a dishwasher to being chained inside a large cage in the blink of an eye.

Then I realised. These were the stone tunnels beneath Commer House in the Isle of Dogs. The ones to which I'd been lured to rescue what turned out to be a splinter of the shape-shifter in the form of Clover – who, you'll no doubt remember, had later been taken by surprise and despatched by Hulse whilst in her vulnerable human form, very likely on the orders of my future self.

The past me, who was currently pressed up against the bars of the cage, obsidian heart in hand, urging it in vain to do its stuff, knew none of that, of course. I wished I could tell him (me), but I couldn't. I couldn't do anything. As before, I was little more than a ghost.

I heard the unreal Clover say, 'It's no good, Alex. You've got to go, before he comes back.'

You're only saying that because you know there's no way I'll abandon you, I thought bitterly, before the past me replied, 'Don't worry. If I can get the heart to work, it'll protect us from that freak who attacked us in Incognito – him *and* his army.'

I frowned. Hang on. Was that what I'd originally said? It didn't sound right somehow.

Before I had time to ponder on it, the unreal Clover said, 'That wasn't who took me.'

The past me looked surprised. 'Who was it then?'

'It was me!'

I turned my head, already knowing what I would see. Barnaby McCallum was stepping from the shadow of one of the arched openings about fifty metres away.

It wasn't the real McCallum, of course. It was yet another splinter of the shape-shifter.

The past me gaped at him. 'But you're dead. I killed you.'

'Appearances can be deceptive.' The shape-shifter in McCallum's form pointed at the heart in my hand. 'Now, I believe you have some property of mine. Perhaps you should give it back before someone gets seriously hurt.'

I frowned again. *What's wrong with this picture?* I thought. Then, as the false McCallum took a lurching step forward, I realised.

No Frank.

Again. He hadn't appeared in my earlier vision and now he wasn't here either.

The past me stood with the heart held above his (my) head, as if it was a rock he was intending to lob at the old man.

'Hang on a minute,' I heard my past self say. 'Don't come any closer. I want to know what's going on. I want to know why you aren't dead. Most of all, I want to know where my daughter is.'

The shape-shifter smiled. It was a warm smile. Reassuring.

'So many questions. Though I can hardly blame you, I suppose. As regards what's going on and why I'm not dead, it's... complicated, Alex. Let's leave it at that. As regards your daughter, I'm pleased to say I have information that will lead to her recovery. Rest assured, I simply want what's best for all of us. What's *right*.'

The past me looked uncertain, suspicious, though I could see that he was desperate to believe the old man.

'How do I know you're telling the truth?' he said.

McCallum rolled his eyes. 'Oh, for goodness' sake.'

And then he came apart.

It was like before – one second he was standing there, the next he became a mass of slithering snakes; of insects, both flying and scuttling, that erupted outwards in all directions. The big difference this time, though, was that Frank wasn't there to throw up a wall of darkness against them. They swarmed, unimpeded, towards the past me in a crackling, rustling, buzzing wave.

I saw the past me swing back to the cage, saw him begin once again to bash the heart against the bars. Although his (my) voice was muffled by the rush of creatures, I could hear him frantically muttering, 'Come on, come on, *come on.*'

Last time this had happened, Frank had stopped a good ninety-nine per cent of the advancing wave of creatures in their tracks. The heart had finally erupted into life only when a weakened shred of the shape-shifter, in the form of a huge moth, had stung me on the back of the neck.

This time was different. This time the creatures were on me before the heart could respond – or at least, before it *did* respond. Watching from the sidelines I was shocked not only by the sight of the creatures swarming over my past self and literally taking him apart (once again there was blood; a *lot* of blood), but also because I had previously assumed, or at least hoped, that with the heart in my possession I was more or less invulnerable; that if ever I was physically threatened, it would respond immediately and protect me.

Not so. Not in this vision anyway.

I came to lying on the kitchen floor, with Clover bending over me. When I'd had the vision where I'd found myself in Pentonville I'd woken up alone in the sitting room, hunched in an armchair in front of the fire, slumped to one side with drool leaking out of the side of my mouth. I hadn't said anything to Clover about that vision, just as I hadn't mentioned the first one to her either, and so as far as she was concerned, this was the second occasion where, for no discernible reason, I'd phased out.

'I'm fine,' I said as she helped me sit up, 'I slipped.'

'You didn't slip,' she said. 'You passed out. Just like before.'

'No I didn't. I'm still a bit wobbly, that's all. I tried to stand up – I was going to get myself a drink – but my leg couldn't take the weight. My knee buckled and I went down. But I'm fine, honestly. It wasn't like before.'

'It *was* like before. You didn't just fall, Alex, you were completely out. I'm taking you back to Oak Hill right now. Something's wrong with you. It might be something ser—'

'*Oh, for fuck's sake!*' I bellowed, shocking her.

My anger was out of proportion, and as soon as the outburst was over I was ashamed of it. I knew Clover was only showing concern, and I wasn't angry with *her* specifically. It was just that I was worried and confused about what might be happening and why, and frustrated by the simple fact that I didn't *need* this, that I had to find Kate and couldn't afford to let anything hamper me.

I apologised to her as humbly as I could, and reminded her that the last time she'd taken me back to Oak Hill, after my blackout at Benny's, Dr Wheeler had found nothing wrong with me.

'I can't afford for them to keep me in,' I said. 'I can't afford to waste any more time having tests.'

'You can't afford to drop dead of a fucking stroke or brain haemorrhage either!'

'It won't come to that.'

'How do you know?'

'I just do. This is... different. Look, just trust me, okay? I'll be fine.'

Finally she agreed to let me be – not that she could have *made* me go back to Oak Hill without bludgeoning me unconscious and dragging me physically out to the car – but she did make me promise that if I had another blackout I *would* go, not only for my own sake, but for Kate's.

I agreed, keeping my fingers crossed that either my visions were finally over or that if I *did* have another one it would happen when I was alone, and she would therefore hear nothing about it.

I was bang out of luck on both accounts.

The next time I *shifted*, only a matter of hours after the argument with Clover, I found myself in a small, rectangular room with a brown carpet and white walls. The room was featureless except for two chairs, which were upholstered in olive-green PVC and positioned side by side against one of the long walls. The chairs faced what I guessed was a screen or a window or perhaps a large painting, concealed behind a pair of pale blue curtains with a pull cord at one side. Although the room could not have been plainer, I immediately felt an unfocused but acute dread mounting inside me – not because I necessarily felt that bad things had happened here, but more from a sense that bad memories *could be*, and *had been*, made here - the kind that could become embedded in the mind like sharp stones and forever cause pain.

Please, I thought, without knowing who or what I was appealing to, *take me away from here. I don't want this.*

But it was no good. I couldn't move, couldn't leave, couldn't even close my eyes.

All I could do was watch as the door in the narrow wall at the far end of the room opened and two people came through.

One was a man in a suit - balding, glasses; I barely registered him.

The other was me.

If I could have gasped I would have done. I looked dreadful. Not only ill, not only haggard, but *haunted* - my face etched with such pain, such despair, that I felt terribly, instantly afraid. Even though I couldn't move I felt my soul, my essence, if such a thing exists, shrinking away from this appalling representation of what I had, or could, become. It was as if the other me had an infection so virulent it could spread through the multiverse, affecting each and every one of my alternate selves.

The other me stumbled and the man in the suit reached out to grab his arm.

'Are you all right, Mr Locke?'

Of course I'm not fucking all right! I retorted silently, and saw a flash of that thought echoed on the other me's face.

But he simply nodded. 'I'll manage.'

'Would you like to sit for a few minutes to gather yourself? Perhaps a glass of water?'

The other me shook his head curtly. 'Let's just get it over with.'

The man in the suit nodded solicitously. Indicating the curtains he said, 'Behind here is a window. Through it you will see a brightly lit room containing a trolley on which the deceased will be lying. The deceased will be covered in a sheet. As soon as you're ready, Mr Locke, and not a moment before, a colleague of mine, who will be standing beside the trolley, will fold back the sheet, revealing the face of the deceased. You will then be required to confirm the deceased's identity - or not, as the case may be. Do you understand?'

The other me gave another curt nod and barely whispered, 'Yes.'

The man in the suit reached for the curtain cord. 'Very well. If you could step a little closer to the curtain? That's it... Now, if you're ready?'

I saw the past me's hands clench at the ends of ramrod-straight arms. Another papery whisper: 'Ready.'

With a faint grinding swish the curtains peeled back. Beyond them was exactly what the man had promised: a brightly lit room, a trolley, a body beneath a sheet. On the far side of the trolley, his face carefully neutral, stood a burly man with close-cropped ginger hair, wearing a blue V-neck surgical top over a white T-shirt.

The other me gave a low moan. The man in the suit glanced at him, but said nothing. A moment went by. The other me shuddered. Then he (I) turned to the suited man, his head moving so slowly it made me think of a rusty automaton coming to life after years of inactivity.

'Okay.'

The suited man's lips twitched in sympathy and support. He turned to the ginger man in the surgical top and nodded. The ginger man reached out, his hands encased in latex gloves, and almost daintily folded back the top of the sheet. The other me moaned again and seemed to sag. Between the other me and the man in the suit I saw the waxy face of the deceased, who the other me had come here to identify.

It was my eldest daughter, Candice.

The shock jolted me back to my own reality. I came to, flailing, screaming out denials, as if that alone would enable me to unsee what I'd seen. I felt a weight on me, holding me down, clamps tightening on my arms. My vision was a blur, a confused smear of colour and movement. I struggled, blinked, and realised that the reason I couldn't see was because my eyes were full of tears. I blinked more rapidly to clear them. My eyes focused.

Déjà vu. Here was Clover again. Bending over me. Hair falling around her face. Large, widely spaced eyes full of fear, alarm... and anger too. Anger at me for point-blank refusing to go back to Oak Hill. Anger at herself for allowing me to persuade her I was okay.

'Alex!' she was saying, and from the way she was saying it I guessed it wasn't the first time. 'Alex, can you hear me?'

I forced myself to stop screaming, to stop saying no. I tried to nod and realised I was shaking so much I could barely control my movements. When I tried to speak I couldn't stop my teeth from chattering.

'Alex!' she repeated. 'Are you with me or not? Do you know where you are?'

With an almighty effort I wrestled free of the involuntary spasms racing through my body. I clamped my mouth shut and closed my eyes tight, then opened them again.

'Yes,' I whispered, and this time felt only a slight judder in my jawbone, as though a low electrical charge was running through me. 'Yes, I know where I am. I'm back. I'm fine. I had another one, didn't I?'

'Yes, you fucking did.' Anxiety was making her cross. 'And you are definitely *not* fine. This time you're going back to Oak Hill. I don't care *what* you say. In fact, you promised, so that's that.'

My faculties were slowly returning. Glancing around I realised where I was - in the bathroom on the second floor - and what I'd been doing when I'd blacked out: washing my hands.

Things could have been worse. If the vision had come a couple of minutes earlier I'd have toppled off the toilet where I'd been sitting, and would now be lying on the bathroom floor covered in my own shit with my jeans and boxer shorts round my ankles.

I moved my head and winced as a throb of pain went through my temple. I put my hand up to the sore spot and winced again. There was a lump there and it hurt like hell. I must have caught it a whack on the sink or the side of the bath when I went down.

'It's not what you think,' I said.

Clover rolled her eyes. 'Don't give me that crap.'

Still lying on my back, I raised my hands, as if warding off an attack from a wild animal.

'No, listen. I'll go to Oak Hill if you want me to. But I want to talk to you first. I want to explain. I should have told you straight away.'

'Told me what?'

'These... episodes. They're not strokes or fits. I don't think they're physical at all. They're... mental attacks. Well, maybe not even attacks. Warnings.'

She shook her head. 'You're not making sense.'

'Help me up and I'll explain.'

When she did I discovered that I'd caught my knee a good one too, probably on the floor when I went down. It was now throbbing like a bastard, and made me cry out when I tried to put my weight on it.

With my arm around Clover's shoulders I limped into my bedroom – the one I'd woken up in after taking a pounding from Hulse and his cronies the first time I'd found myself in Victorian London; the one where a future version of me had appeared on the night Hawkins had died and persuaded me to change history, and because of that had then never had cause to exist.

'So?' Clover said, hands on hips, after I'd flopped with a grunt onto the bed.

I shuffled up the mattress until my back was against the headboard and I could stretch out my injured leg. Then I gestured towards the chair where the future me had once sat.

'Sit down a minute.'

She sighed, but did as I asked.

'Every time I blacked out I went somewhere,' I said. 'I revisited my past – except I didn't. Because on each occasion something had changed.'

She frowned, but before she could say anything I launched into an explanation of what had happened during each of my visions. The longer I spoke the more thoughtful and worried-looking she became. Finally I told her about the latest vision; about how I'd found myself in a morgue or a coroner's office, or wherever it was that someone went to identify a relative's body (I hoped I'd never have to find out, never have to go through the experience for real) and what I'd seen there.

'It was awful, Clover.' My voice had started to shake again. 'I mean, they were *all* awful, but that was the worst. No offence. It's just...'

'I know,' Clover said almost bluntly. 'Candice is your daughter. Your own flesh and blood. Her death – her *perceived* death – is bound to affect you more than... well, more than anyone else's.'

I fell silent. She was frowning, almost scowling. Despite what she'd said I wondered whether I *had* offended her by saying that seeing Candice lying dead in the morgue had been worse than seeing Clover beheaded by the shape-shifter.

I was about to say something, if only to break the silence, when she muttered, 'You say you thought these visions might be warnings?'

I nodded.

'Of what might happen if you don't use the heart again?'

'Yeah.' I used my fingers to count off each specific future action. 'If I don't save Frank; if I don't pay Benny to protect me in prison; if I don't pay off Candice's boyfriend's debt...'

Still frowning she said, 'Except these... scenes you've been shown, these visions... they don't quite tally, do they?'

'What do you mean?'

'Well, take the first vision at Benny's house, and then the third one in the tunnels. If you don't meet Frank, and I die in Benny's conservatory as a result, then you'd never have been lured to the Isle of Dogs to save me, would you? I mean, I'd already be dead, so that future would never happen.'

'So what are you saying? That the visions are false?'

'I think they're... I don't know... fabrications? Dramatic fictions?'

I thought about it. 'You mean they're not *really* real? They're not alternate bits of this multiverse of yours I'm being shown? They're just... what? Dreams?'

'More than dreams, maybe. Worst-case scenarios. But fictions all the same.'

'But they're still warnings? They're still examples of the kinds of things that *might* happen if I don't do what I'm supposed to do – if I miss an appointment, as it were?'

Clover shrugged. 'Maybe. But I'm not sure how it works. I mean, we're *here*, aren't we? We've arrived at this point in our lives. I *wasn't* killed by the shape-shifter in Benny's conservatory.'

'But time is flexible,' I said, thinking again of the future me who had appeared at my bedside on the night Hawkins had been killed, the one whose warning had caused me to change what I might otherwise had done, thus negating the need for me to go back in time and issue the warning to my past self in the first place. 'It's not solid. If things change in the future, then maybe the past can be... I don't know... rolled back. Reshaped. The multiverse, remember. Maybe if I don't do what I'm supposed to do, this present, the one we're living in now, will disappear, or be shunted into another reality or something.'

'And I'll die,' said Clover. 'And Candice will die. And maybe even you'll die too.'

I shrugged. 'Maybe.'

She threw up her hands. 'But how *can* you use the heart again? We've already established that it's killing you. There's no way you'd survive another...' she groped for the appropriate word '...blast!'

'Maybe not,' I said. 'But I have to try. I don't think I've got a choice. I have to find a way.'

'*What* way?' she said, and this time it was her frustration that was making her angry. 'What way could there possibly be?'

'I've no idea,' I admitted.

TWENTY-SIX

PROVING IT

I've always loved the sea.

Even as a kid, spending odd days or holidays in Brighton or Margate, Southend or Selsey Bill, the sea meant more to me than ice creams and sandcastles and fish and chips. There'd be a part of me, even back then, that would respond to it on an instinctive level, that would recognise, in comparison to its dispassionate, eternal vastness, how tiny and insignificant we were, and how petty were our cares and concerns. I might not have been able to articulate those feelings back then, but I felt them all the same. It didn't frighten me or make me sad; on the contrary, it soothed me. Even as young as seven or eight I'd find a place on the beach to be by myself – if there were rocks, where I could hide myself away in a crevice, so much the better – and I'd happily sit and watch the tide coming in and out for hours. I loved its ceaseless rhythmic shushing; I loved the way the sea looked – glossy and dimpled on the surface, like beaten tin, white and foamy and fizzing at the edges, where it crashed against the jagged black rocks. And I loved the way it moved – sinewy and rippling, like something alive. I'd watch it and I'd forget who I was; I'd become mesmerised by it. I'd imagine the breeze blowing in to shore was its breath ruffling my hair. I'd lick my lips and taste a delicious fishy saltiness.

Once, I remember, I was gone so long that my parents thought I'd either been snatched by a kiddie fiddler or swept out to sea. They had people scouring the area, looking for me. They'd been on the verge of calling out the coastguard, alerting the local lifeboat station, when I turned up, drowsy and smiling, all my worries washed away by the tide. My dad ruined my mood by giving me a clip round the ear, which I felt I didn't deserve, and my mum was weepy for the rest of the day – not because of what had happened, but at the thought of what *might* have.

Even that didn't stop me going off by myself, though, seeking solace in the sea whenever I got the chance. I liked my own company. Always have. If I'd had brothers or sisters it might have been different, but I can't remember ever feeling alone, ever envying friends who came from larger families.

Standing on the beach, staring at the sea now, dark grey and choppy, like churning chunks of slate, I was reminded of those bygone days. Back then, of course, it had always been summer; now it was autumn and the sky looked murky and charred, and the wind flying in off the crashing waves felt like blades of ice that sliced the skin but left no marks.

Bygone days. Innocent ones too. The sea still made me feel insignificant, but it no longer had the ability to shrink my problems.

I looked at my watch. It was almost 10:20 a.m. I'd arranged the meeting for 10:30, but had wanted to get here early, to suss out the territory and work out exactly what I was going to say.

Turning my head quickly left and right, I scanned the beach in both directions. The bay was enclosed – backed by cliffs, from the top of which a footpath zigzagged down like a scar, and bordered to left and right by promontories of jagged black rock, against which waves crashed with tremendous force at high tide.

I'd selected the location carefully. I'd wanted somewhere remote, somewhere I'd be more likely to be listened to, where it wouldn't be easy for the other person to just stand up and walk away. There was a café on the cliff top – a rectangular flat-roofed building that was virtually all glass on the seaward side so that customers could enjoy the ocean view whilst sitting in the warmth, sipping their lattes and hot chocolates – but even though it was little used at this time of year it had still been too public for my purposes. I knew the meeting was likely to be difficult. I knew too that if the other person broke his word it was likely to be over before it had even begun. There was nowhere for me to run to here, nowhere to hide.

'I'll tell you everything,' I'd said to him on the phone. 'But only if you come alone.'

He hadn't liked it, but I'd stuck to my guns. And in the end, he'd agreed.

I looked out to sea again. I'd hoped it would clear my mind, but all it did was reflect my thoughts: dark, churning, never still. Its vastness didn't soothe me now; if anything, it emphasised how hopeless my quest was, how impossible it would be to find Kate without help.

'Where are you?' I murmured. '*When* are you?'

The sea roared and the wind howled in reply.

I glanced at my watch again. 10:26. I continued to stare doggedly out to sea, trying to settle myself. There was an imaginary itch between my shoulder blades, and the bruise on my temple throbbed where the cold wind flailed against it, but I refused to turn round. There was no point in it. No point in anxiously scouring the cliff path to see whether he would come, whether he would be alone. For now, at least, my immediate future was in the hands of fate.

Although my senses were attuned I didn't hear his footsteps on the sand, not even when he was right behind me. I only knew he was standing there when he spoke. Even then the wind snatched at his voice, shaving off the sharp edges, making it seem further away than it was.

'Who the fuck do you think you are? Pissing me about like this?'

I turned to face him, the wind buffeting me from behind, as if trying to push us together. Whether DI Jensen's long, knobbly face was white with anger or simply scoured bloodless by the elements I couldn't tell. There was no mistaking his expression, though. He looked seriously pissed off. His lips were pressed tightly together, his eyes so wide and glaring you could see the whites all the way round his pupils. Even his sparse hair, as colourless as the rest of him, looked angry as it whipped about in the wind.

'Thanks for coming,' I said, glancing behind him and seeing that he had, indeed, seemed to have kept his word.

His face curled in a snarl. 'Bollocks to that.'

I didn't respond to his anger. He was entitled to it. Since reporting Kate's disappearance I'd fucked him about big time.

He took an almost aggressive step towards me, half raised a hand as if to punch me in the face. I was wary, but still I tried not to react, and he ended up slashing at the air.

'So what the fuck is this?'

My own hands were in the pockets of my coat, my tension, my nervousness, centred in them, out of sight. My left hand was balled into a fist, my right clenched around the obsidian heart.

'I'm sorry,' I said. 'I know it's unorthodox—'

'*Unorthodox!*' He snorted.

'But I needed to meet you somewhere... neutral. Out of the way. I've got a long, crazy, complicated, ridiculous story to tell, but it also happens to be the truth, which is what I thought you deserved. I'm just... I'm sick of lying. Sick of running. I thought it was time to... confess all. Get everything out in the open.'

He glanced around, as if sensing a trap.

'What are you involved in, Mr Locke? Are you in danger? Is someone threatening you?'

I almost barked a laugh, but managed to turn it into a half snort, half shrug.

'Yes and yes. But it's not as simple as that.'

Before I could elaborate he was at me again, snapping like a terrier.

'Do you know who's holding Kate? Do you know where she is? Is that why you've been so evasive? Because of what her abductors have threatened to do to her if you talk?'

I half closed my eyes, as though his words were sand blowing into my face.

'Please, Inspector,' I said. 'Let me tell this in my own way. From the beginning. If I start to answer your questions, it'll only lead to more questions, and we'll never get anywhere.'

His face scrunched up as if he'd tasted something sour, but he gave an abrupt nod.

'All right then. Go on.'

I took a deep breath.

'Before I start, I need you to promise you won't interrupt, or ask questions, until I've finished. Whatever you think of what I'm about to tell you, I just want you to hear me out. And I want you to know that this story is... well, it's mental, it's like nothing you've ever heard before. It's the sort of story where, at the end of it, you'll say "Do you honestly expect me to believe that?" or "What the fuck do you take me for?" But before you get angry I want you to ask yourself *why* I'm telling you such a crazy story; what I could hope to gain from it.' I grimaced. The words had sounded better in my head. More slick, more polished. 'And... well, that's it really,' I finished lamely.

He stared at me. Then he sighed.

'I'm listening.'

I started to talk. Right there on the beach, as we stood facing each other like a couple of spies in a John Le Carré novel, I told him everything. I held nothing back. I told him about meeting up with Benny, about killing McCallum, about the attack on Incognito, about Lyn, about Frank, about Tallarian, the Dark Man, the Wolves of London. I told it all as quickly and concisely as I could. I offered no opinions, no theories; I just gave him the facts.

How long it took I'm not sure. Half an hour? Forty-five minutes? The whole time the wind blew and the sea roared and the grey beach on which we stood remained deserted. It felt like my own little pocket in time and space. A micro-universe, containing nothing but this location, these two people. God knows what anyone watching from the café above would have thought, to see two men, huddled in overcoats, simply standing, facing each other, for half an hour or more. We must have looked like tiny black flecks on a restless grey landscape. But no one came to see what we were doing. No one intervened. The only other signs of life were the gulls wheeling overhead calling mournfully.

Throughout the telling, DI Jensen barely moved. He just stood there, expressionless, lips pressed together, eyes fixed on me. I told him about Hope, about returning to the present day, about Oak Hill, about the visions I'd been having.

'Whoever sent that email to Clover - the Dark Man, his representative - told me not to tell anyone, that Kate would die if I did. But we've gone way beyond that now. So I decided it was time to wipe the slate clean. Start afresh. That's why I called you.'

The silence when I finished speaking was almost painful. It wasn't really silence, of course, not with the sea and the wind and the screeching gulls, but that was what it felt like.

My throat was raw and dry. I swallowed and winced, tasting salt. I still couldn't read Jensen's expression. The way he stared at me was unsettling, but it was impossible to tell what he was thinking.

'Well?' I eventually said with a half laugh. 'Aren't you going to say anything?'

His lips parted, but he didn't speak straight away.

Then, quietly, he said, 'What do you *expect* me to say?'

I shrugged. 'I don't know. How about: Do you honestly expect me to believe that?'

He seemed to harden – his face, his muscles.

'Are you taking the piss, Mr Locke?'

'I wish I was.'

His face twisted then, and I realised he was trying to maintain control, to hold his anger in check.

'I can't decide whether you're fucking me about or genuinely deranged. I'm going to give you the benefit of the doubt and assume the latter. There is one part of your story I *do* believe, though.'

Heart sinking, I said, 'And what's that?'

'I believe you're responsible for the death of Barnaby McCallum. You know too much about the specific injury that killed him not to be. Alex Locke, I'm therefore arresting you on suspicion of the murder of Mr Barnaby McCallum. You do not have to say anything, but what you do say—'

'He's telling the truth,' said a voice from my left. '*I'm* telling the truth.'

Both Jensen and I turned. The man standing a little further up the beach, about twenty metres away from us, had appeared from nowhere. He had something in his hand, was holding it up to show us. At first, with a lurch of alarm, I thought it was a grenade – and then my eyes widened.

It was the obsidian heart!

I looked at the man again. His hair was grey, almost white. He looked to be in his fifties, maybe older.

Then the scales fell from my eyes and I saw him anew. My entire body went weak and watery. My head swam, and for a moment I thought I was going to faint.

'Fuck,' I breathed. 'Oh, fuck.'

'Who the hell are you?' Jensen barked as the man took a few steps closer.

The newcomer smiled. I couldn't get over the wrinkles that framed his mouth like brackets, the crow's feet that radiated out from the corners of his eyes.

'Don't you know, Inspector?' the man said. 'Don't you recognise me?'

Jensen narrowed his eyes, but I saw something cross his face: a glimmer of understanding – and fear.

'Should I?'

The man nodded at me. His voice was gentle. 'I'm him. He's me. A younger me.' He waggled the obsidian heart from side to side in his hand. 'Show him, Alex.'

I withdrew the obsidian heart from my pocket, held it up as the older me was holding his up. I was fascinated by him (by me), by how he (I) had aged. I wanted to stare at him; I found it difficult to tear my gaze away. But I wanted to see how Jensen would react too.

The DI was trembling, his eyes darting wildly from the older me's face to my own.

'No,' he said, sounding scared. 'It's not possible. It's a trick.'

'It's not, you know,' the older me said, his voice still gentle, sympathetic. 'And I'm going to prove it to you now. Brace yourself.'

He disappeared.

I can't describe how it happened. He didn't shimmer out of existence. He didn't instantaneously vanish like a ghost in a seventies kids' show. If anything, it was a perception thing, perhaps the mind's way of coping with the impossible. It was almost as if, for a split second, I'd lost concentration, phased out, been distracted, and that when I looked back at where the older me had been standing he simply wasn't there any more.

Jensen gave a sort of sobbing groan, and then he fell to his knees in the sand. Clamping a hand over his eyes in an almost child-like way, as if to deny what he had seen, he began to shudder.

TWENTY-SEVEN

COFFEE AND CAKE

Why do I have to be so bloody enigmatic? Why couldn't I just come back from the future, sit myself down and tell myself everything? It was a weird feeling, being pissed off at yourself as though you were another person, but that was how I felt all the same. The only customer in the Cliff Top Café I looked glumly out through the clear patch of window I'd wiped free of condensation, whilst the owner busied herself behind the counter and hummed along to 10CC's 'I'm Not In Love', which was playing quietly on some Golden Oldies radio station. Because all our footprints were still visible on the otherwise smooth grey sand, it was easy to pick out not only the spot, close to the sea's edge, where Jensen and I had been standing, but also the places where the older me had appeared and disappeared.

I stared at the marks left by the older me, a line of footprints maybe ten metres long, like a thin black scar. *Footprints from the future*, I thought. It should have filled me with wonder, but all I felt was frustration and resentment.

At least the older me had saved me from a tricky situation – though not without giving poor old Jensen a mental breakdown in the process. Actually, Jensen had been all right (well, sort of) once he'd recovered from his trauma. Shell-shocked and dazed, he'd decided not to arrest me, had said he was going to go away and think about things for a while; specifically, about how to proceed with McCallum's murder investigation.

'I killed him, but I didn't murder him,' I said. 'It was an accident.

And he *arranged* for it to happen. He *wanted* it to happen.'

He flapped my words away like troublesome flies. 'Yes, yes, so you told me. I just...' He shook his head, defeated. 'I don't know, Mr Locke. For the first time in my career I honestly *do not know* what to do.'

In the end he'd driven away, still undecided. It was the best I could have hoped for, I suppose. Had I been right to tell him everything? It was an impossible question to answer. All I could cling to was that at that time, in that moment, it had *felt* right. It had felt as though I was ridding myself of baggage, preparing myself for action. What form that action would take, and how I'd respond to and cope with it, I had no idea. As always, what awaited me, despite the hints I'd received from the future, was the unknown, and no amount of strategy or planning could prepare me for that.

Open on the table in front of me, between my cappuccino and my slice of carrot cake, was my notebook. I'd started to carry it everywhere with me now, and to jot down everything I 'knew' about the future. Contained in the book were not only reminders of things I apparently needed to do to maintain my timeline – pay off Candice's boyfriend's debt, meet Frank and save his life, that sort of thing – but also thoughts, theories, musings. I picked up the pen lying next to the book, and wrote:

Older me – fifty-five? Sixty? Looking fine, healthy. So does this mean I'll definitely live for at least another twenty years or so? How do I use the heart without it affecting me?

I paused, then wrote down the location, the date, the time that the older me had appeared. Maybe I'd need that at some point in the future to remind myself to come back. Maybe this notepad would become the single most important thing I owned – as important as the obsidian heart itself.

I took a sip of my cappuccino and stared down at the beach again. In a few hours the tide would wash away all evidence of our meeting. But with the heart the past never really went away, did it? It was weird to think that in twenty years or so, if the older me was the me who was sitting here now, I'd revisit this day. I'd pop back into my own past as easily as if I was popping down to the shops for a pint of milk.

But *how?* How would I do it? After the increasingly devastating physical effects that the heart had been having on me whenever I'd used it, how could I risk using it even *once* more? *Was* it simply a case of getting used to it? *Did* it make you sick for a while until you'd acclimatised? Maybe the answer was to take a full medical team with me next time, who could pull me back from the brink if I went into meltdown? Was that even remotely feasible? I thought again about the older me, and it suddenly struck me that if *he* was *me*, he'd know I was having these thoughts right now; he'd *remember*. So maybe...

I looked eagerly towards the door, half expecting it to open and the older me to appear on the threshold. But nothing happened; the door remained closed. I stared at it until the song on the radio changed to 'Virginia Plain' by Roxy Music. Then I sighed and looked back out of the window again.

There was a ghost on the beach.

That was my first impression. There was something out there on the grey sand in almost exactly the same place as the older me had appeared, something white and billowing. I blinked, my eyes readjusting. The patch on the glass that I'd wiped free of condensation was greying up again. I wiped it with the cuff of my sweater.

The ghost was looking up at me. Only it wasn't a ghost.

It was Lyn.

As far away as she was, her features nothing but a dark blur, I knew I was right. Lyn looked just as she had on the other occasions I'd seen her – bare feet, white nightshirt, heavily pregnant. Her blonde hair flapped like a flag in the wind. I imagined her flimsy nightshirt snapping around her tiny body.

I stared at her and she stared back at me, and then she gave a single, decisive nod.

It was all the answer I needed.

TWENTY-EIGHT

WAR

Clover and I sat on the settee in the room where, over a hundred years earlier, Hawkins had bled to death, and FaceTimed Hope. Using a small fraction of my new-found wealth, Clover had been out to buy the iPad while I'd headed to the coast to meet Jensen, and had set everything up while I'd been away. Hope was using one of the computers at Oak Hill to contact us. She really had taken to twenty-first century technology like a duck to water.

When her face appeared on screen, grinning and happy and even healthier than the last time I'd seen it, I felt so moved that my throat closed up and I couldn't speak. For a moment, ridiculously, I thought I was going to start weeping.

'Wow!' Clover said. 'You've had your hair cut. You look amazing!'

Hope's grin became a little shy, self-conscious. She patted her new, stylish bob uncertainly.

'Is it okay?' she asked. 'It isn't too short, is it? It doesn't make me look like a boy?'

I was wondering whether this was the first time I'd heard Hope use the word 'okay' when Clover laughed.

'Of course not! It's fantastic! It really suits you. Doesn't it, Alex?'

I knew she was prompting me because up to now I'd said nothing. I swallowed to clear the lump in my throat, and nodded, overcompensating for my silence with a grin.

'Totally. You look beautiful.'

Hope's grin widened to match my own. 'Jackie's hairdresser came to see me. She's called Cheryl, she's really nice.' She leaned forward conspiratorially, eyes sparkling. 'She's got a *tattoo* on her hand. It's a flower. And she's got *three earrings in each ear!*'

Clover smiled. 'Ladies in this time are a bit different to how they were in your day. How do you feel about that?'

'It's cool. That means good.'

'Are you okay over there on your own?' I asked.

Hope's expression suggested it hadn't even occurred to her to wonder why she shouldn't be.

'I'm not on my own. I've got lots of friends here. Ed comes to see me nearly every day. We play SIMS. But guess what?'

'What?' I said, her exuberance starting to turn my forced grin into a genuine one.

'Look!' She leaned back so we could see more of her upper body and lifted her right arm into view. It no longer ended in a stump just below the shoulder. Sticking out of the cuff of her now-full pyjama sleeve was a pale pink hand. It was only when she held it up to the screen that it became obvious it was prosthetic. She flexed the fingers, making the hand open and close.

'That's terrific,' Clover said. 'How does it feel?'

Hope lowered her arm, her face filling the screen again.

'It feels like a real arm, except lighter. I've been practising with it. Do you want to see what I can do?'

'Yes!' Clover and I said in unison, as if competing to see who could be the most enthusiastic.

Hope looked down at something beneath the lower edge of the screen. Her arm reached out and she appeared to be fumbling with something. Unconsciously she bit her bottom lip, face pensive as she concentrated.

We waited patiently. A moment later the tension left Hope's face and she beamed; it was like watching the sun come out from behind clouds.

'Ta da!' she said, and this time when she raised her prosthetic hand it was clutching an apple.

Clover whooped and clapped.

'That's fantastic,' I said.

'Hold on,' Hope said. A little jerkily she raised the apple to her mouth, tilting her head down to take a bite. She managed to sink her teeth in, but the contact dislodged the apple, which tumbled from her grasp.

'Whoops!' she said, but she wasn't upset. 'I think I need a bit more practise.'

'You're doing brilliantly,' Clover said.

'This time next week you'll be able to pick your nose with that new hand of yours,' I told her.

Hope giggled. 'Jackie says I might be able to come home next week. Ed asked if he could come and visit me when I was home. Can he? *Please?*'

From her beseeching expression and tone of voice you might have thought I'd already said no - though if truth be known, I *was* wary. This was what my encounters with the Wolves of London had done - made me suspicious of everyone, including Hope's new friend, Ed, and his mother, Jackie. But we couldn't wrap Hope up in cotton wool forever. Besides which, Clover was already saying, 'Of *course* he can! Tell him he's welcome any time.'

'Yay!' Hope said, waving her arms - her real one and her prosthetic one.

When the time came to say goodbye I suddenly found my throat tightening up again, my emotions threatening to spill over. Hope might be coming home next week, but if what I was planning to do later today worked out it might be months before I saw her again - and if things *didn't* work out there was the possibility I might *never* see her again.

But I couldn't give an inkling, either to Hope or Clover, of what was going through my mind. I had to hold it together, stay casual.

'You keep practising with that hand,' Clover said.

'Yeah,' I said. 'And by this time next week I want to see you...' I thought for a moment '...catch a ball with it.'

'If I do, can I have my ears pierced?' Hope asked quickly.

Clover laughed. 'We'll see. Though not till you're at least twelve.'

Hope wrinkled her nose. 'When's that?'

'In about five years.'

'*Five years?* That's *forever!*'

Still laughing, Clover said, 'Tell you what, I'll take you shopping for some new clothes. How's that?'

Hope's dismay quickly evaporated. 'Can I choose them?'

'You can. But I have to like them too. Deal?'

'Deal.'

I wanted to add that I'd take us all out for the best meal we'd ever had when she was home, but I couldn't bring myself to promise something I might not be around to deliver – besides which, the thought of a celebration, though God knows Hope deserved one after all she'd been through, seemed like a betrayal of Kate somehow. Daft as it was, it suggested to me it would be a sign I was forgetting my youngest daughter, abandoning her.

Instead, therefore, I said, 'We can't wait for you to come home.' I hesitated, then added, 'We love you and miss you.'

Clover gave me a curious look, though whether that was because my words made it sound as if we were a couple, or because I'd never actually told Hope I loved her before, I had no idea.

'Are you all right?' she asked me after we'd said our goodbyes and Hope had gone.

I nodded. 'Fine. It just... it gets to me now and again, you know?'

I felt sure she'd guess my intentions from my tone of voice or the expression on my face, but she simply nodded, then leaned across and kissed me quickly on the cheek.

'Don't beat yourself up about it. All you can do is your best. Do you fancy ordering out for pizza?'

I shrugged. 'Yeah, whatever.' But I felt guilty, knowing that if things worked out the way I wanted them to, I wouldn't be here to eat it. 'Do you mind ordering it? I'm going to lie down for a bit.'

I expected her eyes to narrow, expected her to ask: *What are you up to?* But she just nodded, smiled.

'Sure. What do you fancy?'

'Anything. Hawaiian?'

'Hawaiian it is. Coleslaw?'

'Sounds good.'

It was a relief to trudge upstairs, to be on my own. I thought if I'd stayed with Clover any longer she'd have heard how hard and fast my heart was thudding and would have asked me what was wrong. As it was, I was panting raspingly by the time I got to my room. Mostly stress, I supposed; despite my aching knee I felt more exhausted now than I'd done after plodding back up the cliff path to the café that morning. I tried not to think about what might happen when I used the heart, based on what had happened so far. I tried instead to focus on the positive – on how fit and healthy the older version of me who had appeared on the beach had looked; on the encouraging nod that Lyn (who up to now had been nothing but a help and a guide) had given me.

It had been that nod that had finally decided me; that nod that, both at the time and now, seemed like the best vindication I could hope for.

I had to use the heart. *Had* to. There were no two ways about it. I couldn't sit back and wait for fate to intervene, if it ever would. I had to see the visions I'd had as a warning, however inaccurate, of what would happen if I did nothing. What was that saying? Faint heart never won fair maiden? I felt strongly that if I was ever going to see Kate again, I had to gamble with the most precious thing I had: my life.

I felt bad about keeping Clover in the dark, but I couldn't risk her muddying the waters with her protestations, not now my mind was made up. I closed the door of my room and crossed to the bed. Lifting the edge of the mattress, I pulled out the sheaf of papers I'd secreted there, glancing guiltily at the door as I did so. I felt as if I was thirteen again and afraid my mum would discover my stash of dog-eared *Fiestas* and *Knaves*. The memory gave me a pang of nostalgia for a time when life was simple and relatively carefree.

Sitting on the edge of the bed, I began to look through the loose sheets of paper. They were all copies of the front pages of British newspapers on the outbreak of World War One. I'd found them on the internet yesterday and printed them out. Here was the stark declaration on the August 5th 1914 edition of *The Times*: BRITAIN AT WAR; here was the *Daily Herald*: WAR DECLARED BY BRITAIN AND FRANCE; and here the *Birmingham Gazette*: ENGLAND AND GERMANY AT WAR.

There were more – all conveying, in slightly different terminology, the same grim news. I stared at them, tried to absorb them, in the hope they would get me into the right mind set, help make my journey easier.

Knowing I didn't have much time, that all too soon Clover would be shouting up the stairs to say that the pizzas had arrived, I spent no more than five minutes looking at the papers. It wasn't ideal, but it would have to do – though perhaps I wouldn't need even this amount of preparation; perhaps, if all this was truly meant to be, simply picturing the date in my head would be enough to allow me to arrive at my chosen destination.

Standing up, I crossed to the desk against the wall on which my computer stood, and grabbed a pen from the plastic desk tidy just beyond the mouse mat. At some point in the future I'd have to travel back to buy all this stuff for the house – a house which, simultaneously, I had yet to purchase but which I'd owned for at least the past one and a quarter centuries.

Such thoughts, mind-boggling though they were, were a comfort. Surely my mere presence in this house, combined with the fact that I owned all this stuff I was yet to buy, was proof that I would survive the coming journey; otherwise, how could it exist?

Trying not to think beyond the logic of that, I scribbled Clover a note on the back of the sheet of A4 printed with the front page of *The Times* from almost a century before:

Dear Clover

I'm really sorry, but I've had to go. I know you'll think I'm stupid and reckless, but I don't think I've got a choice. And I've seen enough evidence to make me confident I'll survive using the heart again – how I don't know, but I'm sure that somehow I will. And if I don't, then it's possible that this reality will dissolve, and you'll be a completely different person, and you may never even read this note in the first place.

But if you <u>do</u> read this note, I hope you won't be <u>too</u> angry with me (though I suspect you will).

Look after Hope, and hopefully I'll see you again.

Sorry about the extra pizza.

Lots of love

Alex xxx

PS If I don't see you again, let me just say that you've been a brilliant friend, and that I feel privileged to have known you. I couldn't have got this far without your amazing help and support.

Dropping the note on the bed, where Clover would see it as soon as she walked in, I took a deep breath, then put my hand into the pocket of my hoodie and wrapped my fingers around the heart. What I was wearing was entirely unsuitable for where, or rather when, I was going, but I was banking on the fact that if all went to plan I'd arrive in this house – in this exact spot, hopefully – as the owner, and so (courtesy of a future me, who would have fixed it up for his past self) would have a full set of clothes and a full identity, appropriate to the era, all ready and waiting.

Would I have servants? Would anyone else be in the house? Would a 1914 version of Clover be waiting for me, as she'd been waiting for me in 1895?

Fuck it, I thought. No more questions. Just do it.

I held the heart up in front of my face.

August 5th 1914, I thought. *August 5th 1914*.

Last time I'd closed my eyes and pressed the heart to my forehead. Should I do that again?

But last time I'd nearly died, so why follow the same pattern? Why—

The shift was effortless. I was aware only of the room momentarily darkening and blurring around me, as if with the onset of night. What I *wasn't* aware of were things moving around, of the decor changing. And yet after I'd blinked, as if to rid my vision of a smeary clot of matter, my eyes refocused and I realised that the room *had* changed.

The walls were now covered with a dark green, patterned wallpaper. The furniture was darker and heavier too, though many of the pieces I recognised from the three months I'd spent here at the end of 1895. There were more pictures on the walls – mostly landscapes in oil. Again, I recognised some of them from my previous occupation, whereas others were new.

The radiators had been added since 1895, but although they resembled the heavy, cast-iron ones with the embossed Art Deco-like design, which warmed the house in the twenty-first century, they weren't the same.

What else? The house seemed quiet, and the dimness outside the window suggested it was either dusk or a particularly murky summer's day.

But what about me? How had *I* fared this time? Tentatively I flexed my muscles, took several breaths in and out. I felt fine, but then last time I'd initially felt fine too. I looked at the heart in my hand. It hadn't changed. Moving slowly, as if what I held was unstable, I placed the heart in the pocket of my hoodie.

The instant my fingers broke contact with the heart my body was wracked with the most excruciating agony. I collapsed to my knees, unable even to scream. Wave after wave of pain flowed through me, as if I was being struck again and again by lightning. I felt as if my limbs, my organs, my blood was on fire. As my muscles spasmed and cramped, I fell forward onto my face.

I started to vomit, and just before my vision faded I saw that the vomit was bright red, that I was puking up nothing but blood. It was happening again, except this time it was worse, and I was alone, and even if the emergency services *were* to magically appear, as they had done before, I doubted they would have the resources, the technology, to save me.

Although the pain was so terrible I could barely think, deep down inside I was nevertheless aware I had made the most appalling mistake, and that I would never see either of my daughters again.

A terrible numbing coldness crept through me, superseding even the pain. I knew without a doubt that the coldness was death, and that its advent was now undeniable, inescapable.

Kate, I thought as the coldness opened up like a vast maw, rimed with black frost, below me. I felt myself unravelling like a thread as I tumbled into it.

I was dying...

I was dying...

I was dead.

ACKNOWLEDGEMENTS

In January 2015 our daughter Polly was diagnosed with Hodgkin's lymphoma, which was naturally a massive shock for us all. As I write these words she is two days away from completing a six-month course of chemotherapy, with three weeks of radiotherapy to follow in September. I can't express how grateful I am – indeed, how grateful we all are – to our many, many friends and work colleagues for their incredible love, support and understanding these past six months. I don't want to name names for fear of leaving anyone out, but we have been inundated with so many gifts and good wishes and offers of help that not only has it been wondrously overwhelming, but it has also made us realise how amazingly blessed we are. Thank you to the medical staff in the Oncology Dept at St James's Hospital in Leeds, and particularly to the nurses in the Teenage Cancer Unit, all of who are lovely. Huge thanks also to everyone who sponsored my wife Nel on her 10k Race For Life run and enabled her to raise over £6,000 for Cancer Research.

ABOUT THE AUTHOR

M ark Morris has written over twenty-five novels, among which are *Toady*, *Stitch*, *The Immaculate*, *The Secret of Anatomy*, *Fiddleback*, *The Deluge* and four books in the popular *Doctor Who* range. He is also the author of two short story collections, *Close to the Bone* and *Long Shadows, Nightmare Light*, and several novellas. His short fiction, articles and reviews have appeared in a wide variety of anthologies and magazines, and he is editor of *Cinema Macabre*, a book of horror movie essays by genre luminaries for which he won the 2007 British Fantasy Award, its follow-up *Cinema Futura*, and *The Spectral Book of Horror Stories*, the second volume of which will be launched in October 2015. His script work includes audio dramas for Big Finish Productions' *Doctor Who* and *Jago & Litefoot* ranges, and also for Bafflegab's *Hammer Chillers* series, and his recently published work includes an updated novelisation of the 1971 Hammer movie *Vampire Circus*, the official movie tie-in novelisation of Darren Aronofsky's *Noah*, and two novellas: *It Sustains* (Earthling Publications), which was nominated for a Shirley Jackson Award, and *Albion Fay* (Spectral Press). Upcoming is *Wrapped In Skin*, a new short story collection from ChiZine Publications, and book three of the Obsidian Heart trilogy, which will be published by Titan Books in 2016.

Follow him on twitter @MarkMorris10

AN ENGLISH GHOST STORY

BY KIM NEWMAN

The Naremores, a dysfunctional British nuclear family seek a new life away from the big city in the sleepy Somerset countryside. At first their new home, The Hollow, seems to embrace them, creating a rare peace and harmony within the family. But when the house turns on them, it seems to know just how to hurt them the most – threatening to destroy them from the inside out.

'Immersive, claustrophobic and utterly wonderful.'
M.R. Carey, bestselling author of *The Girl With All the Gifts*

'Thoroughly enjoyable, master storytelling.'
Lauren Beukes, bestselling author of *Broken Monsters*

'Deserves to stand beside the great novels of the ghostly.'
Ramsey Campbell

'An intoxicating read.'
Paul Cornell, bestselling author of *London Falling*

THE SILENCE
BY TIM LEBBON

In the darkness of an underground cave system, blind creatures hunt by sound. Then there is light, there are voices, and they feed... Swarming from their prison, the creatures thrive and destroy. To scream, even to whisper, is to summon death. As the hordes lay waste to Europe, a girl watches to see if they will cross the sea. Deaf for many years, she knows how to live in silence; now, it is her family's only chance of survival. To leave their home, to shun others, to find a remote haven where they can sit out the plague. But will it ever end? And what kind of world will be left?

'*The Silence* is a chilling story that grips you firmly by the throat.' SciFi Now

'The degradation of modern society as the swarm moves on is reminiscent of Cormac McCarthy's *The Road*. Fans of environmental horror such as Stephen King's *The Mist* and creature feature horror flicks will no doubt love the end of the world as we knew it and the beginning of Tim Lebbon's new one.' Hell Notes

THE APOLLONIAN CASE FILES BOOK ONE:
THE LAZARUS GATE
BY MARK A. LATHAM

London, 1890. Captain John Hardwick, an embittered army veteran and opium addict, is released from captivity in Burma and returns home, only to be recruited by a mysterious gentlemen's club to combat a supernatural threat to the British Empire.

This is the tale of a secret war between parallel universes, between reality and the supernatural; a war waged relentlessly by an elite group of agents; unsung heroes, whose efforts can never be acknowledged, but by whose sacrifice we are all kept safe.

'Steeped in rich fantasy and Victorian authenticity...
not to be missed.'
George Mann

'A splendid start to what promises to be a terrific series,
making fog-shrouded London come alive.'
James Lovegrove

TITANBOOKS.COM

HOT LEAD, COLD IRON

BY ARI MARMELL

Mick Oberon may look like just another 1930s private detective, but beneath the fedora and the overcoat, he's got pointy ears and he's packing a wand. Among the last of the aristocratic Fae, Mick turned his back on his kind and their Court a long time ago. But when he's hired to find a gangster's daughter sixteen years after she was replaced with a changeling, the trail leads Mick from Chicago's criminal underworld to the hidden Otherworld, where he'll have to wade through Fae politics and mob power struggles to find the kidnapper and solve the case.

'A potent mix of gangsters and magic... gripping, fantastical.'
Publishers Weekly (starred review)

'Thoroughly entertaining.'
Booklist (starred review)

'Guns, wands, gangsters and faeries... extremely entertaining.'
SF Signal

TITANBOOKS.COM

BENEATH LONDON

BY JAMES P. BLAYLOCK

The collapse of the Victoria Embankment uncovers a passage to an unknown realm beneath the city. Langdon St. Ives sets out to explore it, not knowing that a brilliant and wealthy psychopathic murderer is working to keep the underworld's secrets hidden for reasons of his own.

St. Ives and his stalwart friends investigate a string of ghastly crimes: the gruesome death of a witch, the kidnapping of a blind, psychic girl, and the grim horrors of a secret hospital where experiments in medical electricity and the development of human, vampiric fungi, serve the strange, murderous ends of perhaps St. Ives's most dangerous nemesis yet.

'St. Ives has to be one of the most fleshed out Victorian characters ever written, and I'm sincerely hoping that Blaylock isn't finished with this scientist adventurer.'
Wired.com

For more fantastic fiction, author events, exclusive excerpts,
competitions, limited editions and more

VISIT OUR WEBSITE
titanbooks.com

LIKE US ON FACEBOOK
facebook.com/titanbooks

FOLLOW US ON TWITTER
@TitanBooks

EMAIL US
readerfeedback@titanemail.com